AN
ILL
WIND

MARGARET HICKEY

AN ILL WIND

PENGUIN BOOKS

UK | USA | Canada | Ireland | Australia
India | New Zealand | South Africa | China

Penguin Books is part of the Penguin Random House group of companies
whose addresses can be found at global.penguinrandomhouse.com

First published by Penguin Books in 2025

Cover photography by Jean Francois Humbert/Arcangel Images and f.ield of vision/Shutterstock
Cover design by Christabella Designs © Penguin Random House Australia Pty Ltd
Author photograph © Colin Usher
Typeset in 12.5/17.5 pt Adobe Garamond by Midland Typesetters, Australia

Printed and bound in Australia by Griffin Press, an accredited
ISO AS/NZS 14001 Environmental Management Systems printer

 A catalogue record for this
book is available from the
National Library of Australia

ISBN 978 1 76134 205 9

penguin.com.au

We at Penguin Random House Australia acknowledge that Aboriginal and Torres Strait Islander
peoples are the Traditional Custodians and the first storytellers of the lands on which we live
and work. We honour Aboriginal and Torres Strait Islander peoples' continuous connection
to Country, waters, skies and communities. We celebrate Aboriginal and Torres Strait Islander
stories, traditions and living cultures; and we pay our respects to Elders past and present.

To my family

PROLOGUE

2 December 2024

Alan is deep in a dream when the alert on his phone jolts him awake. He tries hard to ignore it, clinging instead to the sweat and lanolin, watching Rhonda watch him as she leans against the press. Already, her belly is growing but no one in the shed knows except for her and him. His biceps were like shotputs back then.

The alert again, and Rhonda slips away. Shoulders aching, Alan rolls over, finds his glasses and phone, and with effort sits up. It is just after 5 am.

A malfunction: number 82, back paddock. Briefly Alan considers ignoring it, going back to sleep, trying to find his wife again. But the alert is a red one and the job is new. Reluctantly, he puts on his trousers, his shirt and his boots. This fancy new control feature on his phone is too eager. Technology, you can't trust it.

Even so, the man finds his keys and heads outside, calling for the dogs as he climbs into his ute. He bypasses the roads and instead drives through the paddocks, the sky a thin grey now, a hint of orange in it. It used to be his favourite time of day.

Over the bumpy paddock – the sheep half asleep, the dam a slick mirror, and the dogs' ears flapping in the back – he heads past the two Blakeley gums, their shapes like old-fashioned ladies in skirts. Stars bow out; the sky is clear.

Everywhere farmers like him will have their elbows out the ute windows, feeling the breeze, rattling along, thinking of the jobs ahead. The thought gives him comfort.

At the top of the hill they call Mont Blanc, Alan kills the headlights and looks across the land. He's lived here his whole life, but he'll never get used to this: the sight of them. From this vantage point, the three hundred turbines look like a scene from *War of the Worlds*.

It takes Alan less than a second to locate number 82.

He turns his head away in horror, and then slowly forces himself to look again.

His hands are gripped tight to the steering wheel, and he's finding it difficult to breathe.

Out there, from one of the blades on wind turbine 82, a body hangs.

CHAPTER 1

The sun was sitting on the paddocks and making its presence felt by the time the police arrived. In the golden haze of morning, their flashing lights were unnecessary, but the blue and red in this instance were designed more to encourage the crowd to move than to signal an emergency. Because, clearly, the person hanging up there was dead.

One of the first farmers to call it in, Alan Crowe, stood at the front of the paddock's gates, holding a hand up to signal the officers through.

The gate behind him had a sign on it: *Clean Energy Solutions Australia*.

The police phones had not stopped ringing since dawn. Every farmer in his ute or on her four-wheeler had seen the dangling shape the moment daylight appeared. It was a nightmare for the country station. Belinda Burney's mobile rang again. 'We know, we're there now,' she said, her voice rising. 'Yes! We can see it, yes, we're dealing with it now.'

Will Lovett pulled the police car in beside Alan, turned the engine off and gave the man a nod.

'We need to get that body down now,' Belinda growled as she ended the call.

'How the hell do we do that?'

They stared at each other. The real question was, how the hell did it get *up* there?

'Mr Crowe?' Belinda snapped into action as they both stepped out of the car. She held out her hand to the farmer. 'Senior Sergeant Burney, Belinda. Thanks for keeping everyone at bay.'

'Whole district is here,' Alan said, red-faced and flustered. His hair was sticking up like a rooster; he looked as if he hadn't slept in a week. 'Everyone gawking.'

Belinda, Alan and Will raised their chins so they too could gawk at the body directly above. The feet were pointing down, rotating slowly, drawing a circle in the air. The turbine's gigantic blades were still.

'Senior Sergeant Will Lovett.' Will took his turn to shake the older man's hand. 'A team from Ballarat are on their way, but we'll need to clear this crowd and check there's no one else up there.'

'I don't have keys to go inside.' Alan tipped his head towards the turbine. 'I'm just the overseer – you'll need the wind techie for that.'

'Wind techie?'

'Shane Burrows, local kid. I called him, should be here in a tick.'

'Good work, Alan.' Will rested his hand lightly on the farmer's shoulder. 'You want to sit down?'

'Before you do' – Belinda tilted her head up, shot her tall partner a look – 'can you tell us how you came to know about . . . this?' She waved a hand upward.

Alan ran his fingers through his wild rooster hair. 'Got woken by an alert on my phone. Shane downloaded it for me. It lets me know when any of the units have been opened, or if they aren't functioning or need maintenance. When that happens, I'm supposed to call him.'

'So did you call him this morning?'

'No. Often it's the new gadget playing up. Plus, it wasn't even light, just gone five – didn't want to wake the kid for no reason.'

'Who owns the turbines?' Will asked, even though he had seen the sign on the gate.

'Geordie Pritchard,' Belinda cut in. 'He owns them all.'

'I've called him too, left a message,' Alan said. 'He should be here soon.'

'Thank you, Alan.' Belinda's eyes were drawn again to those rotating feet.

'You're Reg's daughter, aren't you?' the man said, blinking.

'That's right.' She turned her gaze to him, gave a distracted smile. 'I wondered if you'd remember me.' Alan had the air of someone who'd been dropped onto a strange planet and had no idea where he was or what to do.

A hush fell over the chattering crowd as an ambulance snaked its way through them. *Make way*, the flashing lights said, *this isn't over yet.*

'Who is it up there, Alan?' someone in the crowd yelled out.

'I dunno,' the man muttered, then more loudly, 'How would I bloody know!'

'Go sit in your ute, mate,' Will said. 'I'll walk you there.'

Grateful, Alan nodded at him, and they began heading to his vehicle.

'Bound to happen!' another person in the back shouted, and Will strained to see who it was. He caught a glimpse of a woman ducking behind a group of men. The crowd shifted and he lost sight of her.

'Do you have *any* idea who it is?' Will asked Alan, quietly.

'No,' the man said, and then turned his back as a fierce gust of wind suddenly blew in. The turbine blades spun faster. *All that energy,* Will thought, *the power in it.*

Another police car pulled up close by and the young senior constable, Tammy Reyner, got out, her wild curly hair blowing into her face.

'Cordon off the area, will you, Tam?' Will called out. 'We need some order round here.'

'Boss.' Tammy was onto it, shepherding people away, telling them to leave, that there was nothing to see here.

An eager young man broke through the crowd, holding up a set of keys while making his way towards the bottom of the turbine.

'Wind techie.' Alan gave the approaching figure a glance. 'Shane.'

'Okay, good.' Will opened the driver's door for Alan. 'Why don't you go on home, mate? Looks like we'll be able to get inside and up the turbine now.'

Alan climbed in but then just sat, staring at the steering wheel. 'Glad Rhonda's not here to see this,' he said, jerking his chin upward.

'Yeah?' Will didn't know any Rhonda. After ten months, he still barely knew anyone around here. 'Why's that?'

'She said it from the get-go – these turbines, they're killers.'

Tammy had encouraged the gawkers to leave with minimal success, though she did get them to part for Alan to drive off. Will walked over to the wind techie, who was talking to Belinda at the base of the turbine. The young man was decked out in ropes, a vest with harness and a sturdy helmet.

'You must be Shane,' Will said. 'Nice to meet you – and all your gear.'

'One of us has to put this stuff on too,' Belinda said. 'Safety regulations.'

'And gloves.' Will pulled his pair out of his pocket. 'Investigations will be all over us if we muddy the scene.'

'Photos too,' Belinda added. 'I've taken some, but we'll need more of the inside and the view of the body from up there.'

Shane was holding out an extra helmet and harness. 'So, which one of you is coming up?' He glanced at Belinda doubtfully.

'Well, it won't be her.' Will nodded in his colleague's direction and Shane, with a look of relief, passed him the gear.

Belinda tightened her lips and Will steeled himself.

'I *am* capable of climbing up a few ladders, Will.' The police-woman's voice was ominously low.

'This turbine's over a hundred metres high.'

'So what?'

'And you're eight months pregnant.'

Belinda swore and turned away.

'Look, I know you can do it, Bel.' Will spoke more gently as Shane made an effort to tune out. 'But what if you fell or, or—'

'I wouldn't fall,' Belinda replied, stubbornly.

'No,' Will agreed, 'you wouldn't.'

Belinda pulled a face then let out a heavy sigh of resignation, ducking to avoid the pat on the shoulder he was attempting to give her.

'Hey, Will?' she asked her husband of seven years. 'You still scared of heights?'

*

The answer was yes. Will was still scared of heights. Heights made him dizzy, made him irrational, made him feel as if he was going to throw himself off the ledge.

Now, standing in the cramped round space at the bottom of the turbine and looking up at the ladder, Will remembered just how *much* he hated heights.

'You right?' Shane asked. So far, the techie had shown no anxiety about what they'd see when they got to the top. In contrast, the young man was finding it difficult to contain his excitement as he checked his equipment and peered up the vertical tunnel.

'I'm all right. The front hatch was locked, wasn't it?' Will asked, more to confirm it for himself.

'Yes.' Shane was attaching himself via a chain to a rung on the metal ladder leading up. 'The hatch locks automatically when it closes.'

'Who else has the keys for the turbines?'

'The boss, of course.'

'Geordie Pritchard.'

'Yeah. Alan has the keys to the perimeter fence, but not for the actual turbines. He calls me when there's a problem.'

'Right.'

'I have keys too.' Shane looked down at the bunch in his hand. '*Obviously.*'

The two men stared at each other. In the confined area, the moment was almost surreal. Despite the tragic situation and the rising sense of claustrophobia, Will felt a laugh bubbling up.

'I'll just . . .' Shane used a different key from the same set to open a small hatch, where he studied a blinking monitor. 'Just checking to see that the turbine is definitely turned off. Have to make sure . . . and yes, yes, it is.' He glanced meaningfully at

Will. 'So that means whoever is up there knew how to stop the blades spinning before he started climbing.'

'Right.' Will wasn't sure what he was supposed to say to that. Was Shane expecting him to be impressed? 'That's great,' he added for good effect.

'I mean, it's not difficult.' Shane pointed to a button labelled BLADE MONITOR – ON/OFF. 'But you should probably know that.'

'Thanks.' Again, that urge to laugh.

'I deliver the training to everyone who works onsite here,' Shane said, a solemn look on his face. 'Safety is our number one priority.'

Will stared at his feet for a long moment.

'Now, up we go.' Shane grabbed hold of the ladder. 'Stay right behind me.'

Will took some quick photos before placing his phone in his pocket. *Up.* He focused on climbing, one hand up, one foot up, one hand up. It wasn't too bad, aside from the heat and the clanking metal and the lack of air. *It's like a vertical prison,* he thought, *and I'm the fresh meat.*

After a couple of minutes of slow climbing, they came to a platform. Again, the standing room was close.

'I'm usually by myself when I come up here,' Shane explained. 'Not used to it with two of us.'

'What happens now?' Will took off his glasses and wiped them with his shirt. *God, it's hot.* 'Where's the ladder gone?'

'Now for the fun part.' Shane pressed a button on a remote, and Will was astonished to see a low door opening into an elevator.

'It has a lift?' He followed Shane into it, and the two stood with their noses almost touching.

'This one does. Not all.'

'It's like Charlie and the Glass Elevator,' Will observed. 'Or that movie with Bruce Willis.'

'Who?'

'Never mind.' Will closed his eyes as the lift took them up the cylinder, fifty metres, maybe sixty. His stomach lurched; his head began to throb. Might have been a useful photo, but there wasn't room. He was sure Bruce Willis wouldn't be this nervous.

The lift came to a stop, and Shane slid open the steel door. 'One more climb,' he said.

Will it ever end?

'We do have a climb-assist, for the ladder sections,' Shane said, as he mounted the ladder. 'See this cable?' Will looked to the side of the ladder, where a steel cable ran down the entire length. 'You can clip it to your safety vest, and it relieves most of the weight. Try it now.'

Will clipped himself to the cable and was surprised to feel himself being hoisted up the rungs. He still had to climb, but the job was made much easier.

'I didn't show you the assist at the start' – the young man smiled – 'because I figured you'd want to get the feel for the climb.'

Gee, thanks, Will thought. He was beginning to tire of the younger man's superior tone.

They climbed. After ten metres, they reached another platform.

'Nearly at the top,' Shane said, matter of fact.

With each different level, Will had felt a growing anxiety, amplified by Shane's clinical approach and the clanking of metal within the tight space. Now, he followed as the wind techie climbed a short stepladder and through a grate to a wider area.

'This is the cell,' Shane said. 'In a sec we'll be able to see everything.'

Finally, there was room for Will to take some more photos. But the heat! How could anyone work here? Sweat poured down his back in a stinking stream. Shane was pushing more buttons, and suddenly, two hatches above them opened and wind gushed in. Will's stomach muscles clenched. The giant blades of the wind turbine were just below them and stretching out, over forty metres long.

The body hung from the end of a rope, the head bowed as if in prayer. Light brown hair flapped, revealing a small bald spot. The shirt was tucked into jeans; a neat brown belt, blue jumper on top. The corpse swung in the wind, hands coming up then down in a pleading gesture. The one side of the face he could see was a bloated grey.

Bile rose up in Will's throat. He punched some numbers into his phone, then forced himself to look at the figure, to see if there was anything identifiable about it.

'We're at the top – no one else is here, it's safe,' Will said when Belinda answered.

'Okay. Investigations will be on site any moment. You can come down now.'

But Will was looking at Shane. The techie's face had gone a queasy shade of yellow.

'Do you recognise the person?' Belinda asked down the line.

'No.' Will shook his head. 'I've never seen him before. Shane, do you know who it is?'

The younger man stood stock still. It took a moment for Will to realise that Shane had tears in his eyes and was finding it difficult to speak. The techie looked up at Will with a grimace. He opened his mouth, then closed it. 'It's my boss,' he said.

11

'What, your boss of the technicians? Of the wind farm?'

The young man's arms flapped, gesturing across the land and around it. 'The boss of it all. Of *everything*!'

Will closed his eyes. Now he felt the vertigo, the moving sensation, the dizziness. *Get me down*, he thought. *Get me down.*

'The boss of *everyone*!' Shane's voice had risen. 'Like, everybody!'

CHAPTER 2

The Carrabeen police station had never been so busy. Built in 1865 to monitor the lawlessness on the nearby goldfields and the growing population, the stone building had once boasted a staff of ten. Now, there were three. Belinda and Tammy each worked part-time, with Will being the one full-timer.

This morning, there hadn't been enough mugs to go around. Tea bags littered the sink like sandbags after a flood. The Investigations team were in town. Belinda glowered at the mess before fishing out the sodden bags and tossing them into the bin. Investigations. *Argh.* Their shiny new HiLux, and the way the two detectives swanned around, it really got to her. She had no idea why.

Sure, Belinda. She knew exactly why.

On its way to the bin, one of the tea bags had leaked brown droplets all across the vinyl floor. Bending down, Belinda felt the baby inside her twist and turn. She grimaced, took a few long, deep breaths, then swiped at the spots. With some effort, she stood and squeezed the cloth out into the sink with a satisfying viciousness.

The coppers from the Investigations team were already back at the scene on Alan Crowe's old farm. Will and Tammy were there too. By now they'd have figured out how to get the body down and, finally, the utes gathered along the horizon would have driven away.

And what a sight. She'd been transfixed herself. A body, hanging there for everyone to see. At first, she'd thought it was a dummy, some scarecrow-type thing, put up there by kids. Despite the panicked calls from witnesses, she'd only really believed it was a person when she'd stood underneath and seen those boots turning slowly above.

And as for who it was . . . well, that was the real kicker.

Geordie Pritchard: CEO of Clean Energy Solutions Australia, beloved son of the district, public figure, husband and father. Social media was all over it, and it would be the first story on the national news: Geordie Pritchard, dead at thirty-nine.

The Pritchards owned the original homestead on the old Carrabeen Road. Named Yarrobee, it had been built by convicts, and with its impressive bluestone facade and dark windows, it never failed to remind Belinda of a coldly handsome prince. She remembered going there for a school excursion – there was a lake in front of the house, nude statues and a lot of lawn.

Soon after they'd identified his body, Geordie's ute had been found, outside the local fish 'n' chips shop. Narelle, the woman who owned it, said that Geordie had popped in last night – say seven, seven-thirty? – for a potato cake, two fried dim sims, and a chat about the state of the town. He'd seemed to be in his usual good mood. Forensics were in charge of the vehicle now, report pending. Had Geordie then walked to the turbines?

Belinda considered. It wasn't far, three or four kilometres at most on a gentle declining slope, taking the back road out of town past paddocks and grazing sheep. A pleasant enough stroll. Narelle hadn't seen Geordie after he'd walked out of her shop and so far, no one else had either. Sunday evenings were notoriously quiet in Carrabeen. *Dead*, she'd used to call them when she lived here.

The station phone rang again, just as her mobile started buzzing. Everyone from curious neighbours to media wanted an update. Belinda did her best to be polite, but it was diffi-cult not to snap, and she couldn't help thinking back to those boots pointing downwards. Geordie had worn the same brand in primary school, R.M. Williams. Everyone else wore Blund-stones, or in her case, gum boots. Geordie had come to her tenth birthday party. They used to call him Geordie 'Richarse', but never to his face.

She ate leftovers for lunch – pesto pasta with a rocket salad – and then continued the necessary but mind-numbing tasks around the station. She wanted to be *out there*, in the field with Will and the others! It killed her to be stuck at the station, answering phones.

It was nearly two o'clock by the time Belinda texted her husband to say she was leaving the office to visit the school before heading home. He wouldn't be happy – he wanted her to only work the hours she was paid for – but work was work, and she still had two weeks to go before she went on maternity leave. The thought of leaving work made her glum. So, on a whim she texted Tammy and asked her to come around for dinner. Her recently broken-hearted colleague could do with some company.

Before she left the station, Belinda took one more glance over a job application she'd been working on, making a tweak here and there. The temptation to push send was strong. *But wait*, she thought, pulling her hand back from the screen, *no need to rush.* There were still four days to go till the deadline, and anything could happen before then, absolutely anything.

Outside, the dust raised from the harvest was still making the air hazy, and the red-orange gave the surrounds an apocalyptic feel. The top of the old manna gum was pulled hard to the north and the flags outside the station flapped and became tangled in the buffeting wind.

Always the wind. The southwest gales. Belinda had almost forgotten them in the years she'd been away. Maybe they'd pulled her back here, she mused, as she looked at the faint outline of a turbine slowly spinning in the distance. Or maybe yet, they'd push her away.

CHAPTER 3

'Geordie Pritchard!' Investigative Officer Lisa Flittson, the junior member of the visiting Investigations team, shouldn't have been so excited about the identity of the victim, but she was, and Will couldn't find it in his heart to be annoyed with her, because of the two outsiders, she'd been the most amiable.

'Yep, Geordie Pritchard.' Will gave a weak smile and leaned against the base of the turbine. Up above, their boss, Inspector Jeff Kelmendri, as well as two paramedics and one firefighter, were still busy trying to get Geordie's body down. Will was relieved he didn't have to go up there again; just the thought of it gave him a shivery feeling in his legs. Seeing the body hanging there . . . and that bald spot. It made him . . . it made him—

'Geordie Pritchard! His family practically owns this area!' Lisa was positively glowing. 'And he is so smart. Degree in environmental science, expert in clean energy, he's even done a TED Talk! I googled him on the way here. Everyone's talking about that television interview he did last week, on the need for extreme action and personal sacrifice – it's like he was *warning* us he'd do this!'

Will looked at her.

Lisa arranged her face to appear appropriately saddened. 'But yes, I can't imagine, with everything else he had, that he would actually commit suicide.'

Clearly Lisa hadn't been in the job long. Surely, as a police officer, she should know that people young and old, rich and poor, killed themselves all the time.

'I mean, his wife is absolutely beautiful! She's a former Country Road model, and they've got two children, twin girls.'

Belinda wouldn't like Lisa, Will thought. The young detective was too excitable, not professional enough. If Belinda were here, she'd be more serious, have her pen and paper out.

Will fished out his own pen and paper and drew a sketch of the turbine, writing 'Wife and children, Country Road model' on it.

Country Road models wouldn't like this place. Where were the rattan chairs for them to lounge on? They'd be suitably bored here, yes, but not glamorously so. He looked out at the sea of turbines. This country wasn't country enough for Country Road.

When they'd arrived back at the station earlier, Belinda had hissed in his ear, 'Why the hell are Investigations even here?' and he'd first taken her outrage as jealousy. But now, in all of Lisa's excitement, he considered Belinda's question again. Investigations rarely arrived this quickly for a suspected suicide. First, the police would gather information to form the initial report for the coroner, and then other inquiries could take place. But in this case, Investigations had turned up less than two hours after local police had been informed. Why so speedy? Will's stomach gave a rumble, and he couldn't work out if it was from hunger or adrenaline. Either way, he felt a little sick. In the rush this morning, he hadn't eaten breakfast. *Please,* he thought, *please can this not be a migraine coming on.* Morning teatime soon; maybe he'd feel better after having something to eat.

'James Packer went to his wedding!' Lisa's eyes were round.

He guessed Lisa's over-enthusiastic response to the case was the reason they'd arrived so quickly. Geordie was a man of reputation and importance, not just any pleb from the towns.

Will tried to ignore the industrial sounds coming from within the turbine. It made him even more ill to think about how they were getting the body off the blade. Someone had suggested a crane – but there were none in the area high enough, and the scaffolding used to put the turbines up in the first place was now on another paddock miles away, putting up more. One of the SES men had volunteered to crawl out along the turbine's blade to pull the body up, but there was no way they were risking that. So now they were trying, seemingly without success, to haul Geordie in using a telescopic pole with a hook at the end, which a fisherman had brought in.

Will closed his eyes.

When he'd first seen the body up close, dangling at the end of the rope, he'd been too shocked at the sight to question how exactly it could have got there. He'd taken photos for the coroner's report – a rope tied to the skinniest part of the blade, about seven to eight metres along from the cell, hung down maybe two or three metres. Did Geordie climb out along the blade and loop it around before tying the rope around his neck and jumping? Or did he place the rope around his neck while he was edging out there, along that precarious arm, before hooking the rest of the rope on and jumping? Will's mind struggled with every scenario.

Without thinking, he looked up again and saw the pole reach out, nudge the body, pushing it outwards. Puzzled for a moment, he then realised what they were doing: trying to create momentum so the body would swing and they could catch it, to haul it back in.

Shit, Will thought, *I'm going to spew.* He stumbled around to the back of the turbine and leaned over, breathing hard. *Calm down*, he thought. *Calm.* He closed his eyes, focused. Inhale, exhale, inhale, exhale; just like the doctor told him to do when he was a kid. Inhale, exhale. Slowly, he began to feel better. Lisa was nearby, asking if he was okay, and he reached behind his back to give her a thumbs up. Her footsteps faded away. *Calm.* Will opened his eyes, saw his shoes and the brown stubble of the grass. And something else. An empty UDL can lay on the ground, up against the turbine. Vodka & raspberry. He leaned down to inspect it more closely. No rust or embedded dirt, it looked relatively new, completely out of place in the industrial environment of the turbines. He pulled out his phone and took some photos.

Returning to the front of the turbine, he found Lisa shading her eyes with her hands. 'Car,' she said.

In the near distance, a vehicle was speeding up the paddock, straining in the dust, swerving on the soft edges.

'Listen.' Will eyed the gloves hanging out of Lisa's pocket. 'There's a UDL can back there, behind the turbine. Can you make sure it gets to Forensics?'

'A can?' Lisa looked doubtful, her eyes still on the approaching vehicle.

'Yes, a can. I'll need to head back to the station, but you can take it straight there.'

'Sure.'

They both took a moment to watch as the vehicle stalled at the perimeter of the first paddock, before steaming on through.

'What the . . .' Lisa shook her head. 'We've cordoned off the whole farm!'

It would either be the press or a family member, Will thought, as he registered that it was a navy BMW nearing the fence closest to the turbines. No one else would dare to drive so forcefully towards the guarded scene.

He put his hand up in the air, cautioning the driver to go no further. Warning signal ignored, the driver continued, barrelling up the dirt track till it was almost touching the gate.

Will watched as a tall woman exited the car.

'Is that Geordie? *Is that Geordie?*' The woman was pointing frantically to the body suspended in the air.

'I'm going to have to ask you to—'

'Is it *Geordie?*'

'Yes,' he called back, as gently as he could, 'it is.' Technically he should state that the body hadn't been formally identified, but why lie? Everyone knew who it was, and this person was clearly family. It would be cruel not to tell her.

The woman crumpled in the dust beside her car. 'Geordie!' she cried. 'Geordie!'

'It's the wife,' Lisa exclaimed behind him. 'The Country Road model, her name is L—'

'Lucinda,' Will said, flatly.

'Will?' The woman's beautiful tear-stained face looked up.

'You know her?' Lisa asked out the side of her mouth.

'Yeah,' Will said, staring at his distraught ex-girlfriend on the other side of the fence. 'You could say that.'

CHAPTER 4

Carrabeen P–12 College was decked out in the colours of the house sporting teams, and the oval was a blur of brown and gold. *That's right.* Monday was the juniors' athletics festival. Belinda remembered Tammy had told her about it. On Saturday, it would be the seniors' turn. The colours were meant to represent the beauty of the Golden Plains, but to Belinda, the brown and yellow stripes were reminiscent of a bad case of gastro.

Now, at the end of the school day, a solitary staff member was walking along, picking up orange markers from the running field. Dean Hookes, Belinda noted without joy. He'd been Head of PE for years, coaching the school football team, running the athletics and swimming days, organising the student vs teacher netball games. She watched as he bent down to pick up another marker and kick a drink bottle to the side of the oval. By all accounts, the man should be principal, because wasn't that the joke teachers told? 'Two years a PE teacher, in ten the head of the school.'

Orla Witts, the current principal, was standing out the front of the administration building to welcome her. She cut an impressive figure in navy pants and red blazer, her tall, thin figure casting a long shadow down the steps. As Belinda climbed to greet her, it felt like she was on her way to meet a president rather than the head of a regional school. They'd only met a couple of times before; once when Belinda had given a talk on road safety to the Year Tens, and another time when she'd booked Orla for drink driving.

'Sergeant Burney, thanks for coming.' Orla held out a steady hand. 'I'm sorry, the vice principal's been held up; he's been run off his feet with the parents calling, and now he's talking to the department about getting some counselling to the school.'

Belinda nodded. In a town as small as Carrabeen, the ramifications of any death spread wide. Half the students would have families who worked for the Pritchards or who would have known them for years. The other half, she reflected, had probably seen the body as they did their morning jobs on the farm. The hill known to locals as Mont Blanc was covered on one side with turbines, easily the most visible landmark for miles.

'A couple of the students said they saw the body,' Orla added. 'I can't imagine what that must have been like.'

The policewoman followed Orla inside, ignoring the wooden plaques on the wall that honoured high-achieving past students and focusing instead on the new building, with its large windows, open-plan office and comfortable space for interviews.

'Geordie Pritchard paid for all of this.' Orla gave a wave around. 'He went to school here!'

There was a small bronze plate on the entrance: *Clean Energy Solutions Australia.*

'Yes, I remember,' Belinda said. 'From Prep to Year Six. I was in a class with him.'

'Oh, were you?' Orla ushered her into a small office, adorned with photos of the school over the years and motivational quotes by Dr Seuss. 'How interesting. What was he like then?'

What was he like?

'He was a kid then,' Belinda said.

Geordie Pritchard: short and stocky, good at climbing trees, cheeky, smiley. A punch that could stun.

Orla sat down on a low chair and motioned for Belinda to do the same. The space was surprisingly cramped. Belinda had imagined an office from a brochure, with big windows, a desk clear of debris, a state-of-the-art phone, and maybe a photo of a family on holiday.

Instead, folders and books were piled in the corner of a wide desk; certificates and qualifications lined the walls. A small statue of a monk bookended one row of boxes, with a Garfield cat on the other end, and an impressive trophy balanced on top of a pile of folders. A large computer with two screens took up space, but it was the tall principal who dominated the room.

'Our offices are being renovated,' Orla explained, catching her look. 'I've been in this one for years, but it's time to go. Most of Andrew's stuff is in here, too.'

Belinda nodded, wondering exactly how much money Geordie had given the school.

'I can never quite get used to it,' Orla said in wonder, 'how people in this town all know each other. Some of the teachers were students here.'

'Dean Hookes and Julie Smith, yes. I knew them too. They were a year above me.'

'Country life.' Orla smiled thinly. 'It's so amazing.'

Belinda smiled thinly back. When she'd booked Orla for drink driving, the woman had called her a *fucking bitch*. 'How's it been, cycling to work? You must be getting fit.' Orla had three months to go till she got her licence back.

'Very,' the principal replied with a tight smile.

Belinda leaned back in her seat. 'What did the vice principal call me here for?'

Orla sniffed and looked out the window to where Dean, the PE teacher, was now hauling a load of javelins and shotputs into the back of a trailer. He looked hot and sweaty, weathered as a walnut. If not for the footy shorts halfway up his arse, he could well be an ancient Roman preparing for the Colosseum games.

'Theft,' Orla said abruptly. 'Some of the teachers and a few kids have reported things going missing: cash, jumpers, pencil cases, food. Andrew thought it was time we notified the police. He's in charge of staffing, so when teachers hear about the thefts, they tend to go to him.'

'And the kids are reporting stolen pencil cases?'

'Yeah,' the principal said wearily, 'pencil cases.'

'Sounds like the work of other kids.'

Orla held her hands up in a gesture of helplessness. 'We've had meetings about it in assembly – the importance of being honest, how it's not dobbing to come forward – but nothing.'

'How long's it been going on for?' Belinda took out her notepad and pencil.

'A month, maybe?'

'You should have reported it earlier.'

'A pencil case? A five-dollar note?'

'Who has five-dollar notes these days?'

'Julie Smith. She believes the banks are run by the global elite. Only uses cash, and isn't afraid to tell the rest of us to do so too.'

'Right,' Belinda smiled. That sounded like Julie.

'Julie is the one who's been doing most of the reporting. She would have been here now, only she's been in the kitchen all day with a group of kids, preparing food to take to the Pritchards. I told her to go home.'

Julie was the food technology teacher and a self-proclaimed medium. Some locals went to her to commune with the dead, others for her scones.

'So do you have *any* idea who it could be?'

'No.' Orla shook her head. 'Normally, the kids are lining up to dob, and anyway, the teachers hear things – they think we don't know the gossip, but we always do, whether we like it or not. But in this instance, no one is talking. And so, the thefts continue. The kids seem to be as much in the dark as we are.'

'Do you have cameras?'

'Yes.' Orla pointed out the door. 'At admin, and the lockers; outside the main buildings, and the car park.'

'But not inside.'

'Well, no. That would be illegal.'

Through the window she could see Dean was now in a Herculean battle with a high jump mat, trying in vain to load it onto the trailer. Each time he almost succeeded, the wind bucked the mat out of his grasp.

Belinda almost felt sorry for the man. Almost.

'I'm surprised the junior athletics day still went ahead,' she said. 'So many of the kids will have known the Pritchards.'

'It's important to keep a semblance of normality,' Orla replied automatically, before rubbing at her eyes. 'It's been such a shitty few years here: the drought, Covid, staffing shortages. Now this – Geordie's dead and everyone's upset. It's a wonder anyone learns anything at this rate.'

There was a knock on the door and a young woman appeared, blinking nervously.

'Yes, Tayla?' Orla rapped on the desk with her nails.

'Mr Kent's still on a phone call, so I came to ask you, am I right to go now?' She gave an anxious half-smile. 'I have netball training.'

'That's fine, Tayla, you don't have to ask every time. At four-thirty, you can go.'

'Oh! Thank you, Miss Witts.'

'It's Orla – I'm not your teacher any more.'

Tayla flashed a quick smile. 'Oh, well, thank you . . . Orla!'

The young woman shut the door, and the principal turned to Belinda. 'Tayla Schultz,' she said in a dry tone. 'Gap year student. Very diligent.' She gave a quick glance at her watch, and taking the cue, Belinda stood.

'If you could let us know if there are any further thefts, that would be good. Plus, I'd like to talk to Julie at some stage.'

Orla's phone rang, and she nodded at Belinda before picking it up.

Duly dismissed, Belinda caught sight of the gap year student's thin frame in front of her as she entered the corridor.

'Tayla!' Belinda hurried up to her and smiled reassuringly as the young woman turned around.

'I'm Senior Sergeant Belinda Burney from the local station. I was just talking with Orla about stuff getting stolen from around here.' The two began walking side by side to the front door. 'Do you know anything about it?' In her fifteen years' experience on the force, Belinda understood the value of talking to the assistants, the nannies, the temps.

Tayla's eyes widened in alarm. 'Oh, no! I haven't had anything stolen, thank god. *Everyone's* going on about it in the staffroom.'

Ah, the staffroom, that mystical place of intrigue and secrets. Belinda remembered long discussions with her friends about who among the staff would be friends and enemies, and what they spoke about in the confines of that coffee-smelling, sock-smelling room.

'Well, that's good.' They'd reached the entrance and Tayla pushed open the door. They stood at the top of the steps, looking down.

'I went to school here,' Belinda said. 'It's changed so much, I can't believe how new everything looks.' She had a sudden memory of herself and a friend, returning to the school a year or two after they'd finished, triumphant and grown up, determined to impress. But oh, what a disappointment it had been when the few staff they saw barely remembered their names. Cringe. *Triple* cringe.

'It's just the front section that's new.' Tayla tucked a wavy strand of hair back into her tight ponytail. 'Some of the new part is still getting renovated, but the rest of the school is pretty old.'

'How are you finding working here?' Belinda asked.

'I love it!' Tayla nodded emphatically. 'I mean, I mainly work in reception, and I also help out the vice principal, Mr Kent – I mean, Andrew – taking notes for his meetings and organising his appointments.'

'Sounds interesting.'

'Better than school!' Tayla looked back at the building. 'I wasn't much good at any subjects, but the teachers were always really nice, and Mr Kent offered me a gap year position when I didn't get any university offers. He said he'd taken a year out before going to uni and it didn't do him any harm.'

'Oh.' Belinda felt a sharp pang of recognition. 'It's a good option: you can live at home, save some money for when you do eventually want to leave.'

'Yes!' Tayla smiled brightly. 'That's exactly what I thought. I've only got till the end of the school year, and then I'm moving to Melbourne. This job has been great, but really – I can't wait.'

Belinda nodded, then paled as she felt a deep pull in her stomach. Reaching out to the wall for support, she waited for the pain to subside.

'Are you okay?' Tayla's nose wrinkled in concern.

'The baby is kicking.' It really was. In fact, it was in a kickboxing match against her organs, and it was winning.

'Wow.' Tayla seemed horrified. 'I think I actually saw something move there, under your shirt.'

Belinda breathed in and out. After a few seconds, the baby calmed and she looked at where she'd rested her hand, on the shiny bronze plaque.

Clean Energy Solutions Australia.

'Officer!'

Belinda turned her gaze from the plaque to a middle-aged bearded man half jogging towards her, his face pink and hair flapping to one side.

'Andrew Kent,' he said when he reached her. 'Vice Principal. I'm the one who called you.'

'Senior Sergeant Belinda Burney.'

'Pleased to meet you.' They shook hands. 'Thanks for coming,' he said. 'I've been held up by this terrible business out on the wind farm, but I've got some time now if you like.'

Tayla, halfway down the steps, turned back anxiously. 'Mr Kent? Did you need me to do anything, take notes, or . . .?'

'No, no, Tayla!' Andrew waved her away. 'You go home now, you've done enough. Go get 'em at netball!'

Tayla beamed, and with a final nod continued down to the car park.

'Good kid.' The vice principal smiled at Tayla's retreating figure. 'Has a difficult home life, but she's resilient, she'll do well.' He looked at her. 'You have to admire kids like that, don't you?'

'You do.' They both watched as Tayla turned a corner out of sight.

'You must have had a busy day,' Belinda said. 'A death such as this one, it's shocked the whole community.'

Andrew nodded solemnly. 'I arrived this morning from Ballarat to find total mayhem; parents calling in, the education department wanting to send people over, kids congregating here just to talk.'

'You're from Ballarat?' Belinda asked by way of conversation. 'Long way to drive.'

'No, no – I live here,' Andrew said. 'But I had a leadership conference all weekend. Last night was the final dinner and drinks, and I stayed over.' He paused. 'On my way back this morning, I started getting the calls . . .'

A group of boys sauntered past, bouncing a ball. They called out to Andrew, and he gave them a weary but pleasant nod.

'I'm following up on your reports about the thefts.' Belinda wanted to get back on track. The vice principal seemed miles away. 'I've just spoken to Orla.'

'Oh, good, good.' Andrew tucked his belly into his pants and ran a hand down his thin hair. 'So you've already been inside our new building then? Wonderful, isn't it?'

'It is – Orla tells me it was funded in large part by the Pritchard family.'

Andrew looked at the bronze plaque. 'It was. Geordie Pritchard donated all the money to pay for the building, and next week we were supposed to have a celebration for it. The school band has been practising for weeks.'

Belinda remembered the Carrabeen school band – one girl singing mournfully into a mike while a bunch of kids picked their way through a tune.

'Is there anything else you can you tell me about these thefts?' Belinda asked. 'Orla mentioned the pencil cases, the five-dollar notes . . .'

Andrew gave a wry smile. 'Unfortunately, we think it must be some poor kid who needs extra resources at home. We're a public school, and although most kids come from middle-income families, not everyone in Carrabeen is doing so well. This town's not all about wheat money and turbines. Don't get me wrong, we'll continue to monitor the situation – and I'm very glad I alerted you – but this kind of thing is common across schools nowadays.'

'So, what do you plan to do about it? Other than letting me know?'

'We've done a few bag searches – no missing items recovered, but we've confiscated our fair share of alcohol and vapes, I can tell you that.' Andrew shook his head and gave a wry smile. 'But look, we're putting on a free breakfast twice a week, and it's well attended. We give them a hot meal, a comfy place to sit. And we have clean second-hand uniforms if any of them need it.'

'Good of you.'

'Most public schools run programs like it.'

Belinda felt another jump in her lower stomach. She blanched, closing her eyes for a second. When she opened them, Andrew was staring once more at the plaque. 'Did you know the deceased, Geordie Pritchard?' she asked.

The vice principal sighed. 'We met two or three times at board meetings to discuss the new building, and then most recently when we took the Year Ten students to the wind farm for an excursion.'

Belinda took her pen and paper out again. 'How long ago was this?'

'Two weeks?' Andrew Kent frowned, eager to be of help. 'Maybe three? Why don't you come to my office, I'll have the dates there.'

Belinda followed him back up the hall to his room. Inside, there was a wooden desk, some comfortable chairs and a large window. Everything felt shiny and new.

'Sit, sit!' Andrew waved proudly to one of the chairs. 'I've only been in this office since this morning, still getting used to how spacious it is. Mind you, I've got most of my stuff in Orla's at the moment, still moving things to and fro. This office will soon be messy enough. Can I get you a glass of water?'

'No, thanks.' She sat down gratefully. This was more like the type of office she'd imagined.

'Two and a half weeks ago . . .' Andrew was examining a calendar on the wall. 'Yes, that's right. Orla was there for part of it, Dean from PE came along – he's got a bus licence – and Julie from food technology too.'

'And how was the excursion?'

'Oh.' Andrew looked perplexed at the question. He sat down and rested one foot over the other knee, placing a hand on his shin in a casual pose. His trousers rose up to show a white, skinny leg covered in brown hairs. Belinda looked away.

'Let's see,' Andrew considered. 'It was a usual kind of day. Someone gave a talk, a few kids listened. We got to see inside one of the turbines. *I* thought it was interesting. We also heard from one of the wind technicians there, he did a good job.'

'Shane Burrows?' Belinda remembered the young man from that morning.

'Yes – that's right, Shane, former student here. Nice kid.'

'Was Geordie there for long?'

'No.' Andrew shook his head. 'He said hello to the students, said they were welcome to apply for jobs at his company, and then made some joke about the local football and netball teams. We spoke only briefly. I imagine that with his responsibilities, he was a busy man.'

Belinda nodded, looking out across the school oval to where the tops of three turbines were just visible.

'Impressive, aren't they?' Andrew said, following her gaze.

She couldn't deny it.

'And controversial too,' he conceded. 'But honestly, you've got to admire the technology.' He gave a short laugh. 'You'll have to forgive me; I studied engineering before I went into teaching, and I'm a real nerd for machines.'

Resting against the wall was a framed graduation certificate of his Master of Teaching from the University of Melbourne, partially covered by a cut-out image of Homer Simpson with the words, *People can come up with statistics to prove anything, Kent. 40% of people know that.*

'You went to Melbourne Uni,' Belinda said vaguely. 'My husband did too.'

'Did he? How interesting. Best years of your life, I say to the kids.'

'He didn't like it much, actually.'

'Oh? I'm sorry to hear that.' The vice principal cleared his throat. 'I was fortunate enough to live at one of the residences there, Wesley Hall.'

'That's where Will was too.'

Andrew hid his look of surprise well, but Belinda clocked it; she always did.

'How long ago was he there?' Andrew asked.

Belinda counted the years up in her head. 'Sixteen, maybe seventeen years?'

The man's face cleared. 'Ah, we were in different years then. I'm a little older. And it is such a big hall too, of course. Difficult to keep track of everyone.'

They chatted for a while more about how large Wesley Hall was and how different people have different experiences, how university is not for everyone. Belinda felt the vice principal was trying hard to make up for his earlier slip, and she did her best to make him feel at ease, laughing at his jokes and looking interested as he pointed out various plans for the school. *How do they do it?* Belinda wondered, as she agreed that yes, the performing arts were vital to a school culture, and yes again, how for some kids literature just wasn't the right fit. *How do posh people always get you to do the appeasing?* The vice principal had tried to hide his obvious shock at the thought that someone like her was married to a man who'd gone to a prestigious institution like Wesley – but the expression was written plain across his face.

Belinda drove along the main street, the newsagent advertising cheap books, the supermarket with its blinds down, the gum trees shuddering in the wind. Heat mirages rose across the road like a ghostly flood. She flicked the radio on, listened to a song lamenting lost love and wanting to dance till the end of time. *Fuck's sake*, she thought, flicking it off again. People were often surprised that she and Will were a couple because of their differences in upbringing and the way Will towered over her small frame – really, she thought, she should have been used to attitudes like Andrew Kent's by now. Up ahead a kid was riding a scooter on the footpath, fast, the vehicle too small for his long, lanky frame. She slowed down and saw who it was: one of the Razzes. All the Reynolds family were known as Raz; she didn't know why. She'd gone to school with one of the older Razzes. Katy? No, it was Cathy, that's right, although they just called her Raz. The family lived next door to her childhood home in the Bronx, which was the collective name given to the line of houses on Broker Court, two streets from the back of the servo. The Razzes weren't too bad, but there were always a lot of them, and they were loud. Sometimes there were fights in the front yard. Once, her own dad had threatened to punch the face of any Raz if they didn't shut the fuck up during the dog races on the radio. No one took it to heart.

This Raz – the one going too fast on the scooter – wouldn't have been born then. Belinda decided not to tell him off for being on the footpath. There was something about the look of him; those familiar features, thin with long red hair like a rat half-drowned in a dam. Cathy Raz had looked like that. She was a nice girl, Belinda remembered. They'd walked to school together. Cathy was dead now. Drugs, some back street in St Kilda. Dreams of the city not adding up; the escape worse than a return.

Belinda passed the chemist and the bakery. Each business she passed had a sign in its window that proclaimed allegiance for or against the wind farms. 'Say No to Wind Farms' read the one outside the pharmacy, while the bakery had 'Turbines Equal Prosperity' in bold letters on the door. Yesterday, she'd barely registered the signs. Now they seemed to be everywhere, bigger, bolder.

Beneath every country town there is a low hum of action, she mused. Discernible only to locals and dogs. Beneath Carrabeen there was a definite fizz, like an electrical current. One she hadn't stopped to hear until now.

CHAPTER 5

'You've got to be joking,' Belinda said aloud. '*Lucinda* came to the turbines while he was still up there?'

'Yeah,' Will answered. 'I recognised her straightaway.'

He watched as his wife, refusing any help, lowered herself into an armchair and pulled up her top, stopping just below her bra. Privately, Will thought that her belly looked like the globe for an alien planet: the red and blue lines, the strange bumps and hollows; it was a world yet to be explored. He shook himself. The idea that he would soon be a father was a wondrous thing.

'She still beautiful as ever?'

Will looked at his wife but couldn't detect anything other than genuine interest. 'I don't know, I wasn't really paying attention.'

Now that was a lie.

Even when sprawled out in the dirt, face smudged with tears and dust, Lucinda was a stunner. Oh, and didn't she know it! For a second, Will half suspected that the pose had been deliberate; the way her dress billowed around her legs and over the heeled sandals, the way her dark hair fell in waves about her pale face. Lucinda always did love a stage.

He knew she'd married Geordie Pritchard – his mother often liked to remind him – but up until today he'd never seen her here in Carrabeen. From what he knew, she spent the majority of her time in Melbourne, and when at the Yarrobee house, she had little need to come into town.

Now, he handed Belinda a glass of water and sat beside her, propping her swollen ankles onto his lap.

'Liar.' Belinda grinned at him, and he returned it. 'I wonder if this means you'll be taken off the case,' she said.

'What case?' Will looked at Belinda's feet, the toes like fat wriggling worms. 'It's hardly a case, is it? I know it's bad to say, but it appears just a suicide, doesn't it? Albeit a spectacular one. I mean, he left a note.'

Soon after the body had been recovered from the turbine, Kelmendri had informed them that a crumpled note had been found in the back pocket of Geordie's jeans. It was now in the hands of the coroner.

'Have you *seen* what's on this note?' Belinda asked. 'Or are Investigations still keeping its contents quiet?'

'I think they've shown it to Lucinda – privacy for the family and all that. They wouldn't usually share stuff like that, not for suicides.'

Belinda shrugged, unconvinced. She would have liked to see it, private or not – this was still a police matter. Every detail counted.

'And,' Will persisted, 'there's that television interview he gave last week, "extreme actions for extreme times", all the doomsday talk and apologising to his family for not doing enough . . . The bloke was clearly in a desperate state.'

On his way back into town after seeing Lucinda at the turbines, he'd googled Geordie's most recent television interview, the one Lisa had mentioned. It was clear that the CEO had been made for the camera: handsome and confident, Geordie spoke with authority, using the interviewer's name, listening to the other panellist, then politely offering his own view. At an invitation to address critics of the wind farms and clean energy providers, Geordie had turned directly to the camera. 'The time for inaction is over,' he said, grim-faced, chin squared. 'The time for deliberating, for discussion, for diversion is over. Enough! The planet is in serious trouble, and we need to act now, with drastic measures. What will it take for the leaders of this country to take note? What sort of statement would make them actually stop and listen?'

'Statement?' the interviewer cut in.

'A *drastic* statement,' Geordie replied. 'Action, not words.'

Will was silent for a moment, thinking of the turbine, of the day they'd had.

'But that's why it's a case, isn't it?' Belinda asked. 'A man kills himself like that, for everyone to see, and I mean, *everyone*. It's a statement.' She'd also seen the interview.

'Yes, but what does the statement *tell* us?' Will leaned back into the couch, staring up at the ceiling. 'That he didn't like wind turbines after all?'

'He was the CEO of Clean Energy Solutions!'

'That they weren't effective enough, extreme enough to combat climate change?' Will offered other ideas. 'That his business was killing him, and he couldn't cope?'

Belinda shrugged. 'I was up at the school earlier, checking out that report of thefts, and you should have seen the new work they've done. There's practically a whole new wing, all paid for by Geordie.'

'Yeah?'

'The school had invited him to an event there next week, to say thanks. He'd accepted.'

'So what? That doesn't mean anything.'

'I know.' Belinda nodded. 'But—'

There was a shout at the front door, and their younger colleague Tammy trooped in. 'Who's up for a drink?'

'Me!' Will stood to greet her, then headed to the fridge to get two beers. Belinda would be sticking to water.

'How you feeling, Bel?' Tammy sank into a chair opposite her friend.

'Like a whale ate a whale,' Belinda said, as she chomped down on a handful of chips.

When Will returned and passed Tammy a beer, the three sat in companionable silence for a minute.

'On the way here, I was held up by Gordon Highett, that professor bloke who lives out of town,' Tammy said, taking a sip of her beer. 'He said we should look at providing police protection for high-profile defenders of clean energy. That he wasn't feeling safe in the community.'

'What?' Belinda leaned forward, shaking her head.

'Yeah. He said he's been receiving threats for weeks now about his work in climate activism, and up till now he hasn't taken them seriously. But after Geordie, he's starting to rethink his attitude.'

'Well, he never reported them,' Will muttered.

'I know, I said that to him, but he just said' – Tammy adopted an exaggerated posh voice – '"It's what you learn to expect when you put your head above the parapet."'

'What's a parapet?' Belinda asked.

'It's the top of a castle wall.' Will drew a series of lines with his finger in the air. 'You know, where they go up, then down, then up again. They were used for defending the castle against sieges.'

'How the hell do you know that?' Tammy laughed.

'He spends a lot of time thinking about the Roman Empire,' Belinda answered with a smirk.

Will smiled. It was true, he *did* spend some time thinking about the Roman Empire, but he'd learned about parapets during the semester he'd spent studying history in his first and only year of university.

'Do you seriously think Gordon believes that the anti-turbine people hassled Geordie so badly that he killed himself?'

'Dunno what he thought, Bel.' Tammy took another sip of beer. 'Gordon is a bit of an old drama queen, and when I say that, I mean it. He was in last year's production of *Oklahoma!* – and fuck, it was awful.'

Will's mother had made him see *Oklahoma!* in London when he was a kid. All he remembered was that the King of Tonga was present that evening, and they'd all had to stand for him while he was escorted to the front row.

'But what Gordon said, it did make me think about that group, Farms for Future.' Tammy swigged her beer. 'You know? The group who held that meeting a while back, when the wind farm was in the middle of being built.'

'We weren't here then,' Belinda said. 'But Dad told me about it. He would have gone to that meeting if he could.'

'It started off calm, then turned crazy when their main speaker . . . what's his name?'

'Doug Hay?' Belinda suggested. Doug was one of her father's best friends.

'Yeah, him. He started off with his usual stuff, going on about all the farming land that's been eaten up by big corporations and how the little farmers can't compete and how the country is growing in population, and we need more food, but production is being stymied by the new green infrastructure like solar and wind farms.'

Will listened with interest. Almost the end of their year in Carrabeen and he was only just beginning to understand the level of conflict within the community. Every country town had their warring families, Belinda had told him. It was usually over land, but sometimes on whether to upgrade the tennis courts.

'So, yeah,' Tammy continued, still swigging her beer, 'Doug Hay gets everyone into this full-on frenzy and there's shouting and cheering, and someone brings up the ANZACs and there's laughing, and then someone yells out, "Let's get the bastards!"'

'Whoa!' Belinda raised her eyebrows. 'Vibe change.'

'She was told to shut up, but we all heard it. I couldn't work out who said it, and no one owned up.'

Belinda exhaled loudly, putting down her empty glass, and made an effort to pull herself up. Will stood in front of her, held her hands and hauled her upright. She relaxed for a moment into his chest, and peered up at him, smiling. He planted a quick kiss on her forehead.

Tammy mimed a gag.

'Dinner!' Belinda declared, ignoring her. She gave a decisive clap and walked towards the kitchen.

'You didn't cook, did you?' Tammy asked. 'We could have got takeaway, Bel.'

'I put something on this morning when I couldn't sleep.' Weird to think now that while she was chopping onions and garlic and cooking lamb mince, Geordie was dead or dying. At her tenth birthday party, she suddenly remembered, he'd brought her a present wrapped in orange tissue paper.

Will set the table while Tammy talked more about the Farms for Future group, and their opposition, the local Climate Action Group. 'You know who heads it now, don't you?' she said, suddenly glum. 'Marit.'

'I didn't know that!' Belinda looked up, surprised.

'Yeah well, she's only been in town for six months, hasn't she?'

'Forget about her.' Will instinctively hadn't liked Tammy's girlfriend – correction, ex-girlfriend.

'Easy for you to say.'

Will patted her hand. 'Come on, Tammy, there's plenty of fish—'

'Don't say, "There's plenty of fish in the sea!"' Tammy gave a resigned sigh. 'There's not. There's not even a carp in this town. I might as well dig out my lycra and move back to Kew.'

Belinda brought over a steaming dish of lamb topped with baked eggplant and feta.

'Is there any chance Marit'll change her mind?' she asked.

'Zero. She said that she's "not sure about us" – which is code for she's positive she doesn't want to be with me.' Tammy's shoulders slumped. 'I mean, she never introduced me to her family, or took me rock climbing with her mates like she promised a million times.'

Belinda began serving the food as Will held the plates out for her.

'Well, we think you're a catch,' he said, putting her meal in front of her. 'Marit must have rocks in her head.'

'You're full of clichés tonight.' Tammy gave him a weak smile. 'But yeah, thanks. Tomorrow is another day. I guess.'

The trio began eating, and for the first time that day, Belinda felt herself relaxing. She was always like this when she saw her favourite people tucking into her food. Nurturing, Will called it.

But Belinda wasn't so sure that was the right word. More likely, she thought, the need to feed stemmed from relief that when the people around her were eating, it was mostly a peaceful affair. Her father had liked to listen to the dog racing when they ate, and if one of his bets lost, he'd bang the table so hard with his fist that they'd all jump.

'And you know,' Tammy said in between mouthfuls, 'it's bad for me to hang around with you two, because you're like this perfect couple and that is seriously not good for my self-esteem.'

Belinda gazed at Will over the table and the two grinned at each other. When Tammy said stuff like that – and she often did – they knew it was only half in jest.

Will poured Tammy a red wine and one for himself.

'Bloody Marit,' Tammy said, taking a large swig. 'She cares more about her causes than she does any relationship.'

Will and Belinda waited, letting their friend vent.

'And you know what's weird, now that I think about it?' Tammy gestured with her fork. 'Marit was always going on about *serious measures to effect change*. Like, she wasn't opposed to corporate vandalism, smashing windows of businesses or blocking major roads. I could sort of see what she was getting at, but that's something I absolutely do not agree with.'

'And you're right,' Belinda said. 'How's smashing windows or blocking roads going to achieve anything? It just makes people angry.'

Will sipped his wine but said nothing.

'She wasn't a fan of the Pritchards either,' Tammy added. 'Her and Geordie were always arguing.'

'Why's that?' Belinda said, rubbing her neck and stretching out her aching back. 'Geordie was hugely into clean energy stuff; you'd think Marit would love him.'

'I dunno. She's barely spoken to me since we broke up. Brutal.' Tammy stabbed at a forkful of food and shoved it in her mouth. 'Talk about effecting change.'

CHAPTER 6

The next morning, Belinda and Will lay in bed, discussing the day ahead. Outside, a magpie sang, its melodious tune a welcome start to the day.

'Come on,' Will said finally. 'We've got to get moving.'

Belinda sighed heavily and rolled over, then sat up on the side of the bed. Reluctantly, she agreed to stay in town rather than head out to the turbines with Will and the team from Investigations, Lisa and Kelmendri. Will had been the one who'd gone up the machine in the first place, and he might need to go again. With less than two weeks of work left before she went on maternity leave, it made sense for Belinda to focus on the day-to-day running of the station instead.

'Anyway,' Will said, 'I should be back in town later this morning. The Investigations team won't need much longer there working out the logistics.'

Belinda understood that 'logistics' meant: how the hell did Geordie manage to hang himself from a forty-metre blade?

She reached back across the bed to give her husband's arm a squeeze. 'Hey, were you okay up there?'

'It wasn't fun,' Will said, turning on his side to give his wife a one-armed hug, reaching around her huge pregnant stomach, giving in to the warmth of her.

'How did you go with the height?' she asked. 'I never properly asked you.'

'Not good,' Will admitted. 'I was kind of freaking out on the way up.'

'Really? I didn't know you were *that* bad.'

'Oh, I am.'

'You proposed to me on top of the Eiffel Tower.'

'I was scared then too, but more because I thought you might say no.'

'You did not think that,' she said, and Will heard the smile in her voice.

'You're right.' He snuggled into her. 'I knew exactly what you'd say.'

What Belinda had done, in fact, was turn a bright tomato-red before giving him a watery kiss. She'd been unable to speak. They laughed about it now, the cheesiness of the moment – how he'd kneeled on one knee, before bringing out the little velvet box in a self-conscious flourish. Other tourists clapped dutifully, but Will said he'd never forget the bored expression on the face of the person who worked there. Another couple had been waiting to do exactly the same thing, and the man kept looking at his watch while the woman chewed gum nervously. Later, Will admitted to Belinda that he'd googled 'best places to propose' and the Eiffel Tower had come up as number one.

But even so, despite the lack of imagination and Will's fear of heights, they agreed that it ranked highly among the greatest moments of their lives to date.

'Come on, let's go.' Belinda reached her arm out to draw the curtain aside. 'Media'll be swarming the station, and we'll need to start with the door knocks. I know you and Tammy will be doing most of that stuff, but I can help too.'

In consultation with their superiors from Investigations, it had been decided: the Carrabeen police officers would take on the bulk of door knocks and preliminary interviews with neighbours, family and friends of the deceased, in preparation for the coroner and to stave off media interest. For such a high-profile suicide, they wanted it wrapped up neatly.

'And what about you?' Will was murmuring into her lower back, still half asleep. 'I'd never heard you speak about Geordie Pritchard until yesterday, but you knew him, yeah?'

'When I was a kid, and not that well. We were at primary school here, he was two years older. But you know, in small country schools all the year levels merge together. He left for boarding school at the start of Year Seven.'

'Still' – Will pulled her in tighter – 'it can't be easy. You've got this image of him from when you were kids, and then the next time you see him is . . . he's . . .'

Belinda slowly stood, cradling her bump and turning to look at him. 'Well, actually . . .'

Will's phone beeped. With an exaggerated sigh, he too climbed out of bed and gave a mighty yawn as he picked up his phone. 'Lucinda's on her way in,' he told his wife. 'Wants to meet me at the station.'

Belinda nodded, preoccupied with bending over to pull up her socks. Will walked around to the other side of the bed, kneeled down and helped her. 'Want to join me in speaking to her?' he asked. 'I'd like you to.'

'Sure. I've got the midwife appointment at ten, but I can come in before I go.' Belinda focused on her stretchy pants, pulling them wide to see how big they were. It was as if the clothes she was wearing lately were for a different person entirely.

Will looked relieved. He walked towards the shower before turning back to her. 'What was it you were going to say about Geordie?'

Belinda kept studying the pants. 'Nothing,' she said after a short pause. 'Nothing important.'

Because it wasn't important, not really – only that the last time she'd seen Geordie alive wasn't when they were kids. No, no.

The last time was three days ago.

The Investigations team were already heading out of the station, on their way to the turbines, by the time Will and Belinda arrived. They waited at the bottom of the station steps to let them pass, but Lisa hung back, reluctant. 'Lucinda's just arrived,' she whispered excitedly to Will. 'She's distraught! Only wants to see you.'

'Right.' Will looked sideways at Belinda.

'She says you know each other from way back,' Lisa added, moving to join her colleague. '*Do* you?'

'They do,' Belinda answered for him, friendly, but firm enough to put a stop to the questions.

'Well then.' Lisa raised her eyebrows. 'I'll be off.'

'As you were,' Will said, indicating for his wife to walk up the steps in front of him.

'*As you were?*' Belinda gave a short laugh. 'Are we in a British sitcom now?'

Through the open door, Will saw Lucinda standing there, her face caught in a golden reflection of the window. *'Allo 'Allo*, he might have said.

'Lucinda.' He stepped inside. 'How are you?'

The day before, at the turbines, Lucinda Pritchard had been sobbing pretty much the whole time, asking over and over if it was really Geordie hanging up there, to get him down, get him *down*! Despite Will's efforts to comfort her, she'd only calmed slightly when another car pulled up, and two sombre women half carried her back to her vehicle.

This morning, smart-casual in jeans, a white T-shirt and navy blazer, Lucinda was much more composed.

'Tired,' she said, her beautiful features pale and withdrawn. 'And I need to talk to you about Geordie.'

Will held his hands out in a gesture of helplessness. 'There's not much I can say, Lucinda. We're assisting Investigations for the coronial inquiry, but we really don't know anything at this stage. I'm sorry.'

'You were there! You saw him – Geordie – up there swinging like a . . . like a . . .' Lucinda faltered, and for a moment Will thought she might begin crying again. Swiftly, Belinda reached for a box of tissues and handed a couple to the widow, briefly touching the other woman's arm in a gesture of sympathy. Lucinda blinked, as if surprised to see someone else in the room with them.

'Oh,' she said, dabbing the tissues under her eyes with a small, grateful smile. 'Oh, you must be Bella. My mother told me about you.'

'It's Belinda.' Belinda turned on her heel and shut the front door. 'Would you like a cup of tea?'

Lucinda hesitated, then gave a short nod. 'Yes, please.'

'Why don't we talk in one of our rooms, where it's a bit more comfortable? I'll show you.' As she spoke, Belinda smiled encouragingly, motioning for Lucinda to follow her up the hallway.

Will looked at his wife in admiration, her short, strong body in such contrast to Lucinda's tall, willowy frame. Belinda had a gift for taking control of situations, knowing just what to say. If it was awkward having his ex-girlfriend suddenly pop up, she didn't show it.

Despite Belinda's promise it wasn't very comfortable in the interview room, but there was a table and three chairs and a window. Will continued on to the kitchen to make the tea, shuffling about in the cupboards to find a mug that didn't have some sort of motto written across it. The police sergeant before them had been a dull sort who enjoyed dad jokes and considered himself a practical joker. His sudden resignation from the Carrabeen police force had led to the vacancy for a full-timer, enabling Will and Belinda to make the temporary move from Melbourne to Belinda's childhood town. It had been a pleasant surprise when Bel fell pregnant within a few months, and her part-time status worked well as she grew bigger and more tired.

Now, Will rinsed a dusty mug with *I'd Rather Be Fishing* on it, filled it with boiling water and plonked a tea bag inside. Sometimes he fantasised that the former cop had never resigned, and he was just in Carrabeen for a quick visit. It wasn't that he didn't like the country town – he enjoyed the space and the quiet – it was more that he didn't truly fit in, not like Bel. Unless your great-grandparents were buried in the local cemetery, or you were a life member of the bowls club, Will thought, there was little chance of truly integrating. His eyes fell onto another of the old copper's mugs. *Do I Look Like I Care?* it asked. Adding a dash of milk to Lucinda's cup, he carried it back to the interview room.

'I'm staying at the big house here,' Lucinda was telling his wife. 'That's what the Pritchard family call it, the big house.

50

We've got our place in Melbourne, but I was up here when I got a call from the man who works at the turbines.'

'Shane Burrows?' Will asked, putting the mug down in front of her. 'He's a wind technician.'

'Yes, him. He called Geordie's number first, apparently – to tell him to get to the farm because of the body. And then when he couldn't reach him, he called me and asked me to let Geordie know. I knew straightaway there was a problem; Geordie always answers his phone.'

'Did you have any reason to think the body might be your husband's?'

'Not initially. No, of course not! But then, when I couldn't get hold of him . . . I kept ringing and ringing . . . and I just had a bad feeling. By then, of course, every farmer had seen him up there and the rumours were starting.'

Lucinda turned her gaze to Will. 'Everyone's telling me that Geordie killed himself! One of his friends from Hong Kong sent me this long email with information on how to cope after the suicide of a loved one. My own mother is suggesting that the pressure of work must have got to him – but it's not true. Geordie wouldn't kill himself.'

'The Investigations team will look into every angle, you can be sure of that,' Belinda told her.

Lucinda tore her eyes away from Will to look at Belinda briefly. 'It's the twins' eighth birthday next week,' she said. 'We were going to take them to see the fairy penguins on Phillip Island. They've just finished a project on them at school, and Geordie loves that kind of thing – you know, threatened species. We were all going to drive down there at dusk, take hot chocolates and go and see the bloody things. People don't kill themselves when they've planned to see fairy fucking penguins with their kids!'

Lucinda's upturned hand rested on the table, fingers curled, the palm as smooth and white as a shell. Will resisted a sudden urge to reach out and hold it.

'And that piece of paper they claim is his suicide note – it's ridiculous! A bunch of words that don't make any sense.'

'Can we ask you what he wrote?' Belinda probed, conscious of Will's gaze on her.

'It was nonsense, fragmented sentences that mean nothing . . .'

Lucinda fished around in her phone before pulling up an image of a note penned in blue, on what looked like a scrap of paper. She held it out for both of them to read.

What Statement Will it Take?

World in dire state

Time for Extreme Action Not Words

time to pause

listen

Fact is: World is in a perilous state

My family sorry I've not done enough

Let my children down

Enough

Will frowned. Was it meant to be a poem?

'If Geordie was going to write a suicide note, he'd at least make it clear to understand.' Lucinda pulled her phone back and studied the words. 'And what's this shitty "my family sorry" blah blah . . . No mention of our names? His children? And why leave it in the back pocket of his jeans? If it was a suicide note, surely he'd do something grander – like leave it on my dressing table, or somewhere more significant. He'd write something in it to me – something more personal.'

Will thought that Lucinda was mistaking suicide for something else, like a love letter or a poignant break-up note. In his experience, suicide notes were rarely penned with grace. 'Sorry, I stuffed up.' 'Don't go into the shed.' 'The world is fucked. Goodbye.'

But even so, Lucinda had a point. If Geordie was so big on statements, and so wonderful with people, why leave his final thoughts crumpled up in the back pocket of his jeans? And there was something else about the words in it . . .

'Geordie mentioned quite a few of those things in his television interview, the one he did last week,' Belinda broke in, echoing Will's barely formed thought. 'He used some of those very words.'

Lucinda shrugged. 'I didn't see that interview.'

'I mean,' Belinda added pointedly, 'he didn't use "time to pause", but maybe that was more of a directional phrase, like to himself.'

Lucinda wasn't listening. She stared out the window with a vacant gaze.

Will looked at his wife, had a good idea of what she was thinking. She tilted her head in a subtle nod: *Go on*, it said. *You do it.*

'Lucinda,' he said slowly, 'could the note have been a series of dot points – prompts for his speech on TV last week?'

Lucinda turned to him and gave a bitter laugh. 'It could be, why not? He was always jotting random things down – quotes, reminders to himself or whatever. And that' – she jabbed a finger at her phone – 'was *not* a suicide note. If he was going to kill himself, Geordie would have written something far more obvious. He was a businessman, not some tortured poet.'

Belinda gave Will a small smile and he returned it with a quick one of his own. They'd have to check it, of course, go back and verify the note against the interview – but yes, it did seem likely that the 'suicide note' was merely a series of interview prompts. A shiver ran through his body. What did that mean for their suicide theory?

The three sat in contemplation till Belinda broke the spell.

'When was the last time you saw your husband?' she asked.

'Sunday, around six, six-thirty, I think.' Lucinda rubbed a forefinger over her eye. 'He was heading back down to Melbourne for a night or two. When he said goodbye to me, I didn't even look up.' For a moment, her eyes grew wild. 'I can't remember if I said anything to him. Do you think I did?'

The question was directed at Belinda, and it took a second for her to respond. 'Yes, I'm sure you did.'

Lucinda ran her hands along her thighs before clasping them together. She straightened her shoulders and said, 'No one seems to be listening to me, and that's why I wanted to come to you. You'll listen to me, won't you, Will? I know you!'

Will hesitated, feeling Belinda's eyes on him. 'What do you want to say, Lucinda?'

The widow looked at both of them, fierce determination written across her face. 'My husband was *murdered*. And I'm not leaving Carrabeen till I find out exactly who is responsible.'

CHAPTER 7

When Will had excused himself to join Investigations at the turbines, Belinda had been surprised to see that Lucinda, after initially making moves to leave, had hesitated in departing. She'd assumed that her husband's ex-girlfriend would make a swift exit as soon as he'd gone, and it did seem – after her explosive announcement about murder – that the interview was over.

But Lucinda stayed, sipping her tea, her thoughts seemingly elsewhere. Her presence in the room was disconcerting, to say the least. When Belinda had first met Will, he'd been only newly separated from Lucinda and reluctant to talk about his past. That had suited Belinda, who was eager to escape her own. And right up till now – right up till yesterday – their lives had mostly been about the present and, with the baby, the future.

Belinda knew that Lucinda was married to Geordie, and she'd seen photos of Lucinda, of course. Will's mother still kept them dotted about her place, and the few times Will had mentioned his ex, he'd hinted at the sort of life they'd led. The two had been at boarding school together in their senior years and had then both begun attending Wesley Hall, the same prestigious accommodation Andrew Kent had enjoyed a few years earlier. However, she knew Will had been intensely unhappy there – cue the police training academy and meeting her.

A small, unhappy thought popped into Belinda's head: why would anyone be intensely unhappy with Lucinda? She was once a model for Country Road. *I could never model for Country Road,* she thought, glum. *Not even for Suzanne Grae.*

Yes, Lucinda was undeniably beautiful, and Belinda had immediately labelled her 'Vacuous Old Money', or VACs as she and her friend Briley used to call such people. They had other labels too, like PAPs for 'Playing at Poor'. That one was for the wealthy kids at Carrabeen College who wore op-shop clothes (and told everyone about it), did the forty-hour fast (and told everyone about it), who applied for and received scholarships (and told everyone about it), and who went on overseas gap years to help out in orphanages (and told everyone in the world about it). *You know what? Good on them,* Belinda thought, without any real rancour. At least they were doing something.

Plus, she had to admit that Will was something of a PAP. It didn't make him, or them, bad people – they genuinely believed they were deserving of all they got. Poor rich people, or PRP, as Briley used to snigger.

Right now, Belinda was fairly sure that Lucinda would never be a PAP. She wore her wealth proudly, wasn't afraid to mention the expensive education she'd received, or the property she'd bought with her parents' help. And despite her long, lanky features and long, glossy brown hair, and despite the designer jeans and handbag, the navy blazer and the rose-gold earrings,

Lucinda didn't act like a VAC. No, Belinda had to admit that the woman in front of her cut an impressive figure.

'Someone killed my husband,' she said simply. 'I want you and Will to find out who.'

'And do you believe that person lives around here?'

'Oh, yes.' Lucinda looked at her with cool, hazel eyes. 'Yes, I do.'

Twenty minutes later, as she was heading out to her car, Belinda rang Will.

'Lucinda is convinced someone opposed to the turbines killed Geordie. They'd received threats, and she says Geordie used to talk about how much the anti-turbine people hated what he was doing, no matter how much he tried to make amends.'

'Threats?'

'Phone calls. She's kept some of the messages; I said we'll need to have a listen.'

'And by "amends", you mean that Geordie was trying to offer compensation?'

'That's what I reckon.'

'She give you names?'

'Not for the phone calls, she doesn't know who they were from. And she didn't have the specifics on the anti-turbine people Geordie tried to appease. But she did give me a list of groups who were campaigning against his business, all of them opposed to natural energy. And you know which one is written in bold and underlined?'

'Let me guess.'

Belinda didn't give him time. 'Farms for Future. The one Doug Hay runs.'

'You know him, don't you?' Sometimes it was difficult for Will to keep track of who Belinda knew in the town.

'Yep. He's one of Dad's old mates. Good businessman, friendly – and most definitely harmless.'

Will was quiet. Belinda was pretty sure she knew what that meant. He'd met a few of his father-in-law's old mates, and had heard some tales. Harmless wasn't a word Will would have chosen for them.

'Leave me to talk with Doug,' she said. 'He's the sort who'll open up more to people he knows.' *People he can relate to*, Belinda thought. *Not like you, Will, with your rounded vowels and your polo shirts with the little horse on the front.*

The Carrabeen medical clinic was a series of small, newish build-ings on the way out of town. Belinda walked through the sliding doors, saying hello to Oshani the receptionist. Oshani was married to but separated from Belinda's second cousin, Johnny. Johnny was a good-looking man, but his obsession with *Mad Max* had driven the couple apart. There were only so many dystopian-inspired V8s Oshani could suffer in their front yard. Now, Oshani introduced her to Nola, a midwife Belinda hadn't met before, although she'd seen her in the supermarket a couple of times.

Practical and kind, Nola wasn't above a bit of gossip once she learned Belinda was the local cop. And her conversation, as Belinda lay on the table awaiting her scan, was the same one that had the whole town talking: the death of Geordie Pritchard.

'He was a lovely man,' Nola said, as she prepared the gel. 'I met him just the once, at a fundraiser for the hospital, but my aunt has known him since he was a little one and first got shipped off to boarding school. Lovely kid, very bright.'

Belinda gazed at the monitor to her left, trying to make sense of the pulsating blobs.

'It's a terrible loss of course for his family, but also for the town. His company did so much for Carrabeen. This machine you're hooked up to? We didn't even need a fundraiser; Geordie just gave us the money straight up. That's how generous he was.'

'Incredible . . .' Belinda mumbled, still fixated on the screen.

'And all that work at the school, honestly – he's transformed this town! When the school was almost poleaxed by an outbreak of Covid last year, we were able to get straight onto the latest vaccinations because he helped to bring in extra staff from Ballarat.'

Belinda tried her best to ignore the woman and focus on the image. The rhythmic sound of a heartbeat, the whooshing of blood to vital organs.

'And that was in spite of the crackpots in town trying to tell everyone that the vaccinations cause infertility.'

'Did people really say that?'

'Oh, yes!' Nola said cheerfully. 'But thanks to Geordie Pritchard, we got the jabs done smoothly.'

Belinda murmured vague sounds of relief.

'I mean, the man was a saint!'

The image on the screen showed a white shape floating in blackness. It looked a tad creepy – but even so, Belinda was surprised at the rush of affection she felt for it.

'Is it still in breech position?' She'd needed this late-stage scan to check. It would be a nightmare, she thought, to have to have a caesarean and be bedridden for days.

'Yes, but there's still time for the baby to turn,' Nola said. 'No need to book a caesar just yet.'

'That's good.'

'Your baby looks very healthy,' the midwife commented, peering at the screen. 'Do you want to know the sex?'

Belinda wavered. Will was adamant he wanted it to be a surprise. But Belinda didn't like surprises. She liked to know everything in advance: even his marriage proposal hadn't been a surprise – she'd already seen the ring in its maroon velvet box hidden in among his socks. But that didn't make the moment any less joyful – if anything, it made it even better. Never in a million years did she think she'd be proposed to on top of the Eiffel Tower by a man like Will Lovett, whom her friend Briley once described as an Aussie Clark Kent.

She still kept that ugly maroon box in her bedside cabinet.

'No thanks, Nola,' she replied. 'We'll keep it a surprise.'

The midwife's conversation turned to Geordie once more. 'You'll be busy, I expect, with his death.'

Belinda shrugged. *Give it a rest, lady.*

'Well, remember to look after yourself. Your baby is worth more than work.'

'I like work.'

'So do I,' Nola said, more gently. 'But relaxation is good for the baby. What you feel – stress, tiredness – the baby feels too. I suggest you take a good amount of time after the birth to rest up.'

Belinda nodded gravely. 'Of course.' She didn't mention the job application, now fully complete on her laptop, the deadline 6 pm. If she hadn't yet decided on whether to press send, was there any real need to tell Will?

Belinda never found it easy to drive up the street where she'd spent seventeen years of her life. The house at the end of the road behind the petrol station, the one five hundred metres from the tip. Number four, Broker Court. Her old home. Not as bad as number six, but almost.

Reg Burney's front yard was littered with stones in place of a garden and had a broken path leading up to the house, which was built with the shitty fibro sheeting used on all government-built commission houses in the seventies. A broken blind flapped pathetically against the mission brown window frames, the metallic sound instantly transporting her to childhood.

Next door, an old lady sat in an armchair on the porch, her huge arms and legs stuck to it, as if she was a prisoner. Bernice was a Raz, but only Reg Burney called her that.

Belinda gave her a wave. 'Hi, Bernice.'

The woman lifted a forefinger and offered a slight nod in return.

'Dad!' Belinda called as she pushed open the front door. 'It's me!'

'Fucken prostate.' Her father limped up the hall. 'Given me hell.'

Belinda watched as the old man lowered himself into a deck chair in the lounge room, indicating for her to sit on the sagging couch opposite. There was a smell of mice and sweat in the room.

'Has the nurse come?' Belinda sat down.

'Ha! Wendy,' Reg growled. 'Fucken bitch.'

'You'd better not be rude to the nurses,' Belinda warned. 'Otherwise no one'll ever want to come out here.'

'Julie's all right,' her dad admitted. 'She'd come.'

Julie again. Food tech teacher, messenger to the spirits, and also Meals on Wheels volunteer. Was there anything Julie couldn't do?

Reg farted. 'Onions,' he said. 'Give me wind.'

Belinda closed her eyes and tried some slow breathing. *Ask yourself,* she thought, *what would Julie do?*

Her father began rolling a cigarette. His wiry arms were like old willow branches, his face a dried prune. There was not an ounce of fat on him; he was all sinew and bones. In his time, Reg Burney had been a good-looking man. There'd been a photo of him in the paper once, which his mother had cut out and framed, when he'd won a shire record for shearing the most ewes in a day. There he was, a confident grin on his face, leaning over a fence in his short shorts, Blundstones and a blue singlet. Belinda had been told by old locals that Reg looked like Paul Hogan in his day. Born in Carrabeen, his own father had worked as a fencer in the region, and had been a cruel parent. At sixteen, Reg's mother gave him money for a bus ticket, and he pocketed it, hitching with a mate up to Sydney. There they conned their way into working as bridge riggers, returning at nineteen, when his father died and the offer of a shearing job from Hugh Pritchard's father beckoned.

'Cup of tea?' Belinda asked.

Reg nodded. 'Put sugar in it this time, will you? Three.'

Belinda walked through to the kitchen, where plates were piled high in the sink and a vague smell of dank water hung in the air. On the windowsill there was a tin filled with fat Reg had collected from his chops. Dripping, he called it. She threw it out and pushed open the window. In the cupboards she found two tea bags and then hunted for the sugar among the ancient jars of sago and dried coconut. Looking for a teaspoon, she discovered a drawer devoted entirely to plastic bags, scrunched up and tied together. Reg never threw anything away. Was it hoarding or good recycling? She didn't know.

While the kettle boiled, Belinda filled the sink with hot water and began washing the dishes. *He should do it himself*, she thought. He was perfectly capable of doing a pile of dishes, but still, here she was, scrubbing his dirty, baked-on pans, as if she'd been programmed to do it. She'd returned to Carrabeen with Will after Reg received his diagnosis of prostate cancer. Now, as she stood in the grimy kitchen, noting the packet of tobacco on the sideboard, she wondered if she'd been any help at all.

'Hear about Geordie Pritchard?' she called out.

'Yep.' Her dad's gravelly voice carried through. 'Doug told me.'

Doug Hay had been Reg's old shearing mate and, in the vast shire they lived in, was only second in wealth to the Pritchards. The two families, the Hays and the Pritchards, couldn't be more different though. Geordie and his father and his father's father all went to the same boarding school, then university in Sydney and then a stint working in city banks before returning, distinguished and educated, to the family farm; Doug Hay left school early and worked his way up, buying land, working it, never leaving. Bitter rivals now, their feud was legendary.

In contrast, and despite their obvious differences in wealth, landowner Doug Hay and former shearer Reg Burney had been firm friends since primary school, their loyalty to one another unchanged by any inequality in lifestyle. When Belinda's mother died and Reg went to the dogs, it was Doug who kept the young family afloat. Belinda remembered that. One of her earliest memories was of Doug giving her a Beach Blast Barbie.

Unable to find a dish cloth, Belinda shook a couple of cups dry and made the tea.

'What does Doug have to say about it?' she asked, as she carried the hot drinks back out to the living room.

'Not much. But I'm guessing he wished it was him who had strung the bastard up.'

Belinda winced. Her father never bothered to hide his casual cruelty.

'No one deserves that,' she said tightly. 'Anyway, authorities are treating it as a suicide.'

'Suicide my arse.' Reg scowled into his tea. 'You come back home, prodigal sun shining out of your arse, and you go and ruin good farmland to build those fucken eyesores. What did he expect? A Gold fucken Logie?'

'We don't know anything as yet, and it's not helpful to speculate.'

'Like father, like fucken son . . .' Reg muttered.

They sipped their tea in silence. Belinda gazed dolefully at a photo on the mantelpiece of herself at sixteen years old, in her deb dress. With her high hair, heavy mascara and blush, she looked like a startled meerkat. At the afterparty, she'd drunk Southern Comfort and vomited on her partner, a ferrety type with a mullet and a loose tie. Dean Hookes's style had definitely improved with age, but the PE teacher had once been as bogan as the rest of them. He'd been a terrible deb partner, she recalled, rarely turning up to practice and forgetting to buy her a gift. God, she thought, some of the old anguish resurfacing, why the hell had she agreed to go with him?

Reg was looking at her intently. 'Everything okay with you? With the little one?'

She frowned, momentarily confused, till she realised he was talking about her bump.

'Oh,' she said, slightly shocked. It had been one of the few times he'd mentioned the baby. 'Yep. All good. I think.'

She took another gulp of tea before standing up and carrying her half-full cup to the kitchen. 'I'll be off,' she said, rinsing it out and placing it next to the other now gleaming dishes. 'See you in a couple of days, Dad.'

Her father had put his cup down and was focused on lighting his rollie again. 'I wouldn't worry too much about it. Your mother did a fine job of it with you.'

Too stunned to speak, Belinda raised a hand in farewell and walked out the front door onto the stony path. Was her cantankerous old father becoming soft in his old age?

'Eh!' His voice rang out from inside. 'You only put one bloody sugar in this tea!'

Backing fast out of the driveway, she was surprised to see a shiny ute waiting to take her spot. It took her a second to place her father's old friend.

'Hey, Doug,' she said, an elbow out the window, engine idling. 'We were just talking about you. New ute?'

'Little B!' Doug boomed, using her old moniker. 'Yep, picked it up in Ballarat yesterday. Still got that new-car smell.'

'Love it.' Belinda had never owned a new car.

'Just dropping off this old telly for your father,' Doug continued. 'Reg can't watch the dogs on that shitbox he's got in there.'

The telly in Doug's back seat didn't look like a shitbox. In its fancy packaging, it looked brand new. In her father's house, it would be positively space age.

'The old man seems to be doing well, doesn't he?' Doug was always up for a chat.

Belinda turned off the engine. 'He does, although he's not keen on one of the nurses.'

'That'd be Wendy.' Doug grinned. 'She was a hard case when she was twenty; now she's hit her fifties, she's a force to behold.'

'Doug,' Belinda cut in. 'What's this I hear about you heading up the fight against the wind farms?'

'Should be pretty obvious,' the farmer said, affably. 'This area's a food bowl. Can't make your breakfast using AI just yet.'

Belinda agreed; no, you couldn't.

'And,' the old man continued, 'how effective are those bloody things anyway?' He waved a hand in the direction of the turbines, where even from this part of town, you could just make out the tops of them, spinning. 'Hardly going to stop global climate change. Ugly too. Give me a Blakely anytime.'

The Blakely gums, known as paddock trees, held court all over the shire, a reminder of another time.

Her mobile pinged.

'You must be busy,' Doug said, nodding at her phone. 'Shocked everyone, hasn't it – this business with Geordie topping himself.'

'It's very sad for the family,' Belinda answered diplomatically. 'We might need to speak to you, Doug,' she added. 'For the coronial inquiry. It's good to speak to everyone who knew Geordie personally and from a professional, business side.'

Doug continued as if she hadn't spoken. 'I was never a fan of the Pritchards, but I wouldn't wish that on anyone. Poor bastard. Turns out you can have all the statues and manicured lawns you want, but the grass still isn't any greener.'

CHAPTER 8

At the site of the turbines, Will waited while Kelmendri and Lisa deliberated over a phone call they'd just had with the coroner. They were turned away from him, shoulders hunched in the wind, heads close together.

Bit like primary school, he thought, *kids keeping a secret from you.* He knew what that had felt like at ten. At thirty-five, the sting had gone.

Up above, the blades of the turbines were slowly spinning, emitting a kind of low electrical hum. There was something awe-inspiring about them, he decided. Alongside the rolling hills and flat land mainly cleared of trees, the turbines reigned supreme.

Lisa walked over to him. 'Sorry,' she said. 'There's been a bit of a complication.'

'In regards to what?'

'The investigation.' Lisa held her fingers up in quotation marks.

Will sighed. Lisa wasn't giving anything away.

Or was she? The young woman leaned in to him, her eyes wide. 'We were only here in the first place because of who it was and because . . .' She gestured at the turbines without looking up.

'You know that Lucinda Pritchard thinks it's murder, don't you?' Will said.

Lisa nodded, trying and failing to contain her excitement. 'Oh yeah, we know that. She's been calling up every superior in the force she can think of!'

Connections, connections, Will thought. Lucinda's family and the Pritchards would have a few.

'Still' – Will kept his voice neutral – 'there's been no evidence so far supporting that, has there?'

'No,' Lisa said quickly, before eyeing Kelmendri, who was still on the phone. 'But there is one thing.'

'What?'

'The coroner has raised something. Nothing's official yet, but . . .'

'What?'

He could see she was dying to tell him. But before she could answer, her colleague Jeff Kelmendri walked over. 'Will!' he boomed. 'We need to head back to the 'Rat for a meeting – you okay to take the reins here?'

The 'Rat was the affectionate name locals gave to Ballarat, the large regional city fifty minutes' drive from Carrabeen. It wasn't anything unusual to give the town a nickname, but when he heard them say it, Will always imagined a giant rodent chewing on a massive slice of cheese.

'You're going to talk with the farm manager and the wind technician, aren't you?' Kelmendri was saying to him.

'That's the plan.'

'Good work, good work,' Kelmendri answered distractedly. 'Keep us informed.'

'Still haven't found the keys to the turbine,' Will commented. It had bugged him from the very start – if Geordie had used his keys to get up the turbine, where were they now? They'd searched the interior and found nothing.

'No.' Kelmendri turned to him briefly. 'No keys to the turbine. But his car keys were in the console of his ute in town. How did he even get here?'

A wheat truck drove past, and they followed its slow progress along the road. Harvest time; all hands on deck.

'He could have walked,' Will said eventually. 'It would have taken him half an hour or so, but it's doable.'

'Carrying a heavy coil of rope?' Kelmendri asked doubtfully.

'Maybe he hid it somewhere earlier, placed it near the fence-line? Most suicides are planned, as you know.'

Kelmendri looked at his watch. 'Yeah, either he walked – or got a lift here.'

Will told them his theory that the note was merely a series of dot points for his television talk the week before. 'He said almost all of the things on that piece of paper.'

'We'd already gathered that,' Kelmendri said, looking away. 'One of the first things we looked at after checking the television recording. Obviously it doesn't mean much, but good to know.'

Will felt strangely deflated. 'Well,' he rallied, 'what about the UDL can?'

'Eh?'

'The UDL can. It seemed out of place near the turbines. Just one can, fairly recently used by the looks of things.' Will said it slowly, looking at Lisa. 'I took photos of it, requested that someone file it away.'

Lisa's face flushed a deep red.

'Who did you request that from?'

Will didn't answer and there was a long, painful pause.

'From me,' Lisa answered eventually, in a small voice. 'But I didn't do it, I forgot.'

'Well, do it now,' Kelmendri growled, and she hurried away.

The two men looked around, Will reading the older man's thoughts: if this was a criminal investigation, there had been too many people at the site. Ambulance, police, people called in to help with the retrieval of the body. Utes had driven under the turbine; farmers had stood around watching before the authorities arrived. Too many people, and that meant mistakes.

'We thought it was a suicide,' Kelmendri said out of nowhere, meaning they'd thought there was no need to secure it as a crime scene at the start.

'And was it?' Will asked.

Kelmendri looked at him closely. 'Coroner's talking with us in an hour.'

'Keep us updated?'

Kelmendri paused, then nodded. Will wasn't sure how to take the man: was he like a detective in a mystery novel; gruff and damaged, but kind underneath and dedicated to the job? Or was he, as some colleagues said, sick to death of the job and ready to pack it in?

Lisa returned, dismayed. 'There's no can,' she admitted. 'Someone must have cleaned it up already.'

Kelmendri looked furious and addressed Will directly. 'You have photos?'

'I'll send them through.'

'Appreciate it.' The man turned on his heel and, without acknowledging his young colleague, began striding to his car, his phone buzzing as he walked.

Lisa, with cheeks burning, ran after him.

Will checked his phone to make sure the photos were still there. He sent them to Kelmendri's number, and then on to Belinda and Tammy as well. Lisa had stuffed up, but even so he felt sorry for her, and the can might well be nothing. He watched as she was driven away by her boss, her glum face staring out the passenger window.

He walked around the base of the turbines, noting the mass of footprints, the car tyre tracks and the kicked-up dirt. Too many people had been to the site.

There was another buzz on his phone, and he checked it to see a message from Tammy letting him know that the local paper wanted a statement from one of them on the Pritchard case. He called her back, telling her to hold them off. Despite the dearth of interesting cases, country journos still had the deep investigative urge of their metro counterparts. Even more so, maybe, with their ability to hunt out persons of interest. Someone always had a cousin who knew someone in a country town.

'And a bloke from the *Shepp Advertiser* wants to interview you,' Tammy added.

'Shepp?'

'Shepparton.'

Honestly, it was hard to keep up. 'Rat, the 'Go, the 'Gon, Shepp and Wang. Victoria, or 'Vic', was filled with country towns with their own nicknames. Again, Will felt like the new kid in school.

'Tell them no,' he said.

No messages or calls had come through from Belinda. Will felt a rare pang of frustration at his wife's lack of contact. He'd asked for an update on the midwife's appointment but so far had only received a thumbs up. That was Belinda for you, he thought without rancour, forever frugal. He wondered if she'd perhaps gone to visit her father, as was her habit a couple of times a week. He, meanwhile, kept a deliberately low profile where his father-in-law was concerned. He simply could not understand men like Reg Burney, who were content to live in squalor, unashamed by their circumstances. Because Reg, Will thought, was most definitely at ease with himself. His body, the way he moved, even the way he swore, had a kind of majesty about it – and in this regard, Reg was a little like his own mother, the imperious Penelope, who lorded it over the Toorak crowd. At their wedding, despite his and Belinda's best efforts to keep them apart, Penelope and Reg had got along surprisingly well. The only thing Penelope had grumbled about was Reg's lack of a tie. As for his persistent swearing, she professed to find it refreshing. And now Will remembered how she had taken Reg by the arm and proudly introduced him to all her friends, and how Reg, in turn, had allowed himself to be led by her through the milling crowd.

Will was glad that Belinda never forced him to visit Reg. Try as he might – and try he had – his father-in-law clearly didn't like him. One of these days, he'd get up the courage to tell Reg that he hated being called Shiny Shoes. But that day was not today.

He looked at his phone again. A thumbs up meant good news, surely, so that's how he would take it.

It wasn't even 1 pm. Will decided to walk over the paddocks to Alan Crowe's house, rather than drive back along the dirt track and onto the main drag again. He knew it was just over the other side of the hill the locals called Mont Blanc. Locking his car, Will set off, along the flattened grass made by farm utes and then up the bald hill. A quarter of the way up the wind started again, low at first and then in a strong gust, pushing him sideways. Out the corner of his eye, he could see the shadows of the turbines, their long reach extending towards him, the blades spinning and spinning. Will wished he'd worn a better jacket. The wind was smacking him sideways again, and he crouched down for a minute till it subsided. Finally he stood and, struggling on, reached the top of the hill, turning around to take it all in.

The Pritchard enterprise was Clean Energy Solutions and here was its product: the second largest wind farm in Australia, three hundred turbines covering the vast landscape for miles and miles. The enormous structures were stark against the sky, startling even. If you were drunk, or in a different frame of mind, you might even think they were encroaching. Will had once read of a conspiracy theorist who insisted that inside every wind turbine was a computer on the brink of turning sentient. Science fiction, he thought – and then remembered that it was science fiction that first gave physicists the idea of creating the nuclear bomb.

What would H. G. Wells have to say about these structures?

Will pulled his jacket more tightly around him and looked downhill for his car. Squinting, he spotted it, then made out the turbine from which Geordie Pritchard had been found hanging. Turbine 82. Ten to fifteen metres from the fence line, one of the first to greet you at the open gate. A body up there, hanging.

Whatever the circumstances, Geordie's death was a statement of the most public kind. *Look at me*, it said. Or, *Look at what you made me do*. Or, more frightening, *Look what I've done to him*.

Feeling overawed by the machines, Will turned in the other direction and was immediately struck by the difference. On this side of Mont Blanc, the absence of turbines was a relief. The hill was bare save a Blakely gum and a healthy dam, fenced off, with reeds and native grasses growing around it. At the foot of the hill there was a small house and a big shed. Alan's place. As he walked downhill, the house came into view. Its shiny air-conditioning unit at the side and a new carport hinted at money, but the house itself looked like a sad man, its blinds halfway down, the garden poorly tended, one towel dangling from a washing line and flapping madly in the wind.

Will found Alan in his shed, the older man bent over machinery, his face down low, like he was sniffing it.

'Alan,' he called. 'Will Lovett from the Carrabeen police, we met yesterday.'

The man pulled his head out, gave Will a blank stare before nodding in recognition. 'Yes,' he said. 'Hard to forget.'

'Can we talk?'

Alan motioned towards the house and Will followed him, passing under an old peppercorn, its leaves tickling.

'Nice spot you've got here,' Will said. 'Wouldn't know there's the second biggest wind farm in Australia just on the other side of the hill.'

Alan gave a wry smile. 'When we sold the land to the Pritchards, I had no idea that would be the result.'

'If you had, would you have sold it?'

The man gave no response.

They kept walking, dogs bounding up to greet them, keeping pace. Will gave one a pat.

'It's so quiet,' he said. 'Feels like another world.'

Alan stopped. 'You can hear them though. Listen.'

Will stood where he was, cocked his head. 'I can't hear a thing.'

'*Listen!*' Alan insisted. 'You can hear them now.'

Will closed his eyes for a brief second and tried to focus. He could hear the wind rustling through the peppercorn, a loose tin sheet on the shed roof, the dogs panting beside him. 'Nope,' he said, snapping his eyes open. 'I can't.'

'You might need your ears checked.' Alan kicked off his boots as they approached the back door of his house. 'I hear them night and day. Can barely sleep half the time.'

Will removed his boots too, feeling suddenly ashamed of his polished RMs. Hardly anyone wore them around here; Belinda did warn him.

'Cuppa?' Alan asked.

'Be great.'

'Only got coffee.'

'Even better,' Will said in relief.

While Alan fixed them drinks in the kitchen, Will noted the mess of his house in stark contrast to the neat shed, where everything seemed to have a place. Now, he ran his eyes over a cluttered cabinet and studied the dusty photos lining the walls of the lounge room. One of a younger Alan and a red-headed woman standing in front of the Sydney Opera House with the Harbour Bridge behind them, both beaming into the lens. Another of the same woman in flares, pointing to the Twelve Apostles, her hair blown crazily in the wind.

'That's Hugh Pritchard, Geordie's father.' Alan nodded at one of the frames when he brought Will's mug of coffee over. 'And you'll recognise the other blokes, I'm sure.' He reached over and took the photo off the wall, passing it to Will.

In it four young men stood, arms crossed, in shorts, boots and long socks. Only one of them had a polo shirt on – Will guessed that was Hugh Pritchard, a handsome man, tall with a mop of light brown hair. Like his son. Will remembered the top of Geordie's head as he hung from the turbine and fought to banish the image.

'Easy to tell that that's you.' He pointed to the young man on the left, smiling broadly into the camera. 'And,' he exclaimed after a moment, 'that's Reg, Belinda's father!'

Reg was standing to the second right of the group, a cheeky grin, his good looks and confident demeanour on full display. *Like Alby Mangels*, one of Will's aunts had murmured suggestively when she met him at their wedding. *All legs and arms.*

'The four of us were good mates back in the day.' Alan looked without pleasure at the photo. 'Hugh, Reg, myself and Doug.'

'That's Doug Hay?' Will asked, pointing now at the scrawny man on the far right.

'Yep, Doug. This photo was before the Hays got real rich, and well before he stacked on the pounds. The four of us worked for Hugh's family at one point, shearing. Doug worked like a demon and lived off the smell of an oily rag: buying land, selling it, buying more and getting rich in the process. Him and Hugh ended up fighting over acreage and it never mended. Now Hugh's dead, of course, but the feud is still going.'

The wind rattled the tin roof again; the peppercorn groaned. Out there on the Golden Plains, Will thought, the battles – like the fields outside Troy. Greeks versus Trojans, Achilles and Hector – Doug Hay and Hugh Pritchard – it was always the same. Three thousand years from now, there'd be more wars with big men fighting over land.

'I heard that Doug Hay is anti–wind farm.'

'Oh, yeah.' Alan gave a rueful shake of his head. 'Doug's dead against the buy-up of all the land for the wind business. He cracked it at me big time when I started working for Geordie on the maintenance of the turbines, can barely look me in the eye.' Alan waved a hand at Mont Blanc. 'But Doug, owning as much as he does now, sometimes forgets what it's like to run a smaller outfit.'

And it was once your land, Will thought, wondering if Alan would feel any connection to the hills now dotted with machines.

Will sipped his instant coffee, listening to Alan talk about the hard years, the droughts when they had to buy in water, the mouse plagues, and the time when wool and wheat prices plummeted. That was when he'd sold his land to Hugh Pritchard.

Soon Will's mind was wandering. He'd heard stories like this before in Carrabeen; it was impossible to escape them in country like this. 'In my day . . .' But then, every person he'd ever met romanticised the past to some degree. *We played outside more when we were kids; the work was harder, but we made do; we respected our parents; our lives were simple.* And so on and so on.

After ten minutes of the man talking, the subject of his story meandering like a drunk, Will excused himself to go to the toilet.

'First on the right,' Alan said, seemingly surprised to be brought back to the present. 'Down the hall.'

The bathroom was in a poor state. A matchbox sat on the corner of the sink, nearest the toilet, and a thick spiderweb dominated the dark corner of the room. A wet towel hung over the bath, and the shower screen was layered with soap scum so thick it looked like frost. In movies, when cops excused themselves to go to the bathroom, they always rifled through the cabinets. Will checked himself in the mirror above the sink. He didn't look like a cop from the movies. With his thick black hair, skinny face and round glasses, he was more like Where's Wally.

Where's Willy? kids used to yell out to him in primary school. *Hiding in a book?*

He could still check them out. The cabinet, like cabinets in movies, was full of medicine. Packets of pills, tubes of cream, and little bottles with serious-looking labels. Rhonda Crowe was the name typed on all of them. Will closed the cabinet door and rested for a moment, his forehead on the mirror. Alan had mentioned a Rhonda when they'd first met. *Rhonda always said* . . . Sadness pervaded the dirty room. His wife must have died. If Belinda got ill, Will thought he'd have a bathroom like this too. He walked out, back into the room where Alan was sitting quietly, looking out the window.

'Alan,' he said, clearing his throat. 'We're trying to work out how Geordie got up the turbine. You said he had a key?'

Alan put down his mug. 'I'm sure he had keys, but from what I could see, he never bothered with carrying them. Anytime anyone wanted to check on the turbines, he'd call Shane or me. And the bloke had no interest himself in going up them. He loved what they could do, their potential and what have you – but all he cared about was whether they were working, and he left that to Shane Burrows and me. Geordie was a businessman. The logistics were up to the little people.'

'So, what was your job exactly?'

'Haven't been doing it for that long, three weeks or so. Geordie hired me to keep an eye on the turbines, sing out if there's any malfunction. Keep the grass between them mowed, make sure the fences surrounding them are secure. I don't fix the things – that's for the techie – but I shadowed Shane for a day, just to get the general idea. Everyone who works onsite has to do it. And then, like I told you yesterday, Shane gave me a device that lights up if there's a problem, if one of them's not working right.'

'Can I have a look at it?' Will wasn't sure how it would help to view the gadget, but if he could somehow confirm or support the time of death, then the coroner's report would be made easier.

Alan left the room and came back a moment later with a small black box, the size of two alarm clocks. 'See?' He pushed a button, and a grid with dozens of green lights lit up. 'They're all working okay now. But yesterday morning, number eighty-two was flashing red, and when that happens, I get an alert on my phone. I got up to check it out, drove over the top of Mont Blanc and saw Geordie there, almost immediately.'

Will eyed the blinking device. 'What time did the alert go off?'

'Five am,' Alan said. 'It was just getting light.'

'Were there any other alerts that night?'

Alan hesitated. 'Yes, earlier on in the evening.'

'What time?'

'Around ten o'clock maybe. I was still up. There might have been a few before that too.'

'And did you inspect the turbines each time?'

Alan breathed in deep through his nose and gave a long sigh. 'No. I thought it was the machine playing up. It does that, goes off at the slightest.'

Will considered this. 'So why bother go out at five then?'

Alan looked at him as if he was mad. 'I'm usually half awake by then anyway. If I'm not up and in the paddocks by six then there's something wrong.'

Farmers; they're early birds, Will recalled from conversations with landowners throughout the year. *No night owls on the land. Beat the heat of the day, get out into the paddocks before the sun really burns and the tractor becomes a stove.*

'When did you suspect the body was Geordie's?'

'Not till word started to get out. I did think it was strange that Geordie hadn't turned up, because I knew he was in town. I said hello to him on the Sunday; he seemed completely normal to me. So yes, it was strange when he didn't turn up along with everyone else. Usually, something's wrong with the wind farm and he's straight out here if he's home. So no, I didn't think it was him up there – but I was wondering where he was.'

'So you thought it was . . .?'

'Didn't know who it was. Gave me the fright of my life. First thought that it was some sick joke, maybe a stunt or whatnot. But no. Not that. So yep, called you lot, called Shane and Geordie's number too.'

'Where was it you saw him on Sunday?'

Alan cleared his throat. 'Petrol station in town. Would have been around ten or eleven. I was filling up; he was next to me.'

'You have a chat?'

'We spoke. Don't know about a chat. I said it was hot, he said it was hot; I said it was windy, he agreed. Then he drove off, and I went in to pay.'

'You know his ute was found in town, outside the fish 'n' chip shop, with the keys in the console.'

Alan shrugged as if he didn't think that was such a big thing. Perhaps it wasn't. There hadn't been too many car thefts since Will had been in town.

'You have any idea how Geordie got out here that night?'

Alan closed his eyes in thought. 'I wouldn't put it past him to walk,' he said after a brief moment. 'His father always liked a walk, to look at his properties.'

'How long would it take, do you think?'

'Thirty minutes? Good views along the way.' Alan nodded to himself. 'Geordie could have walked.'

'And yet no one saw him?'

'None maybe that you've heard from.'

Point taken. Plus, Will thought now, it wasn't a stretch to think that Geordie could have walked from town to the turbines without anyone seeing him. In the darkness, no streetlight and only the moon to guide him. It had been a cool night, pleasant enough for a walk. The rope, of course, raised other questions, but Will thought he'd wait till Forensics got back to them before he'd trouble anyone with that.

Outside, one of the dogs started barking, setting them all off, riling each other up like teenage boys at a party.

'Rabbits?' Will asked.

'The turbines,' Alan said abruptly. 'When they really get spinning, the dogs notice. They can hear better than us, you know.'

All these sounds, these different levels that humans can't access, Will thought. It was as if there was another world out there; a throbbing, humming universe of warning and potential. Who could tell what it was trying to say?

When it was time for Will to go, Alan offered him a lift back to his car. Will didn't mind a walk, but it was getting on, and as usual he was still forming his questions in a roundabout way. Will took his time; he always had. Belinda, by contrast, was a speeding train. Now, Alan whistled through his teeth for the dogs, who leaped up into the tray of the ute, while the two men climbed in the front.

'So, you were a shearer with Belinda's father?' Will asked by way of conversation.

'I was,' Alan replied, shifting gears. 'I worked with him on a number of jobs. And yes, me, Doug and Reg all sheared for the Pritchards. Hugh too; his father made him work despite being the owner's son. It was a good time.'

All his life Alan's lived here, Will was thinking. Same people, same country. And, he mused, as they rounded the base of Mont Blanc and came in sight of the turbines, what changes had taken place. 'Bet old Hugh Pritchard never imagined his son would build these on your land,' he said.

Alan grunted in agreement. 'You're right about that. Rhonda always said he'd have keeled over if he knew.'

'When did she pass away?'

'Almost a year to the day after these got put up. Cancer.' He waved a disdainful hand at the spinning blades.

'So, what – you're not suggesting that . . .' Will let his words trail off doubtfully.

They'd arrived at his car, and Will stepped out of the farmer's ute into the buffeting wind.

'I'm not suggesting a thing,' Alan replied out the window.

Will had arranged to meet Shane Burrows in between jobs. The technician said to meet him at the crossroads between Alan Crowe's farm and the next town, Arwett.

Funny to meet at a crossroads, Will thought. It sounded like a scene from a Western movie. He saved it up to tell Belinda, then remembered that she still hadn't called.

As he drove, the turbines were to the left of him, like a big kid looking over your shoulder. *Okay, okay*, he felt like saying to them. *You've made your point.* The paddocks stretched on, a faded yellow, the thin dust rising off them catching the light in a hazy sheen. It felt poetic. Sometimes, in moments like this, Will felt tears prickle the corners of his eyes; he wasn't sure why. Maybe it was hayfever.

The place where Shane had told him to wait was a lonely intersection to the south of Carrabeen. Stone fences ran alongside the road, convict built, old but sturdy. Cows watched him, then turned away. Cypress and gums dotted the horizon.

A dusty four-wheel drive pulled up and Shane Burrows energetically jumped out of his car, a young man on the move. Will had been like that a decade ago, rushing about, always on the go. Nowadays, he was faintly aware of a switch in pace.

'Why d'you want to meet here, Shane?' he asked. 'It's like we're about to have a gunfight.'

Shane chuckled, but Will wondered if he'd got the joke.

'On my way out to the Reebra wind farm, got two hundred turbines there.'

'You manage that farm too?'

'I don't manage them exactly,' Shane said bashfully. 'More like I run the tech.'

'Busy man.'

'You bet I am.' He straightened his shoulders.

'Good career, I'm guessing. Lotta work for you.'

'Too much!' But Shane was clearly pleased about it. 'Left school at year ten, worked my arse off, did an apprenticeship with Geordie's company, and now got no time to scratch myself. Got Reebra farm and another one starting up out west.'

'You might end up owning one, one day.'

'I might.' Shane's tone of voice meant, *I will*.

'You a local boy, Shane?'

'Yep.' There was pride in this one word. Locals always liked to assert their credentials by how long they'd been in the area. Longevity equalled respect, mostly.

'Grandparents are buried in the cemetery, parents still in town.' The young man was listing his references and Will dutifully listened. 'They've got the newsagency now. I went to kinder here, then did all my schooling at Carrabeen P–12.'

'Ah, my wife went there.' Will had a few credentials of his own. 'Was at school with some of the current teachers.'

Shane nodded in approval.

'She said there's a good man out there, looking after the kids,' Will added. He couldn't remember the name Belinda had mentioned, the one who had once attended Wesley Hall. 'He's vice principal?'

'Mr Kent, yeah. He's the one that helped me get the apprenticeship.'

Will pulled out his notebook. 'Shane, I need to ask you a few questions about yesterday.'

The young man steeled himself. His jaw clenched. Will remembered Shane's cries when he'd first seen Geordie hanging there. *Go easy*, he reminded himself. *He's just a kid.*

'Can you tell me how many people have keys to the turbines?'

'I've got a set, and Geordie does. There's the master set too, of course. He keeps that in his office.'

The young man realised he'd mentioned Geordie in the present tense and turned away. Will pretended not to notice.

'Right.' Will wrote it down. 'And did Mr Pritchard often use his own keys?'

'Not that I know of. Anytime he needed to show visitors to the turbines – investors and whatnot – he'd just ask me. If he didn't need to go inside them, just drive around them and whatever, he'd mostly ask Alan because he's closer. But Alan only has the keys to the paddock gates, not the actual turbines. I've got the gate keys *and* the ones to the turbines. Geordie has the same, and then there's the master set. So yeah, he'd often call me if he wanted to take someone like an investor to the top of a turbine. Plus, I'm the one who does the initial training for everyone who works on the site – so yeah, Geordie mostly relied on me.'

'Were the turbines ever left unlocked, Shane?'

The young man looked horrified. 'No, they were not! They were always locked! Like I said.'

'Do the keys open every one of the turbines, or is there a separate key for each one?'

'One set for all of them,' Shane said. 'Be pretty confusing to have to carry around three hundred or so sets.'

A strong gust of wind blew up, and Will moved so that his back was to it. 'Geordie ever go with you up the turbine?' he asked, having to raise his voice.

'Never.' Shane shook his head sadly. 'But he liked talking about them – knew everything about the mechanics of them, the science and all that.'

'Do you know if he ever walked there? Like, from town?'

'Eh?' Shane frowned. 'Not that I know of.'

'Was Geordie a good boss?'

The young man looked down, studied the road.

Will waited. There was power in waiting, he knew.

'He was the best.' Shane said it so quietly Will had to lean in. 'He owned nearly the whole of Carrabeen, but you'd never know it. Not one of those types that come back home acting like they own the joint. Geordie was a . . .'

'A friend?'

'Not a friend, not exactly,' Shane sniffed. 'He was older than me – had kids and that. But he sort of made you feel like, like you *could* be friends, if you know what I mean? Everyone liked him.'

Will nodded. He did know what Shane meant. They were a special breed, the Geordie Pritchards of the world; charismatic, universally liked and financially successful. He closed his notebook, confident that he'd never be any of those things, and not at all upset by the fact.

'I mean, I can't think of anyone who'd want to hurt Geordie!'

There was a slight pause as Will studied Shane. The wind technician looked on the brink of tears again.

'You don't think this is suicide, Shane, is that what you're saying?'

The young man jerked his shoulders in a helpless gesture, unable to speak. Will reached over, gave him a pat on the arm.

'What we saw yesterday wasn't easy, mate. Especially if you knew and liked the man.'

Again, a miserable shrug.

'You got people to talk to about what we saw, how you're feeling?'

'Yeah, yeah.' Shane shuffled about. 'Got that.'

They stood at the crossroads, Will searching for words of comfort or wisdom. In the distance, a tractor was making its way slowly towards them.

'Shane, you ever drink when you're out at the turbines? Like a UDL for instance?'

Shane screwed up his nose. 'No. Why?'

'Saw a can out there, probably nothing. Looked pretty new.'

'A UDL?' Shane looked slightly offended. 'No, sorry. But I'm afraid I've got to go – the two hundred turbines!' He jiggled his car keys for good effect.

'Man on a mission,' Will quipped.

Shane nodded uncertainly before hurrying away to his car.

Will waited till the dust had cleared before pulling out his phone. He googled the number for Clean Energy Solutions Australia and rang it. There was a recorded message, stating that the office was closed. After a moment's thought, he rang Lucinda.

'Hello?' she answered in a groggy voice.

'Lucinda, it's Will.' He ploughed straight in. 'I'm trying to find out where Geordie's set of keys for the turbines is. They weren't on him when he was found. And they weren't in his ute.'

Lucinda sniffed. 'Geordie never carried keys around – he was hopeless with them, he'd lose them all the time. But I know there's a master set somewhere.'

Will explained that he'd already called the head office of CESA in South Yarra and that it was closed. 'Can you find someone who can open the office and check out if the keys are there?'

'I'll try his PA,' Lucinda said, suddenly businesslike. 'She'll be able to go in and check for us. Branka lives close by.'

'Thanks.' Will hung up, doing his best to ignore her 'us'. He didn't want any part of 'us'. 'Us' was what he had fled from long ago.

Still, he pondered, as he walked back to his car and pulled onto the road, Lucinda could be *useful*. He knew that.

Half an hour later, on his way into Carrabeen, he still hadn't heard back from her.

Will knew, after going up the turbine with Shane, how the keys opened not only the front hatch, but the lift inside to get to the ladders. In fact, it was a whole set of keys they needed to locate. Because Geordie couldn't have got up there without them.

And what of the can of raspberry vodka? It was a teenager's drink, lolly water. He couldn't see Shane slogging on one; nor could he imagine Alan, the stoic farmer, drinking one. But then again, you never knew. He wasn't averse to a strawberry Chupa Chup on occasion. He sniffed, looked at the paddocks, the brick farmhouses set halfway down them, the cypress trees lining the driveways.

The can had looked recent, he knew that. And it was the only piece of litter he'd seen there. *Bloody Lisa*, he cursed, slowing for a mob of sheep. She should have sent it off to Forensics the moment he'd told her about it. If Belinda had been there, she would have been onto it straightaway. She'd be brilliant in Lisa's place. She'd go over everything with care.

A sudden thought gave him pause. He pulled over to the side of the road and got out his phone, checking the images he'd taken at the scene, flicking to the ones in the turbine, when he and Shane first saw Geordie's body. Forensics would be looking over them now, even as they conducted print analysis and searched for signs of materials, skin, blood. But now, for the first time, Will was struck by something: how clean the interior of the turbine was. No scuff marks, no handprints, no notepads or pens or drink bottles. The surfaces of everything had appeared pristine. It was as if, like for a house inspection, someone knew they were coming and had given the turbine a thorough clean.

CHAPTER 9

Will stood back after ringing the doorbell, feeling slightly foolish. He folded his arms, then put them by his side, then placed one in his pocket and bent a knee in a casual pose.

The door flung open.

'Will!' Lucinda frowned. 'Is there something wrong with your leg?'

'No,' he said, straightening.

'I was just about to call you. Branka got back to me. The master keys are in Geordie's desk drawer, where they always are. She sent me a photo of them, look.'

A phone was thrust in his face, and he stepped back instinctively before inspecting the image. A set of keys, lying neatly in a desk drawer in a city office, other skyscrapers visible in the distance.

'So, you'll need to work out how he got up there in the first place, won't you?' Lucinda asked, beckoning him inside. 'I'm guessing the farm manager had a set.'

'Alan, yes – but only for the perimeter fence.' Will followed her, as she knew he would. It had been like that often with her and him. 'Geordie had another set – we need to find it.'

'Yes, yes.' Lucinda offered him a drink. He wavered, before accepting. 'As I said before, Geordie was terrible with keys. They'll probably turn up somewhere.'

'You know the keys to his ute were found in the console?'

'Ha! Doesn't surprise me,' Lucinda responded without humour. 'As I said, Geordie hardly ever locked his cars, even when we were in Melbourne. Habit, I suppose, from growing up in the country.'

Belinda was fastidious about locking houses and cars, but then again, she was a cop.

On the kitchen table was a copy of a glossy alumni magazine from St Francis of Assisi College. 'Vale Oliver Moffat!' was the leading cover line.

The man's name struck him, and not only because it sounded like a TV puppet.

Lucinda looked at it in distaste. 'Geordie's residential college magazine, old boys' networking bullshit,' she said. 'It's basically all just a plea for money for the new rowing sheds they can't afford.'

Clearly it didn't stop her, or Geordie, from reading it though, Will thought. The magazine had pages folded over and appeared well read.

'The Wesley one came out a week ago too, did you read it?' Lucinda asked, referring to the residential college that they'd both attended.

'No.'

'I flicked through it. Most of it is ridiculous, but it can be fun to see old people we were there with.'

Will had only lived there for one semester. He had no desire to read about the people who'd stayed on.

Lucinda busied herself at the kitchen island. 'Do you know him?' She pointed to the St Francis magazine. 'Oliver Moffat?'

Will looked at the front cover again. No, he didn't. But again, something about the name stuck – an investment banker?

'He was best friends with Geordie when they lived together at St Francis College, Sydney Uni.'

Will had heard of it. It was, by all accounts, a lot like the Melbourne one he and Lucinda had been at. Sandstone, ivy and glass; all of it darkly glittering with secret promise.

'Anyway' – Lucinda placed a cool drink in front of him – 'Oliver died a year ago; cancer. He was convicted of fraud, at his bank in Singapore. Even went to jail. He learned to play cards there, apparently. It's all there in the article.'

Right. Will watched as Lucinda flitted about the room, picking things up, putting them down. She was like a moth, darting this way and that – never settling.

'Must've been hard for Geordie when he found out his old friend had died.'

'If you're suggesting that Geordie killed himself because of it, then I'd have to say that's a stretch, Will. A *real* stretch. I mean, if you died, *I* wouldn't go and hang myself.'

Will didn't answer, just stood there, straight-faced. Even so, he felt his cheeks burn.

Lucinda picked up the magazine and flicked through it. 'The two of them lost touch after uni. Geordie only stayed at St Francis for one and a half years. He was off overseas after that, travelling, studying in England . . .' Her voice trailed off.

Will stared at his drink. There was a long stick of rosemary poking out of it. He gave it a sniff; was it gin?

Finally, Lucinda sat down on a bench stool. 'Oliver wrote a book before he died with all the details. His wife sent it to our people to see what we could do with it.'

That's right; among other ventures, Lucinda's family owned a small publishing company, which mainly focused on coffee-table books: photography, large art books.

'I've already sent your mother an advance copy,' she said absentmindedly.

Will's head gave an involuntary shake. He had no idea Lucinda and his mother were still in contact after all these years. Though it was easy to imagine his mother requesting the book. Penelope would eat up sordid tales of the rich and famous; she'd enjoy the chapters about a financier mixing with jailbirds. No doubt she'd know people in the acknowledgements. She'd see their names, then call them up for long discussions about the Moffats and all their scandals.

Lucinda's hands fluttered at her lap. Again and again, she twirled her rings around her fingers, as if by doing so, she'd bring on some magic spell.

Will remembered her doing that when they were together, twisting her rings around and around. It was the way she thought about things, turning over problems in her mind, working out how best to come out on top. Their parents knew each other, so they'd met as kids. But they'd *properly* met in Year Eleven, his first term of boarding at Chiltern Grammar. She was a day student, already ruling the roost. Will could picture it clearly. There she was, standing at the common room window, her face illuminated by the pink and gold of the coloured glass and the school motto: *Crescente Luce*. He didn't know then that the words meant *Light Ever Increasing*, but in that moment, when he looked at Lucinda's full mouth and long brown hair, there was no need for translation – he'd felt it, a sudden buoyancy in heart and mind.

Will remembered that moment and how she'd been twirling the ring on her finger as she approached him. He'd walked in after a rowing regatta, and she'd marched right up to him and said aloud, 'My god, Will Lovett, you've become a man!'

Others in the common room had laughed and he joined in obligingly, but for the first time he sensed a subtle shift in how his fellow students saw him. Lucinda Howell, addressing him with her full attention; it held sway. The way she'd said, 'You've become a man!' was mocking, yes – but she was impressed too. He'd been stroke in the winning eight three times in a row. But when beautiful Lucinda Howell had said those words, she may as well have anointed him a knight.

Later, she told him she'd been struck by his shyness, his round glasses and blue eyes, how he ducked his head and smiled. It was a different look to the one the other boys gave her, she said. It held little entitlement and no snark. Plus, she liked his height. Not many men were taller than her in heels, but he was.

By the end of that week, they were a couple.

And what else could he remember about Lucinda? Will let his thoughts run free: her cleverness, her style, the way she would walk into English class late with a 'Sorry, everyone, don't mind me,' as though they were all waiting for her to begin – which, in a sense, they were.

Those first heady months of flesh and limbs seemed now like a feverish dream.

'How are you coping, Lucinda?' He picked up his glass and took a sip, hoping she wouldn't see his slightly shaking hands. Why did he suddenly feel like fleeing?

'I'm all right.' Lucinda pushed her hair back behind her shoulders. 'Fortunately, the children are in Melbourne. I've spoken to them, of course, and I'll head there tomorrow to bring them here. It's hard for them to understand . . .' She picked up her own glass and looked at it in surprise, as if she didn't know how it'd got there. 'Geordie and I were often apart – him up here or travelling, and me with the children in the city, or me up here and him there. I know what it feels like to be without him. But this, this!' She waved her hand around and liquid flew out of the glass. 'How do I tell the kids how their father died?'

Will didn't know what to say. He studied the magazine on the table, looked at the image of the other man who had died, Geordie's old friend. Both men born into wealthy families, destined for great things – and now what? Both dead in their thirties.

'How was Geordie before he died?' Will asked, tentatively. 'I mean, did he seem happy?'

Lucinda looked blankly at him for a moment. 'Yes, he was happy. I hadn't seen him that much, he'd been busy working – checking on the turbines, online meetings – and there was some school thing he was opening that he had to come back up for. He was quite excited about it. I wish we had spent more time together, perhaps had dinner more often as a family. But yes, when I spoke to him, he seemed happy.' She ran a hand over her face, wiping her eyes. 'I've told you this already.'

'Why do you think he said he was going back to Melbourne, but then went to the turbines?'

'I don't know. I really don't.' Lucinda lifted her hands up and then dropped them heavily on her lap. 'He said he was heading back to the city for work the next day. Why he suddenly changed his mind, I cannot tell you. I wish I could.'

'Geordie didn't mention anything to you about the people he said were against him, the anti-wind farm groups? You told Belinda about it.'

'Of course he told me about them. We may not have seen each other much, but Geordie and I spoke all the time on the phone.'

Will waited a moment before continuing, 'Belinda said you told her that there were some sort of threats to your family. Can you tell me more about those?'

'Ha!' Lucinda gave a dry laugh. 'If you think phone calls saying, "We'll kill you for ruining our town," and "We'll string you up for what you've done, Pritchard," and "Wind farms equal murder," then yes, I would say that we received some sort of threats.'

'And did any one of you go to—'

'Go to the police?' Lucinda interrupted him. 'At the start Geordie did, down in Melbourne. But then, you know, we got used to them. Geordie used to laugh about the nutters out there, making all sorts of claims, like their lips were vibrating when they were ten kilometres away from the turbines! Or that they could sense movement deep in the earth because of them. Or that birds were attacking each other mid-flight when they were around them. The trolls just never, ever let up. There were even a couple of messages after he died.'

'After he died?'

'Yes, yes – it's on our answering machine here. This place still has a landline, can you believe it? Geordie liked it, thought it kept with the character of the place.' Lucinda gave an exaggerated shudder. 'I only heard the messages a few hours ago when I remembered to check. I'm so used to iPhones.'

'Can I hear the messages?' Will stood, suddenly alert.

'I *was* going to tell you about the timing of them, but there's been a lot on my mind, as you can imagine.' There was a defensive note to her voice now.

'Can I hear the messages, Lucinda?'

She nodded, indicating for him to follow her. In the hallway, on an old teak stand, was a telephone and a separate answering machine behind it. Lucinda pushed a button and then held Will's arm for a second as the message played:

'*We'll kill you for ruining our town.*' Will gave Lucinda a brief look before pushing rewind and listening again. '*We'll kill you for ruining our town.*'

'It's a female,' Will said. The high pitch, the soft articulation.

Lucinda shook her head. 'No, no, it's a male's voice. Young. Listen again.'

This time, Will was less sure. The articulation wasn't that soft.

'There's another one too, a bit earlier.' Lucinda whizzed through the machine, rewinding and stopping. 'Here it is.'

'*Wind farms equal murder. You know that, Geordie.*'

'A different voice,' Lucinda said, and Will had to agree. 'But definitely male this time.'

'When were these calls made?'

Lucinda checked the messages. 'Both on Sunday night. Late. The first one was at eleven pm, the second at eleven-twenty.'

The coroner hadn't yet provided an exact time of death but indicated the body had been hanging for most of the night. Eleven or eleven-twenty could be either before, during or after Geordie's death. When Will asked if he could take the answering machine, Lucinda responded with a wave of her hand.

Will's phone started buzzing. Belinda: she was home. With relief, Will took the opportunity to leave, clutching the machine, and Lucinda walked him to the front door.

Outside, the tops of the cypress trees were straining under the wind. The old branches were buffeted first one way and then the other, as if the elements themselves were confused. Will was a little afraid that a limb might fall on him when he drove down the driveway. He knew people called gum trees widow-makers, but it was true for the cypress as well.

'I don't know why,' Lucinda said in wonder, 'but Geordie loved it here. I can't stand the place – it's so, so *pressing*.'

Will felt that too, the strange constriction of the town. There was so much land and yet the town felt as if it was squeezed in, with its squalid houses, grimy petrol station, the vague smell of mice in the general store.

He was only here because of Belinda, and her father. After Reg's cancer diagnosis, she'd been determined to move here and assist him in his treatment and recovery. Twelve months was their agreement, and then back to the city where his old job was waiting for him. Bel had tried to get him interested in the local sports, but he was a rower and this was a football/netball town. There was no movie theatre, no decent cafe. While there *was* a reputable golf course on the coast one hour south, the only time he'd played there the wind had caught his first ball and carried it right off into the sea. He didn't mind the locals, but he couldn't catch on to their familiar way of talking, their private jokes and shared history. Sometimes, he suspected they were laughing at him behind his back. Once, he'd been walking past the school when he'd heard two men comment that his arse looked as if it was swallowing a couple of straws.

Face it, Will thought, as he bent his long legs to climb into the car, *you don't fit in here. At least there's only two months to go.*

Halfway down the winding drive, he had to swerve sharply around a heavy fallen branch. 'Two months,' he muttered grimly to himself.

CHAPTER 10

Belinda rubbed at her stomach as she selected a pumpkin from the fridge and started slicing. Pumpkins reminded her of her mother. She had a fuzzy memory – she couldn't have been more than a toddler – of picking pumpkins out of the garden, and crying because of their stinging stalks. Her mother had put her on her knee and sung the song 'Hot Cross Buns'. That memory might have been, Belinda pondered now, one of the reasons she was so interested in food. Her mother in the vegetable garden, then the scooping out of the pumpkin, soft and slimy. She'd been so young when her mother died; her recollections tended to be sensory more than anything else. The smell of lavender, the tickle of long hair, the pressure of a gentle hand at her back.

Belinda placed all the pumpkin skin in the compost tub and scooped out the seeds: there was a way to dry them so she could plant them for next year – except, what was the point? They were moving back to the city soon, to their small apartment. This Carrabeen sojourn had been a chance to slow down after the last frantic years of policing in Melbourne – the rampant family violence, the drugs, the youth crime, the murders that didn't make the news. It had been exhausting. One of her biggest cases had been a series of violent home invasions, leading to long hours, endless paperwork, interviews in seedy spaces, documents detailing how easily a hammer can crack a bone. Will had been tired of the work, and worried at her involvement – but what Belinda remembered most was the *thrill of it all*.

The secondment had been so fortuitous. Reg was in need of help with his recovery when the rare vacancy in Carrabeen had popped up. They'd both decided a less pressured year in the country, caring for her father, would do them all good. And it had, mostly. She enjoyed being back in her old town, seeing familiar faces, watching the big skies and the low rolling hills. And as for helping her father – well now, that was never going to be a walk in the park.

Yes, the move had been pretty good on the whole. But sometimes she'd been so bored! It was, she admitted to herself, a large part of the reason why she wanted to apply for the Investigations job.

Belinda filled a heavy pot with water and was just waiting for it to boil when her phone rang.

'Belinda, it's Julie. I got your phone number from your father. There's been another theft.'

'Yes?' Belinda was annoyed that Julie had rung her on her private number. She should have called the station; Tammy would be there.

'This time, it was a lasagne.'

'A *lasagne?*' *My god, I'd kill for a hammer on bone.*

'Well, two slices of lasagne. I let a Home Ec student put her work into a container and she left it there, in Food Tech. When we came back after period six, it was gone.'

Belinda watched the water on the stove slowly boil. 'I'll call you when I'm back at the station. I'm at home now,' she said firmly.

'Yes.' Julie didn't seem to think it was inappropriate to call her there. 'Your father told me you would be.'

Belinda hesitated. She knew Julie saw her father regularly. 'How is he really, do you think, Julie?'

'Better since you've been in town,' the teacher answered. 'But still a grumpy old thing.'

'Agreed.'

'Call me back about these thefts. I've told Orla and Andrew, but it's as if they've lost interest.'

I wonder why.

'Also, your father told me Geordie visited him on Saturday. That was kind of him, wasn't it?'

'Thanks, Julie.' Belinda hung up fast, not liking the sly tone that had entered the woman's voice.

Again, her mind turned to her last meeting with Geordie. The way she'd shouted, the dried blood on his face . . .

Forcing herself to calm down, she read over her job application once more, adding the words 'reliable and trustworthy' to her personal statement, then deleting them. Her fingers hovered over the screen.

What to do?

She should tell Will about Geordie. She should tell someone.

She typed 'reliable and trustworthy' back in again, then deleted 'trustworthy' almost straightaway. There was no need to embellish. Isn't that what Assistant Commissioner Conti had said about her in his speech after she'd got the commendation? 'No need to embellish when recounting Senior Sergeant Belinda Burney's police work on the Seaford home invasion case. Her work speaks for itself: thorough, professional and brave.'

Belinda flushed with pride at the memory. Since then, she'd taken every course in investigations she could, read up on new practice, attended professional development sessions on forensics and crime scenes.

In a burst of confidence, she reached over to her laptop and pushed send. Sure, she was about to go on maternity leave – but these things could be sorted, couldn't they? A short time at home with the baby, Will taking on more of the caring role, as she knew he'd like to do. At least she could give it a try. This job, it was gold; it would be ages before another one like it opened up again.

Everything would work out, Belinda thought, as the water began to bubble and spit. Surely.

'Just do it!' she'd said to Geordie Pritchard the day before he died, staring right at his stricken face. 'It's *nothing* to you.'

CHAPTER 11

When Will pulled up outside their house, Belinda was bent over, head deep in a rosemary bush. With the bulge of her very pregnant stomach hanging heavy, he thought she might topple in and vanish completely.

He called out to her, and she emerged, red-faced.

'Just in time!' she said. 'I've made a pot of tea, let's have a chat.'

Will preferred coffee to tea, but he enjoyed sitting with his wife, watching her pour from a teapot while he added milk to both of their cups. There was a genteel air to it that appealed to his sense of tradition.

Belinda reached up to kiss him, and he bent down, giving her a hug at the same time. He rested his chin on the top of her head, pulling her in. Their height difference was a joke to their colleagues, but to them they were a perfect fit.

'You can have coffee,' Belinda said. 'I made a pot of that too.'

'Of course you did.' He smiled, grateful. 'How was the midwife?'

'Fine, everything good. Still breech. I've got a photo some-where to show you.'

'Will it turn around the right way?'

'I hope so.'

'And does the baby have your good looks, or mine?'

'Hard to tell. It's too squashed. I think it's waving at us though.'

Back inside, Will poured his coffee into a mug and together they looked at the scan. The baby did appear to be waving in a kind of backward gesture, as if to say, 'See you soon!'

'Look at that, she's already saying hello – or goodbye.' Will said. 'Imagine what it will be like when she goes off to university.'

'You don't know that it's a girl. And anyway, he or she might become a plumber.'

'She might.'

'I applied for that job.' Belinda said it in a rush.

Will put down his mug. 'You did?'

'I won't get it,' she said, shaking her head. 'Investigations! I've got no chance.'

Yet you applied anyway, Will thought. 'What will you do if you *do* get it?'

'Unlikely. We can talk about it if that happens. But it won't. I called Ronja yesterday, and she said there's been dozens of applicants.'

Ronja was a former colleague in Melbourne, and one of the few people Belinda respected enough to take advice from. She was also one of Belinda's referees and had encouraged her to apply for the position.

'I won't get it,' Belinda repeated.

Will wasn't so sure. His capable wife had earned respect at the highest level for her police work in the home invasions case a year ago. But with a baby on the way? She was about to go on maternity leave. He wasn't sure how to feel, and wasn't about to congratulate her for applying just yet.

Belinda reached over and squeezed him on the knee. 'Tell me what happened with Alan and Shane,' she said to change the subject.

Will filled her in. He always enjoyed debriefing with his wife. She listened, nodded, and never interjected as others often did.

'It's a shame about the can,' Belinda said once he'd finished. 'But with so many people hanging around the site, it's almost impossible to keep any scene secure.'

Will agreed, then went on to tell her about the keys, how Geordie's own set to the turbines was still missing, but the master set was found in the Melbourne office where it was usually kept.

'We'll need to send someone around there, just to check that.' Belinda was thinking aloud. 'I'll get on to the South Yarra police tomorrow morning.'

'It sounds like Geordie was hopeless with his keys. He could easily have lost them.'

'So what did he use to open the turbine and get up there?'

'I don't know. Shane said they're always locked. Someone had to have opened them.'

Belinda hooked one leg over Will's lap and they sat for a moment, comfortable in their silence, thinking.

'And look what I picked up from Lucinda's house.' Will leaned over her leg to pull the small answering machine from his bag. 'There were two threatening messages sent to Geordie on the night he was killed.'

'You were at Lucinda's house?' Belinda asked mildly.

'Yes, she called me on my way home from seeing Shane – I met him when he was on his way to Reebra.'

Belinda sniffed. Her eyes were on her knees, studying a torn patch of her jeans.

'What does it look like?'

'What?'

'The *Pritchard house*. What's it like?'

'Oh, I don't know.' Will shrugged. 'It's one of those old ones. Stone. Long hallways, dark little rooms going off them. Windows with heavy curtains. A big grandfather clock. All very oppressive.'

He'd put a bit of mayo on the sense of oppression, but his wife was waiting for more.

'Massive concrete pot plants on either side of the front door. Lots of paintings, pastoral scenes. Kind of depressing.'

Will was aware that he'd added in the last part for Belinda's benefit. He hadn't noticed anything particularly depressing about the house.

Belinda nodded. 'As a kid I always used to wonder about Geordie's house. We went there once, for an excursion, but we never went inside. We were out on the lawn, near the lake.'

'It's a dam, I think, Bel.'

'We thought of it as a lake. But yes, it's probably just a dam.'

Will waited. Belinda didn't often offer up her childhood stories. Each one he heard, he filed away somewhere he could access in quiet moments, when he wanted to reflect on the parts of his wife that were still secret, even after so many years of happy marriage.

'Let's listen to the messages,' she suggested, and swung her legs off his lap. He walked to the wall, plugged in the machine.

'We'll kill you for ruining our town.'

And then:

'Wind farms equal murder. You know that, Geordie.'

'The first one is definitely a woman,' Belinda said. 'And the second a man.'

'That's what I said too. But Lucinda thought the first one was a young man.'

'Lucinda's not a cop.'

Will didn't see how being a cop would make a difference when it came to discerning voices, but siding with his ex-girlfriend was perhaps not the best option tonight. Belinda pushed rewind, and they listened again.

'So, two different people,' she mused. 'We really have to check out those groups who hate the wind farms.'

'My thoughts exactly. Tammy and I can do it tomorrow.'

'Let me at least talk to someone,' Belinda grumbled. 'All I've got is the boring school thefts and people coming to the station to ask about lost property.'

'The midwife said you should rest, and you don't want to be driving miles and miles out of town.'

'I know,' Belinda conceded. 'But surely I'm allowed to whinge about it.'

'There are the campers by the creek; we need to check on them after all these noise complaints – if that's not too boring for you.'

'It won't be boring.'

When they'd first arrived in Carrabeen, there were already two old caravans perched along the creek, just out of town. The pretty spot, shaded by willow trees, was listed in camping magazines as a free place to park your van or pitch a tent. Now, the flattened area was fast becoming a community for the homeless: two more caravans, a falling-down tent and a couple of swags closer to the water. There'd been complaints from people who lived close by about late-night parties and fights. Shameful, she thought – not for the first time – that for a shire so full of wealth, there were people who could not afford a decent place to live.

She reached over and gave Will's hand a kiss before standing up.

Between them, they agreed that as well as visiting the campers and keeping an eye on the school thefts, she would talk to Doug Hay again. That would be enough for her to do. Meanwhile, Will would handle Marit, Tammy's ex-girlfriend – who, despite her green credentials, had for some reason been arguing with Geordie. He'd also liaise with the Ballarat detectives and handle anything about the Pritchard case from now on.

'You've got the exciting stuff,' Belinda said.

'You'll live.'

His phone rang.

'It's Kelmendri,' he said, staring at his wife. 'I asked for an update.'

'Well, go on.' Belinda motioned for him to answer. 'Don't leave him hanging.'

'Poor choice of words there, Bel,' Will said as he put his phone to his ear, nodding as he listened, his eyes wide. 'Yes . . . right . . . of course . . .' He wrote something down on the back of an envelope. 'Yes, no . . . I see.'

'What is it?' she mouthed.

'Absolutely,' her husband said into the phone.

'So?' she asked when he hung up. 'What's the story?'

'The coroner has given us an unconfirmed cause of death.'

'And?'

Will looked down at his notes. 'Acute subdural haematoma.'

Belinda held her palms upward. 'Meaning?'

'At some point before he was found hanging, the coroner suspects Geordie suffered a serious injury to the brain, most likely from either a fall or assault.'

There was a brief pause.

'So, he was dead *before* he was hung up there?'

'Possibly. Kelmendri hinted at more news to come. He's not happy. If this turns out not to be a suicide, his life just got a whole lot busier.'

No, Inspector Kelmendri would not be happy. Nearing sixty, the man was eyeing retirement, holidays in Noosa, beers on a sunny beach, far away from the howling alleyways of the 'Rat. Rumour had it his first grandchild was on the way. And now he was faced with the suspected homicide of a high-profile, much-loved, philanthropic clean energy advocate. Cue the press. Belinda closed her eyes. Cue visiting detectives, cue hangers-on and distant cousins claiming grief and demanding answers on the TV networks. Cue it all and more.

'What's next?'

'Meeting in ten minutes, online. We can do it here. Oh, and I forgot to tell you.' Will gave her an apologetic grin. 'Mum called. She's coming for dinner tomorrow; she'll probably stay over.'

Belinda raised her eyes to the ceiling. Penelope was notoriously fussy about food, and her visits were never easy. Her phone buzzed again: Julie. Belinda turned it to silent, and listened as Will played the messages on Lucinda's answering machine once more.

Kelmendri greeted them online without fanfare. Lisa sat beside him, her back straight as if she was in school. Tammy had logged in from the station, her face difficult to see in the fading light from a window behind her. She apologised numerous times, trying to shift this way and that, till Kelmendri told her to turn her bloody camera off.

'So, it was murder?' Belinda asked, straightforward as usual.

Kelmendri gave nothing away. 'It's suspicious.'

'Geordie's ex-wife thinks it was murder,' Will said. He went on to tell the group about the phone calls on the Pritchard landline.

'They are some serious threats,' Lisa said. 'No wonder she's suggesting murder.'

'She's *convinced* it was murder,' Will said. 'No suggestion about it.'

'Yes, but we're investigating Geordie's death as *suspicious*, Will,' Kelmendri barked. 'Don't let me hear you making statements about murder to anyone, and especially not to the press! This is between us for now.'

'Tell us about the injury,' Belinda said, squaring her shoulders.

'Traumatic brain injury, internal bleeding,' Kelmendri explained. 'Coroner thinks it's most likely caused by a fall or assault with a blunt instrument. We're working on the assumption that someone hit Geordie, rendering him incapable of defending himself, and then strung him from the turbine.'

There was a horrible silence as all participants digested the news.

'Was he alive when he was hung up?' Tammy's voice came through the speaker, thin, like a young girl's.

'We don't know that yet.'

'Anything else?' Will asked.

'There were bruises under each of his arms, and along the front of his shoulders. The coroner suggests they come from rope burn.'

'From where he was pulled up the turbine?'

'That's the likely scenario.'

Belinda cleared her throat. 'So, what would you like us to do?'

'We'll handle the bulk of the inquiry – we're checking out all the Pritchard finances and business dealings, and we're liaising with Forensics on what was recovered at the crime scene.'

'You found something?' Will remembered how clean the place was when he'd been up there. Clinical even.

'We did.' Kelmendri leaned forward, his big forehead filling much of the screen. 'And,' he added, 'on the rope there was a fragment of skin that was not Geordie's. It's been sent for DNA testing.'

'That could be from any of the people who helped to get him down,' Belinda said.

'It's highly possible,' Kelmendri answered. 'But they were wearing gloves. Even so, we'll take samples from everyone to rule them out. It will take some time.'

There was a beat as they stopped to consider the other possibilities.

'How the hell,' Tammy asked, 'did he get up there?'

'Or,' Belinda pointed out, 'how the hell was he carried up there?'

It was the question that had first stumped them all. Now, it appeared, answers were starting to emerge.

'In every new wind turbine that's been built around here,' Kelmendri said, 'there's an emergency descender kit, in case someone injures themselves, or has a heart attack or something, and they can't get down. In this case, there's a rope and harness for workers to descend outside the turbine and straight down.'

'Shit!' Tammy exclaimed. 'Imagine that!'

Kelmendri ignored her and continued, 'It seems the suspect has used the emergency kit to get the body out onto the blade, then attached rope to one of the blades using a carabiner, before pushing the body over. It's not rocket science, but the person would have had to be someone who could stand serious heights.'

'Or,' Will added, 'someone who was desperate enough to ignore them.'

'We'll need someone to go up there again – with all the safety equipment, of course – just to see how it's done. Will? You'll go up again at some stage?'

Will hesitated.

'Does he have to?' Belinda asked. 'Isn't there someone with more experience who could do it?'

Kelmendri sighed. 'I suppose. I'll ask around and see if—'

'I'm not doing it,' Tammy said. 'I'd rather shoot myself.'

'I'll do it,' Will cut in, and Belinda gave him a look of surprise. 'Not a problem.'

The Inspector cleared his throat and looked briefly at his notes. 'Right then, about that rope. We're looking into the make of it, and we'll get back to you on that, along with anything else we find. In the meantime, I'd like you to check out the groups that had beef with Geordie. According to his wife, there was one in particular.'

'Farms for Future,' Belinda said, thinking of Doug Hay. 'We're already onto it.'

'Yes, that one. And start talking to the locals about the Pritchards: let's get some information on Geordie, his personal life, yada yada. You lot will be well placed to do that, seeing as you're the locals.'

Belinda didn't like the sound of Kelmendri's 'yada yada'. It smacked of weariness and boredom.

'Yep,' Will answered. 'We can do that.'

For a brief second, Tammy's head came back into view, nodding in a ghostly fashion against the bright light.

'There's a Farms for Future meeting on Thursday night,' she said. 'It was going to be cancelled because of what happened, but they've decided to go ahead, albeit at the library rather than the town hall.'

Tammy had probably heard about it from Marit – or from stalking Marit on Instagram, Belinda thought.

'What about our work here?' Belinda said. 'We've still got a shire to look after.'

'There's three of you, isn't there?' Kelmendri growled. 'You figure it out.'

CHAPTER 12

Belinda drummed her fingers on the steering wheel and bounced up and down on her seat. *Will understands about the job application,* she reassured herself. *He knows you've wanted a position in Investigations for ages. And you won't get it anyway, you won't.* She bounced up and down again, ignoring the bubble of hope that rose at the thought that she might.

But the job application wasn't the only reason she felt a nervous quiver in her gut. Now that suicide looked less likely, all of Geordie's movements would be scrutinised. Everything he'd done recently, every person he'd made contact with . . . Now, that would raise cop eyebrows. Why would a CEO visit an ex-shearer with prostate cancer whom he barely knew? Belinda held the seatbelt out from her protruding stomach and rearranged it so that it was above her belly, not below. And she'd have to explain why she had met with him on the Saturday before he was found dead. She'd barely slept a wink thinking about it.

She turned down the dirt track that led to the bottom of the bridge, and the flattened grass area of the campers. Someone had attempted to put up a tarpaulin with poles that were uneven in length, and despite the morning hour, a man was sitting under it, doing his best to squeeze out the last drop from a cask wine bladder. Belinda climbed out of the car and shouted hello. A woman poked her head out of a van and then poked it back in again.

No one shouted back.

'Hello!' she tried again, looking to the man wringing the cask. 'Got time for a quick chat?'

'No, I haven't,' he replied, concentrating hard on his task. 'Got a meeting with my accountant in fifteen minutes. About the hedge fund.'

Belinda stepped around a fire pit made from tyre rims. 'Yeah? What sort of hedge fund?'

'Fund to fix my fucken hedge.'

Belinda recognised him. He'd been hanging around the camping area for months. Council had already started to suspect people were staying longer and longer. What constituted a permanent resident? There was a growing consensus among ratepayers that the campers needed to be *moved on*.

'We've met before. David, isn't it?'

'Depends who's asking.'

'It's Senior Sergeant Burney asking.'

'In that case' – the man threw the empty cask away in disgust – 'it's David.'

'There've been complaints about the noise, David. A party last night, and another Sunday night. You have a lot of parties down here.'

'Yeah, well.' The man looked about him – the caravan with

its broken window, the dilapidated tarp, the dirt. 'There's a lot to celebrate, isn't there?'

The camp area was quiet, though the tell-tale signs of a party, such as the bottles and cans scattered in the dirt, were all about. A pervading sense of hopelessness hung over the place.

'Can you please tell your friends here to keep it down next time?'

David muttered something else, then suddenly stood and began patting his pockets, twisting around like he had fleas.

'What did you say, David?' Belinda studied the man, who was now spinning furiously like a top.

'I said' – the man stopped and stared at her, his skinny frame as bendy as an old rubber cord – 'that townies come to the parties too. It's not just us making the noise.' The man patted his pockets again. 'Got a fag?'

'Sorry, no. Who comes to the parties?'

David spied a butt on the ground and pounced on it, lifting it up to show her. 'Ta-da!'

Belinda waited patiently while he lit it, then dragged deeply, its glowing tip at the very edge of his brown fingers.

'That woman, big woman with the food.'

'Julie?' Belinda frowned. 'Does she bring food around here?'

'Sometimes. But we don't call her that.'

'What do you call her?'

'I don't know.' David's face suddenly soured. 'How the fuck should I know? What's with all the questions? Fuck me. Am I under arrest?'

'No, David. I—'

A door to one of the caravans opened again, and the same head poked out: long straggly blonde hair and teeth like the Giant's Causeway. 'Everything okay here?'

'Everything's cool, Val, it's cool,' David said.

Belinda addressed the woman. 'Just try to keep the noise down from now on, okay?'

'Will do, mate.'

'And do you happen to know the name of the lady that comes here sometimes, the one who brings food?' *It could be important,* Belinda thought, although she wasn't sure why.

The woman shook her head vigorously. 'Can't think of it, no. No. We mainly call her The Ghost.'

Julie liked ghosts. At school, she used to conduct seances behind the stadium during lunch break.

David's cigarette was finished. He looked at the scant remains in the dirt. 'Got a fag?' he asked her again.

'I don't smoke.' She pointed to her pregnant stomach.

'And a good thing too.' Val's head bobbed up and down, and for the first time Belinda saw her hand, a thin claw clasped firmly around a can of VB. 'In your condition. You gotta look after yourself.'

CHAPTER 13

Professor Gordon Highett's house was a neat redbrick, Federation style. Situated on the main road heading out of town, it was formerly the doctor's residence, when there was once a permanent medic in town. Now, Gordon lived there with his wife Janine and their two Labradors. When they'd first arrived, Will and Belinda had been invited to play a game of tennis with the couple and, despite their relative youth and energy, had been soundly beaten. The Highetts had failed to conceal their jubilation at the win. Even so, in a year when they had barely been invited anywhere, he and Belinda agreed it had been a pretty good night.

As Gordon welcomed Will, he told him that Janine was in France, visiting their youngest, Sophie. Sophie had got into a bit of trouble overstaying her visa, and as usual it was the parents who had to intervene. Gordon smiled in mock dismay. 'Children!' he said. 'You'll soon learn all about it.'

'Bel's due in a month.'

'Exciting times, exciting times,' Gordon murmured, though his tone registered anything but.

'Gordon, we're looking into Geordie's affairs – what he was up to and so forth.' Will could see no reason not to be upfront.

'Aha, I thought I'd see you at some point about this.' He looked rather sternly at Will, as if he'd been waiting for a long time. 'A terrible tragedy.'

'What can you tell us about the anti-wind farm groups in Carrabeen? We're following up on details for the coroner's report, and Tammy mentioned that you had said something about people hassling the Pritchards.'

'Oh, yes.' Gordon nodded gravely. 'The anti-turbine groups are very active around here, and they're growing.'

'You disagree with them?'

'Of course. Public discourse is good when it's civil and informed. But things have become rather nasty of late.'

'In what way?' Will had his pen and paper out.

Gordon offered him a seat on the front porch. The smell of jasmine washed over them.

'I've had a couple of dead rabbits at the front door.'

'Could have been dogs,' Will suggested.

'Dogs don't slit rabbits' throats.'

'Ah.' Will's stomach turned. 'No.'

'I've had threatening messages on my phone: *Land for the people, not rich fuckers* and *Watch yourself,* that kind of thing.'

Will was still recovering from Gordon saying 'rich fuckers' when he was offered a nice cup of tea. He declined as gratefully as he could, then waited as Gordon headed back inside to bring out some other form of refreshment.

A book on gardening and a glossy magazine sat on a low round porch table. It took him a moment to realise that it was the same alumni mag that was in Lucinda's house. Yes, the same one – the smiling student, the expansive lawn and English trees, the imposing sandstone building.

Gordon returned with a tray laden with tea, sparkling water, a cup, a glass and two biscuits. Pushing aside the magazine, he set it down on the table.

'You went to St Francis?'

'I did,' Gordon said. 'A long time ago. The Pritchards went there too. Geordie and his father Hugh. I didn't know them, of course – Geordie was far too young and Hugh was a little older. We kept to our year levels.'

'The man who died in Singapore' – Will pointed to the cover headline – 'he was Geordie's friend there, I believe.'

'Oh yes?' Gordon turned to look at a rose bush. 'I didn't know.'

'I thought everyone in those circles knew each other.'

Gordon looked back at him, a faint smile on his face. 'Well, you'd be familiar with the Pritchards too then, wouldn't you?'

'Pardon?'

Gordon poured his tea. 'It's not difficult to see it on you, you know: the old money. Something about the way you move, the way you stretch out when you sit.'

The ease, that's what Belinda always called it. The lack of hard edges.

Will held his hands up in surrender. 'Guilty as charged.' He leaned over and helped himself to a glass of sparkling water.

'Ha!' The man laughed. 'You're forgiven.'

'Well, what about you – a St Francis student? I bet you went skiing in Europe with the family at least once or twice.'

'Hardly.' The man took a sip of tea. 'I was on a full scholarship. My mother was a single parent from the sticks, but I was dux of our local high school, and a teacher there helped me write an application.'

'Good of him.'

'Her. Teachers like that, they change lives,' Gordon said, and for a few moments the two men drank in contemplative silence.

'Did you enjoy St Francis?' Will asked eventually.

'Mainly, yes. I was a shy kid, very studious. So, while I liked the tuition and the extra classes, I never made any real friends. But that was hardly the fault of the college. I heard about some terrible bullying stories – there was a hazing culture at one point – but I never experienced any of that. Everyone there was very kind. I've kept all the old school magazines, and when I look back on them – which is rarely! – I feel nothing but fondness.'

Will watched as a magpie settled on top of the gutter, hoping for crumbs.

'*Per volar sunata*,' Gordon said suddenly, with gusto.

'Eh?'

'That's the St Francis motto. *Born to soar.*'

'Inspirational.'

'Indeed,' Gordon grinned. 'I became an English literature teacher and a failed playwright.'

Will took a bite of a shortbread biscuit, enjoying the rare moment of geniality with a local.

'And I did like Geordie Pritchard,' Gordon went on. 'He was determined to make a difference. For him, I really don't think it was about the money. He was a fine man.'

'When did you last see him?'

Gordon moved his head from side to side in thought. 'Gosh, it must have been on his last day. The last day. Yes.' Will waited while Gordon paused before continuing. 'I walked past the petrol station when he was pulling in. He said a big, cheery hello. That's why it's difficult to reconcile the idea that he may have been so depressed. The Geordie I knew was always so optimistic!'

Will moved the conversation on, reluctant to discuss the circumstances of Geordie's death. 'Back to the wind farms,' he said, firmly. 'We know there's opposition to them from Doug Hay and Farms for Future, but how has your pro-turbine lobby reacted? I mean, how heated has this topic really got in town?'

'Very,' Gordon admitted. 'The two opposing groups each have radical members, but basically it's pitting landowner against landowner, and people in the towns are just as divided. There are shouting matches in the street – people who think their land is going to be taken over by the government. Others worry farmland will be ruined, that sort of thing. But we keep on going.'

'Right.' Will listened, watching the magpie watching him. Still no crumbs.

'Wind farms,' Gordon continued, 'are the best chance for this country to get to net zero by 2030. We need to be building more of them, and faster. We might find a better way to combat climate change in the future, but right now, renewables are our best option. They may not be everyone's cup of tea, but they're paradise compared to what the world will look like in the future if we don't try.' Gordon finished his tea in two gulps. 'I've got two grandchildren,' he added. 'I want them to be able to snorkel on the Great Barrier Reef and walk through an old-growth rainforest.'

Family stretches on, Will mused. *It stretches on long after we're dead. It's like a length of rope that extends past the horizon, and we're holding on to it for only a short time. If you can imagine where that rope leads, then maybe you can be less selfish.* He'd have a child soon. And suddenly, Will desperately wanted that child to see snow in the Victorian High Country. It was like something out of a fairytale when he'd first seen it: the drooping snow gums; the way the light caught the icicles; the sparkling, twinkling white flakes drifting down.

'Thanks, Gordon.' Will swallowed a burp and looked at the time on his phone.

Gordon crossed his legs and smiled into the sun. 'I grew up in a small town, not five kilometres from the largest coal mine in NSW. When people tell me turbines are ugly, I want to take them back there. "Come!" I'd say. "Let's talk about a blight on the view."'

Will gave a chuckle.

The older man opened one eye, 'You should come to the next Farms for Future meeting. Give you a good idea of who is who in the community. It's on tomorrow night.'

'I'll try.'

Placing his glass neatly on the tray, Will stood. 'Your friend, Marit. She's involved with the wind farms too, right?'

Gordon hesitated, then looked directly at him. 'Friend is a funny way to put it, but yes – Marit and I have spent a lot of time together, along with our clean energy volunteer group. She's a rock climber too, so we share that interest.'

'You rock climb?'

'I used to. Not any more. Not fit enough these days.'

'You're pretty good on the tennis court, Gordon.'

'Bit different to climbing!'

'Well, that's true.'

'And look,' Gordon continued, 'I don't want to disparage Marit. She is very dedicated to the cause. But sometimes I think that . . . that . . .'

Will waited.

Gordon caught his gaze and continued more firmly. 'Sometimes I think that Marit needs to focus. One step at a time. Like a lot of young people these days, she is very impatient, and she's been through some difficult times.'

'She recently broke up with my colleague Tammy,' Will said. 'That's probably been hard for her.'

Gordon raised his eyebrows. 'I'm not sure heartbreak is at the core of her problems, but who knows? Marit is a troubled soul.'

The man did not elaborate any further, so Will said his goodbyes.

'I'll drop you around some of those St Francis magazines I've kept,' Gordon said. 'You might be able to use them somehow.'

'Yes, thank you.' He wasn't sure how.

As he reversed out of the Highetts' driveway, he gave Gordon a wave. '*Per volar sunata*,' he murmured. *Born to soar.* Will watched Gordon settle back down in his porch chair, while the magpie busily pecked at the tasty remainders of their morning tea.

CHAPTER 14

As soon as Belinda switched on her phone, it pinged with a voicemail message.

Julie.

Bloody hell, she thought, as she turned into the main street. She'd been mulling over what she'd learned at the campsite, particularly about a woman bringing food, when, speak of the devil . . . Or rather, The Ghost.

Please come, was all the message said. The request polite but firm. That was Julie: unyielding in her wacky beliefs, but always civil.

It was after school hours when Belinda drove into the college grounds. The students had already left and only a few teachers wandered around outside, shouting their goodbyes. One of them was Dean, her former deb partner, who gave her a startled look of recognition and a quick wave before hurrying on. He'd done that a few times before, when she'd seen him out running. *No doubt he's forgotten my name*, Belinda thought wryly. And why would he remember? He was always one of the cooler kids. He'd only agreed to be her deb partner because of her father. Dean's mother was probably scared of what Reg would do if her son refused to ask her.

She kept walking, around the side of the newly built section to the old part she remembered well. The food technology rooms were connected to the main building but were unrenovated. The Pritchard dollars only reached so far. There was no sign of Vice Principal Andrew Kent or the principal, Orla Witts. They were probably holed up in a meeting somewhere.

'Hello? Sergeant Burney?'

Belinda turned to see Tayla, the gap year student, standing on the netball court, an apologetic look on her face.

'I'm sorry!' the young woman said. 'But can you please sign in? You can just do it here, I've brought the iPad.'

'Of course!' Belinda strode back to her. 'I should have checked in with you first.'

'Oh, that's all right!' Tayla was flustered; her hair had come out of its ponytail and flowed in untidy curls past her shoulders. 'No need for you to sign out again. I'm just trying to get everyone who comes here to sign in – it's part of my contract.'

The young woman couldn't disguise her pride at having a contract. It meant secure work; it meant someone trusted you; it gave you responsibility. Belinda smiled to herself as she leaned over to sign the digital record.

'This place is lucky to have you working here – you're obviously very organised.' Belinda straightened up. 'If you ever want to join the police force, they'd snap you up.'

'They would?' Tayla's face was pure joy. She pushed her hair back from her face, and with a deft movement pulled it into place with a scrunchie that was wrapped around her wrist.

'For sure.' Why not? She was young, enthusiastic. Hopefully she'd get out of Carrabeen, head to the city and beyond. Going places didn't exclude a return to her hometown, but time away had value, gave you perspective. 'You're going to Melbourne soon, right?'

'As soon as the school year finishes.' Tayla sounded relieved. 'I've got a room in a sharehouse organised. It will be so good to have my own bed there!'

Belinda gave her a short wave and pushed open the wooden doors to the old building, wandering down an empty corridor, past the science lab with its strange smell of chemicals mixed with sweat, and on to the home economics room. Julie was inside, wiping down the benchtops.

'Belinda!' She hurried over to her. 'Finally!'

'Has something else happened?' she asked.

'The usual: lunch boxes, lunch money. One of the novels for Year Ten English.'

'Now the thief is *really* getting desperate,' Belinda said with a smile.

Julie's face showed she wasn't impressed. Her voice lowered. 'There's something weird going on here, I'm telling you.'

'Okay, Julie, so what is it?'

'This morning' – the teacher's voice was now barely a whisper – 'I came in and one of the ovens was *warm*.'

'You mean, it had been left on?'

'It *had* been on, yes. But not all night, otherwise it would have been boiling hot.'

'Okay, but could someone have turned it on this morning?'

'I was the first one here.'

Somewhere down the long corridor, a door slammed. This room, though, was incredibly quiet. It suddenly – and unhelpfully – occurred to Belinda that the food technology rooms were the most isolated section of the whole school. Outside the window, the oval was deserted, and further on from that, way in the distance, she caught sight of the faint tip of a spinning blade.

'There's a presence here,' Julie hissed.

Belinda shook herself. It was *Julie's* presence that was unnerving. With her talk of spirits and raising the dead, Julie (and *The Blair Witch Project*) had played havoc with Belinda's mind when they were at school. Her eyes fell on a rack of glinting knives on the nearby counter.

She cleared her throat. 'Andrew told me the school feeds the less well-off kids. Was there a breakfast club this morning?'

'Yes.'

'And were you using the ovens?'

'Yes, to heat up the muffins.'

'So, is it possible that someone left an oven on? And maybe, *maybe* you forgot about that?'

'Not likely!' Despite her indignation, a hint of doubt entered Julie's voice.

Belinda leaned against the doorway and rested one arm across her stomach. 'Look, Julie, there's not much we can do about the thefts, short of catching someone in the act – and as cameras aren't allowed in the classrooms, that's unlikely to happen. One of the kids will need to come forward, or maybe you'll hear them bragging about it – and *then* we can come in and question them.'

Julie didn't look happy. 'But nothing gets *done* about it! The staff conduct a few bag searches every now and then, but they hardly look inside. No one knows anything, and worse – I get the feeling that no one believes me when I say something weird is going on!'

'*Is* something weird going on? It seems like there's been a series of minor thefts, that's all. Nothing strange and, actually, very common in a school this size.'

Julie slammed her hand down on the counter and glared at Belinda.

'It's as if,' she hissed and leaned in, 'someone is *living* here.'

Belinda felt a creeping urge to look behind her. 'Do you have any evidence for that, Julie?'

'The oven, the thefts . . . I don't know . . .' She broke off, unsure.

Belinda's eyes caught the knife rack again. In Year Ten she remembered Julie insisting she'd seen a little girl-ghost at the school.

Belinda collected herself. 'We *are* taking the thefts seriously, Julie. I'm here, aren't I? Do you think it would help if I came to the school to talk with the students?'

'It might.' Though Julie looked doubtful.

'And if you could keep taking note of what's going missing, and when it happens, that would be helpful too. I've kept a record of all the items.'

Julie gave a dismissive wave of her hand.

'Oh, and one more thing, Julie.' Belinda turned back. 'Do you ever take food down to the people camping by the creek?'

'No.' Julie looked away, defensively. 'Of course not. I've got more than enough to do here. Why would I bother to do *that*?'

Belinda drove through the town again, past the run-down general store, the failing cafe, the old theatre that once housed weekly cabarets. Julie's mother had worked the ticket booth there, Belinda remembered. With its heavy red curtains and dark interior, the theatre had been a spooky place. It would have been the perfect spot for the young Julie to indulge her penchant for the supernatural. The Ghost. That's what David from the campsite had called the woman who brought them food. It did sound like Julie, even if the teacher didn't want to admit it.

She was passing the old dress shop, now vacant, and the petrol station, which smelled of rats. *No one ever mentions the townspeople when they write about the country*, Belinda thought. *It's always about the farmers and their problems.* When was the last time she'd read an article about a petrol station in a country town? Or about the grand old pub, with its rotten balcony and wine-stained carpet? What about the post office, or the shop that sold cheese sandwiches thick with margarine in half-frozen white bread? You never heard about them, did you? Most of all, you never heard about the people who lived in the back streets, in the weatherboards and cheap cladding of the town. In the cities, suburbia is a mystery; in country towns, back streets are a myth.

Turning left, Belinda's thoughts were interrupted once more by the sight of one of the Razzes riding his bike too fast along the footpath. No helmet again. She slowed down.

'Raz!' she called. 'Got a minute?'

At her shout, the teenager looked up, registered the police car and made to head off. Then he saw Belinda in the driver's seat and slowed down, his bike wobbling along the path.

'What.' He asked it like it wasn't a question.

'How's the family?'

There was a loosening in his shoulders. 'Okay.'

'Your mum all right?' Mrs Reynolds used to play Daryl Braithwaite so loud, Belinda's father threatened to shoot her, and Daryl too. It was part of the reason Belinda couldn't ever listen to 'The Horses'.

Raz gave a small nod before clearing his throat. 'Seen Blaize the other night.'

'Yeah?' Belinda tried to remember who Blaize was. A cousin? A sister?

'Cathy's kid,' Raz said, looking away, losing interest.

Cathy was the Raz Belinda had known in Year Eleven, the one now sadly deceased. She'd dropped out of school when she fell pregnant, then moved to Melbourne. Blaize must be this boy's cousin.

'She back for a holiday?'

'Dunno. I saw her down the street.'

That's how it was with the Raz family; the comings and goings, the unreliable home address. It made them flighty, but it made them canny too. If you were always searching for solid ground, you had to be acutely aware of your surroundings, to know when to flee and who to trust.

'She wasn't staying with you?'

'Nah. One of the cousins.'

And the lack of concern too – this kid would trust that Blaize Raz knew what she was doing. She'd come back. Or not.

Raz looked at his wrist, which did not have a watch on it.

'Raz, you know anything about the thefts at the school?'

The young man scowled. 'Got nothing to do with it. Why d'ya—'

'I wasn't suggesting you do.' Belinda was quick to explain herself. 'I just wondered if you'd heard anything. I don't know many locals to ask any more.'

Raz put one long foot onto the bike pedal again, considering. 'Nah. Heard nuthin.' He paused. 'Why're you even looking into it? Let the teachers deal.'

Belinda sighed. 'Theft's theft. Plus, I'm the only cop left to *deal*. Everyone else is focused on what happened at the turbines.'

She tried and failed to stop the resentment leaking into her tone. With nine days left of work, it seemed only practical that Belinda focus on the minor tasks that came up at the station. And the work that required less travel.

It may have been practical, yes, but that didn't mean she had to be *happy* about it.

'Turbines,' Raz sniggered.

'What's so funny?'

'Good for clean energy, and a whole lot more. Nice inside them, by the sounds.'

Belinda put a hand on the top of her stomach to ride a wave of nausea and turned off the engine. 'What do you mean?'

'Nuthin.'

She pursed her lips, put on her best cop voice. 'Raz!'

He gave a bored shrug.

'Is it drugs? Is it a place to do drugs? C'mon, Raz, help me out here.'

Raz looked away then back at her, a little pink in the cheeks. 'Sex is what I've heard.'

Belinda opened her mouth to ask him more, but the young man gave her a nod and powered off down the footpath, his long red mullet flowing in the breeze.

CHAPTER 15

Belinda barely had time to change and put a wash on when a cheery hello and the smell of Chanel No.5 floated in through the front door.

Penelope. She'd almost forgotten.

'Bellll!' her mother-in-law said, elongating the 'l' as always. She left her bag in the hallway and opened her arms to give Belinda a brief hug followed by a kiss on both cheeks. 'You're looking *wonderful*.'

Belinda, red-faced and sweating, knew she wasn't looking wonderful, but she smiled. It never failed to annoy her the way Penelope said her name, as if it was actually Belle rather than Belinda. She'd clearly have preferred her daughter-in-law to be an Isabelle or a Charlotte or a *Lucinda*.

'Terrible business about the Pritchards.' Penelope shook her head and pursed her lips. 'Such a good family!'

'Did you know them well?' Belinda busied herself in the kitchen cupboards.

'Not overly.' Penelope sat on one of the bench stools and crossed her long legs, admiring them as she spoke. 'But you know, the boy who died in Singapore – Oliver Moffat – he was my sister's godson and Geordie Pritchard's friend.'

Belinda didn't mention what Will had told her; that according to Lucinda, Geordie hadn't spoken to Oliver since he'd left their shared residential college at Sydney University.

'And you know, of course that Will and Lucinda Pritchard were very close at one stage.' Penelope blinked at her innocently.

'I am aware.'

Belinda's mother-in-law picked up a vase and tipped it upside down to read its origin. 'I would have preferred that Daniel and Will had gone to university in Sydney and lived at St Francis, just as Geordie did. It's an excellent college – jam-packed with Rhodes Scholars – but Will's father wanted his sons to go to his alma mater, Wesley.'

Belinda wondered what Penelope made of the fact she went to Carrabeen P–12. Her mother went there too, while her father only lasted till Year Eight before dropping out. It wasn't a bad school; in a lot of ways, it was very good. Plenty of kids from Carrabeen went on to be bankers, nurses and engineers.

'Perhaps if we *had* sent him to St Francis' – Penelope put the vase down and picked up another – 'Will might have been happier. It was so disappointing to us when he dropped out of Wesley after less than a year.'

Then he wouldn't have met me, Belinda felt like saying. But what was the use? Penelope knew that – the woman was as sharp as a blade.

Her mother-in-law continued. 'I'm only here for a flying visit, just to see how you are.'

'I'm fine, the baby's healthy.' She looked around the kitchen bench for the scan.

'And Will?' Penelope eyed her rounded stomach.

'Will's good.' Belinda eyed her mother-in-law right back. 'He's fine.'

'The migraines?' Penelope's voice wavered.

'Will's *fine*,' Belinda answered smoothly. 'Honestly, Penelope, you don't need to worry.'

Both women looked at the other with rare frankness. For Penelope, Will's migraines were a source of endless worry. Surely, she'd reasoned once, they were related to his early, unhappy years growing up: the bullying episodes, the days he liked to spend alone rather than hanging out with kids his own age. Belinda suspected that Penelope secretly thought his headaches were half imaginary, a way for her shy son to escape the pressure to be sociable.

'It's just that he's always been so – gentle,' Penelope said, searching for the right word.

'That's not a bad thing.'

'Or perhaps I mean unassuming. You know, when he was still a boy, he was already so tall and the other boys, they weren't always very nice to him.' Penelope held her hands out in a helpless gesture. 'He loved books, you know, and birds – not wrestling, or being loud.'

Or being part of a group, Belinda thought. Will didn't love that. Or rather, being part of the group you were *supposed* to be part of.

'Most of that changed, of course, when he met Lucinda and made a name for himself in rowing. But I did worry about him. I still do.'

'Mum!' The front door swung open. Will walked in and gave Belinda a tighter than normal hug. She wondered how much of the conversation he'd overheard.

'Darling!' Penelope fell into his arms with such motherly rapture that Belinda had to look away.

'When did you get here?' Will asked, gently extracting himself from his mother's grip.

'Just now,' she said, smiling at him. 'Belinda and I have been having a nice chat about the baby.'

'Have you now?' Will gave Belinda a wink, and she returned it. 'You betcha.'

Will moved around the kitchen bench, his mother close behind. 'Want a drink?' he asked.

She shook her head, content just to stand there and drink him in.

When Belinda had first met her future mother-in-law, she'd barely been able to stand Penelope's lady of the manor ways. But now, more than a decade later, she understood that Will's mother was lonely after the death of her husband, and prone to acting the part of the careless rich widow to mask her pain. There was something tough about her, which Belinda had to admire. She saw in those traits parallels with her own father and his behaviour in public. The pair were good actors, well aware that life behind the curtain wasn't as glossy as life in front.

Belinda busied herself in the kitchen while Will and Penelope chatted about Will's older brother, Daniel. She'd made a roast pumpkin dish with pine nuts and yoghurt sauce, to be accompanied with roast chicken. It was an easy recipe, but the end result was interesting enough to please Penelope. Belinda found it pleasant to listen to mother and son talking in the next room: the questioning, the lengthy answers, the occasional laugh. She never spoke like that with Reg. Their conversations consisted of her asking questions and Reg grunting. She looked down at her bump. If the baby was a boy, she hoped they'd have a similar sort of relationship to Will and Penelope's, minus the overt rapture.

'And you know Oliver wrote a book while he was dying,' Penelope was saying. 'I think he started it when he was in jail for fraud – his mother says the charge was nonsense, of course.'

Yeah right. Will caught Belinda's eye through the open lounge-room door and they smiled at each other.

'He'd been through a very stressful time, and they had to send him to that retreat near Byron Bay – you know, that one where people go when they need "time to rest". It's called something horrid like Serenity Now. Revolting! Sounds like a warm salmon quiche.'

Does it?

'So yes,' Penelope continued, 'the first chapter of the book is about his recovery at the quiche place. I brought you it. Oh, yes! Here it is.' She retrieved the book from a large cream leather tote bag. 'Lucinda's mother sent me an early reading copy.' She passed it to him.

'Thanks, Mum.' Will looked at it in horror. He liked wartime books, not memoirs by spoiled rich men turned bad.

'I know half the people in it,' Penelope continued airily. 'I'm sure you'll know a few too, darling.'

When the chicken was done, Will helped Belinda set the table and serve up while Penelope continued to talk and talk. Eventually, and despite Will's efforts to avoid it, the conversation veered back to the Pritchards.

'Lucinda's mother is *terribly* shocked, of course. No one expected this.'

'Yes, it's awful,' Belinda said, sitting down with some relief and indicating they should all begin to eat.

'And you know, those people opposed to the wind farms, all those awful ignorant types who—'

'They're not all ignorant,' Belinda cut in.

'Well, those people who are against the turbines.' Penelope raised her eyebrows at Will. 'My friend Suze says that Lucinda and Geordie received all these abusive phone calls to the house. It must have really taken a toll.'

Belinda and Will concentrated on their food.

'Suze knows Lucinda's mother well,' Penelope added, by way of explanation. 'They're in the same mosaic group. Next year, they're going on a workshop to Greece.'

Will cleared his throat. 'This food is great, Bel,' he said. 'Thank you.'

'Divine,' his mother added.

Penelope barely ate. The woman was a sparrow.

'And you know' – Penelope sipped her wine – 'it's not as if Geordie and Lucinda were rolling in money. The business was hard work! Suze said that Geordie was giving money away left, right and centre. Philanthropy is wonderful, but you must have the funds to do it.'

'Are you saying that Geordie and Lucinda weren't that well off?' Belinda frowned. The BMW, the homestead, the land, the place in Melbourne . . .

'Well, they weren't going to starve, if that's what you mean. But I'm saying that it was a lot of hard work, and with all the abuse they were getting, well . . . You can see how a young man with that much pressure . . .' She took a large glug of wine, letting the words dangle.

As Will grabbed the opportunity to change the topic, Belinda found herself distracted by her thoughts. In particular: when she should tell Will that she'd spoken to Geordie shortly before his death.

CHAPTER 16

Regrets and Promises: A Life in Finance
My life, my story

Will gave a snort of laughter as he flicked through the book while drinking his morning coffee. Who would buy this shit? Really, it looked awful.

He'd left Belinda in bed, faintly snoring, her hands sweetly under her face, cheeks like a round speckled hen. The day was bright and blue – and so quiet, save the screeching cockatoos and the occasional car. So different from their Melbourne apartment, where the traffic was constant but almost soothing. When he'd first moved to Carrabeen, he'd wake in the night, startled by the lack of sound. Almost a year later, the silence still unsettled him.

Walking into the bathroom, he found he'd brought Oliver Moffat's book with him. And there was the author, in a photo on the back, looking into the sunset, smiling wistfully. His yacht's name, visible in the fading light behind him, was *Number One*.

Will laughed quietly to himself. He'd been reading a book on the Napoleonic wars, but this was far more entertaining. Brushing his teeth, he flicked to the middle section of Oliver's book, which was devoted entirely to photographs.

There was Oliver with his glamorous wife and children at a ball. There was Oliver sitting in an office overlooking the city. There was Oliver dressed up as David Bowie aboard *Number One* on Sydney Harbour. Ha! Will could imagine Moffat slinking around the harbour like a goanna, slurping cocktails and leering at backpackers in bikinis. He knew the type. He flicked over the page. And there was Oliver in white linen, barefoot on a beach, with the caption: *The moment of epiphany.*

Christ, Will thought, spitting into the sink. *So that's what I gave up – the yachts and white linen, deals in high places, the harbour parties.* It looked nice enough, but Will felt no regret for the decisions he'd made.

After all, he thought, throwing the book onto a pile of laundry, he'd once had an epiphany of his own. Near the end of his first semester at Wesley, Will had been at the back of the dining hall while the Master was making a speech. He'd had a view of all the students seated along the rectangular wooden tables before him, their faces lit by warm candlelight, their faint, bored smiles as they listened to the speech reflected in his own expression. It was all so very, very familiar, and . . . what the hell! He'd thrown his head back in disbelief, struck by the thought: *I know everyone here.*

And it was true. He'd been at boarding school with most of the students, his parents were friends with their parents, they all played rugby on weekends, they rowed in the same crew. He knew them, knew where they were headed, knew where they'd all most likely end up.

And out of the blue, a voice deep inside his gut rose up, saying, *No, No. No.*

Cue leaving university and finding a profession that was so far removed from Art History/Philosophy that he would be catapulted into a new life: the police force. There, it was a revelation to see so many unfamiliar faces, people from backgrounds vastly different from his. The discipline of the job, the grime of the underworld, the people whose concerns were so at odds with everything he was used to.

And then there was Tough Mudder, an endurance course designed to bring the new police recruits together. He'd seen a woman bounding over a wall towards him, running at him through the rain and mud, red-faced and determined. Her small body was weaving around the bigger men and women, her ponytail whipped about in a frenzy. And when he'd looked at her sprinting at him, Will had suddenly felt a lightheadedness mingled with euphoria. An aura – the first signs of a migraine that could come on at any time. Still, the small woman came running, *really running* at him, as he looked on in wonder, saw the shapes and fuzzy lines behind his eyes, saw them rise up behind her in a pyrotechnic show. His legs were starting to shake . . . and he'd leaned over, breathing deep – only to feel an almighty crack when a rushing head collided with his. When he'd come to, lying on the ground, all signs of the migraine were gone. And the first thing he'd seen was Belinda's face, her hazel eyes looking into his with concern, a thin line of blood running down her forehead. His head was on her lap, one of her arms resting on his chest. 'You're okay, you're okay,' she was crooning. 'We bumped heads. You came off worse than me.'

In hindsight, Will thought now, far from being hurt, they were both extremely lucky.

He was glad to be out of the house early today. He poked his head in to say goodbye to his mother, but she was fast asleep, mouth open. What a force she'd been when he was growing up! Far more involved than his studious father, and always so energised by her surroundings. He knew that he'd disappointed her greatly when he left university. It was his older brother Daniel who was her pride and joy – the investment banker who'd finished his studies, now living with his fashionable wife in London. He wondered what Penelope had made of the little room she slept in now, the double bed with the mustard doona, the jar of daisies Belinda had placed on her bedside table, the fresh towel neatly folded on the chest of drawers, the photo of Belinda and Will at their police graduation beside it.

'I'm *bewildered* by your coupling,' an old uncle had said at their wedding, greatly amused by his own joke at combining their names. Belinda had looked like she wanted to punch him, but then the old man had smiled rather wistfully. 'But you certainly have all the bells and whistles,' he said. 'That you do.'

Will walked over to his mother and planted a quick kiss on her cheek. 'Bye, Mum,' he said, pulling the covers up under her chin.

A thin hand reached out and patted him on the arm. 'Love,' she said, drowsy, 'be careful.'

Will returned to his own room and kissed Belinda goodbye on the lips. In response, she reached up and pulled him down for an embrace. 'Have a good day,' she said, her eyes half open. 'Call me.'

He left the house, enjoying the warm breeze and the honeyed smell of eucalypt. Up above, a flock of cockatoos veered westerly in strong formation. Farmers hated them, but he'd grown to love their wild, screeching cries.

CHAPTER 17

'I'm dead,' Lisa said, her mood considerably lower than in the days previous.

Will had just arrived at the station, seen an email from her, and returned her call.

'What are you on about?' he said down the line.

'Kelmendri's *so angry* with me about that stupid UDL can, I think he wants to sack me.'

'I don't think Kelmendri wants to do anything, let alone sack anyone. It's too much work.'

'True,' Lisa chuckled. 'But after all of this, I don't even know if I want to work here. I'm thinking of going back to do teaching.'

'Yeah?' Will wasn't sure why Lisa was telling him this. 'Why were you in Investigations in the first place then?'

'I thought it would be more interesting than regular police work, but honestly – it's still so much paperwork, and Kelmendri is such an old grump. It took me forever to get here. I had to, like, do these *courses*. Plus, my mum went to school with someone on the interview panel, but yeah – I think I've made a mistake.'

Leave then, Will felt like saying. He felt a bristling annoyance at his younger colleague who'd sailed into Investigations, while his wife – so much more dedicated and thorough – would kill for such a job. She'd done all the courses too. 'Maybe you did make a mistake,' he said. 'But back to this case, is there anything we need to know?'

Finally, Lisa got around to the real purpose of the call – giving him updates on forensics. The results hadn't been finalised yet, she told him, but there were some interesting initial findings. She would send them through. Word on the skin fragment was due in a day or so.

As he hung up, an elderly couple strode through the station's front door, their faces tight with anger.

Oh no, Will thought. *There will be a pothole somewhere. There'll be a group of kids riding bikes outside their house late at night. There'll be a neighbour whose dog won't stop barking.*

'We're here to report an eyesore.' The woman spoke first.

'An eyesore?' This was new. Will didn't know whether to get his notepad out or just nod along.

'It's a *disgrace*!' One corner of the man's shirt collar was sticking up, as if also in indignation. 'Tents and caravans, like a circus, right at the start of town.'

'And not a good circus, not like a Bullen's one,' the woman added. 'A really crappy circus, with a load of junk and dodgy people and no cool animals.'

'A disgrace!' the man said again. 'And right on our doorstep.'

Oh, the campers. Will shuffled on his feet. He wasn't sure where he stood in all of this. Was it illegal?

'They have children down there!' The woman sounded almost triumphant. 'Young children among all the squalor and the dirt!'

'So, what are your concerns?' Will asked, genuinely confused. 'That there are children there?'

'They don't attend school!'

'Are you sure about that?' Will vaguely remembered Belinda telling him that some of the children from the camp were enrolled at Carrabeen College.

'It's not a legal campsite!' the man said, and his shirt collar agreed. 'I've looked it up, *I know.* Those people are actually living there – and no one is doing anything about it.'

Will couldn't deny it. When he drove past there, he mostly looked the other way. The sagging canvas tents after rain, the windblown annexes, the sad caravans with their rusting doors.

'And what's more' – the woman's eyes glistened – 'it's *growing.* There're two more tents there today!'

'What do you suggest we do about it?'

'Move them on! Make them go somewhere else!' the woman exclaimed, and the man nodded in agreement.

'But where to?'

'How should we know?' The man shrugged, incredulous. 'That's not *our* business.'

When they left, the door slammed like an exclamation mark.

Will stared after them. What was he to do? He assumed most of the campers were homeless people, unable to make rent in the city. Somehow, they had found their way to the public facilities and barbecue area by the creek.

Clearly it wasn't just the turbines causing upheaval in town . . .

Lisa's promised email had come through. In order to access the file from Forensics, Will had to first put in the password that was sent to his phone, and then respond to a request for a passcode that was sent to an app he had not yet downloaded. He downloaded the app, provided fingerprint verification, received the passcode and tapped it into the file. After selecting a number of boxes with motorbikes in them to prove he was human, and after having aged a decade in the last ten minutes, the file finally popped up.

First, Geordie's ute. Nothing of interest there; plenty of Geordie's own fingerprints and nothing suspicious to add. Interestingly, no fibres from the rope he was found hanging from. So, Will mused briefly, the rope must have been picked up elsewhere. Found, perhaps, or placed near the turbines earlier. None of the scenarios made Geordie's death clearer.

Next, and more interestingly – the DNA from the turbine itself.

After discounting the DNA of the victim himself and all police officers, ambulance services, SES volunteers and wind turbine employees at the scene of turbine 82 on the Clean Energy Solutions farm, Carrabeen Road – no additional fingerprints could be identified.

CHAPTER 18

Carrabeen Library was packed by the time Will arrived just before seven-thirty. He parked on the roadside fifty metres away as Tammy pulled up beside him.

'I never knew this many people even lived here!' she said. Like him, Tammy was a city girl. 'Wish we got this sort of crowd for our road safety information evenings. Remember poor Jason?'

Six months ago, the pair had had to retrieve the body of seventeen-year-old Jason Hannah, killed in a farm accident. He'd been driving a four-wheeler on the side of a slippery dam, had crashed, then drowned.

Will shrugged. There were always going to be accidents on farms, some more easily avoided than others. And road safety information evenings were notoriously boring, particularly for seventeen-year-old boys.

A group of women bustled past them, one talking loudly on her phone, providing directions to someone who was apparently lost on the windy roads. 'Past the silo!' she was saying. 'No, I said the silo. Are you listening, Jacinta? *The silo!*'

'I don't think Jacinta is listening,' Will whispered to Tammy.

The police officers waited for the women to enter the hall before following behind them. Inside, rows of chairs had been set up before a stage, and a few people were already sitting down, while others were mingling, trying to find their friends. At the back, a table was laid out with an urn of boiling water, cups, instant coffee and packets of assorted biscuits. Parents jiggled babies on their knees, an old man spoke loudly into a phone, and a group of women shrieked with laughter. The atmosphere was one of excited anticipation.

Will and Tammy chose to stand up at the back, jostling each other as more people entered the space. A heavily pregnant woman walked in and looked uncertainly about, until a teenage boy got the dreaded tap on the shoulder and begrudgingly offered her his seat.

Up the front, a rotund woman climbed the steps to the stage. Dressed entirely in black, she reminded Will of Queen Victoria in her mourning stage.

'Tap, tap.' Queen Victoria was testing the mike. 'Tap, tap.' She spoke into the microphone again, and about a dozen people gave her the thumbs up. Clearly enjoying the moment, the woman bent in to the mike once more, this time lowering her voice to a baritone. 'Testing, one two.' The crowd laughed and, with a beaming smile, the woman left the stage.

Will scanned the room. Doug Hay was in the front row, reading some notes, ready to speak. No surprise there; as the main cheerleader for Farms for Future, he'd be expected to address the meeting first. There were other locals present, people who Will knew to say hello to, but couldn't remember their full names: like the owner of the servo. Carmel? Will recalled she was the mother of Shane Burrows, the wind techie. He watched her carefully counting the people in the room, checking out who was there. She caught his eye and gave him a quick smile. There was the man who worked at the garage (Rick? Dick?), seated next to his wife, who ran the adjoining cafe. At the far right of the stage, three young men stood along the wall, two with their arms crossed, looking bored. The third one was busy scratching his bum, and flushed a deep pink when he saw that Will was watching. There was a hacking laugh from somewhere in the middle of the room, and Will's heart sank when he realised that it was Reg, Belinda's father. Wearing shorts and a flanny, he looked as if he'd just put down the shears after a hard day's work.

'Welcome, welcome!' Doug Hay took the mike, his warm voice echoing around the room. 'First and foremost, I'd like to acknowledge the traditional owners of this great land we're on today. We at Farms for Future pay our respects to them, and to their leaders past and present.'

Will felt a spark of surprise: he hadn't expected an Acknowledgement of Country from Doug Hay, or the nodding acceptance of it from the crowd. But then again, he hadn't got a lot of things right about the country and the people who lived here.

'And I want to add that the past week has been really difficult for this town, and we want to send our thoughts . . .'

'Please don't say "and prayers",' Tammy muttered beside Will.

'. . . and prayers to the Pritchard family. No matter what our differences about the land and clean energy, we acknowledge his death as a tragedy.'

There were more nods and some 'hear hear's from the crowd. Slouched in his seat, Reg Burney picked at something behind his ear and yawned loudly.

Doug Hay cleared his throat, and Will felt rather than saw the crowd lean closer.

'Farms for Future is about the land, preserving what we've got and protecting it for subsequent generations.' Doug eyed the audience, holding his arms out wide in a gesture of openness. 'Around Carrabeen, we've got some of the best grazing in the whole country, and we're not known as the food bowl of Australia for nothing.'

Reg, interested at last, gave a loud whistle through his teeth. He'd given a similar one when Will first pulled up in his mother's Saab to meet his girlfriend's father. The whistle at first seemed appreciative, but it had a jeering edge.

Doug continued: Carrabeen was a great place to bring up kids; he'd raised four of his own here; they'd all gone through the local school and planned to move back at some point. Will's mind was starting to wander when Doug finally came round to his point: 'I challenge any of you, when you drive on the south-west road from Ballarat, and you climb over the ranges and you hit the open land, I challenge you to find me a better sight than the Golden Plains. Beauty, that's what it is, and it's *our home.*' There was a collective sigh of appreciation in the hall. Will felt it too, the pride, the warmth.

'And now,' Doug continued, 'if the Pritchard corporation has their way, it'll be ringed almost full circle by turbines. How will you feel waking up every morning and getting an eyeful of them when you look out the window?'

There was a low muttering, till someone shouted, 'Not on our watch!' to general applause.

'And what's more' – Doug patted his pocket – 'you can say goodbye to the value of your land if you're neighbouring them. Cos it'll plummet, and that's not good for anyone.'

Money talks, Will thought. *No matter where you are in the world, it talks.* The chatter in the room had become more heated, and Doug had to wait a few moments for the crowd to calm.

'No one wants to buy a farm next door to a paddock full of machines two hundred and thirty metres high!' he said, shaking his head. 'And no one wants to *live* near one!'

A voice from the centre of the room called out, 'Ever noticed the turbines aren't in the sightline of the Pritchard farm?'

Doug nodded slowly and made a pressing hand motion as if to stop further comments on the topic. 'We won't get personal here, but you have made a good point: it's not the wealthy farm owners who'll bear the brunt of this.'

Will raised his eyebrows. It was true what Doug had said, but at the same time, wasn't it also true that some local landowners were becoming wealthy because of the turbines? He'd read that farmers were getting $40,000 a year in rent for each turbine on their land.

Finally, Doug gave his thank yous and then asked for questions. 'We want to be open and honest here. Don't be afraid to have differing views, we want to hear them all.'

'Is it true they're foreign owned?' a woman at the front asked.

Doug leaned in to the microphone. 'If I'm correct, the turbines are made from a Norwegian model.'

'Sounds like my ex-girlfriend,' someone called out, to whoops of laughter.

A middle-aged man with salt-and-pepper hair raised his hand, then waited patiently till the crowd quietened again. 'If you don't mind me saying, Doug, you're one of those in the wealthy category, so I'd say you can afford to say no to the turbines. Whereas for us smaller landowners, it's a buffer against the hard years. We've got kids to put through uni . . .'

Doug nodded. 'I agree it's hard to say no, but if we all stick together, we can—'

'We're not all as rich as you and Pritchard!' someone from the back said loudly.

'He's worked as hard as the rest of them.' Reg turned around to glare at the person. 'Over fifty years he's worked this land. Doug's earned his due.'

There was a brief silence. Reg could do this: rein in a crowd, get people to stop in their tracks. Whether it was through charisma or power, Will was never sure. Perhaps both.

Out of nowhere, a baby started bawling and the young father hurried out of the library with it, a look of relief on his face.

Another hand shot up, this time Shane Burrows' mother Carmel. 'We run the servo in town, and I can say that we've never been busier now that the turbines are here: we've got the workers coming for construction, we've got the businesspeople and the climate people, and we've—'

'Us too!' someone else said. 'Pritchard donated money to the school and to the local bowlo.'

'You want to look at those massive machines all your life?' A lady with frizzy blonde hair stood up. 'That's fine, but you'll get sick from them. They cause cancer.'

'Can you show us the evidence for that?' It was Gordon Highett, his tall thin features regal in the motley crowd.

'I can show you the lumps in my fucken neck if you want to come closer.'

'Hey, hey!' At the front, Doug Hay struggled to calm the crowd, and after a brief nod at the large lady in black, finally made himself heard. 'I don't want to get into the cancer argument tonight, but Julie will be happy to talk with people about it after the meeting. What I want to reiterate is that the wind farms are going to change this community from a peaceful, beautiful part of the world to a car park for turbines. Sure, some people will make money, but no one will choose to live in Carrabeen any more. Besides, it's pretty windy in Melbourne – why don't they build them there!'

Reg whistled again, and others started cheering. It was a cheap shot, Will thought, but the man did have a point. *When it comes down to it, everyone's a NIMBY.*

CHAPTER 19

Belinda was up early, baking. She'd woken at five-thirty and was unable to go back to sleep, thanks to the baby's constant kicking. She'd made a blood orange cake and planned to take it around to her father's place later, maybe have it with him and one of his nurses. She was keen to get out of the house. She'd been asleep by the time Will had arrived home from the meeting, so she still hadn't told him about seeing Geordie or about the conversation she'd had with young Raz, that the turbines were used for teenage hook-ups. The things she hadn't told her husband were adding up. When he was awake, she reassured herself. *Then.*

And now, at not quite 7 am, she was driving away from him, leaving him in bed.

Already, the tractors out of town were up and running. They'd barely stopped all night: harvest meant no rest for the wicked. The farmers and contractors would be driving them up and down the rows, up and down, up and down, listening to the radio, taking their snacks and drinks with them to save time. When she was a young child, her father would let her accompany him in the tractor that he used when contracting for Doug. It was a way to get her to sleep, apparently; the rhythm of it, up and down the fields.

She pulled up at the locked gate with *Clean Energy Solutions* written across it and looked at the turbines.

Reg was an early bird, but even he wouldn't be ready for cake and coffee just yet. Plus, she could do with a walk. The teenage sex stuff Raz had mentioned was a possible link between the school and the turbines.

She examined the fence, not trusting herself to climb over it. Checking first that it wasn't electric, she lifted the second wire up and pushed the bottom one as low as she could before bending down and manoeuvring herself and her bump between the wires. As a kid, she could leap these things, by placing one hand on top of the fence post and vaulting herself over the top wire.

At eight months pregnant, just climbing through was an effort.

Once on the other side, she stood for a moment, stretching her shoulders back and cricking her neck. Today, the turbines were all spinning in the steady wind, their huge blades chopping the air. If she closed her eyes, she could hear them – an electrical hum, not loud but constant. Pulling her cardigan around her waist as best she could, she tied her hair back in an elastic band that she kept on her wrist like a charm. Locating number 82, she walked towards it, thinking. The turbines were on the south side of Mont Blanc, a softly sloping hill that led down into the flat of paddocks and dams. A dry creek bed encircled the base, scraggly gums, grasses and small shrubs lining its banks. In winter it flowed strongly, and she'd seen it in flood a couple of times. When that happened, shallow lakes formed, and seemingly out of nowhere water birds arrived in their thousands. The view, stretching right down to the wild coastline of south-west Victoria, was impressive. Now, just before harvest, the whole scene spread out before her like a golden rippling sheet.

The view of the moon and stars would be wondrous here in the evening. Even more so if you had a new boyfriend by your side and a can of raspberry vodka in your hand. She kept walking, looking at the ground, kicking at the dirt, imagining where would be a good place to sit with a boy to admire the view. The stubble had been mowed neatly, but even so there were little loose stones all around, and she took extra care not to trip.

Lower down the hill, away from the turbines, she thought she saw the place. A large rock sat flat on the ground, visible in the brown grass and dirt because of its paleness. She reflected how nice it would be to sit here with Will. He'd appreciate the view all the way down to the sea, how the land sloped then flattened, the dotted dams and the snaking Hutchins River.

Yes, if she was sixteen and wanted to sit with a boy and drink a UDL, this was where she'd pick. She sat there for a while, enjoying the peace, cradling her stomach. There was something on the ground nearby, a small rectangular piece of plastic. Without standing, she reached over and picked it up, studied it. Interesting: a disposable vape. Cigarettes were too expensive for kids these days; now it was all about vapes. Scanning around, she spied another one just like it, but in a different colour. Whoever had been vaping here had been experimenting with flavours. It smacked of youth and daring. The illicit thrill of trespassing on Pritchard property after dark. And just imagine! Belinda extended the thought. What if you had the chance to actually go up inside a turbine, right to the top, to those wings. Maybe kiss someone while you gazed out across the land.

It would have been easy enough for kids to climb the fence back there. But Raz had intimated that they went up the turbines too. If so, the question was how. And where were the missing keys?

Her phone was ringing: Will. She checked the time; just after eight-thirty. He wouldn't have been concerned about her absence this morning – she was in the habit of getting up and going out walking early – but even so, now the baby was almost due she probably should have told him where she was going.

She was just about to tell him about the vape when he cut her off. Kelmendri had called from Ballarat. Forensics had come back, and yes, it was official: the turbine had been wiped clean. On top of that, the mystery skin fragment on the rope had not been a match with any of the emergency service officers or the police.

'Okay then, so it was definitely murder.' Now the place where she was sitting took on an ugly, dangerous air. Belinda looked at the fence again, wondering if there was an easier way through. 'When will we hear back if there are any matches with other DNA samples in the system?'

'Kelmendri said he's going to try to expedite the process; public interest and all that. Plus, as we know, he's dying to get up north.'

'Yeah . . .' Belinda was thinking about the fence again. 'He really is,' she said absentmindedly.

'And Bel, listen, there's something else. The coroner thinks that the blow to the back of Geordie's head was not what actually killed him. He's ruling strangulation by hanging.'

'So . . .' Belinda suddenly had a sick feeling at the back of her throat. Geordie had been alive when he was strung up?

'Yeah.' Will often knew what she was thinking. 'It's awful.'

She tried to banish the thought of her old schoolmate dangling at the end of the rope, clutching frantically at the noose.

'Also, at the Farms for Future meeting last night, things got heated. I'll need to talk to more people today, so I may not be home when you get back.'

She stared at a tractor making its way along the fence-line in the next paddock over. She forced herself to concentrate on it and its plough lines, and not on Geordie Pritchard, still alive and struggling to breathe. 'Okay,' she said finally.

'Are you out visiting your father or something?' Will asked. 'I didn't hear you leave.'

'I'm at the turbines. I found a vape just across from number eighty-two. I'll tell you about it later, but I talked to one of the Razzes. I think there's a connection between the school and the turbines.'

'You said there was an excursion out there three weeks ago.'

'Yeah.' Belinda returned the wave that the tractor driver gave her as he was passing by. 'But I don't know, I've got a feeling that . . .'

'Yes?' Will was more interested in feelings than she usually was. 'What?'

She heard the station phone ringing in the background and Tammy's voice talking to someone who'd just entered the office.

'Got to go,' Will said. 'See you soon.'

Belinda hung up the phone and forced herself to focus on the present, rather than Geordie's final struggle . . .

Focus.

The wind, the farms, the vape and the can.

Her mind slowed. What did it all mean?

She stood and walked towards the fence-line, watching the dust around the tractor as it moved towards her. She hurried to meet it, and the farmer inside poked his head out the window, slowing enough to have a conversation.

'Reg Burney's daughter, the policewoman, aren't you?' he said, a weary smile on his face. 'I'm Mick. Back in the day, I used to play footy with your dad and Alan Crowe. I was a young fella then! They were both gods in my eyes, I tell you.'

'Yeah? I've never thought of Dad as godly.' Belinda had to shield her eyes from the dust thrown up by his plough.

Mick chuckled. 'You trying to get out?' He nodded at the fence as he drove slowly by. 'Go a bit further ahead, fifty metres, and there's a gap. It's near that bunch of saltbush.'

'A gap – what, a deliberate one?' Belinda had to trot along now, as best she could, to hear what he was saying.

'Fence was built around a gum that's fallen down. Saltbush covers it now.'

'Thanks!' she called back. 'Good luck with the harvest!'

'Be my last one.' The man's weathered face broke into a smile. 'Got turbines coming. One hundred and fifty of them. No more harvest for me!'

'You'll miss it?'

Mick changed gears and the tractor sped up. 'Like hell I will!' he shouted back, giving her the customary forefinger wave.

Belinda walked the fifty metres along the fence, waving away the dust cloud the tractor had left in its wake. Sure enough, under a clump of saltbush, there was a cut in the fence, an almost perfect hole. Belinda saw how it would be visible to Mick as he drove along the fence-line on the other side of the road – but if you looked at it straight on, or weren't looking closely from an angle, the hole would be difficult to make out.

She bent down, parted the shrubs and once again struggled through the fence, although as she didn't have to hold up the wires this time, it was much easier.

She stood back and looked at the hole, thinking how for someone smaller and slighter, getting through it would be a breeze. She took a photo of it and then leaned closer to the wires. There, caught in one of the barbs, was a small piece of blue wool. Snapping more photos, she placed her long sleeves over her fingers and retrieved it as carefully as she could, placing it gently in the inside pocket of her jacket.

The smell of the freshly baked orange cake permeated the car as Belinda drove back into town, her mind buzzing with ideas. The thefts at the school, the raspberry UDL can, the vape, Geordie's death. Far-fetched perhaps, but could there be a link?

And what of the keys? There were three known sets for the turbines: one with Shane Burrows, one with Geordie Pritchard, and one kept at his Melbourne office. Alan Crowe had one for the perimeter fence: he wouldn't be happy about the hole. Land-owners were precious about fences, and rightly so.

She rounded the bottom of Mont Blanc, past the driveway of Alan's farm. From this vantage point, just for a few kilometres, there were no turbines in sight. She toyed with the thought of visiting Alan and telling him about the fence, but decided against it. No doubt Mick would let him know.

On the day before he died, Belinda thought with a pang, Geordie Pritchard had spoken to her outside the IGA in town. It had been Saturday, in the afternoon. She'd caught glimpses of him in town from time to time, but they'd never had the chance to speak. At this time, outside the supermarket, Geordie seemed delighted to chat. He'd remembered her instantly and congratulated her on her pregnancy. He said that he'd heard she was the policewoman in town, that she'd moved here with her husband, and he was highly amused that Will was his wife's ex-boyfriend. Geordie mentioned too that he'd been around to see Reg – wanted to clear up a few things with her old man.

There was a nervous energy to him, Belinda thought, a real desire to please.

'What things?' she'd asked, immediately on edge.

The dog-racing track, Geordie continued without clarifying: he hoped to buy it. The sport was on its way out, and the site itself was perfect for more turbines. He planned to buy the whole thing and dedicate the site to its loyal former patrons, the local identities who made the community what it was. A decent percentage of the profits would flow back to the towns; it was going to be great!

Belinda waited, watched as her former school mate waxed lyrical about his plans. Smiling, he touched her elbow lightly, drawing her in.

'Only thing is,' he'd said, 'the racing track is in financial trouble. The club itself has been running at a loss for years. I got to look at the books, you see.'

'And? What did you see there?'

Geordie cleared his throat. 'There's some patrons who have spent a lot of money there. As in, all their money. Some still owe money, in fact.'

'Dad,' Belinda said, flatly.

Geordie nodded ruefully. 'Yeah. The racing track won't sell till all the debts are paid. They're threatening legal action, the sale of Reg's house to cover the funds he owes.'

'The house?' Belinda said in disbelief. 'When did this all happen?'

'A few days ago. They say they've sent people around to Broker Court, but your father won't even discuss it.'

Who have they sent around? Belinda thought. *People in suits? People wearing balaclavas?* Her father never told her anything.

'Thing is, Belinda' – Geordie stepped back to let a cyclist ride by – 'they don't care who pays the money, as long as it's paid.

I wanted to let your dad know that I'm happy to settle his debts. Then at least he gets to keep his home.'

Belinda turned her head, watching a wheat truck drive past. Two small kids on the footpath held up their arms in the familiar plea for the driver to honk his horn. He did so. The kids cheered.

'What did Dad say?'

'He told me to eff off.'

No surprises there.

'Why would you offer to do this?' she asked.

Geordie held his hands out in a gesture of openness. 'I want the land for more turbines,' he admitted. 'But also, your father worked for my grandfather for years. At one point, our fathers were friends.'

'Right.' A gust of wind swept up the main street, dry leaves swirling in the stone gutters. 'Except they weren't friends for long. Your dad did a stint of shearing and then moved away. I don't get it.'

'Dad became a ruthless old bugger, I know. I'm not like him. I'm not.'

She didn't know how to respond to that.

'I want to help you, Belinda. I know not everyone is as privileged as me.'

The way he said it, his head slightly bowed, like he was acting ashamed. Had he read a pamphlet on how best to declare it?

She sniffed. 'Yeah, well, don't beat yourself up about it.'

'No one needs to know I'll pay for it. Plus, I do want that land for turbines.'

The wind strengthened, and a dry branch broke loose from a nearby tree and hurtled past them.

'So why bother telling me all this – why not just go ahead and do it?' Belinda looked at him, incredulous.

For the first time, Geordie looked uncomfortable. 'I always felt sorry for you, Belinda. You were this smart, funny kid, but your dad, and the house you lived in . . . it must have been so . . . demoralising?'

Belinda felt a sudden rage at the man before her. *It must have been* . . . How would he know? Growing up on Broker Court wasn't always bad.

'Do whatever you want,' she said stiffly. 'I don't want to know about it.'

And what did he want exactly, from coming to see her? A medal?

'So,' he said, smiling again, all pleasant and eager. 'It's a large sum, but I don't mind, and I can't see Reg ever being able to pay it off, or you – not on a police wage!'

Those Pritchards. So bloody imperious.

'Just do it then!' she'd replied, angry. 'It's *nothing* to you. Just do it!'

The thought of her last interaction with Geordie made her feel ill with guilt, over how she'd spoken to the man, how she'd told him to pay off her dad's dodgy debt, and most of all how she still hadn't told Will. She drove along, thinking of Geordie and his business dealings, the way he was so willing to let go of his cash in order to expand. What other favours had he granted, or deals had he made? And who else might he have offended in doing so? Her police brain began ticking, mulling over ideas.

The Pritchard farmhouse, Yarrobee, was close by now. Before she could change her mind, Belinda signalled right and drove till she came to the long, tree-lined driveway of the homestead.

The last time she'd been here was for the primary school excursion, when Dean Hookes had shoved her so hard into the high hedge that surrounded the garden that she'd suffered scrapes to her face and nasty cuts on her arms. She'd slumped to the ground and cried a bit. What had he shoved her for? She tried to remember but could only recall the hard bite of twigs. And something else too – Geordie Pritchard, hearing her cries, running up to Dean, pushing him over, punching him hard in the face.

Belinda pulled up in front of the grand old house and sat there for a moment, engine running. The hedge she'd landed in was still there, full and green despite the heat of summer. No doubt, every evening the gentle ticking of a remote sprinkling system would ensure its lushness remained.

Belinda got out of the car and stretched, unsure of what her next move was. She reached into the back seat and retrieved the cake she'd baked, still slightly warm and wrapped in the tea towel. Too early for morning tea? *Oh well.*

She was just about to walk to the porch to knock on the door when a blue BMW drove up from a dirt road around the back of the main house. 'Belinda?' It was Lucinda in the driver's seat, her face red and sweaty. 'Is there any news? What's happened?'

Remonstrating with herself for not calling first to let the woman know she was dropping by, Belinda explained there was no news, she'd just come for a visit and was hoping for a quick chat. 'I brought cake,' she said apologetically, holding up the offering.

Lucinda considered her for a moment before switching off the engine and climbing out of the car. 'Cake? Well then, I can hardly refuse.' *She's never eaten a cake in her life*, Belinda thought. *And certainly not at nine-thirty in the morning.*

'Sorry, I really smell.' Lucinda wiped her hands down the front of her jeans and sniffed her fingers. 'I'm shifting compost onto the garden beds out the back. It's something to do. I can't sleep. I can't say I'm enjoying it though. Compost was more Geordie's type of thing.'

Belinda waved away Lucinda's concern, but the other woman *did* smell. Rich, rotting compost, all wormy and warm.

'Do you want any help?'

'No, no. I've had enough. Let's go inside.' Lucinda clicked open the boot of her car and flapped her hands in front of her nose. 'Geez. Not the best idea to do it with the BMW, but I'm ashamed to say that I cannot drive Geordie's ute.'

Compost in a BMW? Belinda did her best not to chuckle. She eyed the luxury car with the buckets of compost, mulch and a dirty shovel in the back.

Where are you hiding the bodies? she might have joked to a different person.

Lucinda led her into the house and through to the kitchen; a modern, light space after the relative darkness of the hall. Washing her hands at the sink and then turning on the kettle, Lucinda reached for two glasses, motioning for Belinda to sit at one of the kitchen stools standing alongside the long island bench. Her makeup-free face was lined with tiredness and worry. Belinda could even detect some grey strands in her thick dark hair.

'What exactly are you here for?' Geordie's widow asked, eyeing the orange cake.

'I'm not sure.' Belinda saw no reason to lie. 'I was on my way to visit my father, and I just could not stomach the thought of it. I started thinking about Geordie and decided to come here.'

Lucinda chose a sharp knife from a rack and deftly cut two slices of cake. Placing each slice neatly on a plate, she slid one over to Belinda. It was precise, the way she did it. No nonsense.

'You sound like Geordie,' Lucinda said, running her hands under the tap again. 'Even when Hugh was dying, he never wanted to visit him.'

Belinda took a mouthful of cake. Dammit, it was a little dry. She looked at the tap, hoping Lucinda would fill up the glasses, then offer one to her.

'And I didn't blame him really,' Lucinda continued. 'Hugh was an old prick, always hassling Geordie to invest in this or that, buy up this land, sell this lot. And you know, Geordie never really forgave him for what he did to Millicent.'

'Millicent?' Belinda frowned. She'd never heard this. 'What happened?' Who was Millicent?

Lucinda looked at her hands. 'Sometimes I wonder – if I had been more attentive to Geordie, if I'd listened a little more to how vicious the anti-turbine people could be. If I'd talked to him more – then maybe he would still be alive.'

'You don't know that.' Belinda wanted to switch back to Millicent, but she couldn't think of a way to do so tactfully.

'I was not a perfect wife,' Lucinda declared. 'Not even a very good one.'

'Nobody's perfect.'

Lucinda shook her head, as if clearing her thoughts. 'What about you?' She looked closely at Belinda's face. 'Let's talk more about you. Why don't *you* want to see your father?'

'He's not very friendly. Every time I leave him, I feel worse about myself.' Belinda shrugged, took another bite of cake. And it wasn't just because of his swearing, his casual cruelty, his air of menace and the fetid atmosphere of the house. No, the reason she most disliked visiting Reg was the feeling afterwards that things had stagnated between them. She felt as she had growing up in that squalid house; a sense of entrapment and desperate inevitability.

'I used to think that one day I'd be police commissioner,' she admitted out of the blue. 'And look at me now: a part-time sergeant in Carrabeen, about to go on maternity leave.'

'I used to think I'd be the CFO of a publishing firm.' Lucinda gave a dry smile. 'Now I'm the widow of a murdered CEO, who spends her time composting herbs.'

Lucinda's words brought Belinda back to the present. And how surreal it was to be sitting in the Pritchards' kitchen, eating cake with Will's ex-girlfriend.

'Can I please have a drink of water?' she asked. 'The cake is kind of dry. Sorry.'

Ignoring her, Lucinda worried at the rings on her finger, looking out the window, then back at the untouched cake on her plate.

'We need to find Geordie's set of keys,' Belinda said, after a moment. 'Do you have any idea where they could be?'

'No.' Lucinda grabbed a glass and filled it, then left it on the bench. 'I've tried to think about it. The master set is in the Melbourne office, but I know Geordie did have a set of his own. He used to jangle them all the time, and I'd worry he'd lose them.'

'Perhaps he *did* lose them.'

'What, and someone just happened to pick them up and decide to kill him?'

They were both silent for a moment.

'The coroner's office called me,' Lucinda said at last. 'I know Geordie was hit on the head before he was killed.'

Belinda couldn't tell if Lucinda had been informed her husband was perhaps alive when he was hung up. She reached over and grabbed the glass of water, taking a large glug before she spoke. 'It's just awful.'

'In some ways, it's better.' Lucinda was working her rings again. 'I hope that Geordie was hit really hard and had no idea what was happening. I hope he was dead before he hit the ground.' She began crying, weeping into her hands, softly at first and then louder, leaning over the island bench and gasping in between sobs.

Belinda walked around the bench and patted Lucinda on the shoulder, rubbing her lightly on the back. 'There, there,' she said stiffly, not really knowing what else to say. 'It's okay, you're okay.'

But the woman was inconsolable. She shrugged Belinda off, then reached for a tissue and blew her nose long and hard. The sobs continued.

Belinda stayed by her side, looking out to the buffeting wind, thin clouds racing across the sky. The Golden Plains, they called it – but often the region was as grey and stormy as the North Sea.

After a minute or so, Lucinda quietened. 'Geordie and I hadn't been getting along,' she admitted between sniffs. 'There were arguments.'

Belinda felt a creeping urge to reach for her notepad and pen. She waited.

'I thought he was being reckless with money, and he thought I was too conservative. We were fighting about it. A lot. Geordie had this, I don't know, this restlessness about him, like he wanted to jump out of his own skin. But the man had everything. I mean, look around you!'

The old homestead, the dam that looked like a lake, the lawns, the statues, the land.

'Do you mean reckless with the wind farm business? Did Geordie want to expand it?'

Lucinda gave a shrug of her shoulders. 'He wanted to expand everything. Wind farms, solar farms, regenerative farming, land buy-ups for old-growth forests. You name it.'

'Those don't sound like bad things to invest in. He could have done a lot worse.'

'Well, yes, he had his father's legacy, you know – Hugh Pritchard was famous for his land-clearing and his investments in coal.'

'And Millicent.'

Lucinda looked at her sharply, as if she hadn't mentioned the name before. 'Yes,' she said, unwilling to shed more light on the subject.

The twirling of the rings again. 'Geordie was going around making offers, promising things, suggesting deals.'

Like the one he'd made to her father.

'Geordie knew he was charismatic . . . He wanted to act, to use his . . .'

'Power?' Belinda suggested. 'Influence?'

Lucinda raised her hands in the air, palms upward. 'Maybe. I don't know.'

Belinda looked out the window to the hedge she'd once been shoved into. The BMW filled with compost caught her eye. 'Where were you on the night Geordie was killed?' she asked. 'At the station, you stated you said goodbye to him here at about six-thirty pm when he left for Melbourne, but what did you do afterwards?'

Lucinda gave her a cool smile. 'I had nothing to do with my husband's death. I can assure you of that.'

'Okay. So where were you the night he died?'

Lucinda smiled again, and tapped her rings on the island bench. 'I was here, in this house.'

'Did you see anyone? Speak to anyone?'

'I watched some television. Went to bed early.'

'Did Geordie usually call you when he reached Melbourne?'

'No,' Lucinda said. 'We were beyond the "I've arrived" phone calls. I just assumed he'd made it back.'

Belinda nodded. 'Right. Well, I had to ask.'

Lucinda grinned properly for the first time. 'Maybe you should lead the investigation. That old guy in Ballarat doesn't seem to be asking too many questions.'

'I can't lead it. It's not that easy. There's no way I could ever get a leadership position like that. Some of us don't have that much sway.'

Lucinda raised her eyebrows. 'Don't doubt yourself,' she said firmly. 'From where I stand, Senior Sergeant, you seem quite a force.'

CHAPTER 20

First Will's phone buzzed, then Tammy's, then the station landline. Will's heart lurched as he answered – he remembered all too well from his days in Melbourne the sudden burst of activity when something terrible had happened: a car accident, a triple homicide, cops gunned down in the street.

But it was none of that. There'd been an accident at the silos. An ambulance had been called. *Come now.*

They leaped into action, jumping into their car, lights blaring. An accident at the silo was every wheat farmer's greatest fear.

Please, Will thought, *please let it not be a kid who's fallen into the grain.* He'd heard the grisly tales. How could he not, living here? Grain entrapment, they called it. It took only seconds to sink into the wheat, barely minutes to suffocate. And the two silos out of town, on this clear blue day, reminded him of September 11, the Twin Towers.

Tammy hung up her phone as they neared the silos, the ambulance already parked close by.

'It's Doug Hay,' she said. 'His farm manager was the one who called us in.'

'Christ, what happened?' They jumped out of the police car and joined the ambos running towards the scene. A small group of men were gathered around the base of one silo, conferring.

'We've turned off the chute,' one man called out. 'Can't see Doug, but Simmo says he saw an arm.'

'Is there any way to drain it?' Will asked him. They had to yell over the noise.

'In the process of doing that now.'

The silo in question was one of the smaller types, six to seven metres tall, with a cone-shaped roof. Wheat poured out of a hatch at the bottom in a steady stream.

Tammy and Will were directed to the ladder at the top, where another man was peering down through a hatch. They climbed up after him and took turns to look inside. There was a horrible smell, scratchy and dry. Wheat churned in a grinding whirlpool.

'Fuck!' Will shouted over the din. 'What can we do?'

Tammy leaned down further, and Will had to grab her to make sure she didn't fall.

She pointed down, then whipped her head back at him. 'He's there!' she cried. 'Look!'

And in the swirl, Will could just make out the side of an arm – and, in another second, the top of a head.

Wheat was draining fast.

'How deep is it now?' he shouted to the man who'd led them up.

'Five and a half feet,' the man estimated, and before he'd had a chance to think about it properly, Will jumped down.

Instantly, he was submerged and panic engulfed him. The wheat was heavy, pressing him down. Mercifully, he soon found he could stand. The wheat was up to his chest, and instantly he began thrashing about, feeling for Doug's body. The wheat was clearing, but not fast enough.

Swiping through the scratchy wheat granules, grabbing at it, straining – he felt skin, and the loose material of a shirt. Pulling on it, he hauled the arm up, horrified to feel it lank in his grasp. With supreme effort, Will located the man's underarm and pulled as hard as he could, lifting him slightly. With that effort, combined with the gradual draining, the top of Doug's head came into view.

'I see him!' Will heard Tammy shout from above, and there followed a strained silence as she and the men outside waited to hear confirmation of life.

Frantic, Will clawed at the wheat, scraping it away from the man's face. How long had Doug been in here? Minutes? It had taken them less than ten to get here, and the men had called as soon as he'd fallen in.

'Doug!' Will shouted. 'We're here, mate, you're okay. You're going to be okay.'

But Doug was not okay. His face, clearly visible now, was bright red from exertion and scratched badly from the wheat. There was blood smeared across his cheeks. Will couldn't tell if he was breathing. The wheat was now down to the top of his legs, and he used it as a buffer to hold Doug's head up, while he shoved his fingers in the man's mouth, clearing it of grain.

'Breathe, mate!' he said, and outside the silo, the other men took up the call. 'Breathe, mate! Breathe, Doug, you bastard!'

And finally, Doug breathed. A cough at first, more coughing, and then a wheezing sound as he took in a great gulp of air.

'Water!' Will shouted, and a bottle was thrown down to him. Then suddenly, as all the wheat drained out of the silo, a hatch was opened and hands appeared. Another man was there beside him, helping to lift Doug out of the tin coffin he'd been trapped in.

Cheers erupted as they clambered out. 'Doug! We gotcha, mate! We bloody gotcha!'

Will felt big gentle hands brushing the wheat off his arms, clapping him on the back, patting him on the shoulders.

'Is he okay?' Will blew air out of his nose and wiped his eyes. Someone brought him his glasses, wiping them first on a dirty sleeve. He took them gratefully – one arm was horribly bent, but miraculously the lenses were still intact.

'Well done, mate.' The words were echoing through the crowd.

The two ambos were bent over Doug, inspecting him. After a minute, with help from some of the men, they picked him up and placed him on a stretcher, to take him to hospital.

'He looks all right,' one of the local men assured Will. 'He'll be right as rain.'

'How could that happen?' Will turned to them, puzzled. Doug was as experienced as they came.

Another man in a dusty flannelette shirt shrugged. 'Got here. Saw his truck still running but no one in it. Called out, heard a cry from inside the silo. That's when I called you lot. I managed to climb up and let him know help was coming, just as I saw the top of him disappearing.'

'Must have been a blockage,' someone else said. 'Stopped him from sinking for a bit.'

The ambulance driver gave them all a final wave, and there was a collective sigh as the van drove off.

Wheat lay on the ground in a great pile. The wind began whipping it up, sending it away, mingling it with dirt. 'What a bloody waste,' one farmer said, as the men drifted off, back to work.

CHAPTER 21

Belinda sat down behind the police station's reception desk and flicked through the paperwork she still needed to complete before she took her maternity leave. As she signed off on the agreement to dismantle her email, her station access and her police ID card, it felt like the force was trying to get rid of her forever. An older friend had confessed to her how difficult she'd found returning to work after mat leave; not because she missed the children, but because the technology had changed so much over the twelve months. 'I didn't know whether it was Zoom, Teams, Google Docs or holograms, but I left after three months back.'

Belinda located her laptop case, with the Victorian Police logo stamped on it, checking she had all the different cords to go inside. She took the photo of her and Will off the shelf, washed the mug with 'My Coffee Cop' on it, and put it back in the cupboard. Whole folders of loose-leaf paper filled with rough notes from old development courses were turfed in the bin.

No word on the job application as yet.

She deliberated over a stress ball.

Will had jumped into a churning wheat silo and saved Doug Hay's life. She squeezed the ball hard, then bounced it on the desk and against the wall, repeated the process, catching it in turns.

When she'd first got the call from Tammy, what a fright it had given her. *What the hell! No one jumps into a silo!*

But Will had. He'd jumped straight in.

Like all locals in the Golden Plains, she'd grown up hearing tales of kids who'd drowned in grain, every slight movement causing them to sink deeper. Most kids were scared of monsters and robbers; in wheat country, you were scared of the silos.

When Will had arrived back at the station, she'd been so relieved she didn't know whether to swear at him or burst into tears. In the end, she'd hugged him so tightly she felt his ribs press into her.

Will was at the doctor's now, getting checked over. She threw the stress ball at the wall again, catching it, throwing it. She remembered all too well the first time she'd ever properly laid eyes on him. He was prostrate on the ground, his head on her lap, blue eyes flickering. Already, there was a bump forming on his forehead from where they'd clashed heads. As he lay there in the mud, she whispered soothing words, and it seemed as if something momentous had happened. Here, during her first endurance race, was a beautiful man who'd literally fallen into her arms. She'd been trying to protect him ever since.

Ahh, Will, she thought with renewed warmth. He'd come to Carrabeen an outsider and he'd leave a hero. Locals wouldn't forget the actions of the ridiculously tall, bespectacled policeman who'd jumped into the silo to save one of their own.

She wondered if her father had heard what Will had done yet, the effort he'd made to save Reg's oldest friend. Looking at her watch, she vowed she'd give her dad a quick visit later, having chickened out this morning.

She was checking her phone, willing her husband to call her with news that the doctor had given him the all-clear, when it rang in her hands. It was Lisa, informing her about the fibre she'd found in the hole in the fence. Originally, when she'd sent Kelmendri a photo, he'd agreed that it looked like the same wool as the jumper Geordie had been wearing when he was killed. However, he cautioned her against getting too excited. Forensics and the coroner would confirm that, he said. And, as was the case with everything in this very public investigation, the report came back at speed.

Because, Lisa said, it *was* confirmed: the wool was from Geordie's clothing.

'So, it means that Geordie squeezed through the gap in the fence himself,' Lisa said.

'Or was dragged there,' Belinda added.

'Be hard to drag a man through a gap in a fence, surely.'

'Not if he was unconscious or dead.' Belinda's mind was buzzing. The person had to know about the gap, how hidden it was. It was Alan Crowe's responsibility to look after the fence-line – so why hadn't he mentioned it? Possibly, the man hadn't even considered the gap – he had keys to the fence-line, and Geordie had his own keys. He had no reason to think that Geordie didn't use his own.

Lisa had more information to report. The blow to Geordie's head looked to have been caused by a smooth, heavy object, though nothing like that had been found near the scene.

'Interesting.'

'And in terms of the skin fragment, we've discounted all the workers who got the body down and who were present onsite, so now we can start testing suspects.'

'Do we *have* any suspects?'

'None,' Lisa admitted. 'It's frustrating.'

'Welcome to police work.' Belinda said it lightly, then remembered Lisa was hardly new to the job. In fact, she was senior to Belinda, though she didn't act like it.

'Yeah,' Lisa said gruffly, more to herself. 'I dunno what I was thinking. Hope Troy knows what he's in for.'

'Who?' Belinda felt a rush of irritation that the excitable Lisa had made it into Investigations before her. Didn't she realise how fortunate she was to have the job? Belinda looked at the clock on her phone. She didn't have time to be chatting about people she didn't know.

'Troy Haydar. I was in police college with him,' Lisa continued. 'He got that job in Investigations, St Kilda branch. You hadn't heard?'

Belinda felt a lump in her throat. The deadline for applications was today. How had they filled the position so quickly?

'Everyone knew he'd get it.' Lisa sighed loudly. 'Apparently Kelmendri was one of his referees.'

Belinda was surprised at the sharp sting of disappointment she felt. What had she been thinking, that she'd really be in with a chance? And, in any case, how would it have worked out with the baby due in a month?

'So, what, there were no interviews?'

'No need – apparently he was the best applicant by a mile. Anyway, they don't have to interview if there's no one else up to scratch.'

She said her goodbyes to Lisa and stared at the stress ball. *Oh well,* she tried to reason with herself, *it's for the best.* Then she threw the ball hard at the door, watching it slam instead into the filing cabinet. Papers flew everywhere. *Good*, she thought, and when she'd retrieved it, she threw the ball again.

Belinda was considering packing it in for the day and visiting her father when the front door opened, and a gust of wind blew through the office. A young woman appeared, as if carried there by the elements.

'Hi!' She took off her bike helmet and shook her dark curly hair. 'I'm Marit Leslie.'

'Senior Sergeant Burney.'

'We've met briefly, I think?'

They had met more than once, in fact, when Marit was with Tammy. But Belinda wasn't going to mention that now. 'Yes, I think so.'

'The other officer here, I think he's your husband? He left a message on my phone – so I thought I'd save the hassle and come straight in. I imagine that you'll want to question me.'

'Well, yes.' Belinda was momentarily confused. 'But we didn't need you to come in. We could have visited you at your house.'

'Can we do it now though? I ride past here all the time, so thought I'd pop in.'

Belinda felt resentment rising up inside her once more. Just thought she'd 'pop in', eh? Why hadn't Marit ever come to visit Tammy then? Particularly in the last few days. Her poor colleague was still heartsick. 'I'm pretty busy right now,' she huffed.

'Righto then.' Marit made to put her helmet back on. 'Catch you whenever.'

'Wait!' Belinda looked at the long checklist she still had to complete before she went on leave. 'I may have a bit of time.'

In the interview room, Marit sat across from Belinda and pulled a mock-serious face. 'Do I need a lawyer?'

'I don't know, do you?'

Marit smiled. 'I don't think so, not now anyway – there's a lot of time for me to break the rules. I'm only thirty-two.'

Belinda smiled thinly. 'Tell us about your work in Carrabeen.'

'Non-profit stuff. I'm part of a company that assists environmental projects in getting off the ground, or, in some cases, suggests ways of fighting harmful industries. Last year, for instance, I was in New South Wales fighting a fracking company.'

'So who are you assisting, or fighting, in Carrabeen?'

'I came here to help with the wind farms. Clean Energy Solutions Australia has a number of new wind farms in planning, and I was helping to get those across the line. I was also assisting in publicising the environmental benefits of the turbines.'

'And what are those benefits?'

'Oh, there are too many to count.'

'Humour me. Give me your best ones.'

Marit shrugged. 'Well, wind is renewable, inexhaustible and locally available. It's also free.'

'Go on.'

The younger woman leaned forward, gesturing emphatically with her hands. 'Wind is clean and cost-effective, and generating energy from it doesn't release any carbon emissions. If we want to get to net zero by 2030, wind is our best option. At the moment, it contributes about ten per cent to Australia's total electricity supply, but it has the potential to provide far more than that.'

'I see.' Belinda studied the woman opposite her with renewed interest.

Marit was now waving a hand at the trees outside the window. 'But really, my main point is, if we go on like we are, then the world won't survive. It sounds dramatic, but it's true. We're killing the planet, we don't have time, and until there's a better method, we've got to do what we can.'

'And this is what Geordie believed too?'

'It's not a question of belief, it's science. But yes, Geordie was passionate about clean energy, and wind in particular.'

Belinda hated the word 'passionate'; it brought to mind earnest teachers and career advisors in musty rooms, dispensing unwanted advice.

'We have reports that you had a disagreement with Geordie before he died.' They weren't reports at all, but Belinda remembered what Tammy had told them about the pair when she'd come to dinner.

Marit gave a dramatic sigh. 'I thought that's why you'd want to question me.'

'What were the arguments about?'

'What it's always about with him – wind!' As if in response, a small branch from a tree that had been buffeted all day by the hot northerly crashed into the window. 'Geordie was getting ahead of himself, and asking me to come along.'

Belinda raised her eyebrows, questioning.

'So, at the moment,' Marit explained, 'Australia has more than fifty wind farm projects in various stages. Geordie was involved in at least four of them, all over the country.'

'Okay . . .'

'And two of those are in places where I don't think they should be, environmentally speaking: precious places in North Queensland with rare flora and fauna. A lot of clearing would need to be done there in order for the turbines to be built. I don't think it's right to build in places rich in biodiversity, and I absolutely will not support those particular projects. I told him so on the Saturday.'

'The day before he died?'

'Yes.'

Belinda nodded, writing it down. 'So, Geordie was angry with you.'

'Yes, he was. But I think there must have been something else bothering him too – because he really blew up quickly. It's like he came to meet me already angry about something.'

Another branch, slightly bigger, banged against the window, making Belinda jump. Marit ducked her head, then gave a small smile.

'Do you know of anyone who might have wanted to harm Geordie?'

Marit looked at her curiously. 'I thought it was suicide?'

'We are investigating all avenues.' It wasn't the smoothest of lines, but Belinda didn't think Marit was the sort to run to the papers, or gossip about it with her neighbours. Besides, she didn't seem overly surprised by the news.

'Geordie was a great advocate for the environment, and that made him unpopular with a lot of people. So, yeah – I think there'd be quite a few people who'd want to harm him. I don't own any land or turbines, but I've had dead animals thrown in my yard, had shit put in my letterbox, and twice had my tyres slashed.'

'Did you report all that to the police?'

'It wasn't here. That was at my last job.' Marit fiddled with her helmet. 'But, yes – there are groups here who were dead against Geordie and all he stood for.'

'Can you name them?'

'Doug Hay's group, Farms for Future, is the big one, although there are more radical ones than that.'

'Names?'

'I don't know their names.' Marit put on her helmet. 'There's a woman who goes around telling people that wind farms cause cancer, and that, I don't know, the world is flat and that sort of stuff . . . I wouldn't say she's threatening though.'

'Is she a local?'

'Probably.' Marit was buckling the clip underneath her chin. 'It's usually locals.'

Belinda raised her eyes to the ceiling and let out a sigh. *Never,* she thought to herself, *never insinuate that all people from small towns are stupid, particularly not to a person who is from a small town.*

'What about the pro-turbine people then?' she asked. 'Who here is on your side? I'm guessing you know their names.'

'Our side?' Marit looked amused. 'You make it sound like a schoolyard fight.'

'Who are the pro-turbine people in town, the prominent ones?' Belinda asked plainly. 'We'd like the names of everyone involved.'

Marit raised her eyebrows. 'Okay, if you insist. There's me, Professor Highett, Lucinda Pritchard – although she's often in Melbourne – Dean Hookes from the school.'

'Dean?' Belinda wasn't sure why she was surprised. She hadn't spoken to Dean since she was sixteen.

'Yes, although his commitment to the cause wavers and depends largely on what else is happening around town.'

'Any others?'

'Yes, yes.' Marit mentioned a few more names: the owner of the general store, another couple new to town. 'That's about it,' she said. 'Not as many as I'd like, but what can you expect? Country Victoria – they're hardly going to be greenies.'

Belinda shook her head as she wrote down the names. Honestly! She was growing really tired of the woman. She put down her pen.

'And where were you on the night Geordie died?'

Marit leaned in, a grin on her face. 'Am I a suspect? Now, this *is* exciting. Finally! Something happening around here.'

'Just answer the question.'

Marit considered her for a moment, the smile still on her face. Then she answered. 'I was at home. On my own.'

'So no one can vouch for you?'

Marit shook her head. 'No.'

'Right.' Belinda slammed her laptop cover down. 'You can go.'

'Geordie's death is suspicious, then? It wasn't suicide?'

'As I said, we are looking into all avenues,' Belinda replied in a neutral voice.

'Right, okay then.' Marit smirked and stood up. 'Whatever you say.'

'Why'd you break up with Tammy?' There, she had to ask it. Marit's mocking tone had validated Belinda's growing dislike of her.

Marit stared down at her coolly. 'Tammy has a tendency to want to please, haven't you noticed? It's cringeworthy. If I said I was in favour of hunting endangered animals, she'd order a whale burger the first chance she got.'

Belinda studied a poster for Blue Ribbon Day on the wall. She really did not like this woman.

'Now' – Marit turned – 'can I go? Is that it for my civic duty?'

'Sure, whatever.' Belinda gave a dismissive wave of her hand. 'Your OAM is in the mail.'

She had no idea if Marit was surprised at her hostile attitude. She didn't bother to check.

Once more alone in the office, Belinda typed up the notes on her meeting with Marit, then spent a good thirty minutes stalking Troy Haydar on the socials. It was kind of torture to read how well qualified he was for the Investigations job, how good looking he was and how he'd been commended for duty in a number of cases. Haydar was three years older than her, married, with a wife who stayed at home looking after their small children. Their family shots were sickeningly sweet. And the bastards in HR hadn't even bothered to tell her she was unsuccessful.

Will would be pleased she didn't get it, she thought without spite. He didn't want her to begin a stressful job when they'd just had a baby. It would mean Penelope visiting more, and juggling child and career. He'd worry about her constantly, and she'd have to be on call a lot more than she was now.

Suddenly, she wanted to see her husband badly. Maybe she could catch him at the doctor's. But she'd just reached her car when Will rang. He'd run into Doug Hay's nephew outside the medical centre, and a few of the men wanted to take him to the pub. Did she mind picking him up at the Crown in an hour or so? He felt fine – he felt fine!

Ignoring the vague feeling of abandonment, Belinda decided she'd procrastinated enough about visiting her father. In any event, Reg would be interested in what had happened to Doug, and she wanted to tell him about Will's heroic actions. For too long, Reg had dismissed his son-in-law as a 'toffy townie'.

Well, this should change that, she thought.

In Broker Court, Belinda was half relieved to see that Reg was on his way out just as she arrived, watched over, as ever, by the Raz matriarch from next door. Belinda waited while Reg climbed into his ancient ute. An esky was already placed in the back tray, and Reg threw in a swag effortlessly without dislodging the fag from his lower lip.

'Heading down to the river, too much noise in town,' he explained, local newspaper tucked under his arm.

Belinda understood what he meant. The town was buzzing with excitement after the incident at the silo.

'Down the river?' she asked.

Reg used to do this sometimes, head off for a day or two. He had a place he liked to camp at, not too far away. It was down from Alan Crowe's house – near the turbines but further along, where there was flattened grass, plenty of shade, and the shallow rippling river.

'Yep.'

'How long?'

'Just a night.'

'You going to be okay, with your prostate?'

'Easier to piss outside than in a toilet.'

'What'll you eat?'

'Got some chops. Bit of bread.'

An unpleasant thought crossed Belinda's mind. 'Dad, is this about the dogs? I know about the debt and Geordie's offer, but please tell me you're not in any serious trouble.'

There had been a couple of frightening episodes in the past, when big men involved in dog racing came banging on the door, demanding money. One time, Reg was even taken away in a car and returned two hours later, bruised but defiant. She looked at the state of her childhood home and wondered, not for the first time, if gambling was one of the reasons it had never been updated or sold.

'Fuck, no. Just got to get out for a bit. And I told Geordie to piss off. I don't want him paying my debts.'

'Well, he can't pay them now,' Belinda said, and there was a long, heavy silence.

'Whatever,' he said eventually. 'I don't give a fuck.'

Belinda resisted the urge to argue. She took a deep breath, forced herself to calm down.

'Heard about Doug at the silo?' *And Will,* she wanted to add.

Reg spat out the remainder of his cigarette and stamped on it with his boot. His legs were a pair of dehydrated twiggy sticks, but the man's stance was firm.

'Will you go and visit him?' she asked.

'Doug won't want visitors,' Reg snarled. 'He'll want to be back on the farm. I'll see him then.'

Belinda couldn't help herself. 'Did you hear about what Will did?' She tipped her head.

'Fucken idiot! Could've killed himself.' And without further ado, Reg climbed into the front seat of his ute and drove off.

'Well, goodbye to you too,' Belinda muttered with bitterness. 'Have a nice time, you skinny old prick.'

On the way back to the station, Belinda stopped at the butcher's and bought a kilo of sausages. She'd had a sudden hankering for curried sausages and wondered whether it could be pregnancy cravings. Were they even a real thing? Who knew, but the curried sausages had seemed a vital, pressing thing. At the IGA, she spotted the local paper, the *Chronicle*. The thin rag was usually chock-full of information about field days, farm auctions and local sporting achievements. But on this day, the journo must have had a field day himself: MURDER NOT SUICIDE, the headline screamed.

Belinda made a growling noise. Someone had been leaking information. She read on:

187

Local man Geordie Pritchard was found by the Ballarat coroner to have been murdered before being brutally strung up on one of the blades of his own turbine. The CEO of Clean Energy Solutions Australia was initially thought to have taken his own life after financial turmoil and relentless attacks on the legitimacy of wind farms in rural areas. However, Forensics discovered signs of a body being dragged from the base of the turbine and within its lower sections. A source close to the Pritchard family believes that the forces aimed at disrupting the wind farms need to be more closely examined. Investigations continue.

Belinda couldn't be sure, but the sly tone of the article hinted at other secrets still to come. How did the journalist know all of this? Even she didn't know yet about the evidence of dragging inside the turbine, the hauling of the body. Belinda looked for the name of the author: Austin Dorney. She'd been to school with a girl named Harriet Dorney; could the two be related? Ringing the paper, Belinda put on her best cop voice, friendly but firm. She asked to be put through to Austin.

'Sergeant Burney, how can I help?' The man's tone was casual, but his speed in answering betrayed his eagerness to talk.

'I'm interested in how you got the information for your article this morning. The coroner's report has not been made public.'

'I cannot betray my source.' Dorney couldn't hide his excitement. No doubt he'd waited a lifetime to deliver that line.

'You know the Pritchard family has strong ties in the legal world, and they won't appreciate you publishing information about his death without first consulting them.'

'As I said, I cannot betray my source,' Dorney repeated, his voice faltering slightly.

'Tell that to Lucinda Pritchard.'

The man was silent for a beat, then: 'Lucinda Pritchard is not as squeaky clean as you think.'

Belinda's ears pricked up. 'What do you mean? What do you know?'

'I really can't say, Sergeant Burney.'

'Okay' – she was losing patience – 'do I need to ask you to come down to the station?' Belinda wasn't sure on what grounds, but she was prepared to give it a go.

There was a pause at the end of the line. 'I've been digging deep into the Pritchard family enterprises. There's some surprising stuff there, Sergeant. I'm thinking of writing a book.'

'That doesn't prevent me asking you to come to the station right now.'

The journalist gave a heavy sigh. 'Well, here's a titbit for you: a week ago, Lucinda Pritchard put a motion to the board of Clean Energy Solutions Australia to replace Geordie as CEO.'

Well, that was new – and perhaps, she thought, it may have been the reason Lucinda said they'd been fighting. 'Interesting, but that doesn't mean much in the scheme of her husband's death.'

'And if you are prepared to give me the heads-up on any leads to do with the murder, I might have a few more things to tell you.'

Belinda considered his offer. Technically, she should run it by Kelmendri, but the man was so focused on his approaching retirement, she didn't think he'd care.

'What can you tell me?'

'Ask me a question,' Dorney said, rather grandly.

'Okay. What do you know about Millicent?'

*

Dorney's information was wide ranging, and at times bordering on the salacious, but there were a few gems in it that demanded further attention.

Belinda pondered all he'd told her as she sat by Doug Hay's bedside. It was not time yet to pick up Will from the pub, and she'd been meaning to visit her father's oldest friend.

He was lying in his hospital bed. His big frame under the white sheet mimicked a mountain covered in snow.

'Can I get you anything, Doug? A drink?'

The old man shook his head. The near-death experience had left him in a nostalgic mood. 'You look so like your dad, you know,' he said. 'Fine-looking man in his time.'

There were still hints of Reg's good looks, but 'fine' wasn't a word she'd use to describe him now.

'Everyone says he looked like Paul Hogan in *Crocodile Dundee*.'

Doug laughed, then coughed. 'They say it because not only did Reg look like him, but because he was also a rigger on the Sydney Harbour Bridge – like Hogan was.'

She'd heard it all before, but she didn't mind. 'And then he came home, and sheared with you.'

'Ah, they were all good shearers.' Doug's thoughts wandered again, and Belinda considered calling the nurse, though her father's old friend looked peaceful enough. 'Better than me,' he continued. 'I was too scrawny back then.' It was difficult to imagine Doug as anything other than rotund. 'Hugh, Alan and Reg; we called them the "podium three", because they'd always finish neck and neck in the shearing. And actually, if you got down to it, it was usually Alan who won. Your dad was strong, but Alan was more disciplined. You know he won King of the Mountain three years in a row?'

Belinda had heard of it – the legendary race up Mount Wycheproof, known as the smallest mountain in the world. Runners would race to the top carrying heavy wheat sacks across their shoulders. The winners were lauded as heroes, their photographs plastered in pubs across country Victoria.

'Did he?'

'He sure did.' Doug sank back into his pillows, a dreamy look on his face. 'Usually, it was the spud lumpers from Gippsland who'd win – them or the wheat lumpers from the Mallee. But for three years in a row, it was our man Alan.' Doug closed his eyes, and for a moment, Belinda thought he might have fallen asleep.

But then he opened one eye and continued. 'Your dad might have had a fighting chance in the race, only Reg was usually too hungover or making himself scarce from the local bookies.'

'Bloody Dad.' Belinda didn't know what else to say.

Doug was still reminiscing: 'Sixty-three and a half kilograms of grain on his shoulders, that's what Alan did; running with it, for one kilometre to the top. There were blokes keeling over, spewing, collapsing in the street afterwards!' Doug laughed at the memory. 'But not our Alan! No! He won the toughest race in the world!'

Belinda smiled and looked at her watch. 'Is Alan against the wind farm?'

'Eh?' Doug frowned. 'We back to wind farms, are we? That was quick.'

'Sorry, Doug, I don't have much time.'

Sitting up higher, Doug reached for a drink of water, which Belinda passed to him. 'Alan sold his land to Hugh after he and Rhonda got married. I tried to tell him it was a bad move; he used to own the whole of Mont Blanc! He even tried to sell the land to me once, but I refused. Now he owns just a tiny bit on the north side – good land, very good, but small. But then, even worse, when Geordie built those big monsters, Alan agreed to manage them for him. Sold his soul to the devil, didn't he? I can't forget it.'

'Maybe he needed the money. He doesn't have as much as you, does he?'

'I said he could come and work for me!' Doug looked cross. 'Manage whatever part of the land he liked. But he flat out said no.'

Belinda stared out the window, to where the oak trees in the hospital gardens were being bent sideways by the wind. 'Doug,' she said carefully, 'are you always this angry at people who work for the wind farms?'

The older man gave her a hard stare before shaking a finger side to side. 'I know what you're getting at, young lady, and the answer is no. I'd never do anything as drastic as harass someone till they killed themselves.'

Belinda took her notebook out. 'Some people are very opposed to the wind farms, aren't they? Angry at the farmers who leased them on their farms, angrier at the ones who sold their land to companies like CESA.'

'Yes, there are some who are a bit over the top,' Doug admitted. 'General nutters who cotton on to any old cause. And look – there's lots of reasons for being anti-wind farm; but I don't hold with the whole turbines-cause-cancer-and-Covid brigade.'

'People think that?'

'Oh yeah, they do. Last year we had a nasty bout of Covid at the school, and there was a hardcore group saying it was the turbines causing lack of immunity in kids. Really weird stuff.'

'Okay, so what's *your* beef with the wind farms then?' she asked. Doug was a reasonable man.

'My beef, as you put it, is that we won't have any *beef* left if we keep building these things on prime land. No beef, no wheat, no dairy. I've done my research.'

'But isn't that a little overstated?' Belinda tapped her fingers on her knee. 'It's not like no one has thought of safeguarding food production, and anyway – isn't the average approval time for a new wind farm almost ten years?' She'd done a little research too. 'You're not going to have to dodge turbines on your way to the golf course anytime soon.'

But Doug wasn't listening. 'Maybe a country full of turbines will be good for the vegans, but they still won't like the views.'

Ahh! The views! Finally, someone had mentioned them.

'Do you think that's part of it too, locals having an objection because of what they look like on the landscape?'

Doug gave a weary sigh. 'So what if it is? There's nothing wrong with loving the beauty of the land, appreciating the natural world. Or is there? Seems I can't get anything right these days.'

If you objected to the turbines for reasons of beauty, you were scorned as entitled and self-absorbed. But Doug was neither of those things. Sometimes, it was difficult to pin an exact reason for people's loathing of the wind farms. Harder still to articulate, the actual pain you could feel at seeing a much-loved landscape changed. Better to talk about money, or health, or prime farmland.

The man looked exhausted, but Belinda had one more question. 'Doug, can you tell me the names of the people who are really anti-turbines? People who might do something extreme?'

Doug's eyes were closed, and once again she thought he'd fallen asleep. 'There's a few crazies in town, but they're crazy about *everything*. The really angry ones whose energy is focused on the turbines? I'd say it's a very small number.'

'Yes?' Belinda leaned in.

'Well now, I know that young woman Marit isn't a fan of them being put up everywhere. There's Julie Smith too, the teacher who claims she can speak to the dead. I mean, what does that tell you? There's the owner of the garage, Rick – he hates them! And yes, there's the principal from the school – what's her name?' He thought for a moment and then spoke in a slightly accusatory tone. 'I can't remember – but you took her driver's licence from her.'

Outside the hospital room, Belinda bumped into Shirleen, Doug's wife. After a hurried update on the patient, Shirleen shoved a newspaper into Belinda's hands. 'Take this!' she said. 'Doug normally loves the paper, but I'm not showing him this tripe, it'll only make him more upset.'

'Good idea.' Belinda recalled how he'd groaned when she'd mentioned the wind farms. 'It's pretty terrible stuff.'

'You know that when he was brought in, he was saying he'd been pushed into the silo, don't you?' Shirleen looked at her closely.

Belinda frowned. 'He didn't say that to me.'

'That's because it's ridiculous! Doug shouldn't be up at the top of those towers at his age. His balance is terrible, and what with all the weight he's put on, I'm surprised the ladders held him at all.'

'But I wonder why he didn't mention it to me.' He'd mentioned a lot of other things, Belinda thought, like Alan Crowe winning King of the Mountain, and the shearing prowess of her dad.

Shirleen ran a hand through her short grey hair. 'I think he's come to his senses now that he's had a think about it. He probably feels a bit of a fool. But when he was first brought in! What a hue and cry!'

Belinda wondered whether Shirleen knew how close her husband had been to drowning in wheat. The woman was remarkably upbeat. But then she noticed the redness of Shirleen's eyes, the forced jocularity, the shrillness in her tone. How frightened the older woman must have been to get the call. If it had been Will – and it could so easily have been Will – Belinda wasn't sure how she would cope. She'd go mad, she'd tear the world apart.

Will wasn't a big drinker, so Belinda was not surprised to see him swaying on the kerb out the front of the pub. Two other men she vaguely recognised were standing beside him. There was a general air of congeniality about them as the three men smiled and swayed, smiled and swayed, not talking.

She pulled up alongside them, asking if the other men needed a lift.

They shook their heads.

'No, but your husband's a legend,' the younger one told her, giving Will a pat on the arm. 'Legend!'

'Aww, come off it, Jono,' Will replied, in a tone she had rarely heard him use.

''Sss true, mate,' the other, older man said, nodding. 'Saved Doug Hay, jumped right in.'

'Jumped right in!' Jono repeated in awe. '*Legend.*'

On the way home, Will fell asleep and then, with her help, stumbled from the bathroom into bed. She took off his bent glasses and put them by his bedside.

'My hero,' she said, brushing his dark hair back from his face.

'When you get the job,' he slurred, 'I'll look after the baby.'

'I didn't get it. We don't have to worry.'

'Really!' His eyes opened, but he was frowning. 'That's stupid. You're the best out of everyone. You're *the best*, Bel.'

She gave him a kiss. 'Not this time.'

CHAPTER 22

Saturday morning usually saw Will vacuuming to loud music, a habit Belinda found in equal parts endearing and annoying. On this bright morning, however, her husband lay on his back snoring loudly. 'God,' he'd said in wonder, when he woke briefly before she left for the station. 'I feel like crap.'

'That's the price for being a legend in this town.' She gave him a kiss goodbye. 'You've got to be able to sink the piss.'

'Never say "sink the piss" again,' he groaned.

'I'm popping into the office, I want to pick up the rest of my stuff.'

He was already asleep.

On the way to the station, she saw groups of students, all dressed in the same colours, walking along the footpath. It took her a moment to realise that it was the senior sports carnival and a day of celebration in the town. Food trucks and coffee vans would be onsite to encourage parents' attendance, and there was usually a band playing later on in the afternoon.

This year, the build-up had been tempered, no doubt due to the death of the school's chief benefactor. But still, the sight of the students cheered her. They jostled one another and leaped on each other's backs as they made their way to the oval. Tragedy had struck the town, but the young move on. *Good on them.*

The station phone was ringing when she arrived and stopped just as she raced in to answer it. No sooner had she turned away than it began ringing again. With a sudden, crazed thought that it was another silo accident, Belinda picked it up in a rush.

'Hello? Is this the police station?' A man's voice, cautious.

'It is. Senior Sergeant Burney speaking.'

'Sergeant, hello! This is Andrew Kent, from the school.'

'Right.'

Belinda didn't know if she could stomach any more news about the thefts. Her mind kept returning to Will in the silo, all those grains like a whirlpool.

'Bit of a strange one here for you, but, well . . . we've got a teacher missing.'

Belinda was suddenly alert.

'I mean, he's never ill,' Andrew continued, 'and always so punctual. He was supposed to be here at seven-thirty on the dot to set up the sports day.'

'It is a Saturday. Could he have forgotten?'

'No! He's organised the whole thing, it's the same every year – we always have the seniors on a Saturday. It's a big deal here.'

'Okay.' Belinda waited. It didn't sound too serious. Tammy was often late to the station. It was only just after eight-thirty.

'This morning, he didn't show. Orla's gone round to check – she lives on the same street – but there's no sign of him and he's not answering the door. Should I tell her to break in? Climb through a window maybe? It's probably nothing . . .' The vice principal's voice was outwardly calm, but Belinda detected a rising concern in his questions.

'Who is it, Andrew?'

'Dean Hookes, our PE teacher.'

Belinda nodded to herself, cleared her throat. 'I'm sure everything is fine. He's probably ill or caught up somewhere else. We'll check it out, and please tell Orla not to break in.'

'Okay. Thank you, Sergeant.'

Belinda hung up, a tight feeling in her gut that couldn't be wholly explained by the baby within. Geordie Pritchard, Doug Hay, and now a missing teacher? Carrabeen had never been so busy. Feeling increasingly worried, she called Will at home, letting him know what Andrew had said, and that she was going around to Dean's place to check.

'Wait ten minutes,' Will had said. 'I'll go with you.'

'Don't worry, I'm on my way home now.' She collected the box she'd left the day before. 'I'll pop in and have a look.'

Dean's house was built on a new subdivision, on the Ballarat side of town – locals called it the Toorak end. 'Subdivision' was probably giving the row of just three new houses more credit than they deserved, but that's how they were described. Plus, the sign at the side road read *Creek View Crescent*. The name had a new subdivision ring to it.

Belinda slowed as Orla rode her bike towards her, on her way back to the school.

'Orla!' she called out, and the woman stopped and removed her helmet.

'Yes?' She looked annoyed. 'I'm supervising javelin in fifteen minutes.'

'You didn't touch anything at Dean's, did you?'

Orla's eyes narrowed. 'What do you mean? I knocked, I put my hands on the windowsill to look inside. I peered into his car with my hands on the windscreen. So yes, I touched things. Is that a problem?'

Belinda sighed. 'I hope not.'

Orla swore, got off her bike and adjusted the seat before climbing back on. 'I told Andrew that Dean's probably at some woman's house and has lost track of time, but the man is such a worrier!'

'You think that's what's happened?' Belinda looked across at Dean's front yard, the car still in the driveway.

'Maybe.' A hint of doubt had entered the head teacher's voice. 'We don't talk about personal stuff that much. But it is odd he's not turned up for Seniors' Sports Day. He organised it all and was due in early to get things sorted.'

Belinda nodded and Orla headed off at impressive speed, long legs pumping, head down. It took Belinda a moment to realise that Orla was riding an electric bike, which helped to explain the pace. *Electric bikes in Carrabeen*, she thought. *Times, they are a-changin'.*

Dean's front door was locked. Instinctively, Belinda lifted the edge of a pot plant at the side of the porch and pulled a key out from under it. 'Honestly,' she said out loud. 'Are you *asking* to be robbed?' Pot plant, fake rock, under the mat. In her first year of policing, she'd been astounded by the lack of creativity in hiding keys. People put them in places that were easy to remember – and easy to guess. She let herself in while announcing her presence loudly. No response.

Dean's house was rather sterile, completely devoid of clutter. There was one photo on the fridge, of Dean himself in racing gear, grinning beside an older man. *Port Douglas Triathlon* was the caption. *Ex-Olympian Johnny Taylor greets third place, Dean Hookes.* In the photo, Dean was beaming, clearly proud to be standing alongside the tanned, distinguished former athlete. Belinda leaned in and looked closely at Johnny Taylor, deciding he did look familiar. Bronze medallist in London? She used to know them all; now she couldn't remember.

Inside the fridge, there was a square Tupperware container filled with chicken salad. There were no dirty dishes, the fridge was spotless, and the counters looked newly wiped. Dean was a bit of a clean freak, Belinda concluded. The other rooms were much the same. The bathroom was all white and silver, and there were no drugs aside from Panadol in the cabinet. His bed was made. Sitting on it to rest her back for a second, Belinda wondered how much action Dean got in it. He was, after all, a good-looking man in his thirties. During his time as a pupil at school, he'd been popular with the girls, who were acutely aware of his presence and eager to impress. Belinda never really liked him. Dean's father, she recalled, knew Reg, used to drink with him at the Star. After she'd admitted to her dad that she had no deb partner, she'd been surprised when Dean approached her in the canteen and asked, through clenched teeth, if she'd like to go with him. Why say no to him? She had no one else.

Was she imagining the clenched teeth? she wondered now, as she sat on Dean's bed and looked at his plain unadorned bedroom walls. Honestly, it was difficult to recall.

She opened the drawers beside his bed. Two packets of unopened condoms and a pamphlet on wind energy, published by Clean Energy Solutions. *Interesting combination*, Belinda thought, moving on. *Whatever does it for you, I guess.* She took a photo.

His wardrobe was full of clothes, and there was a laundry basket half filled with items to be washed. All very normal.

Taking two steps back, Belinda sat on the bed again and picked up the pamphlet on wind energy. She opened it to the glossy first page: a picture of a sole turbine in a sunlit paddock, a section on the benefits of wind energy; the job creation opportunities and a future now safeguarded. But then, as she turned the pamphlet over, something else: some tiny writing on the top right of the page. She squinted, bringing it closer; not writing, a phone number. Taking out her own phone, she dialled the landline number and waited till it clicked over to an answering machine. The friendly male voice advising her to leave a message was instantly recognisable. Geordie Pritchard.

After taking a photo of the pamphlet and the scribbled number, she put it carefully back in its place beside the condoms. The baby jumped, and she placed an arm over her belly, waiting till it stopped. Her heart was beating fast, and she was conscious she was feeling something that was somewhere between excitement and dread.

There was little else to see in Dean's house. There was certainly nothing to suggest there was reason for concern. And yet, the uncharacteristic lateness to school, particularly on a sports day, the prepared lunch still in the fridge – it *was* a concern. Was he injured, or ill somewhere?

Belinda stepped outside, locking the door and putting the key back where Dean had left it, although it half killed her to do so.

Dean's car in the driveway was an old Mazda. It was less well maintained than the house, and there was a crack in the windscreen that he really should have seen to. Like Orla before her, Belinda cupped her hands against the driver's window and peered inside. Besides a water bottle on the passenger floor, it was tidy. She tried the door handle and found it was unlocked. *Christ on a bike!*

In the glovebox, a wallet.

For the first time feeling a sense of fear, Belinda opened it. Yup, it was Dean's. There was his licence, credit cards and a card for Clean Energy Solutions. *Shit*, she thought, pulling out her phone and taking some photos. *This is not good. This is not good at all.*

Finally, she clicked open the boot. And the first thing she saw was a neatly coiled circle of rope, the very same kind and thickness that had been used to hang Geordie Pritchard.

CHAPTER 23

Will's hangover wasn't as dire as he feared. He'd woken at 2 am, taken two Panadols and sat on the toilet, feeling a kind of dread for the day to come. But apart from a dryness in the mouth and a vague headache, he wasn't too bad at all. Memories of being patted on the back, bought drinks at the pub, and having the story of his silo jump relayed back to him gave him a rare glow that outweighed any regret at drinking on a weeknight.

Now, he put down his phone after talking to Belinda. Surely her concerns about Dean were a little overblown. It was still morning, and the man was a grown adult. From what Belinda had said about him in the past, Will guessed that Dean had spent the night at some woman's house out of town and was at that moment scrambling to find his way back. It happened. Although, he conceded, never really to him. Besides Lucinda, Belinda, and one other woman named Jayne, he'd never slept with anyone else. He'd been too shy, for a start. The dorky beanpole who was prone to migraines. It wasn't until Lucinda sized him up in senior school that he was finally noticed by girls. He supposed the reason Lucinda had chosen him was because she was after change. Like him, she was used to the same sort of crowd, the familiarity of the confident types, their charisma, their ability to glide over rough topics with ease. It grew boring. Some of them went overseas, lived in communes, did the kibbutz thing. Others went full-on Outdoor Ed, learned to live off the land. But mostly, they always went back to the life; their kids went back too.

To Lucinda, that day in the common room, Will must have seemed like an insider because of his family, but an outsider too. Those thick glasses, the migraines that kept him bedridden for whole days, his quietness and lack of show. Plus, she'd seen him row that day, stroke position in the winning eight. A triumph.

Now, as he finished his cup of coffee and read over his findings about the type of rope that Geordie had been hung up with, Will reflected that perhaps Dean – living in the town he grew up in, teaching at the school he'd attended – was at last busy finding something different, something new.

Maybe the Clean Energy Solutions pamphlet was a reflection of that.

The discovery of the rope in his car, however, was more problematic.

Colin from the hardware shop in town had been adamant. When shown a photo of the type of rope from which Geordie had been hung, he immediately identified it as Manila. It was very common and used for a stack of things: farm work, tying up hay, dragging dead animals. Every farmer in the world needed good rope. Everyone who worked on boats used it, he said, everyone who ever needed towing. Everyone *who ever lived*, he surmised. And this rope, which Colin said was 32 mm, was strong.

Rope, Colin had declared with confidence, was a better invention than the wheel.

Now, Will rang Colin again. 'What about schools?' he asked. 'Would the education department ever use that Manila rope, for school camps or sports or whatever?'

'Funny you say that . . .' Colin hummed a song as Will heard him flicking through some papers. 'My first answer would definitely have been a yes, but you know, these days people like a little something called *evidence*.' Will couldn't tell if the man was being sarcastic or not.

'Right,' he said in response. 'Yes, indeed.'

Will really hated himself when he said 'yes, indeed'. It made him sound like an English lord. He tried not to say it so much now, but the offending phrase occasionally slipped out. Belinda gave him loads about it.

'Here we go.' Colin's voice came back on. 'The type of rope we're talking about, and let's not pretend I don't know why you're asking this . . . I saw it myself, Geordie Pritchard hanging from the blade – who didn't? The *whole world* saw it.'

Colin was a nice enough bloke, but so prone to exaggeration that it was difficult to gain any solid information from him. His own mother was like that, Will thought. Belinda, never.

'So yeah,' Colin continued, 'that type of rope you're talking about is extremely common . . . like my ex-wife Jodie.' He waited for a laugh, and when he didn't get one, hurried along. 'Interestingly, a whole twenty metres of that kind was bought just two weeks ago and invoiced to the PE department of Carrabeen College.'

Will sat in his car, took off his damaged glasses and wiped them on his shirt, thinking hard.

The rope was commonly used in farming and had also been bought for the school, most likely for tug-of-war or some other PE game.

The school, and farming.

His thoughts turned first to CEO and landowner Geordie Pritchard. Next, to farmer Doug Hay, who claimed he'd been pushed into a silo. And lastly, to the missing school teacher, Dean Hookes.

He flicked through his messages. Belinda had texted him a photo of the notes she'd made on Millicent after talking to the local journo.

In the border of the notes, she'd scrawled one name that connected all three men.

CHAPTER 24

Belinda was home with her feet up, drinking a cup of chamomile tea and trying to relax. That's what Nola the midwife had told her to do, and midwives must be obeyed. Especially ones like Nola. *Relax. Be calm. Breathe in, breathe out.*

Oh, but she hated that shit! Who was she kidding? She was itching to get to work. *Sorry, Nola,* she thought, picking up the phone. *I can't sit still, and chamomile tea tastes like wee.*

'Tell me,' she said when Will answered. 'The rope from Dean's car, it's the same type used to hang Geordie, isn't it?'

'Yes,' her husband confirmed. 'And the school ordered some of it two weeks ago. But it's also the same type as every other rope in the area. It doesn't mean anything.'

'Dean is still missing.' Belinda had been ringing the school every couple of hours. 'The sports day's almost over now. Orla says they've called everyone they can think of, but no go.'

'Still doesn't mean much. He is an adult.'

'There's something wrong here, Will. A reliable teacher, his wallet still in his car, his lunch in the fridge, no one knows where he could be. Don't you think it's weird?'

The rope, despite it being commonly used, *had* changed Will's perspective a little. In the city, there might have been cause for mild concern, but here, in a small town like Carrabeen, there was usually someone who'd know where a person was. It was more difficult to disappear. Reluctantly admitting she had a point, Will considered his wife's line of thinking a little more.

'You know,' Will said hesitantly, 'Dean was pro-turbine – we know that from Marit, and the pamphlet you found shows he was interested in what Geordie was doing.'

'And?'

'You told me yourself he was a bit of a bully – didn't he shove you into a bush once?'

'Yes, but that was almost thirty years ago; we were in primary school. Kid stuff. What are you thinking?' Belinda was always interested in his theories.

'Maybe Dean pushed Doug into the wheat? It's not far from his house, and it would be easy for someone as athletic as him to push someone as big as Doug in.' He said it like he didn't really believe it.

'So . . . what, Will?' Belinda asked, mildly. 'Dean tried to kill Doug Hay because Doug was fighting the turbines?'

'I don't know.' He was still mulling over his vague theory, trying to put it into place, see if it was viable.

'What are you getting at, Will?'

'It's your notes from the journo that have got me thinking. Nothing concrete just yet . . .'

Will looked at the names he'd been writing as he'd been speaking to his wife. Doug Hay, Gordon Highett, Shane Burrows,

Alan Crowe and Dean Hookes. Then he wrote two more: Lucinda Pritchard and, lastly, Marit Leslie.

He looked at each of them in turn, frowning, thinking carefully about each person, their character, what they'd revealed so far.

But the one he kept returning to was Marit.

Belinda put her phone down and stood, stretching her arms up high, bending back her neck, rolling it round.

Three pm, and Dean still a no-show.

In Victoria, she reminded herself, an adult isn't considered missing till after three days. For children it was less, but the same statistic applied; 98 per cent of people reported missing return after one to three days. It had been almost eight hours at most. She should wait.

For the fifth time that day, she called the school – but of course no one was there; the sports day was well and truly over. The winners, she'd been told by a teacher who'd answered one of her earlier calls, were Derrimut house; of course, every house at Carrabeen College was named after a variety of wheat.

And as tradition stated, the teacher went on, Principal Witts had presented the winning trophy. Apparently, the kids weren't too fussed who won, but Dean's absence at the time was glaringly obvious.

So strange, that on this important day for his job, he had not turned up.

She closed her eyes, breathed in, breathed out. *Calm. Breathe.*

But no, an idea! She opened her eyes, grabbed her notebook and stared at it for a second, before ringing the small supermarket in town. 'Deb? It's Senior Sergeant Belinda Burney – just want to ask you a question.'

'Fire away.' The woman sounded interested.

'You're usually open at six-thirty am, aren't you?'

'Yep.'

'Did you see Dean Hookes run past this morning? Would have been around the time you were opening?'

'Certainly did. I see him every morning about that time. Guy's a machine. Can I ask what this is about?'

'Thanks, Deb.' Belinda hung up without answering.

Next, she rang Shane Burrows' mother at the petrol station, situated just on the edge of town. She asked Carmel the same question. She too had seen Dean running past the station, just before six-forty.

Grimly satisfied, Belinda hung up and mentally drew a road map of the town. Most mornings, she liked to walk. There was a time she'd liked jogging, but her commitment to it never lasted long. She was too busy – with work, with cooking, with dashing from place to place. Running, Belinda privately thought, would only slow her down.

It was hardly a jogging path, but the thin dirt road that ran around the back of the petrol station and general store was popular with exercisers, primarily because it ran straight for six kilometres, and also because it was so quiet. In her brief foray as a runner soon after they arrived in Carrabeen, it had been rare to ever see anybody on the track, and today, it didn't look much different. Belinda walked to the start of the track, where the soft dirt spread like thick powder. This was the original highway, long discarded. Taking note of the footprints and tyre tracks still visible – kids sometimes used this path to get to the bus – she edged along, taking in her surroundings.

Gold dust wattle, needlewood, prickly tea tree and yellow box grew on the sides of the track. Cockatoos perched in a gum, their stark whiteness dramatic against the blue of the sky. A magpie wheeled by.

This thin wedge of Crown land hadn't been razed for farmland or to make the place 'tidy'. Her own grandmother was like that; she used to say she'd fix up the front verge before mowing the whole thing down. Order, that's what she liked, and no wonder, Belinda thought – with a roaring drunk for a husband, and a brother in and out of the clink. But her grandmother did like this part of town, the small grasses and shrubs that gave home to the wrens. She liked it too.

Belinda had gone almost half a kilometre when she noticed the tyre marks and footprints growing fainter. Here, the kids could cut through to the back of the general store and head to town that way. Further ahead on the track, only a couple of foot-prints remained, and the heavy, long groove of a bike. Stopping for a rest, her hands on her aching back, she looked about her and then continued. She'd only gone a few steps more when she noticed something to her right – an upturned shoe in the grass beside the track.

With a thudding deep in her chest, she pulled out her phone and bent over the running shoe: size 11 or 12, men's. It was now that she should call Will – or someone in Ballarat, that's what Will would do – but, even as she thought that, Belinda kneeled down, cradling her bump, and crawled forward, noting the broken twigs and flattened grass up ahead.

And there, as she half expected, was Dean's body, face down in the grass, the back of his head a bloody mess.

He was clearly dead, but she checked the pulse on his wrist anyway, his hand curved like it was begging. She put her fingers delicately on his, just like she had at the deb ball. A tiny droptail lizard ran out from his sleeve, and she watched it dart onto the dirt, then into the scrub. Dean's fingers were cold. It was very quiet where he lay. If someone walked past on the track, it would be easy to stay hidden. The thought gave her a queasy, creeping feeling.

And then, she heard someone coming. Without knowing why, she ducked her head down and waited. A bike was riding towards her, very slowly. Common sense told her to stand up and shout, but a deeper, more intuitive part urged her to stay hidden. The bike rode past, so slow at one point she thought it might stop. But then, she saw the familiar spinning wheels, the athletic legs circling, as the bike gained momentum and sped out of her immediate line of sight.

Belinda crawled out of the bush and away from Dean's body as fast as she could, fighting a sudden urge to be sick. She spun around to face the track – she had a horrid sense that someone close by was watching her. In the distance, the bike was turning left, back into the main stretch of town. Her eyes scanned over the thick shrub and low wattle as she called Will's number, then Tammy's, leaving messages for both that Dean Hookes' body had been found.

CHAPTER 25

The sun was low on the horizon, the sky a fading orange by the time the Ballarat Investigations team arrived in Carrabeen. But this time it was clear what they were coming for: a murder, the second in a week. Grim-faced and harried, Inspector Kelmendri didn't bother to hide his annoyance at the inconvenience of another dead body turning up weeks out from his retirement.

'Tell me everything,' he growled, looking at the white police tent set up around the low shrubs where Dean's body lay.

'Dean Hookes, long-time local and PE teacher of Carrabeen College. Vice Principal reported him missing when he didn't turn up for work.'

'Eh? Bit keen, wasn't he, calling the cops when someone is late?'

'Dean's usually very reliable, and it was the senior sports carnival,' Belinda said. 'He was in charge of it and was supposed to get there at seven-thirty.'

'After Geordie's death,' Tammy stepped in, trying to be helpful, 'I think everyone is very jumpy around here.'

Kelmendri nodded, looking at her but not really listening.

'Dean had rope in the back of his car which looks like the same one used to hang Geordie,' Belinda explained, and then, after glancing at Will, added, 'It's also used in farming and is very common.'

'And you didn't think to let us know this?' Kelmendri gave her a long, disapproving stare.

'It was earlier today, when we were checking out his place.'

'I don't mean that. I mean, about your plan to search for the body along this track.'

'It was just an idea I had. Nothing concrete. I used to see Dean running in the mornings, when I'd walk along the track. I'd pass him now and then.'

'Nothing concrete . . . nothing concrete. I'll tell you what's not concrete is this crime scene. You climbed in there, beside the body, touched it—'

'Belinda had to make sure he was dead,' Will spoke up.

'Oh, I think she knew he was dead,' Kelmendri said dryly, and again they all turned towards the tent surrounding the body. Two Forensics officers in their white protective suits emerged, one holding a clipboard, the other a plastic bag.

Tammy walked over to them and the three conferred quietly, their low voices indecipherable to their waiting colleagues.

Belinda's cheeks flushed. She felt lightheaded and weak. Under normal circumstances, she'd be cross at Kelmendri for his comment regarding how she'd found Dean's body, but she knew on some level he was right: her eagerness to jump in and take control had overridden her professional judgement.

'We think Dean was a turbine supporter,' Will said, breaking the brief silence. 'He had a pamphlet for CESA, and the phone number of the Pritchard residence.'

'And how do you know that?'

'I found the number in his bedroom and called it,' Belinda answered flatly. 'I thought it was important.'

'Even though, at that point, Dean had only been missing for a few hours?'

'It helps now, doesn't it? To know that?' Will said.

Kelmendri nodded again, wearily. 'Yes, it does. But if we investigated every missing person case in that way, then it would set a dangerous precedent, wouldn't it? Every family would expect the same due diligence, when in the vast majority of cases the person comes home a couple of hours later.'

Belinda thought their Ballarat boss was being a little unfair. Kelmendri obviously wasn't happy about the extra work. Perhaps he would have preferred Dean's body to have been found sometime in the future, when he was safely up in Noosa Heads.

'Getting back to Dean.' Belinda wiped her hair away from her face and rested a hand on her stomach. 'He was running on a track that only locals know well. I'd say that the person who killed him is from around here.'

Kelmendri didn't look at her. 'Murder weapon?' he asked Tammy, who had returned to their group.

'Forensics are saying something heavy,' Tammy said. 'Enough to make Dean fall forward at the first blow. They think he was hit at least twice, not sure what the weapon was yet – but they say something smooth.'

'Right' – Kelmendri looked at his watch – 'is there anything else?'

'I saw Orla Witts,' Belinda spoke up. 'She's the principal of the local school, the one where Dean worked. She was riding her bike along the track near the crime scene.'

'So?' Kelmendri shook his head.

'It's not on her way home, and she was riding very slowly.'

'You didn't think to stop and ask her?'

'I was next to the body, checking his pulse, I didn't have time.' Belinda didn't tell them about the creepy feeling she'd had, hiding in the bushes, watching Orla ride slowly by.

'Talk to this teacher then, and to anyone else who might have seen him,' Kelmendri added. 'But other than that – and I mean this, Sergeant – report *only to me*.'

CHAPTER 26

The lights of Carrabeen College were still on by the time Will and Belinda parked in the staff car park and walked up the steps to the foyer. The school had opened to provide counselling for staff and students, and as a community place to gather after the news of Dean's death had filtered out. Now, solemn-faced locals passed the officers as they streamed out of the school and down the front steps. 'What's going on in this town?' a woman asked them mournfully, and they didn't know how to respond. A couple of teenage girls sobbed inconsolably even as they eyed their phones, and a short bearded man patted Will's back, urging him to find the killer as soon as possible. The space grew quiet as the cars began to pull away.

Tayla stood in the entranceway, staring out at the night sky. She held a tissue to her nose and didn't bother to try to rein in her untidy hair. A thin line of sweat glistened on her upper lip.

'Mr Hookes taught me,' she said, tugging at a loose string of cotton on her top. 'I wasn't very good at sport, so he didn't really know me – but it's still such a . . . such a shock.'

Belinda resisted the urge to pull her in for a hug. 'Why don't you go home now, get some rest?'

But Tayla simply shook her head slightly. As Will strode ahead, down the corridor, Belinda hung back to offer the girl a ride home.

'That's okay,' Tayla said, walking slowly down the steps. She raised a trembling hand in a slight wave. 'I don't have far to go.'

Belinda watched her for a moment as she walked across the car park and into the night. *She's frightened*, Belinda suddenly realised, and she wished she had insisted on taking the young woman home.

'Bel!' Will called out impatiently. 'Come on!'

Orla and Andrew stood, ill at ease, in Andrew's plush new office. Pale and red-eyed, they looked exhausted. Andrew waved the officers into the comfy chairs while he leaned on the desk.

'Do we know how he died?' he asked. 'I heard someone saying he'd been run over, but that can't be true, can it?'

The cause of the PE teacher's death hadn't been made public, but that didn't mean much in a small town. At the first sight of the ambulance, the sealing off of the track, and Forensics in their white gear – *everyone* would know. The community Facebook page would already be lit up like Times Square.

It felt so very long ago that she was sitting on Dean's bed and calling the Pritchard number.

Orla said nothing, and it took Will a moment to realise that the principal was crying softly, her palm over her mouth. Andrew put a gentle hand on her shoulder. 'Orla,' he said. 'You should sit.'

Allowing herself to be led to the chair, Orla slumped down, her face a mask of misery.

'Orla was Dean's mentor,' Andrew explained. 'You become very close in a role like that.'

'Orla, I'm sorry this is so upsetting for you.' Belinda cleared her throat. 'But can you tell us why you were riding your bike on the dirt track where Dean's body was found? It would have been about three-thirty this afternoon?'

Both teachers looked up in shock.

'Orla?' Andrew asked. 'You went straight home after the sports day was all finished, didn't you?'

The principal answered so quietly that Will had to ask her to repeat it.

'No,' she said. 'I didn't go straight home.'

'Why?' Belinda leaned forward.

There was a flash of annoyance in the woman's eyes. 'Why should I have to let everyone know my whereabouts? I'm the principal, not the bloody prime minister! I didn't have anything else to do, so I thought I'd have a hunt for Dean.'

Andrew appeared relieved. 'Well, that makes sense.'

'How did you know to go to the track though?' Belinda asked. 'And why were you riding so slowly?'

'Where were you?' Orla shot back, but Belinda waited, arms crossed for an answer. 'I knew Dean was a runner,' the principal continued, 'it's not a secret. And I had an idea that he might have been bitten by a snake in the morning, before school. It doesn't take long to ride that track on my electric bike; I thought I'd take a look. And the reason' – she gave Belinda another steely stare – 'I was so slow was that I thought, if Dean had stopped for a pee in among the shrubs and then got bitten, he would be difficult to see.' She sat back, defiant.

The explanation was plausible, Will thought. Dean's body was in thick scrub, hidden off the track. Belinda had only seen his shoe after she'd stopped for a rest. 'We think Dean was murdered, possibly by someone he knew,' he said plainly. 'Did he have a problem with anyone, at the school, or otherwise?'

Both teachers shook their heads.

'Dean was well liked,' Andrew said. 'A great colleague.'

'And do you know if he had anything to do with Clean Energy Solutions?' Will asked. 'We have reason to believe he may have been a supporter of the turbines.'

'Dean was a supporter all right,' Andrew said sadly. 'He jumped at the chance to come on the excursion there. He attended meetings in the city too, I think. Went with a lady new to the town, curly-haired. Marit someone.'

Marit again.

Will turned to Orla.

'I don't know.' The principal shrugged. 'It seems like everyone in the school is pro-turbine. I don't see how that helps with anything.'

'What about the thefts?' Belinda interrupted. 'Did he ever report anything stolen?'

'No,' Orla said sharply. 'Dean never reported anything – it was mostly just the kids.'

'What do the thefts have to do with this?' Andrew asked, exasperated.

'Just covering bases.' Will could see Belinda's mind racing.

There seemed little else to say. Will's phone buzzed, and they all stood up as if by order.

'Thank you, officers,' Andrew said, rather formally. 'Please keep us informed.'

Will wasn't sure whether it was their job to do that, but he shook hands with the man and then turned to Orla. The principal stood with her back to them, unwilling, or unable, to say goodbye.

Back in the car park, Will checked the voicemail on his phone. Information had come through from Kelmendri's team in Ballarat, the ones who were sifting through Geordie's finances and emails. 'Hang on,' he said, reading one of them. 'This is interesting.'

'It may have to wait,' Belinda replied, looking back at the school. 'We've got someone waving at us who might actually help.'

Will glanced up to see a large woman with thick Coke-bottle glasses standing outside the lit classrooms at the far end of the school. Queen Vic! He recognised her from the Farms for Future meeting.

'Julie Smith,' Belinda told him grimly, re-locking the car doors. 'She's spooky, but she's honest. And,' she added as they walked back towards the school, 'she does make a great scone.'

Julie must have been the only person in Carrabeen who wasn't noticeably grieving for Dean Hookes. 'It's a shame,' the food tech teacher said soberly enough when she met them outside the older part of the school, towards the back of the glossy new section. 'But – I mean, *you* know what he was like, don't you?' She turned to Belinda.

'Yeah.'

'He was your deb partner, wasn't he?'

'My dad forced him into it,' Belinda admitted. 'He would never have chosen me.'

'No. Nor me. I didn't do my deb.'

There was a moment's pause, as Will looked from one woman to the other, wondering if he'd missed something.

'How come you're still here, Julie?' Will asked. 'Everyone else seems to be leaving.'

'Orla asked me to come in this evening, do a little catering. It calms people, you know, it's a nice touch. I'm happy enough to do it, but when it comes to packing-up time everyone vanishes, and it's the good old food tech teacher who ends up with it all.' She began walking to the back entrance of the school, the police following her. 'I'm glad I saw you just now.'

'Well, we don't want to hold you up,' Belinda said. 'You wanted to tell us something, Julie?'

'Yes.' The woman nodded with vigour. 'It's about the thefts . . .'

'We don't really have time for that now,' Will answered, annoyed. What with the two *murder investigations*.

But Belinda was interested. 'Do you have any more information?'

The woman now gave her a sly smile. 'I do. I'll need to show you.' She looked quickly about and then beckoned for them to follow. Will hesitated, shaking his head behind her back and mouthing to Belinda that they had to go, yet his wife was resolute. *Just one minute*, she mouthed back.

Julie led them up an old corridor. The floor had been cleaned, but there were dark smudges from student shoes, and a faint smell of Pine O Cleen, overlaid with BO.

'Would you like a scone?' Julia asked, as they turned left to enter a classroom. 'There was a batch left over, they might be still warm.'

Belinda gave Will a wink at the mention of the scones, and they followed the teacher into the Home Ec room and sat down at student benches. Julia placed a plate of scones in front of them, and, as if under a spell, they both picked one up and ate.

'I've done something illegal,' Julie admitted with that strange smile again. 'But I hope you'll forgive me.'

Belinda put her scone down – reluctantly, Will could tell, as it was delicious. 'What have you done?'

'No one was taking me *seriously*,' Julie said. 'Not Orla, not Andrew or anyone at the school. Even you, Belinda. I *told* you there was a presence here.'

Will swallowed a laugh. 'A presence?'

'What's so funny?' Julie turned to him. 'It's not uncommon. Haven't you ever felt something that you can't explain?'

The smile on Will's face faltered. 'I don't think so,' he answered, subdued.

Belinda gave him a sidewards glance, and he focused on eating his scone.

'I installed cameras to film what's been going on.' Julie pointed to the window above the door, and it took Will a moment to spot the small black lens. If not for her pointing it out, he would have assumed it was a paint smudge.

'Well, you're right, that is illegal, Julie.' Belinda was firm. 'Were you filming when the kids were here?'

'Not usually.' Julie waved a hand dismissively. 'Mostly just after school and overnight. I've got another one in the hallway too – although that one only captures a small part of the corridor.'

Will was losing patience. He was itching to talk with Belinda about Marit and the other locals he'd been thinking about. School thefts were way down their list of priorities. Besides, this room and the talk of 'presences' gave him the creeps.

'What did you find?' Belinda adopted a gentle, coaxing voice.

Julie opened a laptop and the two officers leaned across, waiting for her to press play.

The first few minutes showed nothing. Just the empty benches of the food technology room, and the view of the window beyond. It was grainy, nighttime, so there was little to see. He could tell Belinda was also getting impatient now. Then the footage shook slightly, as if there'd been a minor tremor in the room.

'Odd,' Will murmured, as the view steadied again.

'Keep watching,' Julie urged, and Belinda took a sharp intake of breath as a dark shape scurried across the bench.

'A mouse,' the teacher said. 'Not proud of it.'

Belinda blew air out of her cheeks. 'Is that all you brought us here to—?'

Suddenly a figure in black crossed the screen.

'God!' Will said, startled. 'What was that?'

Julie rewound the video and played it again.

The dark shape, unmistakably human, crossed the camera's path and went out of view.

'Can you freeze it?' Belinda's heart was thumping wildly.

Once more Julie rewound it and then froze it, just as the figure entered the screen. Tall, thin, a hoodie covering the face, the head turning briefly towards the window. It was impossible in the poor light to tell who it was.

'See! I was right,' the teacher said with grim satisfaction.

'But how could someone get in?' Belinda asked. 'All the doors would be locked overnight, wouldn't they? And there would be security alarms.'

'This is an old part of the school,' Will said. 'There are alarms, but I'm guessing it wouldn't be too difficult to find ways to get inside.'

'Especially,' Belinda added slowly, 'if somebody already had the code.'

'But why would anyone want to sneak into a school at night?' Will asked. 'I mean, I can see how teenagers might do it for a dare, but this has been going on for weeks, and it's not as if anything really valuable has been stolen.'

'That we know of,' Julie added. Belinda could tell the woman was enjoying herself.

'Is there anything valuable in the school that we don't know about?' she asked. The food tech teacher just shrugged.

'What about the camera in the hall, was there anything in those shots?'

'No. Nothing interesting.'

'We'll have to take both of those recordings and cameras,' Will said. 'With definite evidence of trespassing, we can upgrade the investigation on the thefts. Plus, we'll need to search the school to find the entry and exit points.'

Julie looked slightly shocked, as if she hadn't considered that the recordings would now be used as evidence. 'Will I get the cameras back? What's on them is very valuable to many of us in this field.' It took a moment for both Will and Belinda to realise that Julie believed the figure in the video to be super-natural. 'And they were very expensive too,' she added.

Was Julie more upset at the loss of her cameras than she was at the possibility of being charged? Will could imagine Julie fronting one of those TV shows filmed in houses that were reportedly haunted.

'We'll see,' he answered diplomatically. 'But we need those recordings.'

CHAPTER 27

Night was falling over Carrabeen as Will and Belinda drove home. The streets were empty, the shops closed. Both detectives were silent, each caught up in their own thoughts, but jointly rattled by the dark figure on the laptop screen.

By the time they'd reached home, Tammy had rung to tell them that she'd been round to see Dean's parents, who were understandably distraught. Belinda had broken the news to them earlier, in a futile attempt to reach them before the rumours spread. At first they'd refused to believe it, but soon reality set in. Belinda had known Dean since they were kids. There was no way she could have misidentified him.

Now, according to Tammy, Dean's mother was insisting that her son had seemed happier than ever these last few weeks, and had hinted there was a special woman on the scene. Different from his usual type, he'd said. Passionate about the environment.

Passionate. That word again.

From what Belinda remembered, he *always* had a woman on the scene. But even so, this deserved looking into further.

Tammy said that Dean's father had added that his son had been loving getting back into running after a lengthy break – he'd completed the Port Douglas triathlon and had done very well. He was enjoying work; life was good. He had it all ahead of him.

It was brutal talking to them, Tammy said. Dean's father kept looking at a photo of his son, half smiling, half crying. Sometimes he mimicked how Dean used to run, with his arms pumping, elbows close by his side. It was awkward and distressing. She didn't know what to say.

It was, Belinda decided, one of the worst parts of the job, speaking to the families of the deceased.

She texted Tammy back: *Talk soon.*

Belinda slumped onto their couch. There was so much to process. Dean's death, his parents, the videos from the school. But more than anything else, she needed a good sleep.

Will had made toasted tomato and cheese sandwiches for a late dinner, and Belinda took some pleasure in the fact that the tomatoes were homegrown. But she was feeling strange, out of sorts. Dean certainly wasn't the first dead body she'd had to deal with. There had been plenty of car accidents, suicides, overdoses, even murders in the last fifteen years. But this was a murder of someone she knew. Two people, in fact: Geordie *and* Dean.

She could hear Will in the next room, working on the computer, typing up notes. Usually, they never sat apart in the evenings.

She wondered what it would be like when the baby was born. Maybe it would be like the movies, with her always in a dressing gown, exhausted and forgetting to wash her hair. Maybe she and

Will would only talk about baby things, then gradually stop sleeping in the same bed, start growing apart.

It would kill her if that happened. Belinda's gaze fell on their wedding photo, the image of the two of them staring into each other's eyes and trying not to laugh. The photographer had wanted her to stand on a couple of steps, so their heights would be more in line, but she'd said no. She wanted the photo to be just as they were: him looking down at her, her cricking her neck to look up at him. It was perfect, the way her head could rest on his chest. Will was more conscious of the height difference than she was; she couldn't care less.

Listen, kid, she said silently to her bump, *you better not make us hate each other.*

She couldn't believe that her due date was only four weeks away.

Still plenty of time to work, she told herself, cheering slightly at the thought.

Her mind turned back to Julie and the video. To that figure in the recording.

Sitting on the sofa with her feet up, Belinda reached for her laptop. Will had already copied the videos from the cameras, and she opened the file.

First, the still classroom. Then the slight jolting of the screen, then the mouse, then the person. Once more, the jolting of the screen, the mouse, then the person. What had caused the screen to shudder in that way? She banged her hand hard on the couch and watched as her laptop moved slightly. Was it the footsteps of the mystery figure? Although that didn't make sense. The figure in black moved stealthily, looking from side to side. If you were walking past them in the street, you might catch a glimpse of a face, but nothing more. The effect was ghostly.

She clicked on the camera in the hallway, hoping to see the figure walking in and out. Like the camera in the classroom, this one had been set for 3.10 pm, the time when all the students were dismissed and sent home. For the first twenty minutes, there was nothing except a stream of students walking out. At one point, Orla Witts came into view, speaking to some pupils, but then she too was lost from the screen.

Putting down her laptop for a moment, Belinda stood and stretched her arms above her head. God, she was huge. Wandering into the other room, she saw that Will was still busy reading from his laptop and compiling a list of dot points. 'Be with you in ten minutes,' he said. 'The Ballarat crew have found out some interesting stuff on the Pritchards.'

'Okay. I'm looking at the videos from the school,' Belinda told him. 'Can I get you a glass of wine, or a beer or something?'

He declined, so she stood watching the dark pink sphere of the moon hovering above the shadows of the trees outside her window. On their drive home, they'd noticed that there were more campers, down by the creek. Lit by torches and the glowing fire, the scene resembled at first glance a happy gathering of holidaymakers enjoying the night. But the state of the caravans and the falling-down annexes soon corrected that assumption. 'No places to rent in town,' Will had murmured. 'I rang a real estate agent in Ballarat after people came in to enquire.'

'There's no places to rent anywhere,' she'd added. And they'd driven past, trying to ignore the vague feeling of unease that washed over them every time they talked about the growing camp. At least it was a warm night, no rain.

Drink of fizzy water in hand, she sat back on the couch to watch the rest of the recording from the school hallway. There were hardly any students left now, just a few dawdling along, one racing at speed, probably to catch a bus.

And then, something interesting. A kid, who looked perhaps Year Eleven or Twelve, walked slowly into frame, then hesitated, staring at his phone. *He's waiting for something or someone*, Belinda thought. *He's biding his time.*

She watched for a few minutes more as someone else came into view from the rear of the corridor, not the new section of the building where Orla and Andrew had their offices. *Even more interesting*, she thought, as she watched Shane Burrows exchange something with the student. *What the hell is the wind tech doing at Carrabeen College?*

There was a crash as a light branch fell onto the roof and scratched its way down the Colorbond. A gust of wind raced past, rattling the windows. Her thoughts turned to the campers again; would their tents and caravans be able to withstand a really powerful blast? What would happen then? Surely there was somewhere better in town for them all to go.

Surely.

She remembered Julie talking to her, that first time at the school when she'd said that she'd arrived at work to find the oven in the food tech room still warm . . .

Belinda's eyes widened and she gave a half-laugh. *Of course!*

'What's up?' Will entered the room, notebook in hand.

'Shane Burrows is on the video. *And* someone is living in the school roof.'

All night Belinda had been tossing and turning, clearly mulling over her theory that someone was living in the college's roof space. Usually, it made Will happy to see Belinda like this,

231

all enthusiastic and excited. But the dark rings under her eyes worried him.

'When the camera shakes in Julie's video,' she said again, over an early breakfast the next morning, 'it's because that figure has just jumped down to the ground from the roof. I think it makes sense, don't you? Julie did say when I first saw her that she thought someone might be living at the school! And in this video, we don't see the person exit or enter via the hall camera – and we know the after-hours alarms haven't gone off. Besides, the person has been stealing food, maybe even keeping the ovens on for warmth at night. We know there's a rental crisis, we know there's a heap of homeless people living by the creek. Andrew told me there's a lot of disadvantaged children at the school. Some poor kid is probably sheltering there.'

'Shit, that's awful.' Will ate his toast in near silence. Despite all he had witnessed in his years on the force, he still found it hard to believe how badly some people struggled.

'Right,' Belinda was saying, turning to him. 'Andrew will open up the building for us; Orla is on her way. We'll need to conduct a thorough search.'

'Tammy and I will do the search of the roof,' Will said firmly, not trusting that Belinda wouldn't clamber up there herself. 'Why don't you deal with Shane at the station? I'll call him now, tell him to get down there.'

Belinda nodded, satisfied. They'd already discussed the odd appearance of Shane at the school. Was he selling drugs to teenagers there? Julie's video had yielded more than perhaps even she thought. The car keys jiggled in Belinda's hand. She was itching to get started.

'We have to consider that it's possible Shane might have a plausible reason for being at the school – picking someone up or whatever. A girlfriend maybe.'

'That's gross.' Belinda screwed up her nose. 'A girlfriend who still goes to school? He's about twenty-six!'

'Twenty-four.'

'Still gross.'

'What if Tayla is Shane's girlfriend?'

Belinda looked dubious. 'I don't know if he's her type.'

How would she know what Tayla's type was, Will thought, though he found it amusing how protective Belinda was of the gap year student.

Early Sunday morning, and the streets of Carrabeen were busy with kids' sports: netball and football, soccer if you wanted to drive to Ballarat. No rowing, Will noted. Not here. He'd been the star of it in his day; there'd even been talk of an AIS scholarship. He wouldn't care if he never stepped into a boat again. He enjoyed more solitary activities now; bushwalking and swimming. Maybe if they lived closer to water, though, he might take up the single scull.

With Reg, Will had pretended to support the Magpies football club, but he suspected his father-in-law knew he was a fraud. Belinda, however, loved the AFL and would get red-faced from cheering every time it was on.

Andrew Kent was already at the front door to the school when Will arrived. The man seemed nervous, but perhaps a little excited too. 'Is this something to do with Dean?' he asked, and then looked disappointed when told it wasn't.

Will was well aware people got a thrill out of murder, especially if the victim was someone they vaguely knew. But Andrew didn't just 'vaguely know' Dean. The men were colleagues.

'Forensics are looking into how Dean was killed,' Will said. 'But there's nothing to add just yet. We're here for a different matter.'

Will had been informed last night by the Ballarat team that Dean was killed with a rounded, smooth object rather than a stone or brick. The shape of the wound, as well as the lack of fibres, all pointed to that conclusion. It was, they tentatively suggested, much like the wound found on Geordie Pritchard's head. But he wasn't about to tell Andrew that.

'We're here about the thefts,' he added. 'And we have reason to believe that someone is sleeping rough at the school.'

'What?!' The vice principal looked shocked. 'Why do you think that?'

Will still hadn't worked out what to do about Julie and the cameras. The woman would lose her job over them, and despite the wacky stuff, she was by all accounts a dedicated teacher, well liked by the kids. 'It has come to our attention,' was all he said.

Orla and Tammy turned up just as Will was helping Andrew retrieve a ladder from a storage shed near the oval.

'The police think there could be someone living in the roof, above the food tech rooms!' Andrew explained to Orla, failing to hide his excitement. 'One of us will need to go up and check.'

'The *police* will go up and check,' Tammy corrected. 'Not you.'

Andrew looked disappointed; Orla just scowled. 'Did Julie send you here?' she said. 'Is this a ghost you're searching for then?'

'We have substantial evidence,' Will said, though he wasn't sure that was true.

'I mean, shouldn't you be investigating Dean's murder?' Orla glanced at her watch. 'Or Geordie's?'

Will didn't bother responding, but Tammy whispered to him as she helped him with the ladder, 'God, what a *bitch*.'

The manhole in the food tech room was towards the back, near the pantry where staples like spices were kept. It looked to be

234

kept securely in place. However, on closer inspection, Will could see that there was a small gap in one corner where it had shifted, or not been properly replaced. At his height, he only had to step up two rungs before he could prod at it. With Tammy holding the ladder, and Orla and Andrew peering on, he climbed further up and shifted the cover to the side.

'We should have social services here,' Tammy said suddenly, and Will kicked himself that he hadn't thought of it.

'First let me have a quick check,' he said, flicking on his torch and crawling up and inside. 'It might not be anything.'

CHAPTER 28

Shane Burrows was visibly nervous when he entered the police station that morning. 'What am I here for?' he asked, scratching his cheek. 'Is this about Geordie?'

Maybe, Belinda thought but didn't say. She led him into the small interview room where they'd taken Lucinda a few days earlier, and watched as he checked his phone before sitting down. 'Do you want a tea or a coffee, Shane?'

'No, thanks.'

Making small talk as she gathered her notebook and pen, Belinda commented on the weather, how nice it was; warm, no wind.

'Wind is my business,' Shane shrugged. 'So I don't mind it. I get so sick of people whining about it all the time!' He allowed himself a brief smile. 'For half the people here, it's the reason they can afford to go on holidays, and the other half are just jealous.'

Belinda glanced over her notes. 'Would you like a lawyer here, Shane? I mean, we're just having a chat – but you can if you want.'

'Nah, it's all right,' the young man said, his shoulders relaxing. 'Long as we're not here for too long, I've got Reebra to get to.'

'The other wind farm you're managing, is that right?' Will had told her a bit about Reebra the night before, but now wasn't the time to discuss that. 'Shane, can you tell me why you—'

'If it's about the keys, then yes. Yes, I did.' His words came out in a rush. 'I was going to tell you, but you've been busy and so have I and, well – I wasn't sure how much it mattered.'

Belinda had no idea what he was going on about. She waited, letting him do the talking.

Taking her silence for disapproval, Shane continued to stumble on. 'I only gave them out twice. I know they all say it was every weekend, but it wasn't, it was *twice*! That's just how kids talk in the town, you know. And it was only for the last few weekends!' He held his hands up in a gesture of helplessness. 'My friend Limbers, his brother met this girl and . . .'

Belinda suddenly understood. 'The keys . . . you lent out the keys to the turbines to kids at the school.'

'Yeah.' Shane looked on the brink of tears. 'I knew it would be just a matter of time before you found out.'

Belinda's thoughts were racing but she tried to keep her expression neutral.

'At the start I thought it could be a way to make some easy money, you know?' The stress was visible in his flushed cheeks, his reddened eyes. 'I drop the keys off at the school, I pick them up when they're done.'

'So, that's what you were doing at the school? Handing out the keys, picking them up?' Belinda's mind whirled. Not drugs then! 'Pretty dangerous, isn't it?' She kept her voice level. 'Letting teenagers up inside those things. There's a lot that could go wrong.' *They could become trapped in there; there could be a fire.*

237

She remembered footage she'd seen of a turbine in France which burst into flames. The two workers trapped at the top chose to jump and were killed instantly.

'I don't tell them how to use the lifts or anything!' Shane's voice rose. 'They just know about the keys to the lower section, where you can stand up. There's a short ladder that leads to the next platform, but they can't go any further than that. The alarm system goes off when they open it, so I told them they can only be inside for like a really short time.'

Belinda frowned. 'Wouldn't Alan get an alert every time they go in there then?'

'I told him that the system is a bit glitchy, and that it's very sensitive. I don't think he checks it every single time.'

'Right.' Belinda considered that a moment.

'I don't know why kids want to go there in the first place, to be honest,' Shane said, trying to smile.

Oh, I do, Belinda thought. *Sneaking into a turbine, the intoxicating fear that you might get caught. I would have liked to do something like that when I was a teenager.*

'I wish I'd never lent them out! God, I'm an idiot. Will this cost me, like, will I get into trouble?'

'How did you manage to have an extra set?' Belinda tried to temper her excitement.

'Geordie gave them to me.' Shane was visibly miserable now. 'One day, he was on the phone and he was playing with his keys, and he just handed them to me and said, "Take these, I'll lose them." And then, he never asked for them back. I kept waiting and waiting – he never did.'

'But you never offered to return them,' Belinda said. What else had Lucinda told her? *Geordie was hopeless with keys.* She started making notes. 'So, tell me, what was the situation with the school kids and the keys on the weekend Geordie was killed?'

'On the Friday afternoon I gave the keys to Limbers' brother Potty. I just went into the back part of the school, near the stadium.'

'Where do the kids leave the keys after they're done?'

Shane didn't say anything.

'Please, please tell me you didn't get them to leave them under the doormat.'

'No! No, of course not,' Shane said. 'No, I got them to drop them off at school again and I'd pick them up.'

'But that didn't happen in this instance?'

'No.' A look of panic crossed Shane's face. 'When I got the call about the turbine, I didn't know what was going on at first. Alan said there was a body hanging there, but I didn't believe it. I thought it was a prank or something. I went straight there and then went up with Sergeant Lovett and saw it was Geordie. I couldn't believe it!'

Though Shane was distraught at the memory, Belinda had little sympathy for the young man who'd lied to them. They'd repeatedly asked him about the keys. He knew their whereabouts was important.

'I honestly didn't think that it had anything to do with the keys – I mean, I still don't! But when I got to the school, and the keys weren't there . . .' Shane's face paled at the memory. 'How could anyone get up the turbines without keys? I went to the school to try and find Potty, but I couldn't. I asked around and . . . look, I really have no idea where they are!'

'So, tell me, and this time no lying.' Belinda used her steely voice. 'How many keys to the turbines are there, and who has them?'

'Geordie had the master keys, which he keeps in his Melbourne office, plus another set. Those were the ones he gave me. I have my own set, and Alan Crowe just has keys to the fences around the turbines and the entrance gates.'

Belinda remembered Shane moving through the crowd, his safety gear on, brandishing a set of keys. 'So, just to confirm, it was Geordie's keys that you lent out?'

Tears were running down Shane's face. Belinda looked on, straight-faced.

'Shane,' she said after a moment's pause. 'Can you confirm that it was Geordie's set you gave to people?'

'Yes,' he said, looking up at her through wet eyes. 'People are always asking me if they can go up the turbines and—'

'Why didn't you tell us this straightaway?' she cut in.

'I just wanted to make some extra money, you know?' Shane mumbled.

Belinda stared at the young man in disgust as, at her insistence, he wrote down the names of the kids he'd lent the keys to, alongside the relevant dates.

Here was a young man who had it all: a good family, a growing career, opportunities others would kill for.

Greed, she thought. *It makes beasts of us all.*

CHAPTER 29

The place stank. A whiff of mice and damp filled Will's nose as he swung his torch around the roof space above the food technology room. Below, he could hear Tammy talking to Andrew and Orla, their voices muted through the wood and heavy insulation. The space was surprisingly large, and although someone of Will's height definitely could not stand upright, a child easily could, even an adult Belinda's size. The beam of his torchlight illuminated a pile of clothes and Will's heart jumped; at first glance he thought it was a person lying huddled there. He crawled closer. The clothes were adult-sized: a large jumper, tracksuit pants, a dirty T-shirt.

There was a bowl with a spoon in it, and further on, he could see an old mattress and sleeping bag.

At a sudden noise, he shone his torch into the blackness. 'Hello?' he called. 'Is someone here?'

Silence – save a scurrying sound in the dark corners. Will placed his hand on the bedding. It was warm. There were sheets of paper lying scattered about, as if they'd been thrown into the air then left to fall where they may. He picked up one and shone the torch on it.

'Will?' Tammy's head poked through the manhole. 'Is everything okay?'

Will didn't answer. Instead, he carefully took a photo of the paper, wondering why someone living in the roof of the school would draw such an intricate sketch of Lucinda Pritchard.

Finn Norton was known as Potty because in primary school, when his class was compiling family trees, he said his great-grandfather was from Potsdam. That was as good a reason as any, Belinda thought. Potty was just seventeen, going on thirty. He wore a *Peaky Blinders* cap, which looked stupid, and a Ramones T-shirt, which he'd clearly borrowed from one of his older sisters. Belinda didn't mind how he dressed; it was his attitude that irritated. Potty simply thought he was too important for the world.

'Zara wanted to go to the turbines,' he said, giving an affected sigh. 'She'd heard that if you got to the top of one and looked out, you could see the lights of ships on the ocean.'

That did sound pretty good, Belinda thought.

'I said to her, why don't we get the bus to Ballarat and then catch the train to Melbourne? Go clubbing? But no, that's all she wanted to do – look across some stupid paddocks to see the sea.'

You're the stupid one, Potty.

'Besides, she doesn't have a fake.'

'A fake?'

'Fake ID,' he said, looking at her like she was an idiot.

'I am a police officer, you know,' she said sternly.

'So I gathered.'

Belinda's lips grew thin. 'Tell me about that night.'

'I picked up the keys from Shane on the Friday, and then Sunday evening, about nine pm, we rode our bikes from my place to Mont Blanc.' Potty looked a little shamefaced at the mention of bikes. Saying it clearly reminded him of his young age. 'Zara and I had a few drinks and then, you know, just hung around.' He gave a smirk. 'Zara was pretty pissed.'

Run, Zara, run.

'Were you vaping?'

'What? Yeah. It's not illegal . . . is it?'

'Is there anything else you can tell me about that night? You know it was the very next morning that Geordie Pritchard was found hanging from one of the blades.'

'Yeah, I know.' Potty looked excited by the recollection. 'Dad saw him there in the morning and called you guys.'

Along with everyone else in the district.

'So, what more can you tell me?' Belinda pressed.

'At about, I don't know, ten or ten-thirty, we thought we'd try to get up the turbine. We were mucking about with the keys – there's too many of them. We were trying different ones when we saw a car.'

'Which direction was it coming from?' Belinda's pencil was poised.

'From town.'

'What did you do?'

'A runner, of course!' Potty looked at her as if she were mad. 'If you get caught out there, it's serious trouble. So, yeah – we ran through this gap in the fence, got on our bikes and went straight home. But somewhere on the way I dropped the keys. I know when I saw the car and started running I had them on me. They must be in the paddock somewhere. I haven't told Shane yet, he'll go ape.'

Yeah, he'll go ape. 'What can you tell me about the car you saw? Did it stop?'

'Don't know about that, but it didn't pass us.'

'Were its lights on?'

'Yeah, but low. Sort of dim. Can you dim them?'

'Low beams.'

'Well yeah, it had its low beams on.' Potty looked at his watch. 'Is this nearly over, cos I've actually got my brother coming to pick me up? We're catching a band in Fitzroy.'

'Catching a band, are you?' Belinda couldn't hide the scorn. 'Tell your brother you might be a little late. This is important information that you've withheld from us for days. There could be serious penalties.'

'Really?' Potty's face paled.

'Oh yes, maybe,' she said. 'I want you to fill me in about these fakes. But for now, tell me again about that car.'

CHAPTER 30

Will put his shoulder to the stiff breeze and ran up the steps to the police station. Once inside, he could hear Tammy giving Belinda a rundown of the events at the school.

'There was no one else up there,' she was saying. 'Will and I had a good look around, but we're going to go back and give it a more thorough check.'

They had crawled through the entire space, torches flashing, searching for any other traces of people living there, but it did seem to be only the one, and that person was gone.

'Any idea of how they'd get in and out of the school?'

'It wouldn't be too difficult to slip out with the students at the end of the day, or slip in at the beginning of classes,' Will said.

'But how would they climb up the manhole?' Belinda asked.

'There's a storeroom adjoining the Home Ec room,' Tammy said. 'It's got a stepladder in it. We think whoever was up there would have put the stepladder on the bench and then hauled themselves up, then lowered themselves down in the morning.'

'You'd need to be fit to do that,' Belinda commented. 'Or very tall.'

They discussed the layout of Carrabeen College. It was in the shape of a T, with the reception area and the new offices at the front – all paid for by the Pritchards – and the science, maths and food tech buildings running down the back of the school.

'Julie will be pleased she's been proven right,' Belinda commented. 'Although she might be sad you found evidence of a human and not a supernatural presence.'

'It felt like a kind of presence up there in that roof.' Tammy screwed up her nose. 'Like, a really rotten one.'

Belinda filled them in on what Potty had had to say after Shane's admission. Then Will took out the drawing of Lucinda he'd found and placed it on the table in front of them.

'Do you think' – Belinda leaned back after they'd studied the drawing for a minute or two – 'that we can now say there is definitely a connection between Geordie's death, Dean's death and the school?'

Will felt a heaviness in his stomach. He knew this was what Belinda had been inching towards ever since she'd learned that the Pritchards had funded the new building, and found Geordie's number on the brochure in Dean's room. She would never admit it, but Belinda placed a great deal of trust in her gut feelings, which – like the auras he experienced before a migraine and Julie's feelings of a presence – were difficult to explain.

Unlike his wife, Will didn't thrive on work. What he was most looking forward to – what he truly *couldn't wait* for – was the birth of their baby and his paternity leave. He planned to take another week off after that, and he thought about it all the time. What it would be like with just him, Belinda and the baby. They were due to move back to Melbourne in a couple of months. Now she'd made this connection between the cases, he could see how his wife would become consumed.

Tammy pulled a muesli bar out of her bag and started eating it. 'I don't really see it,' she said in response to Belinda's question. 'I mean, so what if Dean had a number for the Pritchards and there's a drawing of Lucinda in the roof. The Pritchards are well known, and not just around here.'

It was a good point, but Belinda wasn't backing down. 'What about the turbine keys? Shane and the school? It is weird, don't you think? I mean, what if the person living at the school killed Geordie?'

'And then drove him to the turbines and strung him up?'

Belinda shrugged. 'I don't know – but come on, it's an interesting theory, isn't it?'

'Where's Lucinda's car?' Tammy asked. 'She'd have a posh one, wouldn't she? Didn't the kid say that he thought the car was a nice one, because it was quiet?'

'Her car is electric,' Will added. 'Those things barely make a sound.'

'Lucinda was moving compost with it when I saw her, because she didn't know how to drive the ute.'

'We should get that car checked out,' Tammy said. 'I'll talk to Kelmendri about a warrant.'

'I can do that if you like,' Will said.

'No, I'm more than happy to. Plus, I've got a good recommendation for a restaurant in Noosa for him.'

'And talking about expensive cars,' Will said. 'Investigations got back to us about the Pritchards' online communications and their finances.'

He told them how the team in Ballarat had combed through the family's business, in particular the investments and dealings associated with Clean Energy Solutions Australia. The value of their landholdings and property was seriously impressive, but the business itself was in trouble. The oldest turbine farm on the side of Mont Blanc had gone through regulations and council fairly quickly, but more recent propositions had proved harder to push through. It was taking some clean energy producers more than a decade to receive approval to begin building on a site, and in the meantime there were legal fees, builders, consultants and compensation to be paid. All of this was daunting enough, but apparently Geordie Pritchard would not stop spending. And not on luxury goods like cars or holidays or anything like that. Geordie Pritchard was giving money to community projects, he was offering to buy land for public housing, he'd proposed a statewide conference on bullying in schools, and he'd bought up land in the Daintree, so it would never be logged or built on. All wholly funded by CESA.

'Interesting,' Belinda said slowly, fiddling with the buttons on her top. Will thought she looked uneasy, and she turned away when he tried to catch her eye.

'Anything more?' Tammy asked.

'Lucinda had made moves to take over the company. It looks as if she was trying to rein her husband in.'

'No wonder.' Tammy whistled.

Belinda didn't say a word.

The winds of Carrabeen created havoc with hair, plans for outdoor picnics and golf matches – but they were a natural cleanser too. One afternoon of a stiff southerly and the streets would be free of debris and dust. Belinda was thinking this as she made her way to the football oval, where the strong winds that afternoon would either favour or hinder the local team. Crowds had already gathered on the sidelines of the netball court, where Carrabeen Division B was playing Darlington, a notoriously rough team, despite the name. Then again, they always said that about Darlington. Belinda had once played in Division C, but only lasted three games after she was suspended for pushing the Goal Keeper over for calling Cathy Raz a 'povo slut'. It wasn't the shove itself that was the problem, but the fact the Goal Keeper was from her own team.

She pondered the memory as she drove. The Razzes lived on the same street as her father; their houses were similar; they had parents who worked in contract labour. Fact was, her family wasn't much different from theirs. Except for one important detail: Belinda had Reg for a father, and Reg Burney held sway. Being poor didn't mean you had no power, it just meant you got it and used it in other ways. Reg was respected for his shearing skills, his drinking capacity, his general attitude of disdain, and the air of menace that clung to him like a barbed wire hug. People in town didn't cross Reg Burney, and they didn't cross his kid.

Belinda had never known her mother. Sharon Phillips had died when she was barely three. Reg had brought her up, with help from his sisters and the families of the town. But mostly it was just her and Reg, till she shot through to join the police.

Darlington was winning 28–20. Belinda bought a pastie from the canteen and watched the game as she ate. Just because she didn't play netball now didn't mean she didn't love it. She was a fan of the Vixens, went to a couple of games each year. This game was better than the scoreboard suggested. Belinda watched on, glad to be focusing on something other than police work just for a while.

The whistle blew, and Tayla Schultz was onto it. Wing Attack covered; Goal Attack covered. Belinda watched, eyes wide open, leaning forward. Tayla threw the ball backwards, just as the Goal Keeper leaped for the intercept – too late! The ball went straight to the Carrabeen Goal Shooter, who put it through the ring.

Half-time was called.

Belinda walked over to where Tayla was sitting on the ground, taking off one of her runners. *Maybe I should take up netball after the baby*, she thought. *Get fit, shove a few people, really stick it up those cocky Wing Attack types* – but then she dismissed the idea. She'd never been a team player, not really.

Tayla looked up at her, red-faced and concerned. She held a dirty white sock aloft, like a flag of surrender. 'Is everything okay?'

'Great game.'

The girl relaxed a little and slowly lowered her sock. 'Yeah, I hope we win.'

'Play like that and you will.'

From nearby, the coach called out for a huddle.

'I need to ask you a question.' Belinda spoke quickly, conscious of the time. 'Can you give me the details of when Geordie or Lucinda came to the school in the last two weeks, and, if possible, what their reason was for doing so?'

The girl blinked anxiously. 'It's Sunday. Was I supposed to be at work today?'

'No, no, not at all! I know it's the weekend, but this is import-ant, and I know you will have kept a record.'

Belinda waited while Tayla shook out her sock and put it back on. 'Sure,' she said. 'I mean, if it's for a police investigation

I guess I wouldn't be breaking any confidentiality. I can access my work computer from my phone, so I can just . . .'

'Tayla!' the coach called to her from the sidelines. 'Hurry up!'

Belinda resisted the temptation to pull out her ID and tell the coach that this was a police matter.

Tayla stood on one leg and hopped over to her bag on the sidelines, where she pulled out her phone. 'There.' She tapped with both thumbs expertly. 'I've just sent my record of appointments to you.'

Belinda gave her a broad smile. 'Tayla, you've just made me the happiest cop this side of Mount Abrupt.'

The young woman gave her a proud smile. It lit up her whole face.

'Go and kick that Goal Keeper's arse for me, will you?'

'Darlington – they're so rough!'

'Be rougher.'

Reluctantly leaving the game, Belinda threw her pastie bag into the bin and wiped her hands on her jeans. In the car, she sat and read through Tayla's neat notes, scanning down for interesting school appointments in the days before Geordie's death. Nothing jumped out at first. There were parent meetings for Orla and Andrew, a meeting with a builder, and someone from the Education IT department about a new system. Julie had met with both Andrew and Orla for fifteen minutes on the Tuesday before Geordie's death, presumably to discuss her concern about the thefts, and a parent had met with Orla about a new enrolment. There were staff meetings. Finally, Geordie's name appeared. He'd been at the school on the Wednesday the week prior to his death, meeting with the principal to discuss the new building, according to Tayla's notes.

On the week of his death, Geordie hadn't visited the school at all.

Belinda checked again. No, nothing else. She put her phone down, disappointed. What was she hoping for? A lengthy catch-up at the school, preferably between Orla and the Pritchards, maybe even with Julie present as well. But no. Most appointments ran for an hour at most.

Still, Belinda's eye lingered over Dean's name on Friday 29 November. The weekend Geordie had been killed. Why had the PE teacher met with Andrew Kent for an hour and twenty minutes in his office that afternoon?

Holding Tayla's notes in one hand, she called the vice principal's number. He answered on the second ring. 'Hello?'

'Andrew, it's Sergeant Burney.'

'Oh, right. Any news?'

The question was an odd one, Belinda thought. Any news on what? On Geordie? On Dean? On the person in the roof?

'Not as yet, we're just following up some information.' She decided to leap straight in. 'Can you tell me what you were discussing with Dean Hookes on the Friday afternoon before the weekend Geordie was killed?'

'What has that got to do with anything?' His voice was surprisingly sharp. 'Dean was a valued staff member. I don't see what a conversation regarding the school has to do with any of that business.'

For a moment, Belinda was a schoolgirl, put back in her box.

'We have two murders to investigate, Mr Kent. One of them Dean's. So "that business" is now very relevant.'

She could hear a long sigh down the line, then a cupped hand as he spoke to someone nearby.

'You should come here,' he said into the phone, reciting his home address. 'I'll tell you everything then.'

Andrew's house was not far from the school, set back on a quiet street lined with elms. The front garden of his home was attractively landscaped with rosemary clipped into spheres, banksias and saltbush. An Audi sedan was parked out the front, a glistening navy blue. Andrew answered the front door before she'd even knocked, then led her into a lounge room, where a little dog yapped at her feet until a woman came and scooped him up.

'This is Fumiko,' Andrew said, turning to the attractive, dark-haired woman.

They said hello, and Fumiko left, the dog yelping in her arms.

'Fumiko's a pharmacist,' Andrew said. 'She thinks I should teach in Ballarat near where she works, but I've still got two years left in my contract here, and I would never break it.'

'So you like it here in Carrabeen?' Belinda was always interested in how people fitted into the town.

'I do,' Andrew answered. 'It took a bit of getting used to after the city – everyone knows you here and all of that – but the kids are great, and the staff are wonderful. That's why Dean's death has hit us hard, we're a really close team.'

If Tammy was killed in such a brutal manner, Belinda thought in a flash, she'd be devastated. Colleagues are not always your friends, but they're a constant presence. They know what you eat for lunch, how cool you like the air conditioning, what parts of the job you love and loathe.

'Did you think about closing the school tomorrow? Maybe the kids need to—'

Andrew cut in, 'Schools should be a place of security, where kids can come and go and feel safe from what's happening around them. It isn't always the case, but we have tried to create an atmosphere at Carrabeen where students and staff feel supported. We provide careful structure and offer a broad range of counselling when something like this happens. We have done all of that, and we will continue to do so.'

His words smacked of an educational white paper, but Belinda could see that Andrew was genuine about caring for the kids. The rings under his eyes, the way his wife had gently placed her hand on his back before she left the room, the hours and hours of overtime he no doubt spent at work. Here was a teacher trying his best to keep a traumatised school community afloat.

But even so . . .

'I'm trying to get a sense of what Dean was doing in the weeks and days before he was killed. I wondered why you met with him on the Friday before Geordie was killed – your meeting went for almost ninety minutes, so you must have had something substantial to discuss.'

The vice principal said nothing.

'Or,' Belinda continued, 'perhaps you were just catching up as friends. I don't know, but it could be important. Either way, we'd like to know.'

Andrew winced. 'Is this really important in some way for the investigations?'

'It could be.' Belinda was firm.

The vice principal thought for a moment, then threw his hands up in the air. 'Dean came to tell me that he was being blackmailed.'

Belinda hoped her face wouldn't show the shock she felt. Motioning with one hand for him to continue, she pulled out her phone. 'Do you mind if I record this?'

Andrew shook his head.

'Go on then.' Belinda clicked record.

'Dean thought that the person blackmailing him was someone from the school, maybe the thief everyone was talking about. Now, I recognise that the culprit was probably the person living in the roof.' Andrew groaned. 'Events seem to be moving too fast.'

'What was Dean being blackmailed about?'

Andrew looked at her directly. 'Dean was having an affair with Lucinda Pritchard. He told me that – and that someone had clearly found out.'

Belinda was stunned. Lucinda and *Dean*? But then she recalled how Lucinda had looked at her through teary eyes and said she wasn't a perfect wife.

Lucinda and Dean. It was difficult to process.

'Who else did you tell this to?'

'Nobody. I mean, I was going to tell Orla . . .' The man hesitated. 'But sometimes I had the feeling that . . . that . . .'

At the door, Fumiko shouted a cheery bye as she stepped out in running gear. They both called goodbye back.

'What were you going to tell me then?' Belinda looked at the vice principal closely.

He shook his head and gave a shrug. 'It's nothing.'

Sometimes Belinda wished she'd been a cop in the seventies. Then you could threaten a witness, beat the information out of them. Instead, she waited.

'It might be important, Andrew,' she said finally, in an even tone. 'What did you sometimes think about in regards to Orla?'

Andrew picked up a little pot with a fake plant inside, studied it and then placed it back down. 'Our principal can be unstable,' he admitted, looking at her. 'She's a terrific teacher, but there are times I worry.'

Belinda returned his gaze. Orla's drinking. She knew all about that. The drink-driving charge, her aggressive manner during the interaction they'd had. *You fucking bitch.*

She changed course. 'So why didn't you reveal the affair to us after Geordie was killed?'

'I had no reason to believe that their affair was connected to Geordie's death, and anyway, everyone was saying it was suicide.'

'What about after Dean's death?'

'Dean was adamant that I not tell anyone,' Andrew said slowly. 'Now, of course, I wish I had ignored his wish and gone straight to you. But, you know, Dean lived in a small town and he *did* deserve a private life, whatever we may think about the morals of it all.' They both gazed out the window onto the street, where the wind was cleaning again – whipping up leaves from the road and carrying them away.

'I could see Dean as a principal one day,' he said. 'And I didn't want to jeopardise his chances. Having a sexual relationship with the wife of our biggest benefactor would certainly do that,' Andrew muttered sadly. 'But yes, I thought Dean had real potential. One time, when Orla was ill, he stepped up into her role and really, the man was very good.'

'Right.' Belinda stood. 'Is there anything else?'

Andrew considered her for a moment and then walked to a small bureau cabinet, opening it and holding out an envelope. 'Dean gave me these when we met that day,' he said. 'I think, under the circumstances, it's best if I now hand them over to you.'

Belinda held up a pot of coffee and poured it slowly into a large mug. She didn't feel like a coffee – it was too late in the day – but she needed to do *something*, and even the smell of the stuff could help her think better. For now, it was quiet in the station, she could work in peace. Belinda looked down at her notes.

Dean Hookes had given Andrew a series of drawings. In the week preceding their meeting, he'd had at least three sketches pushed under his office door in the gym area, sketches depicting him and Lucinda Pritchard in compromising poses. Two of them kissing, her long dark hair scrunched up in his hand, and another of them lying on a desk in an office, his bum in the air. The drawings were all in pencil, clearly amateur – but there was skill in them too. The illustrator had taken care with the shading, the way Lucinda's face was half in shadow, half in light. And there was a definite humour too; Dean's bare bum pointed skyward, the dramatic clenching of Lucinda's hair. Whoever drew them had taken time and care before slipping the final product under Dean's door. They were undoubtedly in the same style as the drawing Will had found in the roof; the artist was the person who spent their nights at the school, eating from the food tech room and stealing from students' bags.

Financial demands had accompanied each drawing: that Dean leave $100, then $50, then another $100 on the shelf in his office before he went home at night. Each time, according to Andrew, Dean paid up. The gym teacher was frightened and upset; he didn't know what to do. However, when Andrew suggested going to the police, Dean had become agitated, insisting no. In the end, they'd agreed to leave it for a few days and to keep a watchful eye out. Andrew had hoped Dean would eventually calm down enough to go to the authorities, but in the meantime he'd assured his colleague that he would keep quiet.

A paper bag flew along the road outside the police station, as if it was late home. Belinda followed its path right down to the end of the street.

Dean was on track to fulfil every expectation of him, Belinda thought. From local stud to PE teacher to principal. His trajectory was set out for him, clear and true.

And then, along came Lucinda Pritchard.

CHAPTER 31

Lucinda wasn't answering her phone so, after a moment's thought, Will decided to drive to her place at Yarrobee. Ever since Belinda had shown him the drawings, he'd been thinking about his ex-girlfriend, and not in a good way. In each drawing, Lucinda was like a character from a cheesy romance; leaning back in Dean's arms, hair flowing down, a wrist raised to her forehead as if in a swoon. Lucinda looking back, her hair sweeping over her face, her lips in a knowing pout. Everything about it was staged, as if she expected a photographer to appear at any moment. And then, as he drove out of town and past the turbines, he thought that was perhaps how it had mostly been with them. Wasn't it all for show, her being with him?

In any case, the images of Lucinda embracing Dean reminded him of model poses – not dissimilar to the way she'd collapsed onto the ground in front of the turbine when she'd first seen her husband hanging from the blade. It had been painting-like – the grieving widow, beautiful and mourning in the dirt.

Her car wouldn't be checked out till Kelmendri agreed to the warrant, but the affair and the business dealings were subjects Will could ask her about. Belinda was taking over matters at the school with the staff, the thefts and now the person in the roof, while Will would stick to the Pritchards and help Tammy liaise with Forensics. Investigations were still in the early stages of looking into the murder of Dean Hookes.

On that note, he called Kelmendri's number in Ballarat. The boss answered after the fifth ring; his customary sigh accompanied the greeting. Will could easily picture his boss in the moment, the sagging head, the drooping eyelids so big they'd fit a Noosa time share inside.

Will filled him in on the discussion in the station regarding Lucinda and Dean's affair. 'It makes sense now, with the phone number in Dean's house – but we're still thinking that with the finances the way they are, and Lucinda opting to take control of the company, there is cause for further investigation.'

Kelmendri was silent.

'And you know, when Belinda spoke to that kid who was at the turbine, he said it was a nice car that drove up. A quiet one.'

'And you're pinning that on the Pritchards?' Kelmendri sounded incredulous. 'A "nice car"?'

'Belinda saw her moving compost in it in the days after Geordie's death. That's odd, don't you think?'

'Perhaps.'

'And now we know about the financial issues with Clean Energy Solutions as well as the affair, we have to talk to Lucinda again. She's personally connected to two men who are dead.' Will rammed the point home.

'And to you, I gather.'

Now it was Will's turn to be quiet.

'It's not appropriate for you to be questioning Mrs Pritchard.'

He had just pulled up in front of her house. In the large bay window, he could see Lucinda's pale face looking out. Again, he was struck by how she seemed to him to be a set of images rather than a complete person. Kelmendri was right. If he did happen to find anything of interest, it would be discounted in court because of their previous relationship. What an idiot he'd been driving out to Yarrobee.

Now Lucinda was walking down the steps towards him.

'We need her car searched, boss,' he said into the phone.

'Forget the Pritchards. Their lawyers are already swarming,' said Kelmendri, ending the call.

Lucinda held a hand up to her eyes, saw it was Will and gave him a relieved wave.

He wound down his window. 'I can't talk to you any more, Lucinda, I'm sorry. I shouldn't have come out here.'

'Don't worry.' Her smile turned to a sneer. 'I've already been instructed not to say a word.'

Belinda flicked through the names she had written down, the people she and Will and Tammy had spoken to in the last week. There was Lucinda Pritchard, Marit Leslie, Gordon Highett, Doug Hay, Alan Crowe, Shane Burrows and the teachers, Julie Smith, Andrew Kent and Orla Witts. After a second's thought, she added Tayla from the school. All locals, or as good as . . .

Something suddenly occurred to her: if someone was so upset at Geordie, why had they chosen to kill him on that particular evening? Lucinda claimed the perpetrator was a local, but locals could have got to Geordie at any time. He came to Carrabeen regularly, and the furore over the turbines had been going on for months, years even. Why now? What had happened in the days preceding his murder that had made someone angry or desperate enough to kill him, and then Dean?

Come on, she told herself. *Think!*

An alert on her phone buzzed to remind her about a haircut the following week and she turned it to silent, wanting to concentrate. *No time for haircuts now*, she thought. *Bigger things to fry than foils.*

Her eyes moved up the list to Dean's name again, and she felt a fresh shock that he was dead. The well-known PE teacher: an athlete, turbine supporter and lover of Lucinda Pritchard. Had he discovered who had killed Geordie, and then been murdered because of it? Or had he been involved in Geordie's death, the lover getting rid of the pesky husband so he and Lucinda could live in peace?

The theory didn't ring true, but Belinda was struck by just how little she knew of Dean Hookes, despite going to school with him, being his deb partner (major cringe) and living in the same town. She thought back to his house, how minimal it seemed, how little of a personal touch there was. There were always rumours of his love affairs, but Dean had never married, never moved elsewhere. An affair with someone as glamorous and wealthy as Lucinda Pritchard must have been significant, and perhaps even dangerously exciting for the long-term PE teacher.

What exactly had Dean done, or seen, that had made someone want to kill him?

Will's uneasiness at how Lucinda had greeted him was lessened somewhat by the welcome he received at the supermarket, where he'd stopped to buy some milk and the local paper. Everyone, it seemed, had heard about his leap into the silo to save Doug Hay.

The woman at the checkout asked if he was going to receive a medal, and when he answered that that wasn't likely, she slapped down her roll of coins in despair. 'Not get a medal?' she cried. 'The greatest hero Carrabeen has ever seen, and you don't get rewarded!'

'Bloke from Bendigo got a medal for saving some kid from a house fire,' the man behind him added.

'A house fire!' The checkout lady made a dismissive sound. 'What's a house fire compared to a silo! There's at least a chance of running back outside in a house fire – but in a silo full of wheat, there's no hope.'

'Well' – Will gave a half-smile – 'there's *some* hope. I'm here, aren't I?'

The woman laughed. 'You are! It's a miracle!'

Another man joined the queue. 'But it's true,' he said solemnly. 'When you jumped in there, you had no idea if you'd make it out dead or alive.'

'Hero.' The checkout lady looked at him with lowered eyes. 'That's all there is to say.'

Will picked up his goods and left, embarrassed but not unhappy with the attention. Ripping off the top of the Crunchie wrapper, he took a massive bite. Honeycomb fragments splattered all over his top, and he didn't care.

At home, his good mood was dampened somewhat by the parcel in the letterbox from his mother. He'd forgotten to collect it on Friday, and now the box was full of bills, brochures and this parcel. He had a good idea what it was. She'd forwarded the Wesley magazine to him every year since he'd left, even though he never asked her to. Will couldn't care less what was going on in the place. He'd been there for less than a year. Nevertheless, with his newfound confidence, he flung himself down on the couch and opened up the glossy pages. Wesley was celebrating its centenary as a college and, as a result, the magazine had included photos from every year since 1924.

Will kicked off his shoes and rested his long legs over the arm of the sofa. He skipped past the Chair's Address and the O-Week reflection, read with interest a small paragraph on tips for excelling socially ('literally just gaslight yourself into thinking that nothing you do is embarrassing'), and then some advice on 'How to Survive a Massive Hangover' ('watch TikToks about how the world is meaningless and small, so you forget your hangxiety'). The photographs were towards the back, and he soon found his cohort. There were two shots of him, each for rowing awards. He was smiling in both, but Will thought that his younger self looked unsure and self-conscious. There were at least four pictures of Lucinda; one of her lounging back on a chair, two at the ball with a group of girls – her knowing smile less exuberant than those of the others. And there was a formal shot, her hair falling drastically to one side and her head slightly tilted. Already, she was acutely aware of how to show her most attractive self.

Will scanned to the list of names in his brother's year. Andrew Kent was there – a few years above Will, just as he'd told Belinda. He looked up their corresponding photos; a casual image of their first year – his brother Daniel grinning up the back, taller than everybody else, and Andrew in the front row, one foot placed over his other knee, his face uncertain, looking the wrong way.

Will made himself a cheese sandwich with some of Belinda's tomato relish. He tried to call her, but she wasn't answering. Perhaps she was at her father's. Maybe, with his newfound courage, he'd go and see for himself.

He looked out the window to where the washing was being spun around on the Hills Hoist like a ride at a fair. It would be dry in no time. He washed his plate and set it on the wooden rack, then walked into the bedroom, where he took off his shirt and changed into a T-shirt. He and Belinda had been together for years, and Reg still made him feel like shit. Every time he saw the man, he felt like a bumbling city-slicker in polished boots. Will looked down at his shiny R.M.s and thought that maybe Reg had a point. In the past, he'd purposefully scuffed them in the dust before he'd entered the house. Sometimes, he heard himself broaden his vowels when he spoke. It was difficult, trying to fit in. Belinda never felt the need to adjust herself for his family, although she must have felt pressure to, knowing his mother. He admired that about his wife, her sense of self. The thought of Belinda gave him courage. *Stuff you, Reg, I like a polished boot.* His hands would never be as coarse as Reg's, his arms never as wiry and lean – but Will was married to the man's daughter, and that had to give him some sway. It was overblown, but the checkout lady's insistence that he was a hero gave him new determination.

He would go and visit Reg.

CHAPTER 32

When he pulled into Broker Court, there was no sign of Belinda's car out the front. Perhaps she'd gone for a walk; he wouldn't put it past her, even in this heat. One of the neighbours, who Belinda called Senior Raz, was sitting on her front porch, smoking. Will gave her a wave, and the woman nodded back, imperious. She blew smoke out of her nose like a dragon.

'Is Reg home?' he called to her.

'Search me,' she answered, and he thought, *Not likely.*

He knocked on the door and then opened it a crack. 'Reg?'

No answer.

He could hear the radio on in the kitchen. Greyhound racing, loud.

The old man was probably having a smoke in the lounge room, listening to it in that rotting deck chair he liked.

'Reg?' he called louder, his eyes adjusting to the gloom as he stepped inside.

The rapid-fire pace of the commentator's voice continued: Say No More was gaining speed; Say No More half a metre behind; Say No More closing the gap.

He walked up the hallway and into the lounge room.

The man wasn't in his chair.

'Reg?'

The race was now close. Nothing in it. Say No More and Bessie's Girl were neck and neck.

There was a business card wedged under the landline phone next to his chair.

Geordie Pritchard, CEO, Clean Energy Solutions. *The offer still stands*, was written underneath it in neat blue ink, and the next words, *Speak to Belinda*, were underlined.

What the hell?

The race continued, loud. Half a length to go. Will couldn't bear listening to it any longer. He stepped over to the old island bench which separated lounge from kitchen and pulled the radio's cord out from the wall.

Silence.

Now he could hear the quiet buzz of the fridge, flies gathering at the window. It was clammy in the room, but despite the warmth Will felt a distinctive chill. He walked into the kitchen. There was broken glass on the lino, and a faint sound of water gurgling down a drain. 'Reg?'

The old man lay on his side, curled up like a child.

At first Will thought Reg had tied a red ribbon about his neck, but the blood and the choking sounds brought him to his senses.

He moved instantly to action.

Reg, barely conscious, was trying to speak. Will pressed his hand on the neck wound and leaned down towards him.

'Fucker!' the old man was gasping through gritted teeth. 'Tried to . . . garrot me.'

Holding his father-in-law up with one arm, Will managed to call an ambulance. There was more blood, coming from the older man's hands, and when Will gently prised one finger open, blood welled into his palm.

'Fucker tried to . . .'

Reaching for a tea towel, Will pressed it firmly on the man's neck, then closed his fingers again. 'Everything's going to be okay, Reg,' he said, cradling him.

'Get me . . .'

'Don't speak,' Will ordered.

And for once, his father-in-law obeyed.

In less than half a day, the story had spread through Carrabeen: how Reg Burney, sixty-nine years old, had fought off an attacker trying to strangle him with a fishing line, using only his bare hands and a bottle of beer. And – the detail everyone added at the end with great flourish – the cigarette butt never left his mouth.

Sitting beside him in his hospital bed, Belinda was already tired of the story.

But still, she could easily envision the scene:

Reg. Lit fag stuck to his bottom lip, in his singlet, elbows propped up on the kitchen bench, drinking a cold stubbie of VB. Dogs on the radio. Her father had been doing this every weekend for fifty-odd years. Reg would have been slightly hunched from his shearing days, bending in to the radio, skinny arms like dried chicken wings.

Footsteps creeping in the background: he wouldn't have heard them till too late. Then the fishing wire about his neck, yanking, cutting through old skin. Reg was pulled backward on the stool, his knees under the bench preventing a complete fall to the floor. And then, through sheer grit, Reg had grabbed at the ligature, wire cutting deep into his fingers. Straining with the effort, and unable to breathe, Reg had smashed his beer bottle hard on the bench with one hand, before shoving the broken half into the attacker's arm. A muffled cry of pain, and the stool suddenly righted again, as the person slipped away. Reg, lit ciggie still in his mouth, had then grasped hold of his throat and fallen to the floor.

Dad, she thought in despair. *What the hell was it all about?*

Will was sitting beside her, his hand on her knee. Reg was now sleeping after being stitched up. For the third time in a week, Ballarat Investigations were in Carrabeen gathering evidence. A general air of exhaustion permeated the little hospital room.

'Is he in on it, do you think?' Will asked, quietly. 'For Geordie? Or Dean?'

The shock hit her like a slap. 'Are you talking about *my dad*?'

'Yes.' He looked aggrieved, but his voice was firm.

'No! Why would you even *say* that?' She shook her head.

'Doug and Reg are very tight,' Will said. 'Remember him saying that he'd do anything for Doug?'

'What, *kill* for him? Are you *crazy*?'

'I don't know, maybe he's involved *somehow*.'

'Jesus, Will!' Belinda felt a rare flash of rage towards her husband.

'Bel, your dad was once a rigger on the Sydney Harbour Bridge. He's strong, he's not afraid of heights. That's all I'm saying.'

'That's not all you're saying, Will, and you know it.'

Will snorted. 'And what about *you*, Belinda? What are *you* not saying in all this? I know you've been hiding something.'

There was an unusual edginess to his voice, which frightened her. She wasn't used to her calm husband being so sharp. 'I saw Geordie's card with your name on it in Reg's house. *The offer still stands. Speak to Belinda.* What's going on?'

Reg stirred, muttering something incoherent. Belinda reached for a glass of water and held it to his dry lips, letting a little bit trickle into his mouth, which was opening and closing like a baby.

'I saw Geordie on the Saturday before he was killed,' Belinda admitted finally. 'We spoke.'

'What about?'

'He said he wanted to buy the dog-racing site, but that they were asking for all the debts to be paid first. Dad owed a lot, like almost everything.' It was a relief to finally spit it out.

Will waited.

'Racing management were threatening legal action, forcing the sale of Dad's house to clear the debt. Geordie said he'd pay it all off.'

'Why would Geordie do that for him?' Will looked at the man, fast asleep.

Belinda raised her hands in a gesture of 'who knows?' 'He said that our dads sheared together. He didn't want to be like his old man. Plus, he wanted that site.'

'What did your father say?'

'Dad told him to eff off.'

Belinda and Will gazed at Reg, fast asleep, so small now on the white bed. He looked harmless, but neither would put it past him to sit up like a zombie and wring both their necks in an instant.

'I said to Geordie *just do it.* He said no one else needed to know.'

'Including me?'

'Including you.'

'But why, Bel?' His words were a plea, and now he did look at her.

'You wouldn't understand.' She didn't return his gaze. 'You really wouldn't, Will.'

'I'm going home.' Will stood, suddenly. 'See you later.'

Belinda muttered bye, but if he heard, he didn't acknowledge it. She stayed where she was, sitting stiffly in her chair, watching her father sleeping.

Will had no idea what it was like, she thought. He would never understand the humiliation of having a shitty house full of shitty things and a yard with a rotting car out front. He had no idea of how the embarrassment grew and grew. How you couldn't have sleepovers at your house; how your friends never came to visit; how, in a rage, your dad sometimes threw things through windows, whether they were open or closed. Knowing that people felt sorry for you. *It builds up, all of that. It does.*

Just do it, she'd snarled at Geordie, unwilling or unable to say thanks. And now she recalled how, as if bidden by her anger, the wind had swiped up a small branch and blown it into his face. He'd batted it away, but it left a scratch, a spot of blood.

He'd walked off then. Given her a 'what have I done that's so wrong?' gesture, then climbed into his ute and driven away. Two days later, he was found hanging from a turbine blade.

Belinda looked at her father now and felt a prickle of shame. Geordie wouldn't even have known how patronising he'd sounded when he'd made her the offer. He genuinely would not have known. She should have been less of a spiteful bitch, but there it was.

And now, she remembered how kind Geordie had been, before he'd mentioned paying the debt. He'd said he remembered her mother. Belinda's mum had found him crying in the playground once; it must have been during his prep year. She'd scooped him onto her knee and told him a funny story about a bear. He'd never forgotten it. Geordie had admitted too, very calmly, that he'd been an arsehole in his younger years, and he didn't want to turn into an even bigger one like his father. He was trying to set things right, one way or another. Paying off Reg's gambling debt was one thing he could do for the man who'd been a loyal shearer for his family over the years.

Geordie *had* been a bit of an idiot at school, she recalled – she had a memory of him once teasing one of the Raz kids for their hair and shitty clothes. But she'd been guilty of that too.

And Geordie Pritchard had punched Dean Hookes in the face after he'd pushed her into the hedge on that excursion.

But when he said, 'I always felt sorry for you,' and then that bit about the police wage; even now she felt her blood rise thinking about it. *Pity.* It's worse than a punch.

To tell Will would be to invite unnecessary drama, and yet again, further put a spotlight on the trainwreck that was her childhood. Will didn't need that. She didn't need to recount yet another failed episode in the sordid drama that was her upbringing. What harm would it have done to keep just this one from him? Up until this incident with her dad, it surely held no relevance in the Geordie and Dean cases.

Or did it?

She *should* have told him. And really, she should have told their boss Kelmendri too. He'd want to know about the dog racing, the debts, Geordie's offer. What a total idiot she'd been. She let out a groan of despair.

Her father was waking. One eye opened, followed by the other, two bright lights in the gnarly old face.

'Hello, Dad,' she said.

He mumbled something, and once again she helped him to a drink of water.

'Do you know who did this to you?'

The old man gave a firm shake of his head, his lips pursed together.

'Was it to do with the dogs? Betting?'

A slight pause, and then another headshake.

'What about the Pritchards?' she tried again, though she thought it would be useless.

This time a derisive snort, the faintest of smiles.

It was no good – she could put the man on a rack, threaten to tear him limb from limb, and he wouldn't confess to a thing.

'Good bloke,' Reg said suddenly, his blue eyes focused on her. 'Looks after us.'

'I told Geordie to pay off your debts,' Belinda admitted. 'But now he's dead, we'll have to find the money somehow.'

'Eh?' His face scrunched up in confusion.

Reg's uncharacteristic fragility made her teary. She leaned in to give him a rare kiss goodbye. 'Geordie Pritchard and the money you owe,' she gently reminded him.

'I'm not talking about Pritcharse,' he said, quite clearly. 'I mean Shiny Shoes.'

CHAPTER 33

On the way home, Belinda stopped by her father's house to pick up some clean clothes to take in to the hospital the following day. On entering, she immediately opened all the windows, trying to dispel some of the musty odour of old men and cigarettes. The house held no sentiment for her; she'd been glad to leave it all those years ago, and she'd be glad to leave it today. But even so, it was with some fondness that she looked at the framed newspaper clipping once again, of her father in his shearing days, when he'd won the award for the most ewes in a day. It reminded her of that song 'Click Go the Shears', and she hummed it as she packed him some clean jocks and singlets, a pair of shorts and a top. That song! Every junior kid at Carrabeen College in the nineties had sung it as part of their lessons, and every single time, she'd thought of this newspaper article. She sang a few lines of it now, remembering the one time she'd been truly proud of her dad.

It was the day in primary school when Reg and Alan Crowe had been invited to come in to talk about shearing, as part of their classwork on colonial Australia, and the shearing pastime of the region. Alan spoke carefully and in a manner appropriate to school children. He told them how to catch a sheep, showed them some shears, and explained the role of the rouseabout, or 'rousey' as they were known. It had been a warm day, and during Alan's talk the kids had been sleepy and only mildly attentive. Belinda had been a quiver of nerves at what Reg would say and do, but when his moment came, she'd never been so proud of him. Compared to the formal prissiness of the teachers and the kindly patience of Alan, her father held court, telling stories barely suitable for the primary class, about the hard drinking and the fights and the heat of the shearing shed. He mimicked swatting flies; he told the story of the good-looking rouseys, and the rivalry among the men. He pretended to be a classer, mincing his vowels and sipping tea from a cup. He told them that in the shearing sheds, they turned the music up to eleven.

Her classmates lapped it up.

Reg had even given them a shearing demonstration, dragging up one of the boys as the sheep and pretending to shear him, making all the kids and teachers laugh.

At the end, her teacher thanked him and played that song, 'Click Go the Shears'. Everyone sang along as Reg leaned against the blackboard. He hated any sort of nationalistic shit. The only music Reg listened to now was Willie Nelson, and only then when he was supremely pissed. Everything else, he said, was 'fucken noise'.

Belinda thought that in some ways, she was the same. She could never get sentimental about places or music, whereas Will would have tears in his eyes at the Qantas song. Now, however, driving back home, she began humming the tune.

Click go the shears, boys, click, click, click . . .

Two of the original shearing crew – Doug Hay and her father – were in hospital.

Wide is his blow and his hands move quick.

Belinda turned the car around and headed for Alan Crowe's house.

CHAPTER 34

Alan wasn't at home so, finding his number in her phone, she called him to let him know she wanted to talk. He said he was in the paddocks and would be 'there in thirty'. While she waited, Belinda walked around the back of Alan's house and up the hill, to where she could see the turbines on the other side. It was hard going, with her huge belly. Twice, she needed a short rest. The top of the hill was a gently sloping mound with only a couple of trees, but the view stretched out below – the cleared farmland, low undulating hills, creek beds, and a lake in the distance. This must have been the spot from where Alan first saw Geordie's body hanging. Looking around, she thought she could see where turbine 82 would be.

She shivered, despite the strong northerly, hot and full of dust. All the turbines were spinning, generating power, building up energy reserves, harnessing it. It was incredible, what they could do . . .

She stood watching as a mud-splattered ute made its way slowly along a dirt track at the base of the hill. Alan, she guessed rightly, as his silhouette through the windscreen came into view. He raised a hand in a wave and, returning the gesture, she walked over to where he was idling his vehicle.

'You wanted to see me? Everything okay with your father?'

'So you heard about what happened.'

'Everyone's heard.'

Alan waited as she climbed into the front cabin, then began driving, one finger on the wheel.

'Did you know that Doug thinks he was pushed into that silo?'

'Eh?' Alan turned to her, startled. 'What makes him think that?'

'I don't know – it's what he said to Shirleen.'

Alan looked doubtful.

'And after what happened with Dad, well, I got thinking – maybe you should be careful, Alan.'

'Now, why's that?' The old shearer's voice was amused. 'Because I used to work with the pair of them, a hundred years ago?'

In the comfort of his ute, with the hum of the radio and the pleasant scenery all around, Belinda began to feel a little foolish. 'You could take a few days and go away somewhere, that's all.'

'I'm not going anywhere. This is my place, my land. Your dad would say the same.'

It was true, he would.

'But don't you think it's weird?' she ploughed on. 'Geordie Pritchard, Hugh's son, is killed. Then Doug is pushed down a silo. And now Dad is attacked?'

Alan considered her for a moment. 'I was once great mates with your father, as you know. And as fond of him as I was – as I *am* – that bloke attracted trouble wherever he went.'

'You're saying that Reg was attacked because of something dodgy he was tied up in?'

'I'm not saying anything. Just that your dad had a knack for attracting types you wouldn't want your sister to meet. The greyhound business, for one. It's a rare bookie that's completely clean.'

'Yeah, I know.' Belinda remembered the heated calls, the shouting over the phone, the men in cheap suits standing outside the house, demanding Reg come out – usually when Reg had made himself scarce, camping by the river 'for a few days of peace and quiet'. Once, he came home with a broken nose, and when Belinda asked him how he'd got the injury, Reg had said that it wasn't an injury, it was a message. 'But,' she said after a moment, 'I think Dad has toned down a little bit. He's less abrasive, and now that his son-in-law's a hero, he might even be beginning to trust us coppers.'

Alan raised his eyebrows. 'Well, that's a turn-up.'

'Yeah.'

'And while I'm pouring water on your theory, love, Doug Hay is – let's just say – a big man. It's not difficult to see him losing his balance at the top of the silo.'

Belinda nodded, enjoying being in the ute, driving along the paddocks, watching the darkening fields, the pink hue of the dams.

'It's a nice bit of land you've got here,' Belinda commented, changing the topic.

Alan looked with quiet pride at the surroundings. 'Best thing I ever did, not selling this patch to Hugh Pritchard. He got everything else of mine, but he didn't get this. And there's almost fifty acres of it.'

The peppercorn's leaves swayed in the wind, a delicate throw-rug of dark lace. Two dogs came racing as he parked the ute in front of the house. Red and white geraniums were planted in big pots by the door, giving the place a welcoming feel. His late wife had probably planted them, but they were clearly well looked after by her widower.

A short, loud beep from inside the house made her jump.

'That bloody alarm system Shane gave me!' Alan gave a frustrated growl. 'Goes off at the slightest.'

'How annoying.' It occurred to her that she should take the alarm system for the IT people to look into, but she wasn't about to do that now; the evening had been too pleasant. 'We may need to get it checked out at some stage.'

'Righto.'

Alan climbed slowly out of the vehicle, and Belinda noted his stooped shoulders and wince of pain, both tell-tale signs of a life spent in shearing sheds. His legs, however, were as strong as a man half his age.

'Doug told me you were King of the Mountain three years in a row,' she said as she clambered out of the passenger side.

'Did he now?' Alan turned to her with a shy smile.

The alarm went off again, high and shrill.

'Geez, I would hate that thing,' Belinda commented, moving towards her own car.

Alan sighed. 'It'll be the death of me.'

CHAPTER 35

Marit rented a house fifteen kilometres out of town, and as Will pulled into her drive, he noted the mass of trees that stretched for miles at the back of her home.

'She rents a house owned by a woman who lives in Barwon Heads,' Tammy had explained prior to his visit. 'The woman grew up on the place, the daughter of farmers who, for whatever reason, chose not to raze their entire land. There's twenty acres of original bushland there, and they're hoping to keep it in some sort of trust, so the trees can never be chopped down. Marit's undertaking a count of some endangered bird while she's there.'

Understandably, Tammy hadn't wanted to join Will on his visit to her former girlfriend. The two were on uneasy terms, and Will, feeling protective of his colleague, had to check his own defensive attitude towards the woman he'd met only once before. Ever since he'd read Belinda's notes on Millicent, written down from her chat with the journalist, he'd been wanting to talk with the environmentalist, but Dean's death and the issues at the school had got in the way.

Before he'd left for Marit's place, there'd been a sudden downpour of rain, heavy pellets ramming into the warm ground, creating explosive little puffs every time they hit the dirt. Now as the rain eased, a slight humidity filled the atmosphere as tiny droplets fell, landing on the windows like silver earrings. The trees buzzed with life.

The bushland on the way to Marit's house may have been beautiful, but the small house was not and appeared to be falling down in some parts. It looked as if she was living in the one section that was habitable. He walked up to the property, unsure where the front door was. An overflowing garden revealed a small pond, thick with mosquitos. The buzzing around it was so loud it took him a moment to register that there was faint music coming from the back of the ramshackle building. He called out hello, and Marit appeared, in an over-sized dress and purple gum boots.

'Come around the back,' she said. 'I'm having a break from writing a grant and I've just poured myself a wine. Would you like one?'

'No, thanks.' He made his way around on a broken path to where there was a little wooden table and chairs set up. 'Nice place,' he said, to be polite.

'My friend owns it,' Marit answered. 'I can't afford to live on the coast, and I like my space, so this is perfect for my work.'

Marit was a small woman, brimming with energy, but there were rings under her eyes and a croak in her voice. Perhaps she wasn't feeling as good about the break-up as Tammy imagined.

'And what exactly *is* your work?' he asked.

'I'm a partner in a non-profit; we work on environmental issues, advocating for clean energy, fighting against fossil fuels, et cetera, et cetera.' She gave a wry smile. 'But you know all of this, I already told your wife. We help fundraise, we work with community groups, we agitate for change.'

'What do you mean by *agitate*?' Will waved away a hovering insect.

'It doesn't mean killing someone, if that's what you're asking.'

'And yet . . .' Will wondered how much he should reveal. Perhaps his next line of questions should wait till they were at the station, though in this environment, among the greenery and the bush, Marit might be more open. 'And yet, you *have* been implicated in the death of someone before.'

For a moment, there was a silence so deep it seemed even the mosquitoes had stopped buzzing. There was almost no wind at all.

'That was a long time ago.'

'The man's family don't see it that way.'

Marit put down her wine glass hurriedly, making it clatter on the table. 'What have you heard?' she said, her voice rising. 'What do you mean?'

'A local journo saw your photo in the paper after a Farms for Future rally. He did some digging. And he already knew about Millicent.'

'Everything I've done is legal,' Marit said in a rush. 'There's no point in bringing it all up now.'

'It's not a question of it being legal.' Will spoke gently. 'It's a question of you lying to us.'

'I never lied.'

'By omission, which is a crime in itself.' He wasn't totally sure if that was true. Belinda would know. 'Tell me the truth,' he said, keeping the same, even tone. 'What happened exactly?'

Marit's voice wavered at first, then strengthened as she began to speak. 'As you know, it was in Millicent, Tasmania, where the old-growth forests are. Some of the trees there have been growing for thousands of years. They were cutting them down.'

'Who were?'

'The loggers.' She looked directly at him. 'Ten years ago, under Hugh Pritchard's direction; it was one of his companies. They'd come in with their tractors and chainsaws and the helicopters, which dropped chemicals to burn away the remaining vegetation. A total tragedy.'

'Marit, what happened?'

'We'd put spikes around the base of the trees, and one of the loggers, who'd arrived early the next morning, died when his axe hit the spike and it rebounded back at him.'

Actually, the man had bled to death after the lower half of his arm was amputated.

'There were press reports that it took hours to get him to a hospital. That you'd waited, while he lay dying.'

'That's not true,' Marit said, turning away. 'We did everything we could. Everything.'

Will let the 'everything' hang in the air. The accusation that while the man lay bleeding, the three activists had argued about what to do, was impossible to prove now.

'After that, and the court case which followed, I left Tasmania and changed my name, even though no charges were ever laid. My real name is—'

'Margot Thurling. You're from South Yarra, you went to Melbourne Girls Grammar.'

'That's right, I'm a rich kid, like you,' she added. 'Believe me, it takes one to know one.'

Will shrugged. He was done with trying to pretend he was someone he wasn't.

'But that doesn't mean I care any less for the environment,' Marit continued, 'or that my views are less worthy than anyone else's.'

'I understand that,' Will said. 'But your livelihood is not dependent on farming, or logging, or mining. You can afford to hold these views, to spend sixty days living up a tree or whatever.'

Marit held her hands up. 'Sue me, I went to a nice school! I'd be able to hire a good lawyer, so I'd probably win. I'm aware of my privilege, blah blah blah. Every day I'm reminded of it. What do you want, for me to whip myself in the streets? I was twenty-two! Anyway, my family doesn't speak to me, so I'm not sure how much of a soft landing I actually have any more.'

Will felt little sympathy for the woman. He could admire her resolve and her commitment to saving the planet, but she'd lied about her previous connection to the Pritchards and, he suspected, in doing so, she may have failed to prevent another death.

'What made you come here, to Carrabeen?'

'Geordie found out that after Millicent it was hard for me to get work anywhere. I'd studied my arse off in environmental research and clean energy, but no one would hire me. My research area was helping rural communities transition to clean energy, but I believe Hugh Pritchard had somehow let everyone know that I wasn't worth hiring. The big energy companies listened to people like him.'

'Who were you with the night Geordie died?' Will asked it abruptly, suddenly tired of her. Of people lying and exaggerating and imagining their own importance. 'The day before, you'd been arguing with him – but what happened after that?'

'Nothing,' she said. 'I didn't leave here all night. I told your wife this.'

'I know, but I'm asking you again now. Can anyone corroborate that you were here the whole night?'

Marit was silent.

'Marit?'

'He can't corroborate it now, but Dean Hookes was here. All night.' At the mention of his name, Marit's lower lip trembled.

'Dean Hookes?'

'We weren't friends as such, but he used to come to the anti-turbine meetings, and I got to know him. This place was a kind of base for the clean energy group in town. So yes, Dean was here that night.'

Will drummed his hand on the arm of the wooden chair. 'Why did you not tell us this earlier?'

'What difference would it have made?' She seemed genuinely puzzled. 'I didn't think it mattered.'

'And you still didn't think so after Dean was murdered?'

Marit sniffed. 'I *did* think about coming to you, but again, what for? The fact that Dean was here on the night Geordie died wasn't going to change anything about either man's death. It would have been no use, and anyway, I didn't do anything!'

'We have two murder investigations underway, and now we know that both men had associations with you. You absolutely should have come to us with this information.'

'But I *couldn't*.' Marit spoke quickly now, her confidence rising. 'If I came to you, or if I told Tammy, I'd have you all looking into my background, and then it would have come out about my past, and then these grants, these crucial environmental actions, everything I'm fighting for, would be in jeopardy. My work is too important!'

'And Dean might be alive.' It was a spiteful thing to say, but Will couldn't help himself. A great environmentalist she may be, but that didn't make her a good person.

Marit looked a little shocked at his comment, and she flushed before she spoke again. 'Dean was a real flirt, but that night he wasn't here for me. I didn't like it much, but it was only a couple of times . . . and they stayed in the back room. It's none of my business what people do in their private lives. I don't care.'

'What – who?'

'That night, Dean was with Lucinda Pritchard the whole time.'

Half an hour later, walking back to his car, Will heard a bird call in the tree above. A gang-gang cockatoo. He held his breath; the rare gang-gang! He was sure of it. It was the red crest, like a feather duster. *Well now. That's something.*

For one evening, Dean and Lucinda had been protected from prying eyes, able to spend the night together in peace. Marit's place was both a refuge for rare birds and secret lovers, and a place of deceit.

'So that means Lucinda is off the hook?' Tammy said, her mouth turned down.

'Looks like it.'

They were sitting in Will and Belinda's kitchen, eating nachos.

'How do we know Marit's telling the truth?' Belinda added.

'Why would she lie?' Tammy said. 'We've already discovered her greatest secret. She only ever cared about covering for herself. Now you've found out about her past with Millicent and that logger who was killed, she wouldn't need to worry about anyone else.'

Will took his glasses off and stared at the lenses. Belinda immediately took them from him, wiping them on her top, polishing them with care. She always did it better than him.

'There you go.' She handed them back with a smile.

He looked at her, grateful. Already, he regretted the way he'd spoken to her at the hospital. She had her reasons for not telling him about Geordie's offer to Reg. They weren't always clear to him, but he trusted that they weren't malicious. Perhaps that was enough.

'There's video evidence of them both arriving at Marit's house and being greeted by her, and then of Lucinda leaving just before six am,' he said. 'I guess that's when she would have started to get the phone calls about Geordie, although she wasn't sure it was him till she saw him up on the turbine.'

Will remembered now; Lucinda had been wearing a strapless dress and heeled sandals. She'd come straight from Marit's house after a night with Dean.

'Where did the video evidence come from?' Tammy frowned. 'Why would Marit have cameras outside her home?'

'To check for endangered birds. There's a nest she keeps tabs on via the camera. It's part of her research; you can even watch it in real time. There are cameras up and down the driveway. Not one car leaves during any part of the night.'

'Real-time videos? Who would watch that? How boring,' Tammy said with disdain.

But it was true. Avid bird watchers, twitchers from all over the world, logged in to see a livestream of the gang-gangs returning to their nest. They probably wouldn't be interested in the humans in the images – Marit wandering about checking the cameras, tending to the garden; Lucinda and Dean smoking on the veranda, drinking wine and then walking hand in hand back into the house. All hours accounted for.

'Kelmendri will be pleased,' Belinda said, glumly. 'His precious Lucinda Pritchard off the hook.'

'And now,' Tammy said, 'we're back to square one.'

CHAPTER 36

Will stood up, stretched, then went to the kitchen and made himself a drink. It was weird to think that soon he'd be back in a Melbourne station full of colleagues and gossip and action. Here, it was so quiet that at times you could hear the wind outside, picking up the leaves and rattling the bins.

One of the things he'd miss about Carrabeen, Will mused, as he sipped his coffee and looked out the doors of the police station, was the way townspeople sometimes dropped by for a chat. When he'd first arrived, it had been odd to have a person lean over the counter and tell him about the rain due that afternoon. Was he supposed to do something about it? Did the person want to make a complaint? But no, every so often a local would come in just to tell him something about the tennis club draw or maybe a problem with their hips. He'd actually started to enjoy these moments, look forward to them even.

So when a skinny woman with hair like a ruined haystack entered the police station and began gossiping about the royal family, he settled in for a chat. He quite liked the royals, and wasn't afraid to admit it. However, after five minutes Will held up a hand for her to stop. There was only so much he could hear about the way Diana used to dance by herself in the palace. 'I'm sorry, but I've got a meeting to go to,' he lied. 'Can I help you with something specific?'

'Where's the lady who works here? The one about to have a baby?'

'Sergeant Burney,' Will said firmly. 'She's at home today.'

'Pity. Dave and me, we read a local paper and recognised that bloke that was hung.'

'What bloke?' Will leaned over the counter.

'The Pritchard bloke. He was down the creek with us on the night they say he was killed. If you give me a lift back there, and you bring the pregnant lady down, we can have a chat all about it with Dave.'

Either it was a new one, or an extension of an old one, but Belinda didn't recognise the first caravan she walked past, with its grimy orange annexe held up with one pole and a long stick, and dirty lace curtains. Every time Belinda visited, it seemed the camper community had grown.

'I could have come on my own,' Will said, as they parked on a stretch of dirt nearby. 'You're not even meant to be on duty.' He'd already dropped Val off, before returning to town to collect Belinda.

'It's okay, I like it when we work together.'

'Me too.' He brought his fingers together in a hashtag 'me too'. She did the same.

Was that politically incorrect? Maybe. Probably. Right now, she didn't care; she was just happy they were back in each other's good books. She and Will, they would always have differences – what couple didn't? It would perhaps have been easier for them both to have married someone else, someone who understood more fully where each had come from. But, Belinda thought as she walked alongside Will, what was class when there was connection? It was nothing. It was rendered as superficial and manufactured as a plastic wand.

David stood in front of the firepit, arms crossed like a body-guard. 'Val read that article in the paper, about the rich bloke getting hung on the turbine. It was murder, eh?'

They must have been the last people in the world to know. 'Yes.'

'Well,' David said, his feet doing a little dance in the dirt, 'he was down here the night of, drinking.'

Belinda shook her head. Will had already told her this, but it didn't make her any less cross. 'Bloody hell, David, why didn't you tell me this last time I was here?'

'Didn't know about any of that then.' The man shrugged. 'If I did, I would've said. Val here will back me up.' His face lightened. 'Val!'

Her head popped out of the van like a jack-in-the-box.

'Eh?' The woman looked at the two detectives as if she'd forgotten why they'd come.

'Telling the officers how that rich bloke, Geordie Whatsit, was down here drinking on Sunday night.'

'Yup,' Val said, looking at Belinda. 'Like I told your mate here' – she nodded at Will – 'we only found out he died when we read the paper.'

'You don't watch the telly?'

'*Friends*,' Val said. 'We only watch *Friends*.'

'Fucken Ross,' David muttered.

Had David and Val orchestrated the conversation? Belinda wondered. There was a touch of pantomime about the whole scene.

'Did either of you talk to him when he came down here?' she asked.

David chuckled, then spat on the ground. 'He was *all talk*, that bloke. Wanted to spruik some new housing he was going to build, let us all live in it, dirt cheap.'

Val threw her empty can on the ground. 'They all say that. Then it's the last we hear of them; they never follow through. Motherfuckers.'

'What time did he leave?'

'Dunno. Nine? Early,' David said. 'He left with that other lady, the big one who brings the food sometimes. I told you about *her*, didn't I?' He looked pleased with himself.

Belinda felt a ringing in her ears. 'Was her name Julie Smith?'

Dave shrugged again. 'I dunno. Like I said before, we just call her The Ghost.'

'You don't know her real name?'

'Oh yeah, I do.' Val was leaning so far out of the van, Belinda wondered if her feet were glued to the floor. 'You only had to ask. But I don't know if it's her real name. Lots of people around here have other names. Like, my name's not even Val. I just liked the sound of it. So it might not be her real name.'

Belinda wanted to shake the woman. *What was her name?*

'Orla,' Val said abruptly, as if she'd heard her thought. 'Means Golden Princess, she told me. But she didn't look like a princess to me. You wouldn't see Princess Di chugging back the lady cans like she was.'

'*À votre santé!*' David called out suddenly, with an excellent accent.

'We called her The Ghost because she scared us out of our wits. Didn't she, Davey? As in Witts, like Orla Witts. Get it?'

'Val, are you absolutely positive that it was Orla Witts, the principal from the school?'

'And what was she drinking? Lady cans?'

'Yeah, we call 'em lady cans, or bitch pops.'

'Eh?'

'Raspberry shit, lolly drinks . . .'

'Right. And Val, are you sure that she and Geordie Pritchard left together?'

'Yeah. And he wasn't happy about it, I can tell you.'

'Why?'

'She was telling everyone about how much she hated those turbines! Said they'd ruin the place. Her house is smack-bang in front of them. She has massive windows that look right at them!' Val shook her head, in apparent disbelief that someone would build turbines in Orla Witts' way. 'I mean, I can see what she means – it'd drive you crazy.'

Orla! Belinda thought. A secret turbine dissenter. In education circles, she wouldn't have ever dared to say that out loud. Except, of course, when she was extremely pissed.

'And I'll tell you another thing.' Val was out of the van now, a new can in her hand, shaking it like a cocktail. 'It wasn't no fucking accident Diana died.'

CHAPTER 37

Belinda called the station as she and Will hurried to their car. 'Tammy, we've got two witnesses down at the river who saw Geordie and Orla leave a party together the night he was murdered. We'll need you down at the campsite; see if you can find anything there related to either of them. There might be other people who can recall more than what I was just told.'

By the time Belinda and Will arrived at the school, Will had called the Ballarat office and spoken briefly to Kelmendri, who'd sounded more weary than excited that they'd made a breakthrough.

Bloody Kelmendri, Belinda thought, still resentful at his role in helping Troy Haydar get the Investigations job over her. His reference on the man's application would have been a game-changer. And still no one had bothered to let her know she was unsuccessful!

School was still in session, and Belinda had no wish to disrupt a class by storming in and demanding to speak to the principal.

So she was relieved when a rather dishevelled-looking Tayla Schultz told her that the principal was in her office, talking to Andrew Kent.

Far from being excited or curious about the arrival of the detectives, Tayla calmly wrote them up in the visitor's book, before escorting them to Orla. 'She's still in her old office,' the young woman explained. 'With all that's been happening, she hasn't even had the chance to move the rest of her stuff!' Tayla knocked, and then opened the door.

The two teachers were leaning over a desk, studying a series of drawings. Both straightened in surprise when Belinda and Will entered.

'We're looking at the plans for the new building,' Andrew explained, confused but polite. 'How can we help you?'

Orla stood beside him, frowning.

'Can we speak to Orla in private, please?' Will asked, which Belinda thought was a bit too considerate. She had no compunctions about interviewing the woman in front of her deputy.

'Of course,' Andrew said, hesitating. 'Unless . . . Orla? Do you want me to stay?'

'I'm fine with Andrew being here.' Orla pulled back her shoulders and sniffed. 'What's this about?'

'What were you doing last Sunday evening, the night of Geordie Pritchard's death?'

'I was at home alone, catching up on work. Andrew was at a conference in Ballarat, and we were meeting Monday morning to discuss his presentation. I wanted to be prepared, so I was reading over the papers he'd sent through on Sunday.'

'That's true,' Andrew butted in. 'You can check the papers I sent through – Orla had done all the reading.'

There was a pause. Will cleared his throat.

'We have a number of witnesses who report seeing you with Geordie Pritchard on the night he died,' he said plainly. 'Is that correct?'

The principal blanched, before quickly recovering. 'I saw a lot of people, there were a lot of—'

'People at the party?' Belinda finished for her. 'You were down with the campers, weren't you, by the river?'

Andrew frowned. 'Orla?'

Orla gave him a blank stare.

'And you left the same time as Geordie,' Will added. 'Why didn't you come forward with that information?'

'I don't think this is the right place to be questioning . . .' Andrew stuttered. 'What is this all about?'

Belinda changed tack. 'Our witnesses say you were drinking heavily at the party; beer, wine, cans. Do you like UDLs, Orla? Lady cans?'

The woman curled her lip.

'What witnesses?' Andrew looked about him, as if they might be hiding somewhere in the room.

Undeterred, Belinda continued. 'Orla, it seems quite convenient that you and the other staff are the ones searching bags for the so-called school thief. Then you're drinking the findings. It's not a good look for the local principal to be buying up booze in town, is it? This is much better.' She rubbed her hands over her stomach and frowned.

Orla slammed her hand on the table and everyone, apart from Belinda, jumped. 'You know I've got a problem with alcohol, Sergeant, *you know*! How dare you manipulate me here, in my workplace!'

'Just answer the question.' Belinda made her voice hard. 'Do you confiscate alcohol from student bags and then drink it yourself?'

Orla looked away. 'Once,' the principal muttered eventually. 'Or twice.'

'Orla!' Andrew exclaimed.

'We'd like to search this office,' Will said. 'There may be stolen goods in here.'

'Pencil cases? English books?' Orla gave a brief laugh. 'You will probably find those things in here, yes.'

'What about alcohol? Stuff you've taken from kids' bags?' Belinda shot back. 'Just because they shouldn't have it, doesn't mean that you should keep it.'

'You'll need a warrant to search this office,' Andrew replied quickly, glancing at his colleague. 'Orla's not hiding anything . . . she's already told you enough.'

The principal shot him a grateful look. 'It might surprise you to know, but me being an alcoholic in my past is not going to shock Andrew. We have no secrets.'

'Only, Andrew didn't seem to know about you stealing from children's bags.'

'I'm not a thief,' Orla said, fast. 'On occasion we have checked bags after reports of theft, but I'm not the culprit Julie keeps going on about. There *is* a thief here, but it's not me.'

Andrew took a step back, so that he was staring directly into his boss's face. 'Orla, do you need a lawyer?'

The woman pulled herself up to her full height. 'Yes, thank you, Andrew. I think I do.'

'The time is four-fifty pm on December ninth. Present in the room is Orla Witts, her lawyer Raymond Derler, Investigative Officer Lisa Flittson and myself, Senior Sergeant Belinda Burney. Can you please state that you understand that anything you say during this interview may be used as evidence in court.'

Belinda found it difficult to contain her excitement. Because here she was, interviewing someone who, at this particular point in time, was the first real suspect in the Geordie Pritchard murder case. This was what she loved police work for! It was annoying that Lisa was here too, of course. They were around the same age, but Lisa was higher in rank – once again, the thought niggled: how the hell did she even get that job?

Outside, the cypress was being blown to the west, its dying branches hanging like broken limbs. *That tree really, really needs to be chopped down*, she thought, not for the first time.

Lisa leaned in slightly, so that she could be easily heard on tape. 'Ms Witts, can you tell us what you were doing at the campsite on the evening of Geordie Pritchard's death, Sunday the first of December?'

Principal Witts looked out the window. She'd wiped her makeup off and had removed her blazer. The effect was startling. It was as if she'd shed her power along with it. Now she seemed timid, almost bereft. 'No comment.'

'How did you get to the campsite? It's quite a long way from your house. Did you drive?'

'No comment.'

Her lawyer gave a smug smile at his notepad.

'If we found you drove, you'll have been in violation of your drink-driving charge,' Lisa pointed out. 'There are serious penalties for that, including a possible prison sentence.'

A startled look crossed the woman's face. 'I wasn't driving,' she said.

'Perhaps riding your e-bike then?' Belinda raised her eyebrows.

Lisa cut in, 'Because that will also incur a hefty fine, if you'd been drinking at the time.'

Belinda shifted on her seat, annoyed at her senior colleague. Lisa might be correct, but the threat of punishment was hardly going to inspire Orla to talk.

'Orla,' she said reasonably, 'it's best you tell us all you know. If things don't go right for you here, it might be difficult for you to continue your teaching career.'

Orla's face flushed red, and Belinda knew she'd jabbed at a sore point. Like her, the woman loved her job.

The principal sat up in her seat, straightening her shoulders. 'No comment,' she said, her voice faltering.

Belinda asked again, this time more gently. 'Orla, how *did* you get to the river that night?'

There was silence, before Orla's lawyer cut in, urging her not to say any more and warning the police officers that his client would be speaking no further.

'I think you drove down to the river,' Lisa said, looking at her notes.

'I didn't drive,' Orla said in a flat tone. 'On occasion, I'd ride my bike down there.'

'So, you rode your bike there that evening?' Belinda asked. 'Your e-bike?'

'Yes. I went back and got it after school on Monday.'

Belinda's face gave nothing away. 'And then, after you rode there, we think you left with Geordie and you killed him.'

'So, what?' Orla looked up. 'You're saying I met Geordie down the creek, and after I'd ridden there on my *bike*, then I *drove* with him somewhere – in whose car, by the way? – then killed him and strung him up to a *turbine blade*? Ridiculous. And for what reason?'

'That is yet to be ascertained,' Belinda said, more firmly than she felt. 'But you are under suspicion of murder.'

'I did not kill anyone.' Orla, too, was resolute.

'Have you ever been violent with anyone, Ms Witts?'

'What is this?' the lawyer exploded. 'You don't have to answer that, Orla.'

'No, I haven't.' Orla stared directly at Belinda, defiant.

'When was the last time you saw Geordie Pritchard?'

'Near the river, at the party.'

Her lawyer raised his eyes to the ceiling and let out a hefty sigh.

'And do you remember talking to him?' Belinda asked.

'Naturally I would have said hello.' Orla pursed her lips.

'And when was the last time you saw him *before* that night?'

'At the school, I think. He came for a meeting about the building. A week before he died? I'd have to check my calendar.'

Belinda nodded and jotted that down in her notepad. 'Would you say you are against the new turbine development, Orla?'

The woman gave her a glare. 'Really? You think I'd murder someone because I don't like the look of the turbines?'

'Please answer the question.'

'I moved here for the quiet, for the beauty. These low rolling hills, the winding creeks, the sunsets and the vast sky – there's something about this landscape. It gets to you. But now, when I look out my window all I see is huge machines. It might sound ridiculous, but it actually hurts to look at them.' Orla touched her chest. 'It does.'

There was a short silence.

'And,' the principal continued, 'I can't honestly see how they are going to halt the global climate crisis. I mean, come on – do you think they will?' She looked at both women in turn.

Lisa went to say something but then shut her mouth.

'We're not here to discuss climate change,' Belinda said.

Orla gave a short laugh. 'I don't like the turbines. But did I hate them enough to *kill* someone? No – of course not.'

Lisa cleared her throat. 'Our witnesses say you were drinking heavily at the party.'

'Who are these witnesses?' The lawyer spoke up. 'People who live down the river, the homeless people? Are you sure they are reliable?'

'*Did* you steal alcohol from student bags,' Lisa continued, 'and then drink it at the river that night?'

'I might have drunk one or two of the cans there, but that does not – it does *not* – mean I killed Geordie.'

'Orla.' Belinda aimed for a softer tone. 'You must know that we need to work out what happened to Geordie on the night he died. We now learn that you and he were at the same party, and that people saw you leave together. We need to know what happened after that.'

'I don't know if I left with Geordie, I can't remember.' Orla was staring out the window now. 'I must have blacked out. Perhaps someone gave me a lift.' She looked back at the detectives. '*I don't know.* I woke up fully clothed in my own bed, hungover and unable to remember everything.' When no one spoke, she went on: 'It happens. Not often, but it does.'

Belinda wrote that down. *It happens.*

'*But,*' Orla rallied, 'I can categorically say that I did *not* kill Geordie Pritchard.'

'How can you say that if you can't remember?' Lisa asked.

If she was that trashed, she probably wasn't capable, Belinda thought.

Orla's lawyer touched his client lightly on the arm, and she drew back. 'You don't have to say anything,' he said.

'We have a few more questions,' Belinda said. 'Then you can go.'

'Yes?' Orla drummed her fingers on the table.

'Where were you in the hours between six-thirty am and eight am Saturday morning?'

'Oh!' Orla shook her head. 'Now you're accusing me of *Dean's* murder! You really are desperate, aren't you?'

'Where were you at that time, Orla?'

'Asleep, like a normal person. Then getting ready for work. I arrived at school just after eight am; you can check.'

'Can anyone vouch for you? That you were at home between six am and eight am?'

'I live alone,' Orla said. 'So, no. No one can vouch for me.'

'Perhaps Dean found out you killed Geordie.' Lisa leaned in. 'And then you had to get rid of him too. It wouldn't have been too difficult for you; you knew where he went running. You could have lain in wait.'

'I mentored Dean! I *liked* him!'

'And then after you killed him,' Lisa continued, 'you rode along the track again – perhaps you left something incriminating there?' She looked at Belinda. 'Or at his house? Wasn't Orla there too?'

'This is pathetic,' Orla snapped. 'I refuse to say any more.'

'Thank you, Orla,' Belinda said, closing her notebook. 'That's all from me.'

'And from me,' Lisa added.

Orla scoffed and sat back. 'It's like an episode of *The Two Ronnies.*'

The lawyer began collecting his papers. 'Okay,' he said. 'My client won't be talking any further.' Without looking at anyone, Orla followed him out of the room.

When they'd gone, Lisa let out a long whistle. 'The principal of the school, can you believe it? And who the hell are those Ronnies?'

Belinda stood and stretched. 'What do you think about her story?'

Lisa shrugged. 'I think Orla rode her bike to the party, got shitfaced, and then went back to her house with Geordie, killing him at some point during the night.'

'Why?'

'Why? If she was a man, you wouldn't ask that. Shitfaced men kill women all the time.'

It was difficult to argue with that one. 'But Orla *isn't* a man.'

'Okay then,' Lisa surmised. 'Orla hates turbines, we know that. They ruin her view. And she is a drunk, prone to getting nasty. You know that all too well. She might have killed Geordie by accident after a verbal altercation, or maybe she came on to him back at her house, and he rejected her, so she hit him with something. Then, after she'd sobered a bit, she strung him up on the turbine to make it look as if it was an anti-wind farm nutter who did it.'

Belinda considered Lisa's theory. It wasn't *bad*, necessarily. Orla was maybe strong enough for the job – if she used the climb-assist, anyway – and she'd have seen how the turbines worked on the excursion. Perhaps the two of them were having an affair. She toyed with the idea, not liking it.

'I don't know,' she said slowly. 'But we should have her office, car and home searched.'

'I'm on it.' Lisa pulled out her phone.

Belinda wasn't as convinced as Lisa that they'd found Geordie's killer. But there was one thing she felt sure of: at least some part of Orla Witts' story was a lie.

CHAPTER 38

When the warrant came through, hours later, Will was pleased to see Kelmendri had agreed they should conduct the search of Orla's home and the school straightaway. It would be far better at night, rather than disrupting school the following day. Even so, with the school lights on, and the presence of two police cars in the front car park, he had no doubt that by morning Carrabeen would be abuzz.

Belinda had insisted on coming, which Will was far from happy about. Four days left till maternity leave, and she was still working around the clock. His old anxiety that she would put either herself or the baby in danger resurfaced, and they'd argued about it. But his wife was determined. The school was always *my area*, she'd said, and he couldn't disagree with that. Tammy was at Orla's house with other members of a search team sent from Ballarat.

Low clouds covered the moon, so it was difficult at first to make out Andrew Kent as he walked towards them. 'Is Orla all right?' he'd asked pitifully. Giving no answer, Will told the man to wait in reception.

Lisa put her gloves on and motioned for the two officers who'd joined them from Ballarat to do the same. Belinda, already gloved up, moved to follow them up the porch steps, when Lisa stopped her. 'Sorry, Belinda. It's just the team from Investigations.'

'What? Why?' Belinda scowled.

'Kelmendri's orders. Plus, we don't need everyone. Will won't be joining us either. You can wait here or watch from the hallway.'

'The hallway?' Belinda seethed. 'We've been part of this investigation from the start!'

'Orders, Belinda,' Lisa said, holding up her hands. 'Not much I can do.'

Belinda shot her a furious look and turned away. Will tried to catch her eye, but she crossed her arms and refused to engage.

So, Will and Belinda left Andrew in the cold reception room and stood sentry outside Orla's old office, reluctantly observing. Lisa first opened the desk drawer and found a vape, and then in the drawer underneath one bottle of vodka and two cans of Southern Comfort.

'Maybe it's her own,' Will said doubtfully.

'Southern Comfort?' Belinda shook her head in disbelief as she stood, leaning in from the room's doorway. 'If those cans haven't come from a Year Ten's bag, I'll shotgun them both right now.'

One member of Investigations whistled when he opened a cabinet on one side of the room. There, behind some Year Eleven science books and a manual on disaster procedures in Victorian schools, were at least a dozen UDL cans of varying flavours.

A six-pack of beer sat alongside them, a broken phone jammed in between.

'Party time,' Belinda said, and Will saw the baby kick.

They'd photographed and documented everything – including the hangover remedies of three paracetamol and the Berocca – when Lisa declared they were done. Despite what Orla was being accused of, Will felt a crushing sense of sorrow for the principal, who was about to lose it all. His eyes kept going back to a trophy – a golden ball on a tall stem. The golden princess with the golden ball. He looked at it now in resignation.

Andrew caught his look. 'Oh yes, Orla's always so proud to hand it out to the winning teams each year. That trophy's been with the school since it started, almost sixty years ago. It'll be pride of place once she finally moves into her new office.'

Belinda stared at it too for a long moment.

Will nodded absently and looked around at the office, where now the search team had been through most of the papers in the cupboards and opened all the folders. It seemed there wasn't any further contraband left to find. His phone pinged. Tammy and the team at Orla's house hadn't found anything of interest.

'That's odd,' Andrew said suddenly.

'What?' Will asked.

'I'm not sure.' He gave a slight shake of his head, then looked down at the hideous red and orange rug near the desk. 'It doesn't matter.'

'The rug used to be under her desk.' It was Tayla who spoke, from behind the police officers in the doorway. Will hadn't heard her arrive. 'It's been moved out a bit.'

'So it has!' Andrew's face cleared. 'Good observation, Tayla. I remember it was a gift from her mother, but she didn't like it, so she put it under the desk. I don't think it will go in her new office.'

'Why would she move it so that it's more visible?'

Why indeed?

'Pull the rug,' Will said, and Belinda, catching on, took a sharp intake of breath.

Lisa carefully lifted the heavy rug from the floorboards, first with her boot, and then, with another officer's help, by rolling it up. It was a big rug, heavy and square.

In contrast, the bloodstain it covered was round, and rather small.

CHAPTER 39

Inspector Kelmendri, sitting behind his desk in Ballarat, was ecstatic. 'Great work, great work, everyone!' He paused. 'You too,' he said, looking briefly at Belinda. 'Great work all round. We've finally got a break.'

Tammy flushed with pride, smiling back at him. She had been super keen to make the trip to Ballarat with Belinda after the events of the previous evening. Will, meanwhile, was content to remain at the station handling all the local interest, though he'd promised to pick her up later once the meeting was finished. Tammy, who had a date in Ballarat that night, was more cheerful than she'd been in months. On the drive there, she'd been rabbiting on about the moment they found the bloodstain, and then the moment shortly after when Belinda had pointed to the trophy as the possible murder weapon.

'The DNA from the bloodstain is definitely Geordie Pritchard's,' Kelmendri continued. 'And Orla's prints were all over the trophy.'

'Well,' Belinda said after a pause, 'she did hand it out to the winning team, and then brought it back to the office.'

The boss ignored her. 'Plus, we know she hated those turbines. It's adding up, but we do need more evidence.'

'She was so drunk she could barely remember being at the river,' Belinda said. 'Can someone that trashed really get a body up a turbine, even with the climb-assist and the lift?'

'Alcoholic blackouts aren't rare,' Tammy said, trying to be helpful. 'Particularly for women. Plus, people can black out and still function, and even look sober!' There was a pause. 'I did a course in alcohol and crime last year,' she added.

'Thanks,' Belinda said flatly, unconvinced. 'And what about Dean?'

'She killed him when he found out she killed Geordie in a drunken rage,' Tammy chimed in. 'That's the most logical explanation.'

'Logical?' Belinda looked annoyed at Tammy. 'We've barely looked into Dean's death yet – the focus seems to be all on Geordie.'

Kelmendri sighed.

'There's more to this,' Belinda said. 'Don't you think that we're jumping to conclusions without much evidence?'

Kelmendri stared at her. 'Orla Witts is, for the moment, and I repeat – *for the moment* – our chief suspect for both murders. The trophy's size and weight are consistent with the head injuries sustained by Pritchard and Hookes. I expect that the coroner will confirm that in a day or so. It was you who pointed it out in the first place.'

It *was* Belinda who'd suggested that the trophy in Orla's office, smooth and round and heavy, fitted the description in the coroner's report for the possible murder weapon in both cases.

But that didn't mean she was pinning Orla for the job. Not right now, anyway.

Belinda turned to Tammy. 'How do you think Orla got Geordie to her office? And then how did she get him to the turbines after she'd killed him?'

'She must have driven them to her office where she killed him, and then she drove him to the turbines.'

'But you searched the car. There was nothing in it. No sign of Geordie.'

'Ever thought that she'd had a clean-up? It happens all the time.'

Belinda narrowed her eyes at her younger colleague. Tammy was really getting on her nerves.

'Well then' – she tried a new tack – 'the skin fragment on the rope. That wasn't a match for Orla, was it?'

'No,' Kelmendri admitted. 'But as you know, Senior Sergeant, it could have been any number of people who came into contact with the rope. Investigations are not always one hundred per cent in terms of the evidence found.'

'And definitely *not* in this case.'

'Enough!' Their boss stood, his huge stomach bursting from his shirt, hairy flesh poking out between the buttons, reminding her of the kids' book *Grug*.

'Orla is our chief suspect, so all eyes on her for the time being. But of course,' he said, glancing at Belinda, 'we have to look into others. Keep on digging into Dean Hookes' background, what he was up to, his finances. I want to know everything. On the matter of the attempted murder of Reg Burney' – now he avoided Belinda's eyes – 'Ballarat Investigations will take over all interviews. Personal issues aside, this is, from initial enquiries at least, a likely payback attack linked to dog-racing debts. Not altogether uncommon, unfortunately. Ballarat is mad for the dogs.'

For a moment Kelmendri's gaze rested on a photograph of his wife and adult children, standing in front of an ocean so blue it was difficult to look at. He was *almost* there, Belinda thought. She could hardly blame him for trying to hurry things up.

'But perhaps I could make enquiries into the attack on Reg Burney?' It wasn't arguing back, and she'd kept it professional by using her father's full name.

Kelmendri waved them to the door. 'Give it a rest, Sergeant. Go and have your baby.'

'"Go and have your baby", *seriously*? "Go and have your baby"?' Belinda's voice rose as she marched down the street, away from the car Will had only just parked outside the station. 'Who the hell does Kelmendri think he is?'

'Our boss,' Will answered mildly, as he hurried to catch up. 'And anyway, you're off work from Friday, so maybe it's not bad advice.'

Belinda turned. 'I know, I know – but I just don't get it. Don't you have the feeling that something is missing?' She searched Will's face. 'It's *too easy*. Kelmendri just wants it all wrapped up so he can get his gut out and lie on the beach.'

Will looked down at his wife. Her red face and pursed lips reminded him of when he'd first seen her, racing towards him, fierce and determined. 'What do you want me to do, Bel?'

She shook her head, before closing her eyes briefly and sighing. Spotting a bench close by, he helped her to sit. 'Let's just have a rest for a little bit,' he said.

Lydiard Street was busy for this time of the morning, and it was pleasing for Will to be amid the bustle of life once more. In the last few weeks, he'd increasingly missed Melbourne. The mass of people, their busy lives, the anonymity. In a month or two, they'd be back there, in their little apartment in Prahran. His mother was already hinting at them moving into her house in Toorak, but he was holding off for now. It did make sense; she had three spare bedrooms and two extra bathrooms. And despite her wealth and bluster, his mother was lonely. But looking at Belinda now, her face tight with concentration and tiredness, he knew that was a discussion for another time. 'Do you want a drink?'

'That'd be great.' She smiled up at him, still thinking. 'An orange juice or something?'

There was a cafe across the road and, patting her knee, he headed over to it. Two women were in line in front of him, in the typical get-up of lycra pants and puffy jackets. Ballarat was much smaller than Melbourne, but in this regard at least the two towns were the same. Will relaxed, listening to them bicker amicably. In Carrabeen, if he just stood in line at a cafe, someone would ask him about their parking fine, or the camp at the creek, or more recently about the murders of Dean Hookes and Geordie Pritchard. It was nice to be anonymous.

'People go on about the rivalry between Bendigo and Ballarat, and it's not even true!' one of the women said. 'Like, I've never heard anyone say anything about it, and I'm from Bendigo!'

'Really? I never knew that.' The other woman sounded faintly offended. 'How did you find the heat?'

'Oh, it was fine! So much better than how cold it gets here. Plus, the wind! I can't stand it!'

Will found himself nodding. Even now, outside, it was blowing a gale.

'But what do you think of Ballarat schools?' the local insisted. 'Everyone raves about them – they're the best in the state.'

'Yes. Yes, you are right,' the woman conceded. 'But Bendigo has the arts! The gallery! View Street!'

Will bent down a tad, to listen more closely. He found he was warming to Bendigo. The Ballarat woman was bordering on rude.

'One more thing.' The local woman held up her hand. 'Ballarat is such a quick commute, just over an hour to Melbourne on a speedy train.'

Ahh, Will thought. *You've got me now, Ballarat, I do like a speedy train.*

The women were served and drifted away, still bickering, while Will was left wondering at the rivalry outside city walls. All the places that had zealots of their own.

'Which do you prefer?' he asked Belinda, when he returned with their drinks. 'Bendigo or Ballarat?'

Belinda screwed up her nose. 'Geelong,' she said as he sat down.

They drank in companiable silence, sheltered from the wind gusts by a large newsstand. It was a pleasure to watch people hurry past, and to feel the warmth of the sun.

'I've been thinking,' Belinda said, 'about why someone would want to murder Geordie on that particular day. If it was a local who did it—'

'We don't know that for sure,' Will interjected.

'Well, if it was – based on the animosity for the wind farms – why choose that day and time? Was it simply opportunistic?'

'What – so someone happened to see Geordie after the party

and kill him there? How did that bloodstain get into Orla's office? It had to be her.'

'But how could she string him up on the blade of a turbine, particularly if she was so drunk? I'm just not convinced . . .' Belinda paused. 'What happened in the days before Geordie died?' She put down her orange juice and listed the events on the tips of her fingers. 'On the Friday he was at home in Yarrobee. Then on the Saturday he spoke to me outside the supermarket, and had an argument with Marit about his turbines. At some point he visited Reg to offer to cover his debt. Then he went home to Lucinda and stayed there. Sunday he hung around at his farm, nothing much. He went to the petrol station where he was seen by Alan and Gordon. Sunday evening, Lucinda said goodbye to him as he left for Melbourne, and he drove into town in his fancy ute. He got fish 'n' chips . . .'

'Then went to the party at the creek,' Will continued. 'Where David and Val say he left with a very drunk Orla Witts. He was never seen alive again.'

'Yes.' Belinda picked up her juice bottle and took another sip. 'Do you think Lucinda is telling us the truth about that evening? We know she wanted to become CEO and take over the business. Plus, she was having an affair with Dean. Did Geordie know, do you think?'

'I don't know, but she's off the hook. She's got an alibi, remember? Marit, and the videos outside the house and up the long driveway? It would be too much of a stretch for her to run the fifteen-odd kilometres from Marit's house to get Geordie into town to kill him.'

Belinda nodded. 'Yes, I can see that. But I really think we are missing something here. I do. I reckon Lucinda might be able to tell us more: she knew Geordie the best out of anyone.'

'Okay, so – what?'

'I don't know. But, Will' – Belinda rested her head on his chest and gazed up at him with mock adoration – 'I do think you are the best person to find out.'

CHAPTER 40

Perhaps Belinda was right, Will thought, as he drove back down Carrabeen's main road after dropping her off at their house. Perhaps it *was* a good idea to talk to Lucinda one last time, about Geordie and the turbines. Despite his reluctance to admit it, he did share Belinda's discomfort at how easily Lucinda had been absolved of any guilt regarding both her husband's and her lover's deaths. But at the same time, he could not believe she was involved in any real sense.

A child greeted him when he arrived at Yarrobee. 'Are you one of Dad's friends?' the little girl asked with great interest.

'No,' Will said. 'I'm your mum's friend. We were at school together.'

'I'm missing school today, and I'm not even sick.'

'Cool.' Will hoped he'd be better at talking with children when his own was born.

'You're very tall, like a skinny giant,' she remarked, before running at speed to the back of the house.

Lucinda appeared in the doorway, leaning against the wall. 'I thought you weren't supposed to speak to me. Isn't everything through the lawyers now?'

'We have a suspect. Orla Witts.'

'Christ,' she breathed. 'So the rumours are true – the principal? Why?'

'We're still investigating. But it appears to be motivated by rage at the turbines. Orla was drunk at the time.'

It sounded weak, even as he said it. 'Geordie's blood was found in her office. But this doesn't mean we've stopped investigating,' he added. 'We still need to know how she got him up on the blade. There are still a lot of questions.'

'Christ!' Lucinda said again. 'Who are these lunatics? Geordie would never have hurt anyone. And are you saying she killed Dean too?'

'It's possible,' Will said.

Without being invited, he followed her into the lounge room. He sat across from her on a piano chair while she sunk onto a couch. There, she rummaged for a tissue in her pocket and blew her nose. There were suitcases and bags lined up near the door.

'Are you leaving?' he asked.

She nodded. 'First Geordie, then Dean . . .' The tears pooled in her eyes. 'It's time for me to go back to Melbourne with the girls. Christmas festivities will be coming up at school, and I don't want them to miss out. They need things to be as normal as possible. Plus, I must get to the office.'

One of the twins ran in, plonked a large bag down and then ran out again.

'I did read that the finances for CESA are in trouble,' Will admitted. 'And that you had requested to become CEO in Geordie's place.'

318

Lucinda curled her legs up underneath her. 'I may not always have appeared to, but I did care about the business very much. I liked what Geordie was trying to do with the turbines, but he was running CESA into the ground.' She looked at Will and shook her head. 'Every time he'd come back from the islands in the Pacific, or from Brazil, he'd be more depressed and more desperate. Wind power! Wind power! He was obsessed with it. That, and the loathing for his family's money – which was ironic really, because that's how he funded the turbines in the first place.'

Will knew people like that. People who were ashamed of their family's wealth – Marit, in her old rented house, came to mind. People who wanted to prove they'd changed, that they were above all their family stood for . . . oh, but look at how difficult it was to become someone new! There was always a version of your former self in your present one, no matter how hard you tried to erase it.

Will felt as if he was creeping towards something important, although he wasn't sure what. Assistant Commissioner Conti always said to get to know your suspects, your victims and their families. He placed great emphasis on knowing what people wanted, how much power they yielded, and whether it mattered to them.

'Why *did* Geordie hate his family's money?' Will asked.

'I don't think he hated it initially. It was more a gradual thing – you know, when he found out about his parents' investments in industries like coal and timber. The tragedy at Millicent. None of that is a secret.'

Will nodded. The Pritchards were known for having a wide-reaching portfolio.

'It was when he was at university, I think, when he was studying environmental engineering. He came to see the world in a new way. His time there really shaped who he was.'

'And yet,' Will remembered, 'you told me that he didn't finish his course.'

'No.' Lucinda looked up. 'By the middle of second year, he was totally over it. He'd come to see the excesses of his friends as equally repugnant to his father's business dealings. He left, and never kept in contact with them again. The rest of his studies he did online or part-time.'

'Was Geordie bullied there, do you think?' Will was reminded of his earlier conversation with Gordon Highett, about his time at St Francis.

'Geordie, bullied?' Lucinda gave a quiet laugh. 'I don't think so. And I don't think he was a bully either. He liked people, all people.'

Will nodded, unsure. Belinda had described Geordie as acting arrogantly towards her when he'd offered to pay off Reg's debts. *I don't think he even knew he was being like that*, she said. *It was just his tone.*

How we speak, he thought. It mattered.

Will paused for a moment. 'Oliver Moffat, the friend who died – was he the one who Geordie fled from, when he left St Francis College?'

Lucinda gave a dry laugh. 'When I told Geordie that Oliver had written a book before he died, Geordie said he'd never read a thing that tosser wrote. He had no interest in it whatsoever, and he was really cross that my family was going to publish it.'

'Lucinda . . .' Will hesitated before continuing. 'Did you ever think that Geordie *did* kill himself? His company was in trouble, the planet is in trouble, and you admitted even your marriage wasn't perfect.' Once he said it, he realised he'd been troubled by the question the entire time.

'No. Absolutely not.' Lucinda was as resolute as ever. 'Geordie was determined to make a difference, to make up for his family's past and his own mistakes. He has his children, who he loved. He wanted to make the world a better place for them. There's a lot of things I don't know, but I know this: my husband did *not* kill himself.'

She started crying softly. 'But you're right. Geordie and I weren't perfect,' she said between hiccups. 'I had affairs, and I know he did too. But I loved him, I *did*, and I know he loved me. Poor Dean, poor stupid Dean – I was never going to be with him, it was always Geordie. We just *got* each other. For a businessman he was hopeless with money, but I would've taken over the financial side of it, and he could have continued finding the projects. People loved him, much more than they ever loved me.'

Will didn't have an answer to that, so he let her keep talking.

'I'd told Geordie that I was having an affair with Dean. He was angry about it! But only because he knew Dean, I think. We agreed we'd never stray too close to home.'

'When did you tell him?'

'On the Saturday. I knew he was going to see Marit, and I thought she might somehow let it slip, she's so lax about stuff like that – so I just told him.'

'How did he take it?'

'Like I said, he was angry. After that, we didn't talk to each other much, and not really at all before he left for the last time.'

So, Will thought. Geordie left Yarrobee on the Sunday, still angry and upset with his wife. He got fish 'n' chips and then might have thought, 'Fuck it, I'm going to have a drink with the campers,' or 'Fuck it, I'll let the campers know I'm going to buy them all housing. Get their thanks.' But try as he might, Will could not put himself fully into Geordie's mind.

In fact, Will felt an infinite sadness for the man who'd seemingly had it all.

'What do you think happened to Geordie, and to Dean?' Will asked. 'Like, really?'

Lucinda closed her eyes and took a deep breath. 'I think Geordie was killed by one of the crazed anti-turbine people. And then Dean must have been killed because he found out who it was, or he'd tried to solve Geordie's death himself and got killed . . . Poor Dean, he really did care for me more than he should have.'

Will thought he should probably get home. Hopefully Belinda would be back from her father's – he was home from hospital – and they needed a quiet night together.

'Will you be all right here, Lucinda?' He stood. 'Can I call someone for you?'

She gave a wry laugh. 'Always so considerate. Maybe we shouldn't have broken up. I could have been a cop wife.'

Their break-up hadn't been mutual. He'd said he was leaving university, and her. But now wasn't the time to remind her of that.

'No, you couldn't,' Will said with a smile. 'I'm on less than $140,000 a year.'

Lucinda smiled back for the first time. 'You're right then, I couldn't.'

CHAPTER 41

Belinda had driven down to Broker Court to check in on Reg. Her father wasn't interested in talking about the recent attempt on his life. Far more important to him was the upcoming race four, the dogs in Ballarat.

'Do you think,' she asked, once she'd made herself a mug of tea, 'that it was someone to do with the dog races, a bookie or someone from your past, maybe all that money you owed?'

'What?' her father barked, one hand on his neck bandage. 'Fuck no. I don't owe any of those bastards a thing. They've got enough from me. I won't give them a cent more.'

'Well, who else, Dad?' She looked at the shearing photograph on the wall, at a newspaper opened at the dogs page. 'Who else would want to hurt you?'

But her father would not talk. His thin lips pressed tight together, his scrawny arms folded defiantly across his chest. It was no use; she knew what he was like when he was in this mood.

There was a tapping at the window, and when Reg lifted his hand in a vague wave, a woman with a tight perm walked in and placed a casserole on the bench. 'For your dad,' she said to Belinda. 'Poor old bugger.'

There were other gifts on the crowded counter: a six-pack of beer, a cake from the supermarket in a plastic box, and a video tape labelled 'Best of *Hey Hey It's Saturday*.'

Belinda chatted to the neighbour for a bit, and Reg gave a nod of thanks as she left the room. It was as if he were a king, with people coming bearing gifts, supplicating themselves to him.

'You've got lots of friends, Dad,' she said, and he gave a snort.

'Wouldn't be friends with half of them if my arse was on fire.'

He wasn't in a good mood, and it was getting dark. She checked that he'd taken the correct painkillers, made sure his bed linen was clean, then said her goodbyes.

It was odd, she thought, as she sat in her car to drive home; her father had always had people surrounding him who wanted him to like them. It had been that way for as long as she could remember. Reg yielded a power born of something close to menace, and that counted in a small country town.

She turned on the engine. Her seat still wasn't right. Every time Will drove her little Corolla, he extended it right back to fit in his long legs. She jiggled the lever, moving back and forth, till it was right again. *There.*

She continued to sit, engine running, thinking about it: the moving back and forth of the seat . . . She was reminded of Orla out the front of Dean's house, on the morning he died. What had Orla said? She'd been irritated as she fiddled with her seat and made it higher.

Belinda's phone rang, and as if she had summoned her, it was Orla.

'It's a funny thing, you know,' the principal said in a dry tone, 'how after you've had an alcoholic blackout you start to remember things in bits and pieces. There's a term for it, but ironically, I've forgotten what it is.'

'What do you want to tell me, Orla?' Belinda kept her voice steady.

'When you asked me about drinking at the river with Geordie – those reminders did trigger some flashes of memory. I think I know how, perhaps, I left.'

'Tell me.'

And Orla did.

CHAPTER 42

Tired of the calls from journalists and locals, Will turned off his phone. He rarely did that, but in this case, the media was really driving him wild. Back home he had a quick shower and, rustling about the laundry basket for some shorts to wear, saw Oliver Moffat's book underneath a towel. *That's right*, he thought, amused: he'd thrown it there a few days ago then forgotten about it. Absentmindedly, he picked up the book and began flicking through some more of the photo section as he lay on the bed.

In one, the budding entrepreneur was sitting on the lawn with a friend. Geordie Pritchard had a lopsided smile on his handsome face, his shirt unbuttoned, his hair fashionably long. *St Francis of Assisi mates* was the caption. Will paused, read it again. Looked back at the image.

Geordie Pritchard. Of course he would appear in Oliver's book. As old friends who lived together in one of the country's most prestigious institutions, he was bound to rate a mention.

Interest renewed, Will turned to the chapter marked *University*, and read a few paragraphs. Oliver was extolling what fun he'd had at St Francis, meeting new friends, getting drunk and vomiting in the gardens. Will snorted: did Oliver Moffat seriously think people wanted to know that? And it was hardly a unique experience. Anyone who'd ever lived on campus would have similar stories to tell.

There was a sudden knocking on the front door. A little distracted, Will snapped the book shut and went to answer it.

CHAPTER 43

The main street of the town was almost completely dark; only the two streetlights in front of the pharmacy were lit. It may as well have been a ghost town, Belinda thought, as she drove slowly through on her way home. Soon, she'd be back in Melbourne, where the streets were busy at every hour. Late-night restaurants, bars, drunks wandering along, taxis driving slowly up and down the street. She missed it, she suddenly realised – but she would miss this too. Everyone talked about how in country towns it was like living in a fishbowl, but they rarely mentioned this: how you could drive the streets, ride your bike, go for a jog – and no one would ever see you. You *could* have a hidden life in a country town; it was possible to drift in and out of public places unseen.

Passing the hardware store and the small park, she turned right suddenly, and slowed on the approach to the school.

Pitch black, the buildings looked like a sleeping giant. But still, it took her a moment to register that there was a light on in one of the classrooms. She slowed down even more. Was it a trick of the light, a reflection from something? But then, when she saw a waving yellow beam, she recognised it as a torch light.

Nine thirty-five pm on a Tuesday night, and someone was in the school.

She felt a shudder of excitement, followed by a prickle of fear. Who would be there at this time? Surely it was too late for a teachers' meeting. Was it the figure they'd seen on Julie's recordings? Had the person living in the roof come back?

Turning her headlights off, she inched slowly to a park at the side of the oval and sat there thinking. She rang Will, and when he didn't answer, she left a message saying that there was a light on in the school and she was going to check it out. It wouldn't hurt to look.

She decided to head towards the back of the school based on the location of the light. Her feet crunched on the asphalt; the building was encased in darkness. The swinging beam of light was further up the corridor, waving to and fro, just a pinprick through the windows. Belinda softly pushed against the doors, unsurprised to find them unlocked. Everything was quiet. She went to yell hello, but hesitated, remained silent.

A brief thought entered her head that she could go now and tell Andrew – his house was close by. No. No need to bother him, she was only checking it out.

God, she thought, as she stepped lightly up the hallway. *Is there anything more eerie than a school at night?* The empty corridors, the echoes, the ghostly smells, the dust.

A light, up there in the hall. She felt a twinge of fear. But still, she continued, edging along the wall, following the light, guided by the dim moonlight coming in through the classroom windows. She was in the older section of the school now, near the science rooms. In the empty classrooms to the side, dark computer screens sat in rows. A chair perched on top of another looked like a ghostly throne. A lab coat hanging from a door gave her a horrid fright. She shook herself. By now, she'd reached the food technology rooms. Julie's domain. She stepped inside, running the torch from her phone over the ovens, the stainless-steel benches, the whiteboard and the knife rack.

There was a flash in front of her eyes and, for a horrible moment, she thought of Julie's ghost, the little girl running down the hallway. Then everything was still.

Why hadn't Will answered the phone? With shaking hands, she went to call him again.

A door slammed, a sudden noise. Stepping close to the window, she could make out the dark shape of trees being whipped about in a gale.

Once again, she reached for her phone, just as the light in the hallway went out. Total blackness now.

There was a crunch of footsteps, and she called out more bravely than she felt, 'Hello? Who is that?'

Nothing, save another creak of what sounded like old floorboards.

Reaching behind her, Belinda placed her hand on one of the knives, and hardly knowing what she was doing, pulled it slowly out, brandishing it with a shaking hand.

A figure stood in front of her.

'Oh,' she said, confusion overtaking fear. 'What are *you* doing here?'

CHAPTER 44

The visitor at Will's door was Gordon Highett, dropping off a stack of St Francis alumni magazines. 'I tried to get the relevant ones with the Pritchards in them,' he said. 'Thought you might be interested.' Gordon didn't want to stay for a drink. He needed to be up early the next morning for a Clean Energy meeting in Ballarat. No rest for the wicked. Will waved him goodbye.

Glancing down at the pile of magazines, Will saw that the professor had left little Post-it notes as helpful bookmarks, and Will turned to one of them now. There was a photo of a young man with a medal about his neck: Hugh Pritchard, class of 1974.

Will stood for a moment, admiring the confident gaze of the young man, his clear enjoyment of the moment. Resident of Yarrobee, future father of Geordie, owner of Millicent – here was a man who would make an indelible mark on his surrounds.

Will put the other alumni magazines on the sofa and returned to bed, and Oliver Moffat's book. Turning on his phone, he saw that Belinda had called. He listened to the message from her about going to the school. He tried ringing her back, but she wasn't answering. She'd be home soon.

Flicking back through the as-yet-unpublished book to where he'd got up to, he lay down and focused on a chapter titled *Regrets*. Here, Oliver laid bare a litany of extra-marital affairs and his stay in prison for fraud, and how they had made him reflect on his privileged life.

Sitting alone in my apartment, Hong Kong buzzing below, I finally had the realisation that my life, far from the heady success I had always strived for, was one filled with regret and shame. I thought back to my school days, the bullying I took part in out of boredom and habit, and then a moment at college, where I led a group of boys into an act so cruel I can barely think of it to this day. Now, at the end of my life, I look back on this moment and I seek forgiveness.

Will's eyes widened and he kicked off his shoes, his head on the pillow. Oliver Moffat had finally got him interested.

St Francis of Assisi College, O-Week. I was in the Welcome group, along with my close friends Geordie Pritchard and Simon McWilliams. We'd been drinking in Geordie's room, and we were bored and cold. There were numerous things we could have done at that point: played a game of basketball, got some much-needed study done, gone out for coffee. But instead, I came up with an idea. St Francis of Pissisi. Why shouldn't we, just for laughs, pick a random student, get them riotously drunk, dress them like our namesake, St Francis of Assisi, and have photographs taken next to his statue in the front courtyard? The kid we chose would probably like it – why not? We would have.

That's what I thought.

There were all kinds of pranks at that time: painting freshers green and getting them to break into girls' rooms, beer-boarding torture, the annual thong slap. But St Francis of Pissisi was something new, and we liked all things new.

We chose the first person we saw out the window, a skinny kid with thick glasses and a bowl-cut hairdo. He was walking in the courtyard, his head stuck in a book. Poor thing, we laughed, he needs some fun in his life! Braving the cold, we picked up our blazers from the pile and put them on, then headed out.

I now know his name was Kenneth Greene.

Will looked up in surprise, then frowned. A deep unease grew in his chest.

The boy was hesitant at the start, but we made him feel like it was going to be fun. We took him back to my room and made the poor kid drink like a fish, mostly vodka and wine. It wasn't as much fun as we'd thought it would be, and after a while, it grew boring, with the kid wanting to stop and trying to get out of the room. I remember saying, 'No. No, Kenny, you need to have some fun.'

Simon was pissing himself laughing, and we found one of the Master's old gowns, coloured green like the Saint himself, and made Ken put it on. The kid was barely upright, but in order for the prank to work, we needed him to wear it and stand to attention, at least until the Master got in from his philosophy class so he, and all the dignitaries, could see what St Francis looked like in the flesh.

Feeling ill, Will kept reading: how the boy had vomited over himself, and then was made to stand having his photo taken while he leaned against the statue, as the Master and the rest of the tutors filed in. *What fucking pricks*, he thought. *That poor kid.* And suddenly memories surfaced of himself as a boy – much

333

younger than Kenneth, but just as out of place – being humili-
ated when he realised he'd pissed himself during class. Oh, didn't
the kids laugh at him – the tall, lanky boy with all the money,
who couldn't take a joke. The beanpole with the glasses who read
science magazines and touched the fence when told, wrongly, it
wasn't electric. *Fuck you, arseholes*, he thought, in sudden fury at
the Moffats of the world. *Fuck. You.*

*Later, we walked back to Simon's room and took off our coats.
It didn't seem right to be wearing the college blazers after what we'd
just done.*

Bastards!

*And as for Kenneth Greene? Well, his parents pulled him out of
college after that first semester. They said he had glandular fever, but
we all knew. Geordie went overseas, and Simon and I stayed, doing
much of the same. If I could see that boy now, I'd like to apologise and
somehow make amends. I hope he is somewhere good, living a nice
life, but I'd understand if he hated us after that.*

Oh god. Will felt a punch to his gut.

Hauling himself out of bed, he moved to the lounge room
again, where he'd left the St Francis magazines. He tried to work
out what year Geordie would have been there, and then looked at
all the ones from 2007 and worked backwards. *Kenneth Greene,
Kenneth Greene, Kenneth Greene . . .* He flipped over pages,
hurriedly scanning the photographs and text.

And there, in a photograph containing at least fifty grinning
students sitting in rows – each wearing the blue and white of the
college colours – was the freshman class of 2003.

Eyes racing across the names at the bottom, he came to the
one he was after: *K. Greene.* Poor guy.

Will held the page right up to his eyes. He took off his glasses, rubbed them and looked again.

A feeling, perhaps, a faint memory . . . but he couldn't be sure. He studied the boy in the photo again, frowning. The face looked different, the body certainly so. But the way the kid was sitting . . .

What to do?

He sent his wife a text: *Call me.*

Next, Will called his brother in London. Daniel was married to a woman named Pi, and they had three girls who, in the rare times he'd seen them, were like a pack of ravaging monkeys, climbing up on things, asking to be piggy-backed, leap-frogging over couches and each other. After he'd seen them, Will always felt a little dazed, as if he too had eaten too many lollies.

For once, and despite the time difference, Daniel answered straightaway.

'Will!' his brother exclaimed. 'How are you?'

'I forgot your birthday,' Will said, suddenly remembering. 'It was yesterday, wasn't it?'

'It was last week, mate. Don't worry about it, I never remember yours.'

It was true, they were both hopeless.

'Did you have a good day?'

'Yeah, went out for dinner, had a few beers.' Daniel had never lost his Australian accent, despite all the time he'd lived and worked in London. 'Looking forward to your move back to Melbourne?' he asked, always affable.

'Yep, we are.' Although tonight, as he'd driven home, that gold on the paddocks, the soft shimmer of pink on the wind . . .

Daniel began chatting about his work and people they both knew.

'Dan, can I ask you something?' Will cut in. 'It could be important. I don't know if you'll be able to help, but how much can you remember about the students in your year at Wesley?'

'A bit. I'm still friends with a few of them, but we mostly drifted away after uni.'

'There's someone I vaguely recognise. I think he was in your year. Does the name Kenneth Greene ring a bell?'

His brother deliberated. 'No, can't remember a Kenneth – sorry.'

Will opened the group photo of the new students at St Francis. 'I'm going to send you a photo of someone, and I'd like to see if you can tell me if you know them. That okay?'

'Fire away.'

Will zoomed in on K. Greene and took a screenshot, then messaged it to his brother.

Daniel never forgot a face, no matter how distant or how many years had passed.

'Got it,' his brother said. 'Yes, I recognise him. He arrived late – second semester, I think. He'd had glandular fever, is that it? But I don't remember him being K. Greene.'

'But you have a name?'

'Sure.'

'What is it, mate? Tell me.'

CHAPTER 45

Andrew Kent's face was a sickly yellow in the glow of the torch-light. 'I kept thinking about that person in the roof. I needed to check if they were back.' He grinned and pointed a finger upwards. 'I've been waiting here to catch him.'

'Why? The person has left.'

'No, they haven't. I can hear them. Can't you?' He paused. 'Someone is creeping around up there.'

Belinda strained to listen as the vice principal watched on. 'I can't hear anything,' she said.

'I know someone is up there!' Andrew made his fists into binoculars and put them up to his eyes.

Belinda rested a hand on her stomach, tried to quell the sense of mounting anxiety. Outside, the wind raged, banging the school oval gates, rattling at the doors. 'The police will sort it out, Andrew. It's not your job to do the searching.'

The hand binoculars trained on her. 'I need to find that person.'

'Why?' Belinda took a quick glance out the window.

Andrew's hands fell from his face, and he looked at his outstretched palms before turning them over. 'Who knows what the person up there has heard? Or seen?'

'It's late,' she said in a rush. 'We can talk about this in the morning.'

'No, we can't.'

There was a long silence, and Belinda heard the thumping of her heart, a rushing in her head. She felt the knife handle in her fist. 'It was you who drove Orla from the river.'

'Orla spoke to you, did she?' Andrew stood in the doorway of the classroom, blocking the exit. 'Surprised she remembered.' He took one step forward, so that he was now in the room. He picked up a laminated sheet with safety instructions on it, then put it down gently.

Belinda took a sharp intake of breath.

'I pick her up when she's pissed down the creek, I keep her drinking a secret from the school. I'm a shoulder to cry on when she's in one of her self-loathing moods, and then she goes and runs to you.'

Belinda could barely breathe. 'So you *did* pick up Orla from the creek on the night Geordie died?'

'Of course I did! Who else? I'm always the one she calls when she's drunk too much.' He suddenly moved towards the first row of benches. He gave another lopsided grin. 'And when I got down to the river, there was Geordie fucking Pritchard! And I thought, well, finally here's a chance to set things straight. Dean had told me what was going on between him and Pritchard's wife – the man had a right to know.'

It was all falling into place. Andrew Kent had taken Orla home and put her to bed. Was Geordie with them? There was a short dragging sound above her, and Belinda looked up. For the first time, she thought she could hear something. But then it was quiet again.

'And so you brought Geordie back to the school to tell him, did you?' She kept her voice level. 'You took him to Orla's office as if you were the principal . . .'

'I said I'd give Geordie a lift to his ute after I dropped Orla home. He agreed. And then, when I asked if he'd like to take a quick look at the new plans, and that there was a nice bottle of whiskey in the office, he said he had some time. That's all I was going to do. Show him some plans – and tell him a few home truths.'

Playing for time, Belinda edged sideways, so that she was closer to the middle of the room, and in running distance to the door. It meant moving closer to Andrew, but she couldn't risk being trapped between the benches.

'Pritchard was happy to look at the plans, but he got bored quick enough, wanted to leave. So I told him then about his wife's affair, and how I knew from Dean that she was planning to oust him as CEO. I poured him an extra-large drink when I told him that.'

Belinda took another sidewards step.

'But he just laughed when I told him,' Andrew continued. 'He already knew about his wife and Dean. And he wasn't bothered about her taking over the company. "You should mind your own business, Kent," he said. That's seriously what he said. "You're not my friend, stay out of my affairs. You're a teacher! You don't know anything about what it's like in the business world."

'That's really what he said. But do you know what was the worst bit? He didn't even *remember* me. Not at all, not one tiny bit.'

Through the window Belinda could see the headlights of a car on the road, and with desperation watched it drive right by the school. *Will!* she screamed in her head. *Where are you?* Andrew Kent was a tall man; not fit, but he'd still be strong. She could try to run past him, but if he put up a fight, she didn't stand a chance.

'What about Dean?' Belinda tried stalling again. 'Did you have anything to do with that?'

Andrew stared at her for a long moment. 'I rode Orla's bike,' he said finally. 'Electric bikes are so quiet. And that trophy, I knew Orla would be handing it out to the winning sports team.'

'You killed him.' Belinda felt sick. 'Why?'

Outside, the moonlight was making strange flickering patterns as the gum trees lining the street were battered by wind. *Think!*

'Dean was a good teacher,' he said soberly. 'But he was going to tell you about his affair with Lucinda, and then he'd mention how he told me about it before Geordie died. He was confused about why, as the days went on, I didn't tell anyone, especially when you were asking questions of the whole town. He said he was going to tell you after the sports day – about his affair with the man's wife.'

'So what? That's not reason enough to kill him.' Belinda looked about her. *Should I run?*

'Dean saw me cleaning the floor of Orla's office early on the Monday morning. He didn't see anything exactly, but he made a joke about it, said I was busy scrubbing her office, trying to get in her good books. As the week went on and you lot started asking questions, he confronted me about it, and let's just say, Dean wasn't making jokes any more.'

'He was putting two and two together,' Belinda breathed.

'Poor Dean. I didn't want to hurt him, I always liked him. Everyone liked him – far more than they like me.'

His self-pity was something she could work with. She made her voice softer, more sympathetic. 'But it's always been like that in schools, hasn't it? The popular PE teacher, everyone loves them.' She took another step, to where drawers lined the bottom of the benches. 'And that time when Orla was sick. Dean stepped into the principal role, didn't he? Not you – and you were next in charge! That's so unfair. Didn't Orla think you were up to it? What a bitch.'

Andrew gave a twisted grin. 'I know what you're doing. It won't work.'

Belinda took a quick glance out the window, hoping to see a car, a person – anything! But there was nothing.

A drawer was slightly open behind her, and she felt around until she came upon what she thought were the pointed edges of a meat tenderiser. She held her other arm up, and with a shaky hand held aloft the knife again. 'Let me go.'

Andrew shook his head.

Heart thumping, Belinda took a step forward.

'Geordie didn't remember me. But I remembered him. I remembered *all* their names.' Andrew's face had taken on a strange, excited glow. 'They were embroidered on their fucking blazers!'

'Andrew, I called for back-up. The police are coming.'

'No, they're not.' He rounded on her, arms wide as if he was about to embrace her. 'I mean,' he said with a sad smile, '*it's all in good fun, isn't it?*'

Picking up his phone, Will tried to call Belinda again. Then, when she didn't answer, he grabbed his keys, calling Tammy at the same time.

'Get to the school!' he shouted down the line at her. 'I think Bel's in trouble.'

Andrew Kent was edging closer, metal torch raised high.

In a flash, Belinda whipped out the tenderiser and flung its metal head hard at the window, smashing it, sending shards of glass across the room.

Three things happened at once.

An alarm sounded, shrill and persistent.

Andrew lunged on top of her, bearing down his metal torch.

And, just as Belinda began to lose consciousness from the blow, a figure fell through the ceiling like an avenging angel.

Will raced up the steps of the school, just as Tammy pulled up. 'Get back-up,' he yelled, not waiting for her. 'Now!'

He heard an almighty crash that sounded like a window breaking at the rear of the school, followed by a lengthy scream. Will ran full pelt down the corridor, heart in his mouth, long legs pumping. 'Bel!' he roared. *'Bel!'*

Another scream. Will reached the door of the cookery room. Andrew Kent was holding a shard of glass in one hand and thrashing about on his knees, as someone, not Belinda, clung wildly to his back.

Will drew his weapon. 'Police!'

Andrew turned around. There was an odd grimace on his face.

The woman on his back edged away, and Andrew slumped to the floor.

Will could finally see Belinda in the corner, hands covering a wound on the side of her head. 'I'm okay,' she called to him.

Will turned his gaze back to the vice principal. The man's legs were spread out before him, his chin on his chest. The glass fragment in his hand had cut deep into his flesh.

Then he saw his wife walk over to her saviour. 'Are you all right?' she said to Tayla Schultz.

CHAPTER 46

Ballarat Chronicle, 11 December 2024
Local teacher charged with two counts of murder
Vice Principal of Carrabeen High School, Andrew Kent, has been
charged with the murders of local businessman and CEO Geordie
Pritchard, and popular teacher, Dean Hookes. Police are still
investigating, but the motivation for the brutal killings is believed
to date back to Kent's time as a student in Sydney and an attempt
to cover up previous crimes. Mr Kent was charged following an assault
on a police officer at the school on Tuesday night.
Details to follow.

The article was rushed, Belinda thought as she read it. The jour-
nalist still hadn't discovered the exact links between Andrew and
Geordie – their shared schooling, the terrible bullying incident.
Austin Dorney had arrived at the school as the police car with
Andrew in the back was driven away, and as Belinda and Tayla
were led into ambulances. But the journo wasn't there in time to

hear the man insisting that he hadn't strung Geordie up on the blade. He'd driven his lifeless body to the turbines and left it lying at the bottom so the anti-turbine people would take the fall. That was it. He was adamant he hadn't set foot inside the turbine.

'Divine intervention!' he'd screamed, as he was finally driven away. 'That bastard Pritchard! It was like a miracle, like St Francis of Assisi was helping me. Divine! *Per volar sunata!*'

'I don't believe it,' Tammy had said, when she'd visited Belinda in hospital the day before. 'Kent had access to the kind of rope used; he admitted to killing Geordie and Dean as well as setting up Orla to take the fall. He hated Geordie for what was done to him at college. *Of course* Andrew hung him up there! He's definitely strong enough.'

Tammy had a point. Andrew had gone to great lengths to frame Orla – slyly pointing out the rug covering the bloodstain, his references to the trophy/murder weapon, the insinuations of her alcoholism and unpredictability.

'Why should we believe anything that man says?' Tammy had declared. 'His name isn't even Andrew Kent.'

Belinda considered this question now as she rested in her hospital bed. Maybe because Andrew was a dedicated teacher, and maybe because he'd already admitted to so much. He knew his career was over and that he'd be going to jail. Why not admit the final, most incredible part of Geordie's murder?

Belinda turned to face the young woman in the hospital bed beside her. Tayla was asleep, her strawberry-blonde hair covering her face, one fist over her mouth like a child. The girl had been living in the school roof for more than a month. She had it tough at home. She'd enjoyed Julie's school breakfasts for years and, though she hadn't expressed it in so many words, Carrabeen College was the safest place she'd known. With Andrew's help, ironically, she got the gap year position, and then further prospects in Melbourne. But Melbourne was weeks away, and she didn't want to be at home with her mum's new boyfriend. So why not *stay* at the school? She knew it inside and out – had crept into the school's roof space on weekends as a kid on a jaunt with friends, had thought more than once that it wouldn't be a bad place to hang out: showers in the gym, food from the kitchens, free WiFi. There was nowhere else to go. And the school was safe. *Safe.*

It had been, Tayla admitted, a little lonely, sometimes a little scary at night, but she spent her time drawing and reading – and watching with interest the meetings that took place after school hours in the old building.

And then, seeing Dean Hookes and Lucinda Pritchard! It was just an innocent bit of blackmail, for some pocket money. She never would have dobbed them in.

'Then, after you guys worked out someone was living in the roof, Mr Kent became obsessed. It was hard to even get down from there. He was watching the whole time. It was so scary. Maybe he thought I'd seen him kill Geordie. But I hadn't, I swear!'

Belinda thought over the case. What had been established: Potty and his girlfriend had seen Andrew's car approach the turbine and fled, dropping the keys. The vice principal, intent on dragging the unconscious Geordie through the gap in the fence, had not even noticed. And if what he was saying was true, that he did not hang Geordie up on the blade – 'if' being the operative word – then someone else had.

But who?

'Belinda?' Tayla spoke from the next bed.

'Yes?' She suddenly felt an overwhelming tiredness.

'Do you really think that I could get a job with the police?'

'Absolutely, you'd be great.'

'Even after I was sleeping in the roof, and after I'd black-mailed Dean?'

'Police aren't perfect, Tayla,' Belinda said, sinking into sleep. 'You can be sure of that.'

CHAPTER 47

Thursday morning, and Will was signing a Stat Dec for a young man who wanted to transfer his money from one superannuation to another. His mother had told him that he needed to merge the two accounts, and he needed a Stat Dec to do it. Half an hour before, a Channel 9 helicopter had hovered over the school, but this fellow – his name was Ewan – was far more concerned about his financial dealings. Will was tempted to ask him what he thought of the recent murders. 'Do you reckon it was the vice principal who strung him up there?' But wisely, he did not. There was enough gossip around town as it was: people saying Belinda was half dead, that it had been Dean living in the roof, that Andrew had been framed by Orla and that it was she, not him, who was guilty of murdering Geordie and Dean. But the gossips hadn't been at the scene. The gossips hadn't heard what Tayla and Belinda had heard in that room as he confessed.

Will signed the form for Ewan and wished him good luck,

and the young man sauntered out of the station, oblivious to anything outside his own little world.

That's a talent most young people have, Will thought, *the ability to move on.* Older people, not so much. Unless, of course, you were Kenneth Greene.

He collected his keys, locked up the station and got in his car, determined in this instance to move on from his fear of heights. Shane Burrows was meeting him at the turbines – one more thing to tick off – to confirm how Andrew/Kenneth had got Geordie up there and hung him on the blade. Swallowing his regret at volunteering to take on the task, Will grinned at Tammy, who was just pulling in.

'Good luck with it,' she shouted. 'See you when you get back – we can have a beer to celebrate wrapping up this shitstorm.'

Will wound his window down and stuck out an elbow. Someone he vaguely knew waved to him, and he waved back. Since he'd helped to recover Doug Hay from the silo, people greeted him more often.

He hadn't told Belinda what he was doing today; she was still at the hospital on doctors' advice, and he didn't want to worry her.

The gate to the turbine farm was open, and Shane drove in. The young man hadn't been charged with anything yet, but Will couldn't see how he would get off completely scot-free. He'd hampered the investigation by not telling them earlier about his scam with the keys.

Shane's face was solemn as he handed over the safety gear, and they spoke little as they made their way up the turbine using the climb-assist and the elevator. It would be difficult, Will thought, but certainly not impossible to get a body up here; aside from the first section, where you'd have to drag and then lift the body upward. But then there was no further lifting of the full weight.

When they reached the top, Will felt the same gripping fear he'd had before. The space felt tight, choking.

'Get ready,' Shane said, and he pushed the button that opened the hatch, revealing again the enormous expanse of the blades, and the landscape beyond.

'Okay.' Will's voice was shaky, but firm. 'So we know that Andrew must have clipped his vest to this rescue device, then dragged the body out onto one of the blades using the rope he brought up with him.'

'He would have used that rope to help him get the body up in the first section, before the lift.'

'Yes,' Will gulped, looking out to the blade. 'Once out there, he hooked the rope around the skinniest part of the blade and looped it onto one of the carabiners in his safety vest.'

'It was probably already around Geordie's neck,' Shane added. The two were silent for a long moment. 'There was no wind that night,' Shane said finally. 'Lucky for him.'

Will took a deep breath. 'I want to take a few steps out there – just to see how it could be done.' *Or to imagine what it would be like*, he thought. Because at the moment, dragging a body out on the blade just did not seem possible.

Shane fastened the rescue wire to a carabiner on his safety vest and tugged on it for good measure. 'See?' he said. 'It's as safe as houses. If worse came to worst and you fell, this thing would catch your weight and we could haul you back up – or down. There's enough wire for it.'

'Good to know.' Will forced himself to look along the blades. He glanced back, nervous, and tested the rescue wire again.

Shane caught his expression. 'Go on!' he said. 'Just take a few steps out there, you won't fall.'

Will nodded.

'It's perfectly safe,' Shane added.

He nodded again.

Then he took one tiny step, then another, then another.

God, it was high. The wind whipped about him, and he had a sudden fear that the blades might start spinning. But no, he told himself. Shane had stopped them when they entered.

Will forced himself to look down, heard the rapid beat of his heart, saw the plains extending all the way to the sea. The horizon rose up at him, and he trembled. *Enough.* It could be done. And he'd conquered his fear, at least a tiny bit. He turned, inch by inch, focusing on his feet, till he was facing back towards the turbine. Finally, he looked up.

Shane stood directly before him, blocking his path.

'Shane,' he said. 'Move. I need to get back.'

But the wind technician stood there, pose relaxed, arms by his side. He had no safety device connected to him.

'Move,' Will said, more forcefully this time, and to his horror a strong gust of wind whipped up from below.

'Will I get into much trouble?' Shane said, leaning in.

There was a rising panic in Will's chest.

'With the keys?' Shane's voice had a pleading note in it, and he held his hands up, questioning.

'I heard Julie make these phone calls on the night Geordie was killed.' Shane said it sadly, then moved closer still, before lifting one boot to inspect something on the sole. 'Maybe if I tell you that, you'll let me off for the other stuff? I was at her house, and I heard her on the phone to the Pritchards, like, threatening to kill them. It was the night Geordie died.'

There was an intense ringing in Will's ears. He gripped the wire with both hands. Wind smacked into his face.

'So – am I in big trouble?'

Will felt like screaming. 'No,' he said, and the ground seemed to rear up at him.

Shane opened his mouth to say something more, then turned on one heel and walked back into the turbine.

Will followed close behind.

Once inside, he unclipped the rescue wire and moved straight to the ladder.

'Julie's my friend's aunt. Don't tell her I told you.' Shane's face was pale as Will began climbing down.

'Shut the fuck up!' Will cut him off. 'And yes, you're in all kinds of trouble, you little shit.'

CHAPTER 48

Belinda had listened in horror as Will told her over the phone what had just happened up on the turbine. 'You went out on a blade?' she kept asking. 'My god, Will, you're mad!'

But now, after hanging up, and after being reassured that he was fine, she ruminated on how the body was carried to the top. Heaved up the first bit, then put into the elevator . . .

Andrew was still insisting he'd merely left Geordie's body at the base of the turbine, hoping that the anti-wind farm brigade would get the blame. So had someone found Geordie's body and then carried him up there?

Minutes ticked by while she thought.

Shane Burrows? From what Will had said, Shane wasn't all that stable, but he knew the turbines better than anyone. He was certainly strong enough. But Shane's DNA wasn't a match for the skin fragment found on the rope, and what's more, he admired Geordie – and relied on him for work.

Lucinda? Lucinda was strong; her arms were toned from

the gym. There was the climb-assist feature in the turbine. But Lucinda loved her husband, however unconventional their relationship was. And she had the business already; she could do whatever she wanted. Besides, she'd been with Dean that night – Marit's cameras confirmed it. So not Lucinda.

Belinda's mind drifted further.

Marit then? No, Marit was already fighting Geordie on a number of fronts, and she too was at home, as her bird camera testified. She didn't need to perform a stunt like that.

Because that final stunt showed real hatred of Geordie Pritchard.

Or a hatred of the turbines, at least.

Orla then? Orla was against them. But no, Belinda shook her head. The woman was so drunk that night, she'd barely been able to move. Andrew's attempts to frame her were now over, he had confirmed that. It had been ridiculous to truly suspect her in the first place.

Doug Hay? She dismissed that thought quickly. He'd been home with his wife, Shirleen. They'd been FaceTiming their daughter in the UK till late, watching their granddaughter's dance concert. And Doug wasn't fit enough to haul Geordie up the first section of the turbine. No way.

Julie? Julie was big and strong. She disliked the turbines, was deeply suspicious of them. She told whole crowds that they were dangerous to health, that people died because of them. Julie was a dangerous woman; Belinda was only beginning to understand just how much. She remembered, now, Julie's sly smile when she showed them her recordings. How much sway exactly did the woman hold over the town?

Power. That's what this was all about.

Belinda took a sip of water, put a tentative hand on the stitches in her head. Then lay back on her pillow, thoughts running rampant.

Something was missing.

She kept coming back to the one idea she least liked. But it was there, bubbling.

Eyes closed, she was in the process of role-playing her theory in her mind when she heard Will enter the room. She put up her hand to stop him interrupting her thoughts.

After a few moments of silence, Will couldn't wait any longer. 'What are you thinking about?' he asked.

Belinda opened her eyes and smoothed back her hair. 'Shearing.'

CHAPTER 49

Wind was swirling and whipping the air when Belinda and Will pulled into Broker Court. Will tugged at his shirtsleeves, trying to calm his thoughts.

Reg was sitting in a chair on the porch, fag perilous between his fingers, neck wrapped in a dirty bandage.

'Dad,' Belinda said slowly, when he turned towards them. 'Tell us about Rhonda Crowe.'

Reg let out a wheezy laugh, which turned into a hacking cough. He held a skinny hand to his throat. 'Wondered when you'd figure it out.'

Will and Belinda waited while the old man took a sip of his drink, and a long drag on his ciggie, before continuing. 'Rhonda Crowe used to be Rhonda Reynolds, or Rhonda Raz. She worked for the Pritchards as a rousey. We all used to watch her, you couldn't not. The girl had arms like pistons from throwing the fleeces.' He gave a thin whistle through his teeth and sat back, enjoying the moment.

'Dad.' Belinda leaned forward. 'Rhonda.'

'She was a smart one.' Reg puffed on his cigarette, smiling into space. 'Liked to use the big words, but she only had eyes for Alan, never for Doug or me or Hugh. The man was an ox. I was more of a rooster. The two of them used to go down the creek after we'd finish for the day. They thought it was a secret, but it's hard to keep anything hidden in a workplace like that. After a few years, and to nobody's surprise, Rhonda and Alan got hitched.'

The wind started up even stronger. Will could see it coming, through the bushes and the gums on the side of the road. Now, it was making the blinds in the house bang against the window.

'They were happy,' he continued. 'Had a boy, a few years before Hugh's Geordie was born. But Alan's boy was born dead.'

Will watched as Belinda placed a protective hand over her stomach, her face visibly shocked. *Each generation holds its secrets,* he thought. *We don't know about the lives of our parents and their friends; we're too caught up in ourselves.*

'It was the same year as the drought, and what with the wheat prices, and him and Rhonda not able to do anything, their farm went to shit. Alan sold most of his land to Hugh Pritchard, even though Doug tried to stop him; by then, Douggie was moving high up in the world too.'

Bang, bang. The blinds kept making the same, maddening noise. But Belinda and Reg didn't seem to notice.

'Years later, Geordie put up the wind turbines. Then Rhonda got sick with the cancer. She died a year later. Alan always blamed the turbines – he held them and them alone responsible for her death. All that stuff Julie had to say . . . he believed it, was growing more paranoid about it as he got older.'

Julie and her conspiracies.

'Alan hated the turbines, and yet,' Will said, 'he worked for Geordie Pritchard.'

'Had to make a living, didn't he? His land's worth a mint, but only when he sells it.' Reg spat something into his hand and studied it, before rubbing it into his palm. 'Couldn't shear forever, though Alan would have liked to – probably could, if he had to. The man is still as strong as you like.'

Strong, Will thought, but still sixty-seven, almost the same age as Reg. That said, Reg had managed to fight off whoever attacked him. And that newspaper article, which mentioned the dragging and hauling of Geordie's body up the turbine. That language could have resonated with some in the town. Who knew the old history?

Catch and drag, that's how shearers began the process. Catch the sheep first, then drag it along the ground before lifting it up to your knee. Mature sheep could weigh 60 to 80 kilograms. Rams: double that. The catch and drag – it took strength, it took skill.

'Reg' – Belinda called her father by his first name – 'do you think Alan strung Geordie Pritchard up on the blades?'

Reg slowly nodded. 'I do,' he said. 'And he knew that I knew it. That's why the bastard tried to top me.'

She let that thought settle for a moment, then: 'But not Doug?'

'Nah, Doug's a fat old bastard, if you haven't noticed.' Reg gave a bark of laughter. 'He fell in that silo fair and square. And he's too caught up in himself and his business to twig the mention of dragging in the paper. Even if he did think of it, the rest doesn't compute. But the old ones in town, we know the secrets.'

The three were quiet a moment, listening to the blinds bang against the window, to a car driving slowly up the road.

'I read the article when I was out camping near that old spot by the creek,' Reg continued. 'And what do you know? Alan popped down there too – and he wasn't quick enough for me not to see what he was trying to hide in an old treacle tin. I knew then, for sure.'

'What did you find, Dad?' Belinda leaned in to him.

'A set of keys.' He grinned, then winced and felt the bandage about his neck. 'Pritchard's keys.'

Will and Belinda sat back in their seats, looking at each other, eyes wide.

'And don't fucken worry, I didn't touch them. Used a hanky. Took a video too.' Reg grinned again. 'Seen enough of *CSI*.'

Belinda shook her head. 'Dad, you're unbelievable.'

'Got them under the sink in a plastic bag.'

'You've got them here?!'

'Old mate was looking at me with binoculars from the top of the hill, when I took the tin out. I saw the glint of them on top of Mont Blanc. Alan knew that I knew what he'd done. My guess is, he hoped to kill me, and then the keys would never be found. Or if they were found, I'd get the blame.'

Will took off his glasses and rubbed his eyes. 'Why bother trying to kill you though?' he asked. 'Alan knew that you'd work it out – so what? You hadn't told anyone. Plus,' he added, 'he'd know you'd never speak to the cops. You hate them!'

'When someone tries to fucken garrot you with fishing line, you begin to see things differently, I can tell you that. And besides' – Reg's blue eyes twinkled – 'my daughter and her husband are cops. I might finally be coming around.'

*

It was dusk by the time Belinda and Will drove to Alan's house near the top of Mont Blanc. Warm, with little wind. The dam was a shimmering lake; the paddocks were gold and a gentle grey.

Alan wasn't in his shed. He wasn't in his house either. Feeling the grip of dread, Will opened the bathroom cabinet. Most of Rhonda's medication had been removed.

They finally found him at the creek. The place where he and Rhonda used to go – the running water, the grass shrubs, the drooping gums. Julie had always said that Rhonda's cancer medication would kill, not cure her, and in this instance, the old man had counted on it.

He was sitting there, back to a tree, legs outstretched, head to one side as if in sleep. There were empty bottles beside him and his wedding photo cradled on his lap.

CHAPTER 50

One month later

Belinda was dozing in the passenger seat beside him when Lisa called from Ballarat to give them an update. Vice Principal Andrew Kent, formerly known as Kenneth Greene, had been charged with two counts of first-degree murder, and common assault. His lawyer was fighting to have the case heard in a different jurisdiction, but so far with little success.

Lisa had confirmed she was packing it in – Investigations wasn't for her. She was going to do a Dip Ed, maybe major in PE.

'And that means,' Lisa said over the car speaker, 'there'll be a vacancy coming up in five or six weeks' time. It would be Bendigo or Ballarat based. Either of you interested?'

'I'm not,' Will said. 'Not a chance.'

Belinda was half awake. Was she interested? She looked out of the window as the paddocks raced by, the tractors going up and down their lines.

She turned to Will, tired but thoughtful.

'Should I go for the job?' she asked him after Lisa had hung up.
'Do you want to?'

'Maybe, but do you think it could work?'

He put one hand on her shoulder and gave it a rub. 'We'd make it work,' he said.

'What, and live in either Ballarat or Bendigo?'

Will shrugged, watching the golden paddocks race by. 'Both have their pros and cons.'

'You'd have to stay at home with Edie.'

'I'd love that. I really would.' In the back of the car, their daughter slept peacefully, though Will had no doubt she'd be squawking soon.

Edie was three weeks old, born via caesarean in the Carrabeen hospital. A breech baby, like her mum. Now, they were on the way to Melbourne to visit Penelope and to move some of their stuff back into their old unit. It wasn't an overly long drive, but the landscape had never felt so big.

What must Alan Crowe have thought as he looked at Geordie's body at the foot of the turbine? There was rage in him, there must have been that: here was the man whose chief project had killed his wife, and the son of the man who'd bought his land for a pittance.

Now developers would be lining up to buy his remaining land – it would be worth a mint. The sloping land, the paddocks beyond. Land for the wind. And as for his will – well, that was the thing that got everyone talking.

Alan had left it all to Rhonda's family. Her sisters and their children and their children and so on. Colin from the hardware store reckoned there were at least fifteen of them in town who'd get a sizeable cut.

Those hardscrabble Razzes. They'd finally have a piece of the pie.

Will licked a fingertip and held it out the window to the sky. One thing was certain: the wind had changed.

EPILOGUE

1 December 2024

It's Sunday, and that means Alan goes to the IGA. Sundays used to be quiet in town, but not any more. There's sport, shopping, mass. Alan likes to see people he knows there, even if it's just in passing.

The dogs are in the back, and he drives along the old Carra-been road, feeling the sun on his brown forearm and the wind on his face. Mick is there, in his tractor on the other side. Alan gives him a nod as they pass by. Harvest should be good this year. Plenty of rain, heat coming at the right time. Shearing in this area is mostly done now, and the few shearers that are left will be moving on.

He gives his shoulder a rub, remembering the way he'd listen as Doug and Reg would prattle on. His whole body hurts now, but he's learned to accept the pain. With every ache, memories come back to him: Rhonda, Reg, Doug and Hugh. Running with a wheat bag on his shoulders past the crowds, the sound of Reg on his heels, calling him a fit bastard, while he strides on ahead.

Alan doesn't look at the paddocks to his left, but he can still see them. Out the corner of his eye, they're there – the enormity of them, the white flitting in and out, in and out. There's a creek at the bottom of the paddock. He used to catch fish in it, and on his side of the hill there's a spot where he and Rhonda used to take a picnic and a beer on summer nights. There's a tin there too, where he and the boys would keep their tobacco. The creek is almost dry now. Last time he was there a big brown snake crawled over his boot, and he let it go, watching its fat tail sneak under a bush. He's killed dozens of browns in his time. They don't scare him. The creek is where he spread Rhonda's ashes.

Julie Smith pulls out of the servo just as he pulls in. In her dusty little Corolla and with her black hat on, she looks just like a witch. Rhonda used to go to her for readings, and advice on her health. Tarot and that, a load of bullshit, but Julie did know her stuff about those turbines. Good woman, wise.

Gordon Highett, the fancy bloke who lives in the old doctor's house, walks by, and he says hello. Gordon's not a bad bloke, but he shouldn't wear those pointy shoes. It's Carrabeen, not Milan. The morning is hot. There's Mallee sand in the wind; Alan can feel it biting into his skin.

He's almost finished filling up when a shiny LDV pulls in next to him. One of the new electric vehicles. It can only be one person, and he's not surprised when a pair of R.M. Williams boots lands on the concrete floor. Alan glowers; he'd prefer Highett's wanker shoes.

'Alan!' Geordie Pritchard beams. 'How are you, mate?'

Alan doesn't appreciate being called 'mate' by a man thirty years younger, and one who is certainly *not* his mate. But Geordie is his new boss, of sorts. 'Good enough. You?'

'Fine, fine.' Geordie runs a hand through his hair and gives a laugh. 'Still a habit to pull up to the petrol pumps, when I only came in for the paper!'

'It runs all right then?'

'Yes.' Geordie nods vaguely, looking suddenly bored. 'How's the job?'

Alan has been working for Geordie this last fortnight, maintaining the land around the turbines. 'No issues. Two small alarms on the beeper, but Shane told me not to worry. He said there'd be a couple of falsies at the start.'

Geordie looks to the side, watching as another car pulls up. 'Fair enough.' He stares over Alan's shoulder to the street beyond. 'Fair enough.'

It's annoying, the way the younger man doesn't bother to hide his lack of interest in the conversation. Alan would like to leave, but he remembers the concrete pylons he'd spotted by the creek.

'You building something down the bottom of the hill?'

'Apartments!' Geordie answers with glee. 'There's enough space, and the builders reckon it's a prime spot. Public housing. Could fit at least six there, we reckon.'

Alan feels a lump in his throat. That spot by the creek.

Geordie catches his expression. 'Ever think you should have kept the land that side of Mont Blanc instead of selling it to Dad?' The man seems genuinely curious. 'Would have been better for you to hold on to it. Worth a fortune now.' He gives a brief laugh. 'Don't worry, I know how it feels – I did the same thing with the Reebra land. Every time I drive past it!' Geordie gives himself a mock stab to his heart. 'Hindsight, eh?'

Alan cannot speak.

'Anyway, see you, Alan!' Geordie gives him another wide smile before heading into the shop. 'Take care, mate.'

Alan stands there for a long minute, breathing in, breathing out. There is no ache in him, none, only a hard ringing in his ears and a pressure building. Like an automaton, Alan pays for the petrol, then drives away. The dogs are in the back and the northerly comes in hard, spitting dirt and dust.

Ever think you should have kept the land instead of selling?

The *temerity* of it, that's what Rhonda would say. The *arrogance*.

Alan drives, thinking about when he sold his land to Geordie's father Hugh as the drought wore on. There'd been no money; they couldn't pay the mortgage; there wasn't enough to tide them over like there was for the Hays and the Pritchards. At the same time, a mouse plague had hit the region – little grey bodies drowning in the buckets each morning, their mangled corpses and the guts from when they ate their brothers who got stuck in traps. They'd climb into your bed at night, have babies in your shoes. Rhonda wasn't afraid of mice, but she grew thinner as they became fatter and more daring.

Would have been better to hold on to it.

But how?

They'd tried to make it work. He went back, did a season shearing, and Rhonda made dresses for the locals, but no one was buying, and he was too slow now for the farmers who hired him.

The papers liked to suggest that the farmers were struggling, but it wasn't *all* farmers. The ones who'd had money behind them, who had the land gifted to them, the ones who'd married up, the ones with big acreage: *they* were okay, they could eke it out.

Ever think you should have kept the land instead of selling?

Forty-one years ago, Rhonda gave birth to a dead boy. Alan left their home and went first to Doug Hay, offering to sell him his land, and then to Hugh Pritchard once Doug refused. The whole south side of Mont Blanc and a hundred acres beyond. Pritchard Senior snapped it up. It was a steal.

Would have been better to hold on to it.

Alan is almost home now, and he eyes the turbines with a rage he hasn't felt in years. When Hugh died and Geordie took over, the younger man had them erected, and almost immediately Rhonda got sick. It couldn't have been a coincidence. Julie had told them all about the side effects and the things the government didn't want you to know.

Don't worry, I know how it feels.

No, Pritchard, you fucking *don't*.

Alan kicks off his boots and heads inside. His head is thick with rage, thoughts of the turbines and Rhonda and the teeming mice and the Pritchards.

When the alarm goes off at around ten that evening, Alan hasn't been to bed. He's been walking around his property, tinkering in the shed, unable to rest. He hasn't taken his heart medication. The beeping sound jolts him into action. Jars him. Fucking turbines! They don't let him rest. They never had. He's on edge; his nerves are shot.

Ever think you should have kept the land?

The carelessness of it! The *temerity*.

The alarm beeps again, and he jumps. He can't think straight.

Those damn turbines! He wishes he could drop a bomb on the lot of them.

The alarm again, *beep beep*: maddening.

Alan drives up to the top of his hill and then gets out, scanning the property below. Nothing.

But then, in the thin moonlight, he makes out the shape of a car, parked on the side of the road at the turbine gates. Alan frowns, strains his eyes. Yes, there's a car there, and after a minute, its interior lights come on briefly so he can see the figure climbing into the front seat. Hard to make out, but definitely a man. The car begins moving, driving slowly along. It takes Alan a moment to realise that the headlights are not on.

Odd.

Still jumpy and rattled, Alan drives down the hill, opens the gate and manoeuvres onto the track surrounding the turbines. Their big alien structures tower above him. He can barely see a thing. There's the gap in the fence near to where the car was stopped. He bends down, takes a look. And as he stands up, he steps on something: a set of keys. He recognises the shape of a few of them; they look like his fence line keys. He pockets them, gets back in his ute, does a U-turn in the paddock, and drives slowly back along the row of turbines.

And there, in the headlights, is something lying at the foot of one of them. Alan kills the engine and walks over to investigate. First, he thinks it's a bag of discarded clothes; then he gets a fright when he sees someone sleeping there. He shines his torchlight on them.

Geordie Pritchard. Dead.

He considers this for a moment.

The moment lengthens.

Something in him snaps.

He pulls out the keys. Studies them, then selects one.

He's sure it's this one.

Opening the hatch is easy; the door swings inward as if inviting him in.

It feels as if something is happening, like he's meant to *do* something. As if everything since Rhonda's death has come to this.

His mind is all over the place. His blood starts to fizz.

He looks down at the body, at the shiny R.M. boots.

Hugh used to wear them.

Ever think you should have kept the land instead of selling?

Alan nudges Geordie's body with his foot.

And then, before he knows what he's doing, he's catching Geordie up under his arms and dragging him through the hatch door.

And if, later still, he imagines he sees the younger man's eyes flicker slightly, he won't give it much of a thought – because Geordie is dead, his own son is dead and Rhonda is dead, and *everyone needs to know.* Julie is right: turbines kill.

That night, Alan falls into a deep sleep, and dreams of Rhonda in the shearing shed. When the alarm goes off again, he knows what he must do.

He hears the low growl of Mick's tractor in the paddock across the road. His neighbour is starting already, getting a jump on the day. And all over the Golden Plains, the tractors will be starting up, going up and down their lines, getting the harvest in.

The thought gives him courage, and as he pulls on his boots, Alan finds that the air seems to have a sharp clarity to it. He feels a wild jubilance, which is terrible and exciting at the same time.

The morning is dark, just a thin patch of light in the east – nectarine. It used to be his favourite time of day.

He hears them then, the low electric buzz of the machines – and above it too, other sounds: the early morning call of the magpies and Mick's tractor making its way up and down the lines.

Alan's not looking forward to what comes next.

But you reap what you sow, he thinks, *you reap what you sow.*

Alan Crowe whistles to the dogs and they come running. He holds out his hands to them and up they leap into the back.

The day begins.

ACKNOWLEDGEMENTS

In the writing of this book, I was lucky enough to spend time in the Golden Plains and the Wimmera regions of Victoria. What magnificent landscapes! The huge, open skies and vast plains – I love them, and the communities there.

Experts on wind turbines will know that I have taken liberties with certain machinations and dimensions. Please forgive me in the name of fiction. Any truly glaring errors are all my own.

As always, I'm grateful to the team at Penguin Random House for their expertise and support. Particular thanks to Beverley Cousins, Kalhari Jayaweera, Claire Gatzen, Veronica Eze, Hannah Ludbrook, Tanaya Lowden and Adelaide Jensen.

Thank you to the talented staff at my school for their patience. I'd also like to thank my Year 12 students for their good humour and interest. No matter what anyone says, the kids are all right. Remember, be bold in your writing.

I am grateful to my writer friends for their encouragement, my farming friends for their advice on all things wheat and harvest, and the friends who listen to my ideas and are not afraid to tell me whether they are good or bad.

Thank you to Nicole Bilson for her longstanding support and to James Gallagher for chats about turbines and wind.

A huge thanks to booksellers, literary Instagrammers and readers who take a chance on buying yet another Australian rural crime, and to the libraries and festivals who back us every time.

Finally, thanks to my brilliant husband Bernie and to my three sons, who have not read one thing I've ever written. It's okay. I forgive you.

Margaret Hickey is an award-winning author and playwright from North East Victoria. She has a PhD in Creative Writing and is deeply interested in rural lives and communities. She is also the author of *Cutters End, Stone Town, Broken Bay* and *The Creeper,* and a collection of short stories, *Rural Dreams. Cutters End* was awarded the BAD Crime Sydney Festival's Danger Prize, and was also shortlisted for the Ned Kelly Award for First Fiction.

Powered by Penguin

Looking for more great reads, exclusive content and book giveaways?

Subscribe to our weekly newsletter.

Scan the QR code or visit penguin.com.au/signup